THE HOUR OF EVIDENCE

Deceived

The Liberty & Property Legends in reading order:

HEARTLAND
On the Side of Angels

EMPIRE FOR LIBERTY
Dangerous Lullaby

FIRST COUNTRY
Tinged with Rose

THE HOUR OF EVIDENCE
Deceived

THE HOUR OF EVIDENCE

Deceived

TERRI SEDMAK

THE
LIBERTY & PROPERTY
LEGENDS

Visit www.terrisedmak.com
Official website of THE LIBERTY & PROPERTY LEGENDS
A Saga of The West & Gilded Age America

Credits: *We Will Not Be Slaves*, Sons of Liberty Traditional;
The Two Rivers, Emma & Eginhard, A Fragment, Palingenesis, To the Avon, Hawthorne, It Is Not Always May, The Spanish Student by Henry Wadsworth Longfellow; *O you whom I often and silently come* by Walt Whitman; *Les Miserables* by Victor Hugo; *This Lime-Tree Bower My Prison, Kubla Khan* by Samuel Taylor Coleridge; *The Good-Morrow* by John Donne.

Cover and seal graphics: Blow–Up Design Pty Ltd

THE LIBERTY & PROPERTY LEGENDS™
Tank & Ferry Entertainment
Sydney, Australia

Published by VIVID Publishing
P.O. Box 948, Fremantle
Western Australia, 6959
www.vividpublishing.com.au

National Library of Australia Cataloguing-in-Publication entry:
Sedmak, Terri
The hour of evidence : deceived
ISBN: 9781925341133 (pbk.)
Series: The Liberty & Property Legends
A823.4

For WS
A world of dreams awaits.

'The birthright we hold, shall never be sold,
but sacred maintained to our graves,
and before we'll comply, we'll gallantly die,
for we must not, we will not be slaves, brave boys,
for we must not, we will not be slaves.'

Sons of Liberty

~ CHEYENNE, MARCH 1885

The day I came into this world I was not alone. I arrived some small period of time after my twin, Celina. Although we're not identical — and I've heard Mama say many times only by the grace of God that didn't happen — ours is a truly unique connection, so much so if we want keep our lives hidden from one another we have to choose to block the other from our mind or not be bothered to look. We have the sight, you see; twins' sight, that is, such as only we two share, and blocking Celina can be more trouble than my life is worth, so as a rule I don't do that.

On my side, once I am assured she is healthy as a horse and happy as a pig in mud, which she almost always is, being married to Mr Harrison Kennedy an' all, I don't feel the need to interfere in her life unless she were to ask me, and you can't find a rarer occurrence. Simply put, her social world, though sometimes amusing, is not my glass of sweet tea and she holds all the necessary expertise to survive it and flourish. On her side, though, Celina, being older by that small period of time, cannot help but peer and poke into my existence as if she were entirely necessary to it and I can't do without her.

Now considering my life mostly feels as though I am living from one scrape to the next, occasionally her help does have its advantages. I am entirely used to it. I don't shut her out, and she won't butt out. We are entwined in this special way and long ago folks closest to us came to accept it. I can't even imagine what would ever come between us.

Recently, she complained my life and times in Cheyenne were becoming so sticky with complications she felt determined to steer me through them. After assuring her this wasn't necessary, I told her that in spite of all the heartache, there is real courage; and some victories, some justice, too. But the driving force behind this unspeakable ordeal had yet to be uncovered and tried.

There will come a time when the truth will rise up through the mire of lies and murky wrong-doing to reach the surface and show its sad yet radiant light. And I believe that hour is coming.

~ EMMALINE ROBERTS

'A small group of determined people can change the course of history.'
Henry Wadsworth Longfellow

These are they, and some are not necessarily determined to do good! - ER

LUKE TAYLOR - part owner of the Diamond-T Ranch

ETHAN BENCHLEY - half-owner of the Diamond-T Ranch

Ethan & Red Sky's son TIP BENCHLEY

SARA TAYLOR - Luke's mother, part owner of the Diamond-T

JOHN KEATON & his wife, AMY KEATON, own Keaton Ranch

John's sister and Sara's friend EDITH EDWARDS - lives in NY

TRESSA TAYLOR KEATON - Luke's cousin; her son, ADAM

RICHARD TAYLOR - owner of Taylor Mining, Aurora; Luke's uncle

CAROLINE TAYLOR - Richard's wife *(courageous mama & grandma)*

BEN TAYLOR - Richard's son, heir to Taylor Mining, Luke's cousin

RAINA MONTGOMERY - heiress from Denver, wife of Ben Taylor

JENNIFER SULLIVAN - very rare female doctor

The SEVERINI FAMILY - Signora Rosa, Alfredo & Gianni

CLIFF RYAN - Laramie County Sheriff; also deputy US marshal

'MAC' McNamara - deputy & acting sheriff, Laramie County

CAM FARADAY - prosecuting attorney

JOSH BRIDGER - assistant prosecuting attorney

Judge AMBROSE B. CALLAGHAN

JACOB HUNTER - reporter for The Bugle *(not a nice man)*

FATHER NUGENT - Parish Priest, St John the Baptist Church

STURROCK & BUCHANAN - defense attorneys *(The black suits)*

Mr QUAID - Editor in Chief of the Tribune *(necktie always crooked)*

LOREN BODECKER - tycoon *(the less said the better)*

TERENCE DONNELLY - associate of Loren Bodecker *(a killer)*

DILLON KERR - attorney *(obnoxious)*

LAMONT - mysterious associate of Kerr

Albany County Deputy CHASE DELOIGHT

MAVERICKS - Donnelly's team of deadly sharpshooters

Compiled by Emmaline Roberts at The Tribune for Celina Kennedy.

Sara...

Edith Edwards' Residence
Manhattan, NY

Sara hurries in from the cold, her newspaper tucked beneath her arm, frost nipping at the tips of her gloved fingers even as she enters the brownstone. Breathing a contented sigh, for the warmth of Edith's comfortable home embraces her, she boots the door shut, sweeps off her splendid mink hat, a Christmas gift from Edith, and tosses it onto the entry hall table.

Not for the first time does she ponder on the unrelenting depth of a New York winter; she eases off her gloves trying to recall those Wyoming winters that were so harsh she never ventured beyond the ranch for weeks but for some reason she can't clearly recollect them. She takes the New York Post from under her arm and berates herself for her lapse into the soft side of life. What would Morgan, with his ranch and his cattle and his frontier dreams, taken from her sixteen years ago this summer, think of her now?

Laurette appears; she possesses many a capable string to her housekeeper's bow, and has been a wonderful companion for Edith for many years now. Everything runs like clockwork but not one thing feels managed; it only feels like home. Sara particularly likes the woman's wry sense of humor; she's used to it back home on the Diamond-T, with Ethan, Tip and Luke...

That she misses them goes without saying, a feeling that creeps up on her, like now for instance, and draws her away from reality to visit the land of memory. How long has she known Ethan? – since she was eighteen; thirty years. Goodness, better keep that under her hat; people will think she's old. Yes, Ethan and his Texan ways and those awful red long handles of his have been a part of her life for all but her childhood. And missing his Red Sky is something she has experienced every day since that beautiful woman passed from this life five years ago, or is it six?

And the blood brothers of the Diamond-T? Tip, the intelligent and strapping son of Ethan and Red Sky, is family to her; and adventurous, determined Luke, her son and Morgan's, as proud as she is of him, as much as she loves him, will the day ever come when he does one thing she expects of him?

"You been out again in the cold, Mrs Taylor? I swear one day you'll come back in the shape of an icicle."

She looks up. "Don't worry about me, Laurette. I find the cold exhilarating." She removes her muffler and coat. Laurette takes them from her arms. "Thank you."

Laurette eyes the newspaper. "All for some news. Tsk." She lifts Sarah's hat from the table and starts shaking snowflakes off it. "Snowin'. Still?"

"Just a short flurry, probably from the trees. Spring *will* arrive, won't it, Laurette?"

"Any day now," says Laurette with a sideways grin as she strides away with the cozy gait of a rotund woman. Most things in Edith's home are cozy.

A voice carries from the parlor. "Is that you, Sara?"

She hurries along. Edith, dearest friend and kindred spirit, is sitting by the hearth in her favorite armchair with yet another book. And tea things are set out.

"Look at you," Edith exclaims. "You mouth is blue. Come have some tea. Laurette just made it."

She does all the correct things instead of launching into her news. She ignores the newspaper. Sits herself down. Sips her tea. Composes herself. Never mind what her son has got himself mixed up in now!

Edith's bright blue eyes dance. "So, now, what news? Although I can't imagine anything more dramatic than a telegram from your own son announcing his marriage and you not believing it."

"Will you please forget that?"

"Forget it?! Sara, my dear, your son told you he was planning to be married and you didn't believe him."

"He wouldn't marry anyone after... after Kelley. How could he?"

"As her loving aunt, who half-raised her, no one could have wanted her happiness more than I."

"Why, Edith, you make it sound as though she and Luke wouldn't have been happy together."

"Well, not if he was..."

"Was what?"

"I was going to say in love with the woman he's just married."

"And who would she be, if indeed he is married?"

"Who can say," Edith murmurs, looking into her teacup. "But it must be so."

"And even if it is so, I could not have made it back to Cheyenne in the time he gave me, despite you telling me I would have. He said he would write and he hasn't."

"Perhaps he's too busy with his new bride to write his mother a long and informative letter..."

She feels unsteady at the thought of that. Her teacup wobbles and she sets it down. She pushes the thought from her mind and takes up the Post instead. "When I read you this you'll change your mind. It is not a bride that has him occupied. Listen to this..."

"Is that the finance section?" Edith says, quirking an eyebrow.

"Mm. And don't you start."

Edith grins. "Very well. Although I'm beginning to see where Luke gets it from: leave no stone unturned."

"Edith, hush now and listen."

Edith bows her head.

She proceeds. "FRONTIER ENTERPRISES COLLAPSE AS BODECKER TO STAND TRIAL FOR MURDER. Organizations across Nebraska, Colorado and Wyoming Territory are headed for hard times as their leader, business tycoon Loren Bodecker, faces a jury on charges of conspiracy and murder. The prices of shares in Bodecker's numerous companies have plummeted."

"What trial, Sara? And who is this Bodecker person?"

3

"Listen... Last summer a determined group of Bright River ranchers calling themselves the Alliance challenged local Wyoming cattle rancher Ed Parsons who was subsequently indicted for harassment, conspiracy and murder. Convicted on all counts, Parsons was incarcerated in Cañon City Prison, Colorado. Since that trial, further investigations into the murder of one of the Alliance's young women, Miss Kelley Keaton, took on extraordinary significance when Loren Bodecker's involvement in the murder was discovered. After many significant arrests, including Mr Bodecker's, the trials are set to run for several weeks while a jury in Cheyenne seeks to adjudicate on a plot thick with conspiracy and murder, and deliver a verdict on Loren Bodecker's fate.

"Wyoming prosecuting attorney Cameron P. Faraday, whose bid for a bench trial failed, is pitted against the formidable team of defense attorneys Buchanan and Sturrock, renowned for their hard-hitting cross-examinations of key witnesses. It is not expected to be an easy task for Mr Faraday to convince the jury of Mr Bodecker's involvement in the crimes; most people who live and work in Wyoming will have their livelihood in some way connected to Bodecker's many enterprises.

"Although Mr Bodecker has been sacked from the positions he once held on the board of many companies and alternative arrangements have been made without significant damage, the outlook for Mr Bodecker's own companies looks increasingly bleak. Company managers are working around the clock to keep these businesses afloat, begging shareholders, the business community, commercial centers and industry for patience and understanding. Staff layoffs in Bodecker's smaller companies have been widely reported as the situation begins to bite and is expected to worsen.

"While buyers of Mr Bodecker's coal and cattle in the main are steering clear of the disgraced tycoon, Mr Bodecker is reported to have insisted that his Wyoming coal is some of the best coal in the country and any current drop in demand will soon be overtaken by need. Coal production and sales are expected to resume pre-trial norms within weeks. As the price of cattle per head is already traveling a slow decline, it is difficult to tell what pressure the market is bringing to bear on Bodecker's woes.

"However, without Mr Bodecker's tight control it remains to be seen how his enterprises will emerge from this disaster. Already numerous takeover bids have begun, particularly in Denver, for Mr Bodecker's three silver mines, electric power company and several other businesses. Denver magnate Alistair Montgomery has begun takeover proceedings for two of the silver mines and has stated that he would be happy to absorb Mr Bodecker's electric company into his own. Smaller businesses dotted across Denver are already under new management, Denver Jewels the most significant. This exclusive jewelry store, Mr Bodecker's pride and joy, clearly could not prevail without Mr Bodecker's immediate direction. An anonymous party bought out the store after exerting significant pressure on the tight group of shareholders and the small board which oversees its running, although rumors persist that the buyer is Mr C. Lamont.

"Meanwhile, across the Atlantic, European investors have retreated, and while significant buyers of Mr Bodecker's silver and coal are honoring their current contracts they are reported to be considering looking elsewhere in the future.

"It was thought that Bodecker cronies all over would be shoring up their leader's businesses, but this is not the case, giving credence to the long-held suspicion that loyalty to Loren Bodecker is not what it seems. 'Now is the time to get out with impunity' was the rumored declaration of some of Bodecker's business associates.

"A spokesman for Denver's Chamber of Commerce said, 'I can't speak for the rest of the world, but whatever the outcome of the trial, Mr Bodecker is finished in Denver. Any interests he had in this city are gone for good. Denver hasn't got time to wait around while a man goes on trial for murder. It'll be all gone before the month is out.'

"Manifestly, without Mr Bodecker's famous heavy-handed direction, those left in charge cannot cope with the onslaught. On what will be left of Loren Bodecker's empire when a jury of his peers finds the man guilty or not guilty one can only speculate."

She lowers the newspaper.

Edith murmurs, "Oh, my."

Trembling, she says, "I have a bad feeling about this, Edith."

ONE

...the hand of the hour clock moves round...
To the land of promise and of light...

Henry Wadsworth Longfellow
The Two Rivers

Cliff

Cheyenne, Wyoming Territory
Saturday
Voir dire – the selection of the jury

Cliff exits the county jail, leaving its dazzling collection of lately accused murderers, extortionists and general badass under the watchful eye of hired prison wardens, and heads to the courthouse; he wants to check in with Cam and in due course finds Wyoming's intrepid prosecutor coated up, hands deep in pockets, taking some fresh wintry air on the courthouse steps during a much needed recess by the look of it.

"Cam…"

He receives a nod, a half smile and the remark, "Longest winter I can remember."

"Me, too. How goes it?"

Cam sighs white clouds. "You need ask?"

"Yep. I'm the sheriff," he grins into a host of white clouds himself. "It's my job to ask."

"Ah. Your attempt at humor I gather. Well, challenging I anticipated. But even this is not quite what I was expecting."

"You sensibly argued for a bench trial, which even the governor was in favor of, but Buchanan and Sturrock insisted on trial by jury and Bodecker wasn't going to sign away an opportunity like that, so now finding a jury is…"

"The nightmare we knew it was going to be and exactly what Bodecker was hoping for. A whole bunch of people who think he is sunshine itself."

"How many have been dismissed?"

"Honestly, I've lost count. And we're running out. There's not a huge number of folk without a vested interest. And Buchanan and Sturrock have no intention of playing fair."

"Want to know what I think?"

"By all means."

"Between you and the evidence and the witnesses, your case is a lot stronger than anything Buchanan, Sturrock and those black suits of theirs can mount, no matter who is on the jury."

"Thank you, I appreciate that. But wouldn't you want to protect your financial future?"

"Mm, I would, and I do, but maybe under the weight of the evidence I might start to think that my financial future was looking a little shaky anyhow, and a lot of innocent people have died. This trial is about the murder of innocent people, Cam. And murdering the innocent doesn't sit well with anyone."

"You have just talked yourself into a job. We have jurors one to six. You can stay and help me with the rest. It'll be good practice."

"Huh. For what exactly?"

"Just be in court in ten minutes. And what are you looking so cheerful about anyhow?"

"I spoke with Emma this morning. In the bookstore."

"I see. And that went well then?"

"It was nice."

"But have you told her yet?"

"Told her?"

"That's it. Told her about…"

"Ah, not as yet."

Cam frowns and scratches the side of his face. "See you in ten minutes."

Two hours later

"Your thoughts?" Cam murmurs.

"Jurors seven, nine and ten are the ones to watch." Cliff looks down at the list on the paper in his hand.

Juror Number Seven: Arthur Washburn, 61, rancher

Juror Number Nine: Peter Daniels, 54, shopkeeper

Juror Number Ten: Jeff Reeves, 35, boilermaker

"The Judge upheld Buchanan's appeal against my objection to those three."

"I noticed. If you can convince *them*, I think you've won your case."

"That's a big call, Sheriff."

"Maybe. At least I figure you have a benchmark. This trial won't be a picnic for anyone. Murder, prostitution, drugs, Bodecker... As Mac would say, it's got the lot and then some."

"And now we have a jury. Even so, Buchanan and Sturrock are still appealing for separate trials for Bodecker and Donnelly."

"The Judge is standing firm."

"After your North Platte photographs, he's not budging."

Emmaline

Emmaline canons into Ashcliff as she is entering his office and he is leaving it. Her breath catches in her throat.

"Emma," he declares, his hands gathering her in before she stumbles backwards. "Are you all right?"

In the seconds between her subsequent exhale and his release, she manages to mostly recover herself.

"I'm so sorry," she mutters, all too aware her senses have filled up with him and wishing they wouldn't. Every second with him is larger than with anyone else, like it has the universe inside it, stars, galaxies, other worlds... which would be fine if she wasn't so tantalized by the prospect of other worlds. "I know testimony starts this morning... I need to talk to you about something."

He looks cool and efficient, just as he should. "I'm due in court... so are you... How did you get through the mob out front?"

"The picket line?"

"Very well, the picket line," he concedes with a sigh.

"Well, I didn't cross it if that's what you're thinking. I told them that in the name of worker solidarity I would write a story for the paper on their plight and they waved me on through."

"Emma," he reproaches.

"I told them just the facts. No bias. They accepted."

"They're desperate."

"Well, it's not their fault their jobs are lost or threatened."

"It's not mine either."

"I know you care about their plight."

12

"What has that got to do with anything?"

"Not a thing in relation to what I need to talk to you about."

That handsome forehead creases above those pretty blue-green eyes of his. He closes the door of his office and waits for her to begin. She hasn't called him Sheriff Ruthless in a long time, but today he looks like he has slipped straight back into character.

"Mr Quaid..." She takes a breath and suddenly feels warm. Her cheeks feel flushed and her sable hat seems to be overheating the top of her head, so she removes it and hopes her hair will do.

"Go on..." he says, shifting his feet and folding his arms.

"He found out that Luke and Jennifer were married. He... he cornered me and asked what I knew about it."

"You had to tell him."

"He fired..." She swallows – hard. "He fired me."

"Well, it's hardly surprising."

"And that is all you can say?"

"If you want your job back, Roberts, go back and fight for it. Right now, I have two prisoners to get into court without anyone shooting them or trying to set them free. I'm sorry he fired you, but it's probably just a knee jerk reaction."

"I deceived him."

He gives her a long look, which despite its steeliness makes her insides flutter, and says, "If you want your job back, go and fight the mongrel for it, Emma."

"That's your advice?"

He goes to the door and wrenches it open. "That's my advice. Sorry, I have to go." And then he walks out on her.

Indignation hits her like a heat wave. Like a hot knife it stabs and jabs her all over. Always wanting the last word! *Maddening!*

Ouch! Sheriff Ruthless. He can be brutal...

Not now, Celie.

...and you being so damsel in distress an' all. Doesn't he know by now how to treat a southern gal?

The discomfort intensifies as she strides past him in the outer office where he is deep in conversation with Mac. He doesn't even notice her. Only Saturday they were sharing *Les Miserables* like best friends...

Best friends? You and that prime piece of Yankee? Emmie, are you serious?

Celie, I'm busy.

You're always busy.

Hush now, I got somethin' important to do.

Don't let me stop you.

Good Lord willin' and the creek don't rise.

Here comes the South! Atta girl.

Once Bodecker's disgruntled employees have given her safe passage through their number, she marches back to the Tribune, right up to Mr Quaid's door.

She takes a deep breath.

Knocks.

And barges in.

"I thought I told you to clear out," he barks at her.

Good thing he can't see her hands shaking. "And I heard you – a person would have to be deaf… But, well, I have a job to do."

"I'll get someone else."

"There is no one else who knows all the players and the facts as well as I do. You can't deny it."

"You're a witness in a major criminal trial, for God's sake; you don't have access to the courtroom except when you're giving testimony and when Faraday's finished with you. I intend doing it, now scram and go play witness for Faraday…"

"You can't cover and write up the whole trial by yourself."

"Get lost, Roberts."

She grits her teeth. "If you want *Empire for Liberty* you better keep me here."

"If I… say, who do you think you are? That story's mine!"

"I'll fight you for it in court."

Mr Quaid is clearly apprehensive about her legal acumen and connections, because he falters, noticeably. And she moves in for the kill…

"There's a trial about to start. Who knows, the trial of the century in these parts! Do you want your *best* reporter to help you cover it or not?"

Emmaline

"The witness is sworn in, Mr Faraday, and you may begin."

"Thank you, Your Honor. Please state your name and place of residence for the court?"

"Emmaline Elizabeth Roberts. My current address is Mrs Nan Morris' guesthouse on 19th and Warren. My home is in Orlando, Orange County, Florida."

"Please outline your formal education for the court."

"Once I had graduated high school and undertaken two years prep in Baltimore, I entered university and completed a degree in Liberal Arts, majoring in American and European Literature. I graduated in 1882. While I studied a post graduate course in writing and literature in Boston, I began freelance writing. I sold several pieces to east coast and southern journals and won a literary award for a piece entitled *Voice of the Mockingbird, Songs and Poetry of the South.*"

"Your occupation now, Miss Roberts?"

"I am a journalist."

"And what is your current position?"

"Investigative reporter for the Cheyenne Tribune."

"How long have you held that position?"

"Since the twenty-sixth of January."

"And you were hired by the Tribune's editor Charlie Quaid?"

"Yes, Mr Faraday."

"Why was Mr Quaid interested in a reporter from Florida?

15

"The advertisement for the position stated that Mr Quaid was looking for a journalist from regions beyond the Frontier in order to gain a fresh and impartial view of the matter for investigation."

"Why did you answer Mr Quaid's advertisement?"

"I was hoping there would be less gender prejudice in the West than there is in the East and the South. To sell my stories I had to use a man's name. I was hoping to establish myself more securely in my profession as a woman."

"Did Mr Quaid show any gender prejudice, Miss Roberts?"

"No. I think he thought my gender an advantage."

"Please explain."

"I believe he thought he would get the fresh and impartial view he was looking for."

"A great many people believe that a woman is not capable of being impartial."

"I sent Mr Quaid copies of my previous work. As much as I enjoy the odd gothic romance, Mr Quaid could read for himself that I didn't write them."

"So, what did Mr Quaid want you to investigate?"

"He believed the investigation into the murder of Miss Keaton here in Cheyenne last Fall was progressing at a suspiciously slow rate. He suspected it might be deliberate. He wanted a fresh face and a fresh attitude in town to investigate his suspicions. On arrival I had to familiarize myself with countless files and newspaper articles on the Bright River Alliance and Ed Parsons. And I began my investigation."

"And what did you uncover?"

"I suspected that you, Mr Faraday, and Sheriff Ryan had kept part of Luke Taylor's file from the Parsons' trial. I didn't know what, but it had to be important. I set out to track down the file."

"And how did you go about that?"

"The evening after I arrived in town, I tracked Sheriff Ryan to your house. I stood outside in the snow peering in the window at you and Sheriff Ryan studying what I realized was the file. I knew there was something suspicious about that file and I had to know what it was. As I watched and waited, I remember feeling stiff with cold and I shifted my position."

"And then what happened?"

"A gun exploded; a bullet flew past my face stinging my cheek. If I hadn't moved at that last second, it would have killed me."

"And then?"

"The young man who shot at me was apprehended by Sheriff Ryan and Deputy McNamara. The following day I was called to give evidence before His Honor. On the way back to work, I was walking down town with Sheriff Ryan, who felt it necessary to protect me. I stopped on the sidewalk. For the second time someone fired a gun at me and this time the bullet would have killed me but for the actions of Sheriff Ryan."

"What did he do?"

"He took the bullet instead of me, in the arm. And he shot and wounded the gunman, who was positioned on the roof on the opposite side of the street."

"What if anything did Sheriff Ryan say to you regarding this?"

"He said: *A single bullet from a rooftop on the opposite side of the street. I think we might have Miss Keaton's killer.* And he said: *I didn't shoot to kill.*"

"What did you do next, Miss Roberts?"

"I went back to work and I wrote an article about what had happened to me and what I believed was at the core of it."

"Would explain this please?"

"My investigation and subsequent attempts on my life centered on the question: why was the Bugle, obviously a soap box for the Republican Party and the cattle kings, and ideologically opposed to Miss Keaton's opinions, so happy to print every single one of her controversial letters? I wrote of my belief that there was a connection between Ed Parsons and Loren Bodecker, a belief that was enhanced by the request of the man who attempted to kill me for Bodecker's lawyer to defend him."

"How was your article received?"

"It was well-received by townsfolk. But Mr Bodecker's lawyer, Dillon Kerr, threatened to have me prosecuted. He said: *My client is one of the most powerful men in this territory and as such I am a powerful man. If you persist you will probably rue the day you ever set foot in Cheyenne.*"

"To sum up: on the commencement of your investigation into Miss Keaton's murder you yourself were almost murdered twice?"

"Yes… that's correct."

"And on being apprehended your would-be assassin requested Mr Bodecker's lawyer to represent him?"

"That's also correct."

"Your Honor, this is all I have for Miss Roberts for the present time. I wish to recall this witness later."

"Very well, Mr Faraday. Mr Buchanan, you may proceed with your cross-examination of the witness."

"Thank you, Your Honor. Miss Roberts, you have an excellent memory."

"You need one in my line of work."

"Clearly, you are a well-bred, well-educated young woman, why is it that such a young woman finds herself scampering around in the cold and dark looking for clues?"

"To investigate sometimes I am required to scamper."

"How is it, Miss Roberts, that your impartial view suddenly draws the anger of one of Cheyenne's most respected attorneys in Dillon Kerr? – because it is so one-sided and slanderous?"

"Objection, Your Honor. Mr Buchanan is asking a question and then proceeds to answer it for himself."

"Sustained. Wait for the witness to answer, Mr Buchanan."

"Yes, Your Honor. Miss Roberts?"

"My view is separate from that of anyone else in town because I don't have any vested interests in Mr Bodecker's companies, or anyone else's except the Tribune of course, my employer."

"You weren't afraid of drawing Mr Kerr's anger?"

"His threat, his demeanor, was alarming."

"I see. And yet you continued on in your job."

"Of course."

"Rather reckless, don't you think?"

"No."

"No? A woman scampering around town dodging bullets, allowing other people to be hurt. I put it to you, Miss Roberts, that you are reckless."

"You've known me for all of two minutes, Mr Buchanan."

"Indeed. Miss Roberts, all of us here, in fact, people in general, know that a woman is not capable of defending herself and requires someone else to do it. An investigative reporter in a frontier town should be a man who can defend himself, don't you agree?"

"I have worked at the Tribune for two months now. Not one of its employees carries a gun or any other weapon. Investigators ask questions, that is their job. If they get hurt in the course of that job because they have made a strike at the heart of a matter, then clearly their attacker has a serious problem with having their business uncovered."

"How do men take to working with you in their profession?"

"Most get used to it."

"But a male reporter, with a family to support, would be better off with your job than you. You snatch the food out of hungry mouths, in taking a man's position."

"Apart from the stated fact that Mr Quaid didn't want a man for the job, I also need to eat."

"Order, order..."

"Miss Roberts, you're an observant young woman, where do you think most women your age are now?"

"Objection, Your Honor... what is the relevance?"

"Objection overruled. The witness will answer the question."

"I do not take your meaning, Mr Buchanan."

"My meaning, Miss Roberts, is that most young women your age are either at home with their parents or tending to a home, husband and children of their own, and here you are recklessly scampering about after dark, caught up in matters that are none of your business, and taking the job of a family man."

"Oh, my."

"Oh, *my*, Miss Roberts?"

"We have a saying where I come from. *Don't ever go gittin' above your raising*. You'll be thinking that what I've done in taking a job and working to put food in my mouth myself rather than leaving my papa to do it is going against everything I was taught. But I wasn't raised that way, Mr Buchanan."

"Miss Roberts..."

"No, Sir. I feel your point keenly, since no child should ever go hungry. However, let me say this: I'd much rather it was me who faced death than the father of several small children who could very well have been left fatherless, orphaned and dependent on the charity of others. To be a child without a father, to be orphaned that way, your papa murdered in the street, or very likely to be, well, I can't bear to think about it."

"Order, order… order!"

"Has Dillon Kerr ever hurt you, Miss Roberts?"

"No."

"Injured your reputation?"

"He's attempted it, but that kind of thing requires a skill he doesn't possess, so the answer is no."

"Do you possess such a skill, Miss Roberts?"

"My skill, Mr Buchanan, is investigating the facts and writing them down so people can read them. I do not need to injure anyone's reputation; the facts speak for themselves."

"No further questions for this witness at this time, Your Honor."

"The witness may step down."

Cliff

"Proceed, Mr Faraday."

"Thank you, Your Honor. Sheriff Ryan, on the twenty-fifth of January this year you went to Cañon City for what purpose?"

"To interrogate prisoner Ed Parsons at the State penitentiary."

"Why?"

"It was part of my investigation into the murder of Miss Keaton."

"What led you to believe Ed Parsons would be useful?"

"Her murder happened directly after Parsons was convicted and sentenced. I considered the murder too close to that event not to be connected to Parsons."

"Your Honor, I have here People's exhibit 1: Sheriff Ryan's hand-written report of his interrogation of the prisoner Ed Parsons, dated twenty-sixth of January, 1885. I offer it into evidence. Sheriff Ryan returned to Cheyenne on January twenty-seven."

"Thank you, Mr Faraday."

"What did your interrogation reveal, Sheriff Ryan?"

"Mr Parsons started out by insisting he did not know who killed Miss Keaton. I put it to him that he knew who orchestrated the killing. He said it wasn't him and I said that I knew it wasn't him. He asked me how I knew.

"I told him I had in my possession a piece of evidence that someone else was involved. He was abusive and insulting, trying to put me off. And I revealed to him that Luke Taylor's file contained a sketch of Loren Bodecker's face. Parsons went white with shock.

"I told Parsons that for Mr Bodecker's face to be in the file Luke would have to have seen the two of them together. I put it to him that Loren Bodecker might know who murdered Miss Keaton. He said *why don't you ask him and find out?*

"When I told him I intended to, he took fright and told me I didn't know what I was doing. He seemed afraid for his life. He begged me to leave it alone. When I put it to him that he got his friend Loren Bodecker to help him take revenge on the Alliance, he said *so you know; bully for you.*

"I considered this confirmation of my suspicions that Mr Bodecker was involved in Miss Keaton's murder."

"Why did you wait so long to go to Cañon City after Miss Keaton's murder?"

"I spent many weeks after Miss Keaton's murder making discreet observations of Loren Bodecker and his business organizations. To accuse a man of his standing of murder without investigation and evidence would have been unthinkable."

"What did these observations reveal to you?"

"That Mr Bodecker's wealth and power had made him ruthless. No one ever dared question his operations. He despises small ranchers and homesteaders, seeing their contribution to this territory as meaningless. His Association members had developed a reputation for harassing these people, and there were many incidents of harassment which I spent time investigating."

"And did you discover a connection between Ed Parsons and the accused Mr Bodecker?"

"Ed Parsons was a member of Mr Bodecker's association. Mr Bodecker had helped Ed Parsons buy out the Bright River Register, the local newspaper. Ed Parsons' attempts to get rid of the Alliance – itself a small group of independent ranchers – are well known."

"So this was the basis for your trip to Cañon City?"

"Yes."

"Mr Ryan, tell the court when you first crossed paths with Miss Emmaline Roberts of the Cheyenne Tribune?"

"The day I returned from Colorado, January 27th."

"Was that the day the first attempt was made on her life?"

"Yes. She had followed me to your residence and was spying through the front window. I was inside and we were discussing the day's events and Luke Taylor's file. We heard gunfire outside the house. I went out to investigate.

"My deputy, Tremaine McNamara, who everyone knows as Mac, was holding a young man by the collar. Miss Roberts was on the ground. I helped her up and led her inside. Her cheek was grazed by the bullet. Mac took the shooter down to the lockup. I followed later with Miss Roberts. I had the doctor attend to her wound and took her home. Then I went back to the lockup to interrogate the shooter."

"Who was the shooter?"

"The shooter was Gordy Jacobs, aged nineteen years, and he was from Laramie. The gun was in his hand at the time of his arrest, the bullet wedged itself into the wall of the house and was a match for his gun."

"Your Honor, People's exhibit 2: the statement given by Mr Jacobs to Sheriff Ryan after the shooting."

"Thank you, Mr Faraday."

"Continue please, Mr Ryan, with Mr Jacobs' interrogation."

"Gordy Jacobs admitted firing the gun at Miss Roberts. He said it was his job and he wasn't supposed to miss. He admitted to having shot at other people, not usually missing them, and at other times shooting to scare people, such as sheepherders.

"He admitted he missed shooting Miss Roberts because she moved just as he pulled the trigger and Mac stopped him before he could shoot again. I asked him about his boss and he said he didn't know who he was, just that the orders came from someone in Laramie called Maverick.

"He said he didn't shoot Miss Keaton and didn't know who did, that Maverick's sharpshooters don't know each other. He said he'd never seen Maverick and got the job by answering an advertisement in the paper with an address to reply to. It was a Laramie address, this he remembered.

"When asked what would happen if he got caught, he said he never heard of anyone getting caught. If he didn't contact Maverick at the right time, someone else would be sent to finish the job. To contact Maverick he had to send a telegram with these words: *Maverick. Laramie telegraph. Nighthawk lullaby.*

"When first apprehended he was charged with attempted murder but declined an attorney. Later he said he'd rather be in prison, meaning Maverick will kill him, and saying: *Maverick pays well for the job or make you pay if the job ain't done*. Mac and I gathered a list of all the sheepherders shot or killed. Mr Adams from Dickson was the first; no one ever discovered who killed him, but he was shot by a single bullet to the head – Maverick style. His young widow, Edwina, and son, Colin, survived but were forced to sell."

"Objection, Your Honor. I would contend that this mode of assassination is not exactly unheard of; in fact, it is not common to anyone in particular."

"Your Honor, I would argue that this mode of assassination is precisely the style Maverick uses and that is what Sheriff Ryan is describing for the court."

"Objection overruled. Continue, Mr Faraday."

"Mr Ryan, we heard Miss Roberts testify that you took a bullet meant for her. How did that come about?"

"The day after the first shooting she was required in court to give evidence at Gordy Jacobs' hearing. I escorted her to and from court. On the way back from court she stopped on the sidewalk. I stepped in front of her and the bullet struck me."

"How do you know the bullet wasn't meant for you?"

"Because I had walked a couple of steps beyond Miss Roberts. I recovered those steps in an attempt to stay by her side."

"You feared another attempt would be made on her life?"

"Yes, I was sure there would be."

"After you had been shot, what happened?"

"I wasn't seriously wounded. I looked up for the shooter, spotted him on the roof across the street and shot him in the shoulder. Mac and the boys retrieved him from the roof and took him down to the lockup."

"And who was the shooter this time?"

"His name was Swinton Carter."

"And he asked for a lawyer immediately. What was *his* name?"

"Marvin Tucker, who is one of Mr Bodecker's town lawyers."

"Is it true that you sent *Maverick. Laramie telegraph. Nighthawk lullaby* after the shooting?"

"Yes."

"For what purpose?"

"I wanted to see what would happen, and to get some margin of safety for Miss Roberts."

"Did Swinton Carter ever admit to shooting Miss Roberts?"

"No."

"What was his demeanor after his arrest?"

"He became frightened when I asked him what would happen to him if and when Maverick found out that Miss Roberts was still alive and he had failed to do his job."

"You kept a close eye on Miss Roberts for a time after this?"

"Yes."

"Your Honor, this is all I have for this witness for the present time. I wish to recall Sheriff Ryan at a later time."

"Very well, Mr Faraday. The defense may proceed with its cross-examination of the witness. Mr Sturrock..."

"Thank you, Your Honor. Mr Ryan, would you please tell the court the condition in which you found Mr Parsons when you visited him in prison."

"He had pneumonia."

"He was extremely ill, was he not, languishing in his cell?"

"He was ill. I asked the guards to take him to the infirmary."

"And you spoke to him from his sick bed, did you not?"

"That's correct."

"Isn't it true that he was so ill he would have said anything just to get rid of you?"

"No, I don't believe so."

"Mr Ryan, I contacted the prison warden who informed me Mr Parsons remained in the prison infirmary for six weeks, so I'd say he was very ill."

"Objection, Your Honor. Mr Sturrock is an attorney, not a doctor and not qualified to make such an assessment."

"Objection sustained."

"Your Honor, Defense exhibit 30: a written report of Mr Parsons' medical condition, written and signed by the prison doctor and authorized by the warden."

"Thank you, Mr Sturrock."

"The report says, Mr Ryan, that Mr Parsons had been extremely ill and would not have been up to visitors on the day you interrogated him, but you did anyway, did you not?"

"No one stopped me from interrogating Mr Parsons."

"He coughed and spluttered and had trouble breathing, did he not?"

"At times."

"Mr Ryan, either he coughed and spluttered and had trouble breathing or he didn't, which is it?"

"In the interests of accuracy, counselor, he coughed and spluttered and had trouble breathing at times."

"He had a fever, the report says, and people with fever tend to hallucinate and exhibit an unfocussed state of mind, do they not, Mr Ryan?"

"It's possible."

"Isn't it entirely possible that Mr Parsons was exhibiting signs of febrile dementia?"

"I am not familiar with that term."

"And neither is the court, Mr Sturrock. Please explain it."

"Of course, Your Honor. Febrile dementia is characterized by confusion and disorientation brought on by a prolonged bout of high fever due to pneumonia and the condition going untreated."

"Thank you, Mr Sturrock, proceed with your questions."

"Yes, Your Honor. Mr Ryan, it is reasonable to say that Mr Parsons was confused and disoriented by febrile dementia, as I have just outlined for the court. So isn't it entirely possible that Mr Parsons said whatever he allegedly said to you because one, he was in a state of febrile dementia, and two, he wanted to be rid of you. Isn't that possible, Sheriff?"

"I am well-acquainted with Mr Parsons. He certainly wanted to be rid of me, not because he was ill, but because I was challenging him with the truth. Truth he didn't want to hear."

"And what if I were to tell you that the prison doctor's report of Ed Parsons' medical condition shoots your *opinion* to pieces?"

"I am not responsible for what the prison doctor wrote in his report; only for my own actions and what I witnessed. Mr Parsons was perfectly competent at the time of my visit with him."

"The doctor's report and your testimony are conflicted, Mr Ryan. Is that not a concern to you?"

"I have not seen the contents of the report, nor do I know the date of it or anything else except what you have described to me here and now. I cannot remark on anything further regarding it."

"Let's remedy that, shall we? Your Honor, if it would please the court to show the witness the prison doctor's report…"

"The clerk will give the witness the prison doctor's report… Proceed, Mr Sturrock."

"Thank you, Your Honor. Read the report for yourself, Mr Ryan. What is the date? It is the same date as your visit, is it not?"

"It is."

"And as you read down the page, you will see that the prison surgeon details his examination, making a diagnosis of pneumonia, with symptoms of fever and febrile dementia, does he not?"

"He does."

"So I put it to you, Mr Ryan, that whatever Mr Parsons had to say to you on that day is unreliable and, furthermore, you put words and meaning into Mr Parsons' mouth in order to have in your possession some kind – any kind – of evidence for your sluggish investigation."

"None of that is true."

"But your investigation was going nowhere, you needed something to hang your misplaced hunch and prejudice towards my client upon and this was it, was it not?"

"No."

"Well, I am loathe to break it to you, Mr Ryan, but it looks very much that way, to the court and everyone here…"

"I was there, counselor, and I know what Mr Parsons said and how he said it. And I have no prejudice towards the accused, I deal with criminal evidence and only criminal evidence, and that's what I uncovered and acted upon."

"You uncovered a man in prison who was ill and would say whatever was needed to be rid of you, that is all."

"Objection!"

"Yes, Mr Faraday?"

"Your Honor, we've been over this…"

"Mr Sturrock?"

"Yes, Your Honor?"

"How much longer do you intend to pursue this line of questioning?"

"Until I am satisfied, Your Honor."

"And that would be about now, wouldn't it, Mr Sturrock?"

"I am merely trying to get to the truth, Your Honor."

"Your Honor, Sheriff Ryan is under oath; is my learned colleague implying that Mr Ryan is committing perjury?"

"What say you to that, Mr Sturrock?"

"Only that I am moving on, Your Honor."

"Continue, counselor."

"Thank you, Your Honor. Now, Mr Ryan, regarding Mr Taylor's famous file which you spoke to Mr Parsons about... there were faces and objects that proved not relevant to Mr Parsons' trial, were there not?"

"That's correct."

"Can you give the court a number... five, ten, twenty?"

"There were eight."

"Eight! And by the process of diligent investigation you eliminated them one by one, did you not?"

"That's correct."

"You deemed these entries as random and insignificant, including that of my client, did you not?"

"The significance of their appearance in Luke Taylor's file did not hold enough sway in the case to convict Ed Parsons of murder, conspiracy, bribery, extortion and cattle rustling. It doesn't mean that their appearance and then elimination can be generalized as random and insignificant."

"But you would have seen my client's sketch in the file and been skeptical of its inclusion, would you not?"

"Its inclusion surprised me."

"Why?"

"Because of the accused's standing in the community."

"And because if *you* are seen with a convicted man, Sheriff Ryan, and you often are, no one draws the conclusion that you are in cahoots with him, isn't that so?"

"That is so."

"Sheriff Ryan, during the time you interrogated Gordy Jacobs didn't you deprived him of water to drink?"

"No, he was given water to drink."

"You deprived him of food to eat, did you not?"

"There was no deprivation. Prisoners under interrogation are not given food."

"But he was tired and hungry and you persisted, didn't you?"

"You would have to ask Mr Jacobs for the exact condition of his person at the time, but his condition was his to own, and I certainly did not make him that way."

"But you persisted with the interrogation, didn't you?"

"Yes."

"Mr Jacobs never had access to an attorney, did he?"

"If he had asked for one, he would have got one."

"You neglected to make him aware of his rights, did you not?"

"That's incorrect. He was made aware of his rights."

"But you deprived him of food and rest. In essence, you extracted a confession from a defeated man whom you scared into giving the answers you wanted, did you not, Mr Ryan?"

"Certainly not. Gordy Jacobs was given water. It was late at night. I didn't have the resources to go out and buy the man a three-course meal. Nor am I in the habit of consoling prisoners – particularly one charged with attempted murder – telling them not to worry and everything is going to be all right. As I said, upon his arrest his condition was his own and not my doing, and he made his confession without duress or coercion."

"Mr Ryan, what kind of gun did Mr Jacobs allegedly use to shoot at Miss Roberts?"

"It was a Frontier six shooter, caliber .44-40."

"And how many of those are there across the West?"

"Impossible to count."

"And yet you are so certain that it was his bullet you found in the side of Mr Faraday's home."

"Well, no one else has ever shot at Mr Faraday's house in the five years that I have lived here and the bullet hole was too fresh to predate five years. The wood was freshly splintered."

"And yet there are such six shooters and their bullets from one end of the Frontier to other, are there not?"

"Yes."

"Now, Mr Ryan, has *Swinton Carter* ever admitted to shooting at Miss Roberts?"

"No."

"And is it true that he has no legal representation at present?"

"He had legal representation up until two weeks ago. His Honor remanded him in custody until a date for his trial could be set. That date occurred during the time his attorney Marvin Tucker decided to leave Cheyenne and himself return under arrest."

"It is quite likely that the man is innocent and that you are detaining him indefinitely without legal representation and without the hope of a speedy trial. The young man has curled up into his shell, Mr Ryan, scared and unsure of his future. You shot him, Mr Ryan, didn't you?"

"I wounded him in the process of defending an innocent woman from attempted murder. That is my job."

"Miss Roberts stopped without warning on the sidewalk, did she not?"

"Yes."

"It was obviously in her own best interest to keep walking, was it not?"

"Yes."

"If she didn't want to be shot at then why did she stop, Sheriff Ryan?"

"Objection, Your Honor, Sheriff Ryan is not required to answer for Miss Roberts, nor is the inference that Miss Roberts knew she would be shot if she stopped appropriate or reasonable."

"Objection sustained."

"Nothing further for this witness."

"You may step down, Mr Ryan. Call your next witness, Mr Faraday."

Luke

"You may begin, Mr Faraday."

"Thank you, Your Honor. Mr Taylor, why did you return from San Francisco at the beginning of February?"

"For personal reasons, and because I'd left the investigation into Miss Keaton's murder to yourself and Sheriff Ryan and I didn't think that was right."

"And what did you discover on your return?"

"I discovered that the sketch of Loren Bodecker's face in my file held a significance I was not aware of, that it *was* significant."

"Your Honor, People's exhibit 3: the page from Mr Taylor's file with the sketch he made of Mr Bodecker in the Fall of 1883."

"Thank you, Mr Faraday."

"I offer this exhibit into evidence and ask that the jury be allowed to view it."

"Objection…"

"Your Honor, what could my learned colleague possibly be objecting to?"

"Why don't we ask him, eh, Mr Faraday? Your objection would be on what grounds, Mr Buchanan?"

"I contend that this sketch of my client in Mr Taylor's file is hearsay."

"Objection overruled. I will allow it. The jury will view the evidence… Proceed, Mr Faraday."

"Mr Taylor, can you explain what you mean when you say you discovered the sketch of the accused's face in your file held a significance you were not aware of?"

"Last year, during Ed Parsons' trial, I had not been made aware of who Loren Bodecker was and what the association between the two men could mean for the Alliance and Miss Keaton's murder."

"You didn't know who he was?"

"I had heard of him but I had never seen him. So, no."

"How did his face come to be in your file?"

"Last year, during the latter period of Ed Parsons' harassment of us, my partner Ethan Benchley told me…"

"Objection. Hearsay…"

"Your Honor, this is purely the mechanics of how the sketch got to be in the file."

"Overruled, Mr Buchanan. Go on, Mr Taylor."

"My partner Ethan Benchley told me he'd been to see Ed and a man he'd never seen before was there. I asked him to describe the man and I sketched his face."

"And this man was Loren Bodecker."

"That's correct, although I didn't know it at the time."

"Objection! If it pleases the court, Your Honor, I maintain this sketch is hearsay despite how it came to be. How can we be expected to determine what Mr Benchley saw and didn't see?"

"Your Honor, whether Mr Buchanan likes it or not, the sketch is the spitting image of his client, all the more skillful considering it was done from someone else's description."

"That's my point, Your Honor."

"Mr Buchanan, if you had a problem with the sketch you should have come and seen me in my chambers before the trial began. But to satisfy you and your colleagues, Mr Benchley will be required to take the stand to give testimony as to how he came to see Mr Bodecker and how the sketch came about."

"Thank you, Your Honor, and now, if I may, I would like to cross-examine the witness on another part of his testimony?"

"If Mr Faraday has finished with the witness for now."

"I have, for the present, Your Honor."

"So be it. Proceed, Mr Buchanan."

"Mr Taylor, you said you returned to Cheyenne for personal reasons, what were they?"

"Objection…"

"Sustained."

"You just stated that you didn't think it right to leave the investigation into Miss Keaton's death to the professionals. What did you possibly think you could do? This is Cheyenne, Mr Taylor, not the Range."

"Where I come from, when you pledge your loyalty to someone, you don't give up on it, even if that someone has passed on. Miss Keaton didn't deserve to die, she was my friend and an Alliance member and I wanted to make very sure she got justice for what was done to her."

"A noble sentiment indeed. You were a *very* close friend of Miss Keaton, weren't you?"

"Yes."

"So close, in fact, that you were at one time engaged to be married?"

"Objection… what is the relevance of…"

"Overruled."

"Mr Taylor?"

"No, we were not engaged to be married."

"Promised then."

"In a manner of speaking."

"Interesting. But you couldn't see eye to eye on a great number of things…"

"Objection…"

"Objection sustained. A relevant question is required, Mr Buchanan."

"Such a question is forthcoming, Your Honor. Mr Taylor, your relationship with Miss Keaton broke down, didn't it?"

"Objection. Your Honor, there is no relevance to the case in this line of questioning. We are not here to examine Mr Taylor's personal misadventures."

"Objection sustained. Anything further, Mr Buchanan?"

"Yes, Your Honor. Mr Taylor, you are no stranger to Cheyenne, you have been coming here for years. More than ten years, would you say?"

"Yes."

"So in all that time you had never seen my client before?"

"No."

"Why should we believe you?"

"Because it's the truth."

"And if it is the truth then, and the sketch of my client is as Mr Faraday put it 'the spitting image' of him, either you are extremely talented or we are being asked to believe the incredible. And why should we? ...You are very quiet, Mr Taylor. Come, speak up!"

"I'm a rancher in the next county. I spend most of my life with horses and cattle and family, occasionally I see the neighbors. And I like it that way. When it's time to take the cattle to market I drive them to Laramie and put them on the stock train. Then I get on the passenger train and come to Cheyenne. When I get here I see the couple of friends I have in town. We have a drink at the saloon and play some cards. Unless Mr Bodecker has changed his style of living, when would we ever cross paths?"

"And yet..."

"And yet, counselor, Mr Bodecker came to Ed Parsons' place. So we did cross paths, in a manner of speaking. Not because I changed my routine, but because *he* did, and in that moment of difference, a thing happened... my partner Ethan saw him. You see what I'm saying?"

"Mr Taylor..."

"In all those years, we never crossed paths, but when we did it was a telling moment, the one moment I needed to fully comprehend for Miss Keaton's sake and didn't."

"Your Honor, I request that these remarks be stricken from the record on the grounds that they are prejudicial balderdash."

"Order..."

"Your Honor, my learned colleague asked Mr Taylor to speak up. And he did."

"Order... order... I'll have order in this courtroom... Now, Mr Buchanan, your request is denied. Anything further, counselor?"

"That will be all for now, Your Honor."

"The witness may step down."

"Your Honor, the People call Mr Ethan Benchley to the stand."

Ethan

"Please state your name, residence and occupation."

"Ethan Benchley. Rancher. Diamond-T Ranch, Bright River, Wyoming."

"Mr Benchley, when was the first time you ever saw the accused, Mr Loren Bodecker?"

"Well, Mr Faraday, I reckon that would be the Fall of 1883. I went over to Ed Parsons' place to ask Ed about some harassment he'd seen fit to unleash on us and Mr Bodecker was there with Ed talking and drinking."

"Objection. Your Honor, the witness' statement infers guilt by association…"

"Facts are facts, Your Honor."

"Your Honor, if Mr Bodecker was there that does not mean he was carrying out the same activities as Mr Parsons. Businessmen meet for all sorts of reasons."

"Objection sustained. The witness will not infer guilt by association."

"So, Mr Benchley, you didn't know who he was?"

"Never seen him before in my life."

"What did you do?"

"Well, I was kinda steamed up inside because Ed had sent the murderer Wilson Cutter to intimidate the Keaton women while John was away retrieving his stolen cattle, which Ed was also responsible for, so even though I was suspicious, I thought it best to be civil to the stranger. After all, he looked like a big shot and I was on my own…"

"Objection. Again the inference…"

"Your Honor, at that time the Alliance was engaged in a battle for survival. Any associate of Ed Parsons couldn't help but be seen as a potential threat to them. At the very least, as Mr Benchley just testified, viewed with suspicion."

"I see your point, Mr Faraday. However, there is no crime in being seen with someone of any persuasion."

"Your Honor, the association between Mr Bodecker and Mr Parsons goes to the heart of why the sketch appears in the file."

"Be that as it may, I would ask the witness to refrain from such inferences in his testimony."

"Yes, Your Honor. Please continue, Mr Benchley."

"Well, I went home, told Luke and his mother about this new feller…"

"Objection…"

"Ah, about this feller I'd never seen before at Ed's place. Luke was keeping his file on Ed at the time and he wanted me to describe the man so he could sketch him. I did so to the best of my ability. Luke's handy with a pencil and pretty soon the man's face comes to be on the page. It looked just like him. Luke put the sketch into his file. That's how Mr Bodecker's face came to be there."

"Thank you, Mr Benchley. Your Honor, I reserve the right to call this witness at a later time."

"Your witness, Mr Sturrock."

"Mr Benchley, we have heard how my client's image got into Mr Taylor's file by *chance*, did we not?"

"Chance?"

"You walked in unannounced and happened to find my client, did you not?"

"Sure."

"So my client's image got into Mr Taylor's file because of a chance meeting between you, did it not?"

"Yes."

"And how long were you and my client in the same room?"

"Can't say for sure… maybe fifteen minutes."

"And how close did you get to my client?"

"How close?"

"Was it one foot, five feet, ten yards, for example?"

"I didn't measure it. About from me to you, counselor, six feet for the most part."

"And you never saw my client and Mr Parsons in the same place at the same time at any other time since, did you?"

"No."

"Mr Benchley, how long did it take for you to describe my client to Mr Taylor at the time of the alleged sketch?"

"About ten minutes."

"You are a rancher, are you not?"

"Yes."

"And part of your job as a rancher is to describe things in intimate detail to other people, is it?"

"Well…"

"Yes, or no."

"No."

"You don't do it on a daily or even weekly basis, do you?"

"No."

"You are aware that Mr Faraday and Sheriff Ryan knew of the sketch's existence in the file through Ed Parsons' trial, are you not?"

"Yes."

"And you are aware of why they chose to ignore it, are you not?"

"I've never heard them say why."

"You are aware, though, that my client Loren Bodecker is considered one of the most respected and important men in the West, are you not?"

"Yes."

"And therefore you would see it as ridiculous that my client could be involved with a man such as Ed Parsons…"

"Objection, Your Honor, the defense is leading the witness."

"Objection sustained."

"Your Honor, I have no further questions for this witness."

"The witness will step down. This court is adjourned for the lunch recess."

Faraday

Glancing out his office window, sandwich on its way to his mouth, Faraday double takes as he glimpses Cliff sending the picket line, which has been parading by his doorstep all morning, on its way.

"Brave move, sheriff," he murmurs.

"Did you say something, Cam?" Josh asks from the other side of the room where he's been fussing with witness files for the last five minutes.

"I said you should eat something," he replies, turning and indicating the plate of sandwiches at hand.

"I have already. And, yes, Cliff is showing an uncharacteristic lack of sympathy, but he's concerned they are getting too close to the defendants."

"And the defendants' sympathizers."

"Indeed."

He returns his gaze to the street. That picket line amounts to a bunch of very unhappy people and, if pushed too hard, possibly capable of anything.

"So, Cam, Ben Taylor is next on the stand, followed by his mother..."

"Caroline, yes... And, she's nervous."

"Having to face Donnelly in court, it's not surprising. But I have confidence in her, Cam. She's a brave woman."

He nods his agreement. "Well, let's get Ben on the stand."

For this session, he has Ben give testimony in three specific areas. Ben chooses to be terse and straight to the point.

First, regarding Loren Bodecker's interest in Richard Taylor's mining business…

"They had made a deal to expand the business into Wyoming coal. My father was taken by the venture. Even so, I felt uncomfortable about Mr Bodecker's smooth and superior manner."

Secondly, on a personal level…

"I needed to go west to visit with my sister whom I hadn't seen in twelve months, even though my father would see this as betrayal, because my sister had married Mart Keaton against his wishes.

"My desire to see my sister outweighed my father's predictable disapproval, and with my mother's blessing I left for Wyoming."

And, lastly, the point to which he had been building, what happened on Ben's train journey to Cheyenne…

"I met Donnelly. He came right up to me, a man I had never seen before. Sat down at my non-smoking table without an invitation and started smoking. Announced his name at *my* suggestion. I recognized the name from the business meeting with Bodecker the day before – his Cheyenne partner Donnelly.

"Donnelly knew who I was, which considering we had never even met before was supposed to unnerve me. It didn't. He mistook my journey to Wyoming for wanting to see my cousin Luke who he called a nuisance and a troublemaker. He seemed to know a lot about him, and details about my sister and the Keaton family. He spoke in a superior, menacing tone, always fishing for information, or gloating about what he thought he already knew. After he finished harassing me, Donnelly alighted the train at a small town one hour out of Omaha."

He reserves Ben for another appearance and since Sturrock and Buchanan have no questions for cross-examination, Ben steps down.

When he calls Caroline Taylor to the witness stand, he watches Donnelly's face freeze like pond ice. Caroline has not confronted the man since that fateful morning when her life changed forever; everything that has occurred since has filled her with terror and she is trembling on the witness stand. Her fear will make sense to the jury once she relates her story.

"My son Ben left for Wyoming, my husband became enraged and left the house. I went to the kitchen to make myself tea. A man was there…"

"Is that man present in court, Mrs Taylor?" Faraday asks.

"The man sitting next to Mr Sturrock, there. That's him." She stabs a precise finger in Donnelly's direction. "That's the man who insisted Ben went to Wyoming to see Luke, and when I refuted this he didn't believe me and accused me of lying. He wasn't pleased that Ben had decided to make contact with Luke who he called Ben's *no-good cousin*.

"I asked him why he was bothered about such things, and what he answered I'll never forget as long as I live. It has never left my mind and for days and days afterwards it went round and round in my head… I couldn't sleep or eat…"

"What were those words that tormented you, Mrs Taylor?"

"He said: *it ain't a good move to ally himself with the friend of the small time operators in Wyoming, not if he wants his daddy's business to succeed, if I were you I would get him back pronto. Get your boy back and keep him out of Wyoming.* When I asked what would happen if I couldn't do as he asked, he threatened me and that tormented me, too, even worse."

"What was that terrible threat, Mrs Taylor?"

"It was: *there's a lot at stake, your old man's business, your children's lives.* My children! My children, Mr Faraday."

"And, Mrs Taylor, was there anything else?"

"There was more: *your husband is an association member now and it's all a question of loyalty. Taylor is an enemy of the association and we wouldn't want divided loyalties.*"

"Did you understand to which or to whose Association he was referring?"

"I understood it to be Mr Bodecker's."

"How so?"

"In my husband's world the Association meant Bodecker…"

Buchanan stands at once. "Objection, Your Honor. Mrs Taylor's understanding is in fact an assumption. There are many associations in this world…"

"Your Honor, this is a perfectly intelligent connection made by the witness at this point, one born of commendable knowledge of her husband's business affairs."

"Mrs Taylor?"

"Yes, Your Honor..." says Caroline, turning to the Judge.

"Did Mr Donnelly make specific mention of whose association he was referring to?"

"Not specifically, Your Honor."

"Thank you, Mrs Taylor. I'm afraid, Mr Faraday, Mrs Taylor cannot state specifically that Mr Donnelly is referring to Mr Bodecker's Association. Objection sustained. Anything further, Mr Faraday?"

"Two further questions, Your Honor. Mrs Taylor, what did you do when Mr Donnelly finally left your kitchen?"

"I was so terrified from that time on I kept all the doors locked and I never left the house."

"Did your husband ever return home?"

"No, he never did and I didn't know what had become of him. I was frightened for myself and for my husband and my children."

"Thank you, Mrs Taylor. Your witness, counselor."

Sturrock rises and cross-examines Caroline for thirty long minutes regarding that short and terrifying meeting with Donnelly in her kitchen, about her husband and his business and the way he conducts business. Soon the jury knows everything about the Taylors' Omaha kitchen, from the state of the lock screws on the backdoor to the pattern on Caroline's china plates and what type of cuisine was served on them every day of the week.

Caroline answers Sturrock with unwavering courage and patience; she's a little rattled but no cracks appear, as Faraday would expect from a native New Englander; she steps down, by this time looking like an efficient wife, although trembling from head to toe, until such time as he wishes to recall her.

After all that minutiae about dishes and china plates it's hardly surprising when Judge Callaghan adjourns earlier for the day than expected.

Cliff

Early evening
Nan Morris' guesthouse

Cliff knocks. Nan Morris answers, smiles warmly with her greeting, tells him she will find Emma without him even asking for her, and invites him inside to wait.

"Thank you, Nan, but I'll wait here if it's all the same."

"As you like, Sheriff, but it's cold out." She looks past him, between his shoulder and the wide crack in the door, to survey the darkening street, which is deserted; she appears confused as she turns, closing the door behind her.

Her black cat appears from somewhere, pounces across the frosty ground up onto the porch, its white paws flashing, and begins to wind itself around his pants. He bends down and scratches the animal on the head; it starts purring, pushing its head against his legs. They could be here a while so he decides to make himself comfortable.

He sits himself down on the chilled top step, making sure his coat is tucked under his behind, and continues to stroke the interested cat, finding the whole thing beneficial for the churning feelings inside him. The general thinking is that this is one reason people have pets, not only as companions but also to soothe them. Being denied a pet of any shape or form as a wishful child made him curious, but then as an adult he's always been uncertain whether to believe the general thinking, something he finds himself reassessing at this moment.

Just as he is about to share with the cat that he doubts the object of his visit is going to show, Emma emerges wrapped in a cream-colored woolen shawl large enough for two people.

Her approach is circumspect; she stops by one of the posts that hold up the porch roof and winds her fingers around it, glancing warily at him and the cat.

"What do you want?"

"Will you sit down while I tell you? – otherwise I'll have to stand up and disturb the cat..."

After a full minute of amusing indecision she sits, but leaves an elephant-sized gap between them.

With firm pressure the cat places both its front paws on his thigh, blinking up at him, purring like mad.

"I feel the need to quote Victor Hugo at this point... *God made the cat to give Man the pleasure of caressing the tiger.*"

"I think this tiger wants to jump into your lap."

That's not happening. He pushes the animal away.

"Oh, don't do that... Victor Hugo would be stricken." Emma gathers it up; she strokes it, its black fur rippling beneath her fingers, and very soon it blinks and purrs contentedly. "Well?"

"I came to ask, did you get your job back?"

"Oh... Yes. I did."

He smiles down at his hands; she might look like satin slippers but in some ways she's as tough as old boots.

"I'm glad," he says. "And I'm sorry I had to be so rough on you."

"Oh?"

"But it worked, so maybe you could forgive me..." He turns his head her way to find her fathoming gaze upon him, with what is left of the afternoon light gently illuminating her face. "I wanted to take you by the hand and tell Quaid to get over himself, but you don't need me to do that. You lost self-confidence, momentarily..."

He wants her to know that he understands how much her father's revelations of his infidelity and the deception surrounding her parents' marriage woes are hurting her, and how difficult it can be to keep personal problems from affecting your working life.

"Yes," she murmurs and looks at the cat. "And then I... I was annoyed with you and Mr Quaid felt the sting of it."

"Ah…"

"You manipulated me," she says, her voice wobbling.

"If I'd given in to those pleading eyes of yours…"

"I did not plead with my eyes."

"And the hat just about killed me. But we both had our jobs to do, there wasn't much time…"

"Don't say anymore. I forgive you."

Abruptly, she looks up, no doubt hoping to dismiss him. He's learning to steal himself against the times she brushes him off. But the afternoon is so peaceful after the hectic day in court and down in the lockup, and she reminds him of the evening star, the first prickle of diamond light in a mauve sky.

"You did well in court," he says before she can speak. "Buchanan realized you'd made a valid point – better you than a family man. Shut the argument down in hasty fashion."

"Yes, it worked. It's not comfortable being on the stand."

"No, but it didn't show."

Without warning the cat springs from her lap and down the stairs; once she has watched its flight, Emma stands up on the step and brushes fur from her skirt.

"Silly old cat…" she murmurs.

He reaches for her hand, pulling her across the space and right down beside him, catching her gently.

"Ashcliff…" she gasps as she falls against him.

That's him. Her Ashcliff. And now that he's got his arms around her and that enormous shawl, he's beginning to feel warm all over. While he's got her stunned he locates an opening in the shawl and slides his hand inside that warm parcel to find her waist. "I'm going to kiss you, Emma."

"Well, I'm much obliged for the warning." She looks like she's considering the prospect, while she catches her breath, her golden eyes suddenly a little smoky beneath those long bowed lashes.

"You're not running away."

"You did help me keep my job."

"So I did."

And when it's happening, when the kiss is finally happening, when her soft lips melt like the sweetest caramel beneath his, when his arms gather her closer, all his doubt scatters and sublime confidence steps in.

Emma, his evening star.

If this is his reward for helping her keep her job, he'll take it.

The day's tension is about to slip away never to return when the cat startles them apart. One set of paws is latched onto his thigh, the other on Emma's knees. Tail high, snaking a warning. If he's not careful there could be damage...

"Oh, my..." she gasps.

A pair of yellow eyes pierces the purple dusk.

"What made him do that?" she whispers.

"Cats are territorial," he murmurs, giving the cat and its swishing tail the respect they deserve. "I don't think he approves of my intentions..."

She gives a laugh and looks at him. He takes his eyes off the cat to look back.

"Oh?"

"Call off your cat."

"Chicken."

"You don't want me to hurt it."

"What are you fixin' to do – shoot him?"

"Crossed my mind."

"Now there's a headline: Sheriff Ryan shoots skittish cat in self-defense." Emma gets to her feet, spilling the animal to the ground and leaving his arms empty; the cat hisses and looks put out, its tail puffed up like a raccoon's, then darts off.

"Intentions?" she asks, looking down at him, trying to right her shawl.

"To be with you."

"Oh. I see. And... and that's all?"

"Had a long, hard day. When I see you... when I'm with you..."

"We could do better than the porch in this weather..."

"Well... You had better get in out of the cold... er, excuse me?"

"Why was it hard?"

So. He hadn't misheard her.

Casually he gets to his feet, disguising the moment-seizing urge that has just gripped him. "Taking men like Bodecker and

45

Donnelly to and from court – they are going to make a lot of enemies, probably already have. Though they may be scum they still have a right to a fair trial and that means no one taking the law into their own hands."

"I should have guessed it was something like that."

"Mm," he says, taking the edges of her shawl and enclosing her tighter into it. Catching her smiling up at him, he grins back. "As enticing as your pity is, I don't need it."

"Don't suppose you do. Still, won't you come inside and warm yourself by the fire? The other boarders are attending a meeting at Father Nugent's and Mrs Morris is delaying supper by one hour. I was reading…" She starts to move, expecting him to follow. Which is the bait – her, or the reading part?

Touché.

"Perhaps you can explain something to me."

"I doubt it."

"From *Les Miserables*."

Oh, she's very good.

Inside, the guesthouse is like another world; he's come in from the frozen wilderness into Emma's world of warmth and fragrance. She waits politely while he removes his hat, gloves and coat. Then she is quick to the hearth; he follows at a more leisurely pace – a more wary pace… they switch places as spider and fly so often he can never really be sure which he is at any given moment.

When he enters the living room a few moments later, she is standing before the hearth, having draped her shawl on a chair, wriggling her fingers. *Hurry up, flames.*

He joins her. And warms his back.

"Good?" she says.

"Perfect. So, what did you want me to explain?"

"Oh, yes…" She ducks to the armchair beside the hearth and picks up the copy of *Les Miserables* (Volume Two) he had given her a few days ago. A red hair ribbon marks the page. She holds it out to him and points. "This passage here…"

He reads it; explains what he thinks it means; closes the book on the ribbon; hands it back to her.

"Really?"

"Just one man's opinion."

She's very serious with him for several moments, and then a smile breaks out on her face. "I can't believe how well you know this book. Was it your Bible before…"

"Before the Catholic one you gave me?"

She laughs. "Yes. You talk like a democrat but inside beats the heart of an anarchist."

"Not true."

"How did that happen?"

"Apart from the fact that it's not true, I don't know."

Her smile widens.

A moment later he watches it fade.

"When Nan Morris came to tell me you were out on the porch, I was sitting here reading and endeavoring to get my mind off my parents. Think I've read that passage at least a hundred times. It's one I find elusive. I thought if I got my thoughts locked onto something elusive it would be a distraction."

"Thoughts wouldn't lock?"

She gives her head a shake.

He studies the sadness in her eyes, observes and understands the resultant weariness. An idea comes to him. "May I have the book back?"

She hands it over.

He flicks through it until he finds the page he wants. Then he puts one arm around her shoulders and holds her close; with his other hand he holds the book eye level behind her shoulder. Lamplight and firelight combine on the pages and illuminate the written word.

"Comfortable?" he asks.

The light of surprise in her eyes gives way to curiosity. "I am."

He smiles.

She returns it.

"*Book 5: The End of Which is Unlike the Beginning,*" he reads. "*6. The old are made to go out when convenient.*"

He glances at her; her eyes have not left his face. He never imagined that he would woo the woman he loved with books. His grandmother's words, so odd and eccentric in isolation, lay forgotten until Emma came along and made sense of them. Their meaning seems obvious now. Now that he has the One in his arms.

He reads in a soft tone, so only she can hear, without applied affectation, without imbued meaning. Hugo has done the work.

Marius and Cosette are in love. They have no idea what it is to be in love; they discover it with each other. It happened within one glance and remained.

For months they are constantly in each other's thoughts. One evening Cosette goes into the garden. Marius has found his way in. He declares his feelings. He adores her. She almost faints. He catches her. She tells him she loves him. They kiss. A kiss that is as intended by Mother Nature as are all her other designs; birds that sing, the sun that rises... Their souls are laid bare to one another and they talk and while they talk and by the end they possess one another's hearts and souls.

Then they tell one another their names.

He glances at Emma from time to time; her eyes tell him how intently she listens; she grins when Cosette swoons and Marius catches her, then she lays her head on his shoulder.

By the time he reveals how Marius and Cosette are enchanted with one another, his voice sounds choked. Their names he discloses in a whisper.

Emma...

After a moment she lifts her head from his shoulder and looks up at him. The sadness, the weariness, has been replaced.

He closes the book and folds her in both arms.

And now they have arrived at the same place they had come to after their dance at the wedding. The exact, same place.

Before her *kiss not me* eyes, rose-tinged cheeks and parted lips he is helpless. Every particle in his body wants to lay them down in front of that fire.

"We've been here before," she says.

He grins into those eyes. "So we have."

"Hot, isn't it?"

"It is," he agrees. "But pleasant."

She smiles and whispers his name...

James, not Ashcliff...

"Who?"

"You," she smiles.

"James?"

"I think so..."

"Then who do you see?"

"A determined Yankee boy who's trying to steal me away."

He holds her closer; tighter. "Come away with me then."

"Where?"

"Emma, my love, you know where."

The place that didn't even exist until the first time their gazes locked and a new world came into being. Their own Eden. Where each assignation is sweeter than the last. Where he wants to give her everything. And never wants to leave.

"I'm not your..."

But in the intense heat of the moment their lips collide.

He is torn away from Cheyenne and dispatched.

This is the magic in her; the wonder of her and the beauty; the longing he shares with her as he kisses her, makes love to her: she dispels the confusion over life's purpose and so appears a renewed James Ashcliff Alejandro Alvarez Ryan, likely the person he was always meant to be, a man who fulfills the expectation of every one of his five names. Why wouldn't he want to steal her away? No one he has ever known has come close to putting all this on the horizon of his life. She is the unwritten poem in his lonesome heart; the melody of his forgotten soul.

He knows she feels what he feels.

She cannot hide it.

Alas, she is still fighting it; she breaks away, looking troubled, and looking for air. "Y...you can't read to me ever again."

Still deep in the kiss, he puts his lips to her frown...

"An...an...and you can't kiss me like that again."

"I dream about kissing you..."

And it's the thought of what they'd be like when she finally stops fighting that makes him smile.

Her starry eyes view his smile with a curious kind of unease.

"You were right, Emma. You said we could do better than the porch. This place is much better."

"I didn't mean… you know, I didn't mean…"

"I think we can say at this point resistance is futile."

Her eyes flash hard at him, stopping his heart as well as all the other romantic intentions going around in his head at that moment.

She backs out of his arms. "The others will be home soon."

"Emma…" His instincts have him reaching for her hand.

Her eyes begin to shimmer with the emergence of tears.

"Emma, don't…"

"D…don't call me Emma."

He has to concede. And he does so with a sigh.

She pulls her hand free. "Thank you for stoppin' by, and for helping me keep my job. Excuse me." Attention to good southern manners paid, she hurries away, leaving his arms empty.

But leaving him warm.

And so much better than he was half an hour ago.

But wondering. And curious. And concerned…

And yet so much better.

Thank you for stoppin' by? It wasn't exactly *do call again*, but neither was it *don't come back*.

This befuddlement could go on for some time. Better he take himself off home. Eat supper. And pour himself an Old Crow.

A large one.

TWO

...the hand of the hour clock moves round...
to the land of darkness and of dreams!

Henry Wadsworth Longfellow
The Two Rivers

Luke

"Mr Taylor, we have heard testimony from your ranch partner Mr Benchley as to how the sketch of Mr Bodecker came to be in your file. After Miss Keaton's murder, you went to San Francisco, then in fulfilling your pledge of loyalty to her you decided to return to Cheyenne. On your return from San Francisco what significance did you place on discovering what Mr Bodecker's face could mean to finding out who shot Miss Keaton?"

"Objection."

"Overruled."

"I discovered that Mr Bodecker's face in my file was the catalyst for the investigation into Miss Keaton's murder. That it gave direction to what seemed like a hopeless case. I was convinced that if the investigation you and Mr Ryan then proceeded to carry out had been conducted while Miss Keaton was alive, given the significance it was due then, she would not have been murdered."

"Objection..."

"Overruled."

"I see. What did you do next?"

"I got angry and was upset and distracted. I continued on my personal business which should have taken me to St Louis via Denver, but instead I got on the first train out of town and went to Omaha, thinking I'd go south from there."

"What happened in Omaha?"

"I got off the train late in the afternoon to stay over in town, settle myself down before I continued my journey, and I thought I would call on my uncle who lived there."

"Who is your uncle?"

"Richard Taylor."

"What is his occupation?"

"He owns a mining company. Taylor Mining."

"When you got to his house that evening what did you find?"

"I found my aunt, Caroline Taylor, alone in the house, terrified and confused. My uncle was nowhere around. And neither was my cousin Ben. Both men I planned to confront about my cousin Tressa's treatment since her marriage to my friend Mart. But there was only Aunt Caroline, very scared and alone. She told me what Ben had done and how her husband was angry and she hadn't seen him for days. Over the course of the evening she told me about the visit from a stranger and the threats she'd received if she couldn't bring Ben back from Wyoming. She had sent numerous telegrams, offering Ben any incentive she could think of, but he wired her that he would not come, and that his father should investigate a man named Donnelly."

"Your Honor, People's exhibits 4a and 4b: Mrs Caroline Taylor's telegrams to her son Ben Taylor, exhorting him to return home, and People's exhibits 4c, 4d and 4e: Ben Taylor's telegrams in response to her requests, including the plea to investigate the accused Mr Donnelly. I offer them into evidence."

"Thank, Mr Faraday. Please continue."

"What else did your Aunt Caroline reveal about the visit from the stranger in her kitchen?"

"Although she wasn't certain the stranger in her kitchen was Donnelly, her instincts were telling her he was. She got scared when she remembered she wasn't supposed to tell anyone."

"And what did you do?"

"I took pity on her and offered her my help. She told me of Loren Bodecker's admittance to the board of her husband's company and the extensive plans they had for expansion. I told her I had doubts about Bodecker, since I'd learned the significance of his face in my file, and that if this Donnelly was a partner of Bodecker and Ben keeps begging her to investigate him then we need to get back to Cheyenne and start putting together all the pieces of the puzzle. I also thought she'd be safer and happier with Tressa and Ben.

"But she was able to tell me there was a chance Mr Bodecker was still in town and where I could possibly find him – the Paxton Hotel. I took her to another hotel where she could be safe and then went to find Bodecker for myself."

"You went to the Paxton Hotel?"

"Yes. I was able to distract the desk clerk and find out that Loren Bodecker and Donnelly were still registered. Rooms 204 and 205. I got up to the second floor via the service hall. Just as I was working out what to do next, two men stepped out of the elevator. I recognized one of the men from the sketch in my file. It was Loren Bodecker. The other man I didn't know."

"And is this other man in this courtroom?"

"Yes, that's him. Mr Donnelly."

"Continue."

"Bodecker says, *What news of Cheyenne?* Donnelly answers, *You ain't gonna like it.* Then they went into room 204. But they don't close the door, as if one of them isn't staying long; the door is ajar. I put my ear to the crack and the voices are muffled. If I want to hear I must get in. Very carefully, I push the door back, small increments 'til I can see inside. The two men are on the other side of the large room and engrossed. I make the door wide enough to squeeze through and then I hide behind a large armchair. I stay there, listening to their conversation. From this position I can hear very well.

"Then, suddenly, a blonde girl opens the door wide and saunters in. From her dress and made up face and the way she moves I believe her to be a prostitute. She's young, just a kid. She sees me behind the chair, I put my finger to my lips to ask for her silence. She agrees by pretending she doesn't see me and by not letting on I'm there. Bodecker tells her to sit down and wait 'til he's finished talking business."

"And what did his business entail?"

"Donnelly is telling Bodecker about Aunt Caroline being too scared to leave her house, about Ben who isn't taking any notice of her pleas for him to come home, about Maverick not being able to get the job done and about the boys in the lockup. Bodecker blows up, yelling, *Are they talking, Donnelly? They better not be talking*. Donnelly tells him to relax and says he's got someone *to clean up the mess*. Bodecker accuses him of making the mess and starts yelling *get Marvin Tucker off the case*, that *he'll never handle it*. He says he wants *Maverick to stay out of Cheyenne, that Sheriff Ryan probably knows about the whole operation by now*. He accuses Donnelly of *making mistakes, bad ones*, and orders him to do nothing unless it's what he tells him to do. Donnelly asks what to do about *Taylor*. Bodecker says that my uncle, Richard Taylor, has enough to think about with Ben running out on him, but he's happy with the way the business is going. They reckon Ben is in Bright River by now. And they think that I am still in San Francisco.

"Donnelly says they should have made their move sooner. They discuss the prospect that Maverick is set to follow Ben to Bright River and laugh that he was warned not to go. Bodecker says that as long as you, Mr Faraday, and Sheriff Ryan don't know who Maverick is, there won't be a problem and that it's Donnelly's job to see that it doesn't happen. Donnelly is to return to Cheyenne and tell Dillon Kerr to take care of Swinton Carter.

"Donnelly says they should have used Maverick against the Alliance two years ago... that it would be all over by now... that Parsons was an expensive waste of time, that it was a mistake, even though he knew the Alliance.

"Bodecker tells Donnelly to get to work and then says, *no matter what that Tribune reporter prints about me I won't be setting foot in Cheyenne*, and that Dillon Kerr can fix it.

"Donnelly leaves after this. Bodecker comes after the girl and orders her into the bedroom. A couple of minutes later I was certain he wasn't coming out again. So I left."

"What did you do next?"

"The following morning, early, I got Aunt Caroline and myself on the first train to Cheyenne. My aunt was unhappy about traveling second class as she wasn't used to it, but it seemed safer to me. We were a few hours out of Omaha when Bodecker's blonde prostitute comes up to me. All I can think of is if she is here then

Bodecker or maybe even Donnelly ain't far away. I asked what she was doing here and she told me *she'd come into some money* and she was *going to find a place called Bright River*. I told her I was happy for her but to go away. She takes herself off to the dining car. I explain to Aunt Caroline that she's Bodecker's whore and if she's run away he might come looking for her and that she knows me because she saw me in his room last evening.

"I am suddenly very concerned about the circumstances Aunt Caroline and I find ourselves in. We agree that getting to Cheyenne with the information I'd discovered last evening when listening to Bodecker and Donnelly, and delivering it to Sheriff Ryan, are *the* most important things to be done. I was extremely concerned for my family and the Alliance. Aunt Caroline has a stake in this, her daughter, her son and grandson. She says that if anything happens to me she will go straight to Sheriff Ryan. I tell her to lie about me, disown me, betray me, if that's what it takes, but get the information through, although I might have to do the same about her. She was very brave and said she understood. We agreed. It was the best we could do.

"By the afternoon we are very tired, but we see the girl again and she doesn't look good; she looks pale and sick. Aunt Caroline is concerned about her. She says, *dreadful things trains, one hears the most alarming tales.*

"Aunt Caroline and I conceal ourselves behind newspapers. My aunt decides to go to the rest room. But suddenly she sits down again and starts shaking. She tells me from behind her newspaper that the stranger from her kitchen is coming our way. I take a look. It's Donnelly. I feel uneasy and try to steady Aunt Caroline. Donnelly goes straight by us; he goes to the blonde prostitute's seat and indicates with a nod that she should follow him. Aunt Caroline and I hold our breaths and hide behind our newspapers. Donnelly doesn't see us. A few moments later the blonde girl gets up and leaves again. For some long minutes I feel sick at the thought of what might be happening to the poor kid with Donnelly, so I remind Aunt Caroline of what we agreed to and go after the prostitute. That was the last time I saw my aunt.

"Two cars along I hear the blonde girl's voice in the corridor. I

57

tuck myself out of the way because I recognize Donnelly's voice also and I'm alarmed. The girl is offering him money. While they are arguing I try to take a look. I see Donnelly slam the girl against the wall of the train; her head thumps and falls forward. Before I can do anything, even take a breath, I hear a snap and Donnelly lets go of the girl and her body falls to the floor. Donnelly steps over her, takes the money she was offering him and stuffs it in his pocket. He walks off, leaving her there. I wait for Donnelly to leave the car and then go up to the girl. She's dead.

"But while I am feeling for her pulse and looking her over, two passengers raise the alarm. A guard appears and pulls a pistol on me and tells me to stay still. I try to explain what has happened but he says, *a passenger just reported screams coming from here*. He tells me we're just outside North Platte and I can tell it to the Sheriff. I have to hand over my own pistol and sit on the floor beside the dead girl and wait."

"Thank you, Mr Taylor. Your Honor, I ask the court's permission to recall this witness at a later time…"

"So granted. Mr Buchanan, anything from you?"

"Your Honor, I request a short recess before I cross-examine Mr Taylor. I need to confer with my client."

"Recess granted. Ten minute adjournment, gentlemen."

"Thank you, Your Honor."

"All rise…"

Buchanan

With the courtroom cleared of judge and jury, and half the gallery outside taking some fresh air or gone for a smoke, and while two heavily armed guards patrol the back of the room, Buchanan takes a slow breath and releases it.

Bodecker leans across, not so patient. "What's going on, Buchanan? Why'd you call a recess?"

He aims his gaze squarely at Bodecker. "It doesn't matter what anyone else has against you, Loren, if I can't destroy Taylor on the stand in ten minutes' time your chances of winning this are slim at best. His ability to recall facts and details and the way he relates to the jury explain why Faraday and Ryan went to the lengths they did to protect him."

"Taylor's a fool."

"Is that what you truly think, Loren? Because Taylor is as smart as they come and you need to think again."

"Bullshit."

"Afraid not, Loren. Not this time."

"Then destroy him. Do whatever it takes, no matter how long it takes."

Faraday

Faraday hands Luke the water pitcher. "Drink all of it, you're going to need it."

"What's going to happen?" Luke tables the pitcher.

"I think Buchanan's been playing nice up till now." He leans across his desk and peers into Luke's wary face. "Expect anything."

"What exactly do you mean by that?"

"Just this. Considering everything you just said, how you said it and the way the jury believed you, I'd say we cannot expect anything less than a serious attack on your credibility, before you get too further along in your testimony."

"How serious?"

"I know you can handle it, don't doubt it for a second, but I'm just warning you. Grant you, it was always going to happen, but after your damaging testimony, I think he's bringing it forward."

"Then why did we stop? I could've kept on going..."

"It's a big story, Luke. The jury needs to see and understand it from every angle. See and understand why you all stand together the way you do. Henry Wadsworth Longfellow once wrote *a small group of determined people can change the course of history*. It's no mean thing and I intend for that jury to appreciate it. We cannot break Bodecker with anything less than a powerful demonstration of the enormity of the evil he's perpetrated."

"Then I agree. I'm ready. Why did Buchanan ask for a recess?"

"To consult with Bodecker."

"About what?"

"Destroying you, my friend."

Luke

"Mr Taylor, let us examine the episode you had with hallucinatory drugs and opiates several weeks ago…"

"Objection! This is outrageous from Mr Buchanan, blatantly assuming facts not in evidence."

"Approach the bench, gentlemen… …"

"Your Honor, I must insist…"

"I hear you, Mr Faraday; however, given the manner in which the prosecution is presenting its case, given that Mr Taylor is key to it, I will allow Mr Buchanan this line of cross-examination. First, I assume that Mr Taylor's brush with drugs will be placed before the jury at some point in your case; if it so happens that it doesn't, I will instruct the jury accordingly. Secondly, you have the opportunity to redirect at its conclusion. Step back, gentlemen…

"The prosecution's objection is overruled. The witness will answer the question. Order, order… I said order! Continue, Mr Buchanan."

"Yes, Your Honor. Allow me to reiterate, Mr Taylor. Is it not true that several weeks ago you had an episode with certain drugs and opiates?"

"Yes. But they were forced on me when I was kidnapped and held against my will in North Platte. I did not take them voluntarily."

"I see. What were the physical effects of these drugs?"

"I went blind, I was sick, experienced hallucinations…"

"What kind of hallucinations?"

"Mostly that I was flying."

"Mostly? What else?"

"It was weird, confusing, scary... strange dreams..."

"What dreams did you have, Mr Taylor?"

"About the woman I loved."

"Well, that conjures up all sorts of wonderful imaginings. Were these dreams erotic in any way?"

"Objection. Your Honor, is this really necessary?"

"Overruled, Mr Faraday. The witness will answer."

"Some were."

"I see. Did you develop, for example, the inability to tell reality from fantasy?"

"That did happen. But when I was rescued and was no longer given the drugs this disappeared."

"I have it on good authority, Mr Taylor, that excessive drug taking also causes memory loss or deficiency..."

"Objection. Your Honor, is Mr Buchanan's good authority the medical encyclopedia he has recently written?"

"Objection sustained. Mr Buchanan?"

"Your Honor, I have here a volume published by Professor Jean-Paul Geraux who is an expert in the field of the effects of drugs of addiction on the human body."

"Your Honor, does my learned colleague intend to call Professor Geraux as an expert witness?"

"Mr Buchanan?"

"If I may be allowed to recite from his book, Your Honor, I'm sure the gentlemen of the jury will be satisfied..."

"Read on, Mr Buchanan."

"Professor Geraux states in his introduction, and I have the words underlined, that *delusions, paranoia, memory loss and memory deficiency are common and often long term side-effects from the ongoing consumption of addictive drugs*, drugs such as those Mr Taylor took."

"Objection, Your Honor; in the first place, Mr Taylor did not take the drugs; he has just testified they were forced upon him during the period of his captivity and deprivation of liberty..."

"Objection sustained. Mr Buchanan?"

"Allow me to rephrase, Your Honor... such as the ones that affected Mr Taylor."

"I see you have another objection, Mr Faraday?"

"Yes, Your Honor; secondly, Mr Taylor did not consume addictive drugs long term. The period of time he was given them was three days at best. Thirdly, I have here – which I offer into evidence now, since Mr Buchanan has jumped ahead – People's exhibit 5: the medical report by Doctor Arthur Kincaid who treated Mr Taylor in North Platte after he was rescued from the man who drugged him. In it, Dr Kincaid states that Mr Taylor suffered from blindness, sweating, muscle cramps, nausea and vomiting, shaking and tremors, and an aversion to soup because that's how some of the drugs were administered."

"Come, Your Honor, who's to say that Mr Taylor didn't suffer delusions and keep them to himself..."

"Your Honor, Dr Kincaid is a reputable and experienced physician. He would have noticed if Mr Taylor was delusional. In fact, he says in his medical report that Mr Taylor showed remarkable courage and fortitude during the withdrawal, and approached his sufferings with clarity of mind and a determined character!"

"If neither party intends to produce their expert witness at this juncture, and Mr Faraday has the medical report from Mr Taylor's physician, objection is sustained. Let's move on, Mr Buchanan."

"Yes, Your Honor. Mr Taylor, do you suffer from side-effects now?"

"No."

"For how long did you suffer side-effects?"

"For several weeks."

"And in those weeks did you suffer melancholia?"

"Some doctors called it that."

"And of what did you despair in that melancholia?"

"Objection. Relevance, Your Honor."

"Your Honor, it is relevant to Mr Taylor's state of mind. A mind bent on telling all it knows about my client. I'm just trying to ascertain whether it is a sound mind or not."

"Objection overruled."

"What, Mr Taylor, did you despair of in your melancholy?"

"That I would never see Jennifer again."

"Doctor Jennifer Sullivan?"

"Yes."

"Objection. Your Honor, how is this relevant?"

"I must admit I'm curious, Mr Faraday. And we are going to find out. However, I would caution Mr Buchanan at this point that I will not tolerate any malicious words against the good doctor. Be very careful, Mr Buchanan."

"Noted, Your Honor."

"Objection overruled."

"So, Mr Taylor, you were pining away for Dr Sullivan?"

"Pining? I guess I was pining."

"How long had you been involved with Dr Sullivan, Mr Taylor?"

"Objection..."

"Objection sustained."

"When you returned to Cheyenne, why didn't you go and find Dr Sullivan, Mr Taylor?"

"At the time I was under a bench warrant prohibiting me from leaving town."

"So Dr Sullivan came to you?"

"She came to Cheyenne to find me, yes."

"And she found you much altered since last seeing you?"

"Objection. Calls for the witness to speculate on Dr Sullivan's findings."

"Objection sustained."

"Why were you bound by a warrant to stop you leaving town?"

"Objection, Your Honor. Mr Taylor does not have to..."

"Objection overruled."

"Mr Taylor, wasn't it because the Sheriff of Lincoln County, Ralph Walker, believed you murdered the sickly young blonde prostitute, Cadie McClements, on the train, and then bashed one of his deputies in order to escape custody?"

"Order, order... please answer the question, Mr Taylor."

"Sheriff Walker might have thought that, but it is not true. I didn't do either of those things and he knew I was innocent. The Judge has since rescinded the warrant."

"But you have yet to face Sheriff Walker of Lincoln County?"

"That's correct. And I will do that with confidence."

"How inspiring! What happened when Dr Sullivan came back into town, Mr Taylor? Isn't it true she found you living in the tenements in a thoroughly depressed state as a result of your bout with the drugs?"

"I was living there, but the melancholia went away when she came."

"How touching! Did she give you some medicine and make you all better?"

"Objection. Your Honor…"

"Objection overruled. Mr Taylor will answer.'

"No, she didn't give me any medicine."

"So, what was her success then?"

"I asked her to marry me and she accepted…"

"Order! Order! I will have order in this courtroom! Order! Or I will clear it immediately…"

"Well, well, Mr Taylor, this is a revelation."

"Gentlemen of the Press, Order!"

"Just how many people know this? Clearly after that reaction from everyone in here, I'll wager not many."

"The people that need to know. That's all."

"But who is on the guest list, Mr Taylor?"

"Objection. This guest list is not relevant, Your Honor."

"Objection sustained."

"When is the happy event to take place, Mr Taylor?"

"Last Thursday."

"Order! Order!"

"How very clever…"

"Order! Or I will clear this courtroom!"

"How very clever of you – all of you – to maintain such a monumental secret. And the reason for the secrecy would be?"

"To stop the newspaper journalists hounding us."

"Of course, you are *so* famous, there was bound to be unnatural interest in such an event. Luke Taylor, the cornerstone of the Alliance, weds Cheyenne's celebrated female doctor. A charming news item. Most people enjoy fame, why not you, Mr Taylor?"

"Because my weddin' ain't everyone's business."

"This clever subterfuge must have taken great organization. What else do you keep secret, Mr Taylor? You take this court for a fool? What *else*? Drug dependency, delusional behavior, memory loss… you are hiding behind the good doctor, aren't you?"

"No…"

"She will vouch for you, won't she?"

"There is nothing to vouch for."

"I could put her on this stand and get her to testify to all your shortcomings except for one small thing. You are married and a wife cannot be forced to testify against her husband. How very convenient. How very clever. Your Honor, I request the court…"

"Now hold on there, counselor. I don't hide behind women…"

"At this moment, Mr Taylor, your actions speak louder than your words. I suggest you choose both wisely."

"And this coming from a man who is defending a murderer… that's rich…"

"Your Honor, the demeanor of this witness is argumentative. The effect of the drugs on Mr Taylor's memory, actions and temperament is still questionable. I request the court order a medical examination of the witness before we proceed."

"In order to assist the jury, Mr Buchanan, I will grant your request and order a medical examination of Mr Taylor. Dr Gus Prewitt usually carries out all court examinations. Mr Faraday, have his report in the morning; better still, I will see Dr Prewitt on that witness stand."

"As the court pleases. One question, Your Honor."

"Go ahead, Mr Faraday?"

"After Mr Buchanan's hysterics over a simple wedding which has resulted in Mr Taylor's need to defend the silly accusations thrown at him, may I be permitted to redirect?"

"By all means, Mr Faraday."

"Mr Taylor, how long have you known Jennifer Sullivan?"

"We met in Spring last year."

"And how long have you loved her?"

"I fell in love with Jennifer the moment we met."

"And how long has she loved you?"

"Also the moment we met."

"And why have you not been married before now?"

"Because I kept putting defense of the Alliance before her."

"Did she ever resent you for this?"

"No, never."

"Why did you marry Jennifer Sullivan last Thursday?"

"Because I couldn't live without her any longer."

"And has she ever offered advice on how to cope with drugs?"

"Only to say I wasn't dependent. I was still the same person. I was just sad."

"And are you still sad?"

"No, I am not."

"And we can see that you are not. Nothing further, Your Honor."

"The witness will step down. People, we are adjourned until ten o'clock tomorrow morning."

Luke

"The black suits pummeled me."

"You did extremely well, although I think you can kiss your privacy goodbye for the time being." Cam stands as lookout for Doc Prewitt by his office door.

"I guess that had to come."

"I'll walk you home after the doctor's examined you."

"I don't need a bodyguard. I got Ethan. Look at him prowling around out there. He'll flatten anyone who comes near me."

Cam saunters back to his desk, saying, "That's precisely my point. Look, I'll feel better when I know you are safely back in Jennifer's arms."

He sighs and rubs his eyes. "I got pummeled."

"You didn't, you know," Cam says after quiet consideration. "You were beaten up slightly, but the jury believes you too well to be convinced by Buchanan..."

Just then Cliff arrives at the door with Doc Prewitt at his elbow; he stands back to allow the old Doc to enter first.

"Well, let's get started. Mr Taylor, how are we?"

"Never better, Doc."

"Excellent. Er, you two will have to leave..."

*

He gathers Jennifer into his arms and, just as Cam said, he feels safe from the black suits, memory tests and thoughts of tomorrow.

Almost.

The shadow of anxiety likes to remind him from time to time it's only hiding from Jennifer. At least he thinks that's what it is; at times he has the sensation that something sticks close to him. His head aches at such times. For now, Jennifer soothes it all away...

"You shouldn't worry about tomorrow. It will come along and it will pass and whatever happens in between we will manage it."

He gives a soft laugh. "I have a sage for a wife."

"I'm only telling you what you would be wisely telling me if I were the preoccupied one."

"I'd only be worried about it if you weren't here when I woke up in the morning, and the next morning and the next."

"You know you told the whole world you loved me today, under oath... You went from keeping it a secret from me, then from your family, then from town – and now, it's a secret from no one."

"Think I've had enough of secrets."

"There is still one left."

"Well, that one tells the world all by itself."

THREE

The Princess Emma had no words
nor looks
But for this man of thought
and books.

Henry Wadsworth Longfellow
Emma & Eginhard

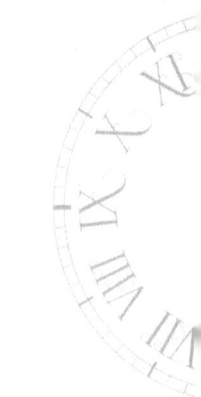

Cliff

"Have you seen this, Cliff?" Mac is holding up the morning's Tribune. "The Tribune's latest scoop. Lotta talk of Luke and Jennifer about this mornin', lotta talk, but this should silence most of it."

He takes the newspaper from Mac's outstretched hand.

DOCTOR SULLIVAN & ALLIANCE HERO MARRIED!
CHEYENNE'S SECRET ROMANCE EXPOSED IN COURT
'A Love That Saved A Life' by Emmaline Roberts

He retreats to his office to read it. And it's quite a substantial piece. Quaid has given her whatever she wanted to finally nail the scoop for which he once had other plans. Emma had even scooped Quaid himself. It must be galling him.

Except that it doesn't read like a news scoop. He grabs his hat.

Mac steps in front of him. "Where are *you* headed? Court in twenty."

"I know, Mac. I'll be back in five."

Against his back he hears the words, "If you're going where I think you're going…"

And then he's out the door before the rest, although he thinks it sounds like *shouldn't't've shown ya the darn thing*. In truth, he doesn't care how long he takes.

On entering the Tribune building he pegs his hat; several of Quaid's staff acknowledge him while he heads to Emma's section where she sits at her desk, writing. His breath catches. The mistress of his heart. Such tender feeling as he's never known humbles the county sheriff in him. Oh, there was no mercy in Cupid's arrow when it struck; he is unfathomably captivated by this woman, a woman in possession of the ability to concentrate while surrounded by people as if she's the only person in the room. He has high hopes of breaking that concentration with just two words…

"Good morning…"

Her eyes dart up… and stick. There's a certain look in her eye in the pleasant silence that follows. And there is no mistaking it.

"Sheriff Ryan. Is there something I can help you with?"

Buoyed by this modest success, he ambles up to her desk while a pretty shade of rose pink stains her cheeks.

He puts his behind in the chair she keeps beside her desk, and adjusts his coat to cover the peacemaker exposed on his right hip, speaking softly, "So you got to write your romance."

She tables her pencil; half turns toward him. "You read it?"

He allows his gaze to wander across her face. "I read it."

Her eyes dance; golden, sparkling eyes. "Mr Quaid and I had yet another disagreement, this time about the headline. I wanted *married* and he wanted *wed*. In my opinion *married* has more meaning in this case. *Wed* sounds as if the weddin' is the important part and not the marriage. I think Luke and Jennifer are definitely more interested in the marriage."

"After Luke announced to the world in court yesterday that he can't live without her, I'd say so. When did you do this?"

"I spoke to them after Luke had his memory examination. Mr Quaid held the presses back an hour. I had most of it already written; just had a few adjustments and additions to make."

"You should ask Quaid for a raise."

"I'm narrowly holding onto my job at the moment."

"No, you're not," he tells her gently. "It's good, Emma, really good."

"I guess you have to be in the right mood."

He doesn't say anything; he's too busy remembering the mood, and the cat and the porch and the purple dusk…

"Is… Is that why you came down here?"

… and the look in her eyes after he read to her. And *that* kiss.

"Mm," he says. "I was moved."

The pink deepens. "That is exceptionally kind of you, but don't you have prisoners to get into court or something?"

"Kind? So that's what they call it where you're from."

Her mouth twitches as she picks up her pencil and pretends to write something on her copy page. "I have a deadline, so if you don't mind..."

"May I borrow that paper and pencil?"

Her gaze meets his, and, for a moment, she weighs up his request. As she slides paper and pencil his way, she whispers, "I can't begin to estimate the grave quantity of suspicion this is raising right this minute."

"Quantity of...? Oh, you and me..."

While he writes her a note, she returns to her copy. When he's done, he places his note next to the tip of her pencil, forcing her to stop and read... *You are amazing. May I call you Emma again? Will you have lunch, coffee, peach pie, supper with me? Please circle any or all.*

Again her mouth twitches, then she scribbles on the note and slides it back without so much as a glance. Whereupon he reads: *Yes to the first and no to the rest. You should go. I mean it.*

He pockets the note.

"I mean it," she says through her teeth this time, working on her copy.

"I know. Thanks for your time. I enjoyed myself immensely. But then I always do when I'm with you."

"Likewise I'm sure."

Luckily for Emma, he manages to wipe the grin off his face before he runs into Quaid as he's leaving.

"Ryan, what are you doing here?" Those dark rings under his eyes wouldn't be the result of grappling with his compliant girl-writer turned investigative reporter becoming somewhat of a celebrity and getting her own way, now would they?

"Er, he was just leaving, Mr Quaid."

Cliff shrugs. "Just leaving."

"Why did you arrive in the first place?"

"You know, Quaid, that's the trouble with you. You are so suspicious of everything and everyone. I came to congratulate your star reporter on her latest story. Quite the scoop."

"Rub it in, Ryan," he says drolly. "And to think you begged me to get rid of her the day she started."

"Water under the bridge."

"Your humility kills me."

"If you two are fixin' to argue about me as though I'm not here, could you at least wait till I'm not around," Emma says.

"Not in my philosophy, Roberts, you know that. But since Ryan here admires your work so much, follow him back to his lockup and get me a good description of how the prisoners are faring this fine morning. You also have my permission to harass him with any questions you see fit to ask."

"Yes, Mr Quaid."

"Mind you still make deadline."

"Of course, Mr Quaid. Goes without saying."

Cliff watches Quaid, well pleased with himself, stride away.

"Go ahead. Don't worry about me." Emma is dropping a handful of pencils into her satchel.

"I'll wait." With the temptation to help her into her coat, wrap up her scarf and tie her fur bonnet ribbons under her chin thwarted by jamming his hands in his coat pockets, he says, "Describe a good description."

"You know, pale faces, haggard looks, sagging shoulders, melancholy eyes." She shoulders her satchel and walks towards him. "Or maybe arrogant glance, proud demeanor, spitting chips..." They start walking. "Sour as grapefruit, bitter as lemon, larger than watermelon, greener than watermelon skin, thick-skinned as watermelon..."

"A fruit metaphor."

"I adore fruit, watermelon being my favorite. Will you let me take a look at the prisoners for a good description, Ashcliff?"

"No, I don't think so."

"That's not a definite no then..."

"This is. No."

He should be rushing back to the lockup. They dawdle. He should have his mind on his job. His mind is definitely elsewhere. If townsfolk are curious about them, it doesn't register. That is until she stops to tell a small group of reporters they have collected along the way that she has an exclusive and they need to back off. He keeps a poker face, folds his arms and surveys the street. And while the reporters trudge off shocked and peeved, *he* suddenly feels ten feet tall. She fibbed to be alone with him.

As they stroll she tells him about the finest day she ever had eating watermelon, when she and her twin sister Celina were ten, describing a childhood blissfully ignorant of the precarious brink on which it sat: her father's inevitable betrayal of her mother and his leaving the home.

And then she says, "I'd like to show you something, if I may? I only noticed it myself this morning…"

He senses she's taken the helm of this encounter and he's beginning to like it.

"Oh, you probably don't have the time," she adds.

"No, I have plenty. Show me." After all, one good fib deserves another.

She picks up the pace a bit and they arrive at Mae Jewell's. Here she stops and turns to gaze into Mae's millinery store window.

"Look, Ashcliff," she says, "look at that…"

Although any experience with Emma is worth Judge Callaghan's displeasure at him holding up the biggest trial in the town's history, he probably shouldn't be window shopping. However, the air of wonder in her tone and the expression of pleasure causing her face to glow are irresistible, and he steps up to the window and looks in.

Hats, gloves, muffs…

What on earth is he supposed to be seeing?

Is she wanting to buy more of this?

"Who would have thought…" she chuckles.

She glances at him, and then double-takes.

"Ashcliff," she reproaches him. "It's my hat… well, not *my* hat, but a copy, on that head mannequin. See the sign beside it… PARISIAN~DESIGN SABLE HAT FAVORED BY TRIBUNE REPORTER EMMALINE ROBERTS, FOR THE SMART WOMAN ABOUT TOWN, MADE TO ORDER. Isn't that simply amazing?"

Her gentle excitement radiates in waves that wash over him.

"I was just dying to show it to you. Silly, I know, but, well..." and she sighs... "This kind of thing never happens to me."

He grins at her; she smiles back with bashful, self-deprecating humor. Now her excitement hovers in the air between them, aquiver like a hummingbird... he feels it in his chest.

Her gaze darts back to the hat.

"What do you say to that?" she asks, her tone more subdued.

All but three words have deserted him. And he can't say those, not here. Not if he knows what's good for him. Think carefully, a voice in his head advises. Choose wisely.

He clears his throat. "It looks better on you?"

"Oh, Ashcliff."

If she keeps saying his name with that southern accent, he's going to lose his train of thought altogether.

He grins again; says what he intended to say. "Wear it with pride."

A giggle escapes her.

And him, a chuckle.

"I will," she says before she steps away and waits for him to join her on the sidewalk.

County Sheriff's Office

He walks her in by the back gate; too many people linger out front. On the path to the back door of his office, and across the compound, the gallows, where Wilson Cutter was hanged last Fall, passes within sight. Maybe she won't care to notice it.

"Were you there at Wilson Cutter's hanging?"

And maybe she will.

"I was. I walked him to the gallows."

They stand beneath the covered walkway, which affords a view of the jail yard and leads to his office door on the right and the jail entrance on the left. The sun never reaches here, which is fine in July but certainly not today. The object of her assignment, the prisoners, seems to have eluded her for the moment; her focus is all on the gallows. A cold, whistling wind causes her to shiver, but this too seems to go unnoticed.

"What a day that must have been," she mutters.

"It was dawn, the town was shrouded in a heavy gray mist," he tells her, lifting his gaze to the gallows. "Cutter had been 'saved' by hellfire preacher Jim Jamison…"

"I've heard of him."

"So he figured himself well ready for death. But there was no glorious ending. He swung on the end of the rope like any other murderer."

She looks at him. "Is that the real you talking, James Ashcliff Ryan?"

He starts at this and gazes back at her. What to make of her sometimes… but she did ask him a question. And right now he can't answer it.

"Have you seen anyone hanged, Emma?"

"I live in the south. You wouldn't believe the things I've seen."

"Have you?"

Her expression grows restless; her gaze reverts to the gallows. Maybe he shouldn't have asked; but maybe his gut is telling him this is a conversation they need to have…

"I've seen innocence hanged on a tree, justice hanged, the constitution of a free people hanged, I've seen fruit on a tree that had no business being there. Time we stopped hanging folks…"

Her gaze meets his and there is a deep pain in her eyes he's never seen before; not even the hurt her father caused her. He swallows hard, lost for words.

"Would you hang a man for the color of his skin, James?"

"No, Emma, I would not."

"Neither would I, but I have."

"Then so have I."

"No, James," she whispers and takes a step towards him; he thinks she is going to take hold of his hands, but checks herself. "You haven't."

Just then one of Mac's prison guards comes towards them along the walkway and tips his hat.

Still reeling, he manages to return the compliment.

Emma steps back and with startling composure greets the man. "Good day, Sergeant Myers."

"Mornin', Miss Roberts..." His deep voice rumbles out of his large frame and full-bearded face, resounding under the low walkway roof.

"How are the prisoners today?" she asks.

"Little change from when you asked me yesterday afternoon," he rumbles in reply.

"Quiet and sullen again?"

"I kinda like morose today."

"Morose! That's a fine description, Sergeant."

"Thank you, ma'am. I try. And I'll thank you to keep my name out of the papers."

"Off the record, of course, I know."

"If you'll excuse me, ma'am... Sheriff..."

"Sergeant," Cliff nods. Emma does the same.

The unsmiling Sergeant Myers continues on his way and enters the jail; the door clangs firmly shut behind him.

"So near and yet so far," she sighs.

He's in two minds whether to continue their conversation as he closes the door behind them and pegs his hat.

"So," he says, watching her removing her hat while she heads straight for his desk where something has caught her eye. "What questions do you want to ask me for this exclusive of yours? Ah, don't touch anything on my desk..."

"Wouldn't dream of it."

Oh, yes, she would.

"My desk is off limits, even for...." he's saying when he catches up to her. Then he sees what she's holding, what she's picked up. The ill-fated silk rose. "...you."

She looks up; their eyes meet.

"You kept this," she murmurs.

"You remember it."

"Well, you gave it to me. Why did you do that?"

"You gave it back. And it's pretty, like you. Although if I had to do it over again I would've asked Pat to make a watermelon."

"Don't people question why their sheriff has a pink silk rose in a glass tumbler on his desk?"

"Why, thank you, Ashcliff, for telling me I'm pretty as a rose," he says, gently mimicking her accent.

Her cheeks turn the color of it. "It must remind you of Emma by Jane Austen; why do you keep it here?"

"Romance."

"Romance?"

"Mm. Romance."

"What romance?"

"The one you and I are having. Our romance."

Her eyes flash at him and for the longest moment emotion wells up and up until she looks like she'll explode. And then she does, in the most bewitching manner. "This is about the hat, isn't it? You're not the only one who feels things, Cliff Ryan. You want me to lose my job at the paper?"

"No, of course I don't." Instinctively, he reaches for her, draws her to him.

"Then why do you needle me? It was going so well, and then you just have to needle..."

"Emma... don't be mad."

"And I won't be lectured to about romance by a sheriff packing two peacemakers, a silver Derringer with pearl grips tied under his right sleeve..."

"How do you...? Never mind. And the Derringer belonged to my uncle!"

"...three sets of the most uncomfortable wrist manacles ever made, and I should know since I've had the displeasure of wearing one of them..."

"My cousin Phillip has its twin, not that you're probably even remotely interested..."

"...and an eleven inch bowie knife!"

"I'm working!"

"That makes two of us!"

He releases her and she pulls away from him at precisely the same moment.

Looking confused and frustrated, she lets out a grunt, throws down the rose on his desk and heads for the rear door.

"What, no questions?" he taunts her.

She stops, turns and retraces her steps. Tension drills his body at the sight of her in full flight. When she grabs the lapels of his coat and glares into his face like she wants to use the derringer on him, he has to swallow his frustration in a hurry.

"Do you know how many women on the streets of Cheyenne turn their heads when you pass by, how many of them watch you, how they talk and giggle together after you've gone? Do you, Ashcliff, do you know?"

Is his jaw on the floor? Because he feels like it is.

"You could have any of them. They live here. They want to be here. Their lives are conventional and ordered. They're Yankee, mostly, and they like you. Choose one."

Tears fill her eyes and fall freely down her cheeks.

With a final look of desperation, she drops her face into the space between her hands on his chest where she has a cry.

And while she's doing that, he puts his arms around her, feels as though he's crushed a nut with a sledgehammer, and thinks awhile about what she just said.

For a ruthless sheriff and an ambitious reporter they are astonishingly vulnerable to one another. Maybe they're neither of those things. Beneath the exterior they present to the world at large who are the two people that their admiration for one another is so bent on uncovering?

"Emma…"

"What?" she sniffs.

"Look at me?"

"I need a handkerchief."

"Take mine. Inside pocket of my jacket, beneath the Derringer."

He feels her small hand fishing for the handkerchief and keeps her within the circle of his arms while she fixes her face. When her tear-bright eyes meet his, sheepish and uncertain, his pounding heart shudders to a halt and melts.

"I'm sorry," he murmurs.

A little stricken sound escapes from her lips.

He strokes a wisp of her hair back into place. "Emma, I stopped paying attention to what you just described a long time ago. I don't see them that way. And it's complicated…"

There's a sharp knock on the rear door.

Anything either of them might have said next disintegrates like a popped bubble as their gaze jolts in that direction.

"Mac," he murmurs. He looks back at her soft profile and pulls himself together. She'd shown him at Mae's window what made her happy to be in his company, what she needed from him, and how he could steer her thoughts in the same direction as his – by steering his in the direction of hers.

"Emma. I saw *you*... everything about you dazzled me."

Her gaze swings back, the golden sparkle in her eyes giving substance to his declaration, and he isn't finished...

"You are the brilliant star in my night sky. And there isn't anyone in this world I like better than you or see more clearly."

She looks down, her fingers smoothing a corner of his handkerchief. "I don't know what to say to that..."

How could she think that there would never come a man unintimidated by her intellect, entranced by her beauty and bewitched by her spirit who couldn't help but fall in love with her?

"I'm not giving up on you, Emma."

The handkerchief is returned to his pocket.

"Maybe you should," she murmurs, but it's light on conviction.

"Not when seeing you is the best part of my day."

Her gaze flies up and his stomach rolls over.

"Ashcliff," she reproaches him, her eyes flirting with his. "Where do you get these lines from, a book?"

"My heart. Memorable?"

"Yes," she grins. "Very."

"Then my heart shall think of some more..."

Another knock, sharper this time.

"Take out your notebook, Emma," he says and releases her. He heads for his office door. When he turns around, she has her hat under her arm, her notebook and pencil in hand and a wry smile on her face. He winks at her, opens the door and says, "And that, Miss Roberts, is my final word on the matter. Thank you and good day."

He turns away again and surveys the scene in the outer office. It's busy; and beyond, out in the street, even busier. Thankfully, no black suits in sight.

When she leaves, a piece of him is going to leave with her, and the only way he'll get that part of him back is if he sees her again. And so it goes, when the soft rustle of skirt and the gentlest of fragrances pass by; her head is down and she's writing as she walks; she stops in the middle of the outer office, finishes her scribbling and rips the page out of her notebook, folds it in quarters and turns back; she hands it to him, her poker face perfect.

"What's this?" he murmurs.

"Relevant information. Good luck in court. And don't watch me leave..."

"Wouldn't dream of it."

When she's gone again, he closes the door. He unfolds the page and reads...

O you whom I often and silently come where you are that I may be with you, as I walk by your side or sit near, or remain in the same room with you, little you know the subtle electric fire that for your sake is playing within me. ....?

The back door opens and Mac strolls in. "Having fun?"

"Wouldn't miss it for the world."

"It'd be helpful if you didn't have to do your courtin' in the middle of a trial the size of Texas."

"I know," he concedes.

"I got you a ten minute delay."

"Thanks, Mac."

They head into the jail.

"Uh. Walt Whitman..."

"Come again?"

O you whom I often... "It's Walt Whitman."

"Looks a dead ringer for Loren Bodecker if you ask me."

"Resembling an unripe grapefruit."

"Yep. That's our resident sour and nasty sonofabitch."

Faraday

"So, Dr Prewitt. Would you please tell the court your findings?"

"Certainly, Mr Faraday. I questioned Mr Taylor extensively about the episode in question. Seems to me he was poisoned. He has what we in the medical profession call a hypersensitivity to opiates..."

"Hypersensitivity. Explain in detail, if you would, Doctor."

"To be sensitive to a substance means you are adversely affected by it and by inducing it or coming in contact with it causes symptoms and side-effects such as vomiting, nausea and headaches. A simple example would be that certain folk are sensitive to strawberries and when they eat them they break out in a rash. But Mr Taylor is hypersensitive to opiates, so if not managed correctly his side-effects are very severe, in fact potentially fatal, and this would have increased the toxic nature of the intense cocktail of drugs he was given. His body reacted severely, trying to reject the toxin while it succumbed to it. He would have been critically ill."

"So hypersensitivity is extremely dangerous."

"Indeed. Elimination of the drug from Mr Taylor's poisoned body would have been painful and difficult, and may have killed a weaker individual."

"What conclusion can be drawn regarding his recovery?"

"This hypersensitivity would likely indicate that there is no likelihood of dependence and therefore once the poison left his system he would make a full recovery."

"A full physical and mental recovery?"

"That's correct. His mental recovery took a little longer because the effects of the drugs tend to make a person depressed and melancholy. But the young man also experienced a severe trauma and, as anybody here knows, that also takes time to recover from. It may still impact from time to time. However, I performed extensive tests on the lad. He is fit and healthy. His melancholy has lifted. He responded in an appropriate manner to all my questions. He can recall details and facts from any time in his life, including the dreadful experience.

"I've been a doctor a long time, Mr Faraday. I've seen a lot of patients with all kinds of conditions that need treating. Mr Taylor needs no treatment. And his memory is fine. If I were him, I would rather not remember some of the things he has experienced in his young life."

"Thank you, Doctor. Your witness, Mr Buchanan."

"I have no questions for the witness." Buchanan's ambivalence is grating; after all, it was on his insistence that they put Luke through the test.

"The witness may step down. As we were in the middle of your cross-examination of Mr Taylor yesterday, Mr Buchanan, do you wish to proceed with it?"

"If you have no objection, Your Honor, my learned colleague Sturrock will take over the cross-examination of Mr Taylor."

"No objection. Recall Mr Taylor to the stand."

"Now, Mr Taylor, there were no witnesses on the train to what happened to the blonde prostitute, Cadie McClements, were there not? No one except you?"

"No one else came forward if they did."

"So it is your word against Mr Donnelly's as to what happened. The two passengers saw you over the body, did they not?"

"I was checking her pulse. And they came along."

"The fact remains that it is your word against Mr Donnelly's and two witnesses saw you over the body. In fact, in your testimony you stated that you followed Miss McClements from the second class car for two more cars. You were stalking her, were you not?"

"Certainly not."

"But you followed her, did you not?"

"Yes, but..."

"You either followed her, or you didn't, which is it?"

"I saw which direction she went; then I went looking for her because I was concerned for her. Aunt Caroline and I had seen her being harassed by Mr Donnelly. I knew what he was up to. She was Mr Bodecker's whore. Donnelly decided to get in for his share..."

"That is utter conjecture, Mr Taylor. Your Honor, I move that these remarks be stricken from the record."

"Your Honor, Mr Sturrock opened up this can of worms."

"Motion denied, counselor. The witness will continue."

"When Caroline and I first saw her on the train, Miss McClements looked happy and bright. The next time she looked sick and pale. Donnelly appeared, tapping her on the shoulder and ordering her around. He knew who she was and what she did because he was there in Bodecker's hotel room when Miss McClements arrived. He got to her. I'm positive if a proper investigation had been carried out after Miss McClements was murdered, a doctor would have found bruising on her body because there certainly was bruising around her neck."

"Caused by you, Mr Taylor!"

"No, a bigger hand. A much bigger hand."

"And that is why we have doctors and experts to look at these things, not ranchers and cowboys..."

"Objection, Your Honor. Mr Sturrock is being argumentative."

"I will answer that, Your Honor."

"Very well, Mr Taylor. Go ahead."

"Mr Sturrock might be interested to know that ranchers and cowboys, farmers and homesteaders, because we're located miles from the nearest doctor, have become clever at diagnosing and treating all manner of things. Fractures. Bruising. Concussion. Cuts. Fever. Influenza. Headaches. Burns. We've devised and improvised many ways of treating these and scores of other conditions. We're extremely careful to understand why and how something has happened, so we can stop it happening again. We are extremely resourceful people. We pay attention to the details and we don't let a life, any life, expire without asking why. I saw Miss McClements die; she fell to the floor like her life was worth nothing to the man who broke her neck. The animals on my ranch are treated with more respect than Donnelly treated Miss McClements."

"Order! Order! That person who clapped at the back of the gallery will be escorted out of this courtroom if it occurs again. I hope I have made myself very clear! Proceed, Mr Sturrock."

"Yes, Your Honor. The fact remains Mr Taylor there were no other witnesses to what happened, were there?"

"There are always clues left behind. The sheriff should have gathered them up and followed them to the proper conclusion."

"I am so glad we have you to tell us these things."

"Objection. Argumentative."

"Sustained."

"So, Mr Taylor, what method did you use to discover the room numbers of my clients in Omaha…?"

Two hours of Sturrock's labored cross-examination and even the Judge is fading; he calls a recess for lunch. Luke is pale and quiet as they head back to the office to take stock of the morning.

"Are you all right?" Faraday asks his key witness.

"I could eat a steer. How about you?"

"Maybe not a whole one."

"No, I mean are you all right."

He chuckles. "Perfectly fine…"

"Where's Jennifer?"

"She was in the back of the courtroom for a while, I don't know… Are you sure you're all right?"

Luke rubs one eye with the heel of his wrist. "I'm just getting started." When he spies George standing by Josh's table looking out for him, his expression lifts. "There she is…"

Twenty minutes into the next session the afternoon appears as though it will be a repeat of the morning. He stands to object to Sturrock's latest question.

"Objection. Your Honor, again I must object to this line of cross-examination. It is argumentative. And I gravely question the relevance of it. I have no doubt that the members of the jury have made up their minds about Mr Taylor's character by now, and this line of cross-examination only displays Mr Sturrock's lack of confidence in their individual and collective ability."

The Judge does his best not to look relieved. "I find merit in Mr Faraday's objection, Mr Sturrock. I believe you have argued with the witness long enough."

"Your Honor, the witness is required to give direct answers to my questions. I do not ask for long-winded and detailed diatribe. Your Honor, please instruct the witness to answer appropriately."

"Your Honor, my learned colleague seems to think that ranchers and cowboys are delinquents. He seems to think that yes and no are all they should be capable of. Anyone would've thought that by now he would have ascertained that with Mr Taylor this is far from the case."

"Mr Taylor?"

"Yes, Your Honor."

"You will give short, succinct answers."

"I'll do my best, Your Honor."

"Continue, Mr Sturrock. If this line of cross-examination again proves argumentative I will shut it down immediately."

"Yes, Your Honor. Mr Taylor..."

Luke gives yes or no answers to four successive questions. On the fifth he sits back a little and starts weighing his answer.

"You know, when Mr Ryan was bringing me home from North Platte, all I could think about was how desperate I was to go home to my family, to make sure they were all right. I think I gave him a hard time. He never once complained about having to take care of me, or make decisions that might affect his job, or about the danger the situation had put him in."

"Your Honor, please instruct the witness to answer the question."

"Mr Taylor, please answer the question."

"I'm getting to it, Your Honor. Mr Sturrock's questions get me thinking and I get lost in all my thoughts. For instance, sometimes in life you have to do things, things you don't like or want to do, but you have to rise above it. And you have to consider not only the value in that, but also how your actions will affect other people. I regret not dragging Miss McClements out of Bodecker's room that night. She'd never have got the money to pay for her train ticket. She wouldn't have been on the train. She wouldn't have run into Mr Donnelly. She wouldn't be dead.

"But I might be dead. And my family might be dead. Maverick was about to unleash his destruction upon the Alliance and I had to do something to try and stop it. But I should have stopped Miss McClements, too. That's what my conscience tells me. And then I think, we all have free will to make our own decisions. She wanted to find a place called Bright River. I guess to her, living the life she did, it sounded like just the kind of place where she wanted to be. I think she was about eighteen. And she had a whole life to live."

"Your Honor, will you instruct the witness to answer the question."

The Judge turns to Luke. "Were you answering the question, Mr Taylor?"

"I forget the question, Your Honor. Would Mr Sturrock mind repeating it?"

A study of the gentlemen of the jury reveals their gaze is fixed upon Luke as though he is the latest preacher in town. One has a tear trickling down his cheek. The questions have ceased to be important. The jury wants to hear the stories, even jurors seven, nine and ten.

Time to interject... "Your Honor, may we put an end to this charade? Mr Sturrock is stalling this trial with his cross-examination of this witness. One would almost be inclined to think he can't bear for the trial to proceed. I move that the witness be asked to step down."

"Mr Sturrock," the Judge barks. "I'm inclined to agree with Mr Faraday at this point."

"In all fairness, Your Honor, I have every right to cross-examination of this witness in the best interests of my client."

"However, Mr Sturrock, I am going to ask the witness to step down."

The groan from the gallery echoes around the courtroom.

The jury looks somewhat nonplussed.

That evening at supper...

"Are you all right, Cam?" Meg asks.

"Supper's good," he says.

"You look exhausted, can you even taste it?"

"You know I love chicken."

"It's beef."

"The black suits..." he mumbles, his thoughts drifting again.

"Jen said that Luke won the battle today with Buchanan and Sturrock."

"Mm, he did... but not the war."

"One battle at a time I always say."

"And you'd be right."

"Eat your supper, my darling."

Cliff

"In my very humble opinion, I think you are almost ready."

"Honestly?"

"You're smart enough to join the priesthood," Nugent prattles and then laughs at his own joke. "And you have demonstrated your commitment. You're a fine fellow and I can't ask for more. There's a little work left to do before Easter, but I think you'll manage it."

"Thanks, Father."

They shake hands.

"Ah, it means that much to you, doesn't it... Don't worry, I know this isn't about Emmaline. Speaking of which, you're going to be needing a sponsor for Confirmation. I know the right and proper long-standing tradition is that you have a male sponsor, but she got you into the church and the honor should go to her."

Cliff frowns. "I know you mean well, Father, but Emma won't agree to that."

Amid sharp knocking on his front door, Nugent starts chuckling. "You think so, do you? Am I the only one who knows how she feels about you? Excuse me, while I get my door."

A moment later Nugent's voice carries through to the kitchen: "Speak of the devil! Ah, but you'd be an angel most surely."

"Sorry, Father...?"

Emma.

"How are you gettin' on? Come in, Emmaline, come in."

"I won't disturb you, Father, I came for that copy you wanted in Friday's Tribune."

"Yes, it's here somewhere. Come in while I find it. Cliff's in the kitchen. He has something he wants to ask you. Off you go..."

Must you, Nugent? He looks up to find his sweet, feisty Emma adorning the normally stark and holy doorway. Words desert him.

"You wanted to ask me something?" she inquires cautiously.

He clears his throat. "Emma..." And rummages in his brain. "So... When was the last time you went to confession?"

No other pair of eyes could have registered both shock and amusement so exquisitely. It's enough to make him forget where they are. Her cheeks pink up like rose petals as she searches for a response, which eventually comes along... "The serious Catholic always knows how long it has been since their last confession."

"And the not so serious?"

The pink deepens as she gasps, "Sweet tea and vittles!"

Nugent strides in. "Confession, did I hear you say? Now why would you two lovely people be needing to bring up confession?"

"Er. No reason. None at all. Ashcliff seems confused, Father..."

"Only since you walked in, Emmaline, and I suspect it happens to the lad a lot."

"You do? It does?"

Nugent winks. "Now, here is the copy. Times for all the Easter services. And my article on the meaning of Lent and Easter. I'm sure the Bishop would heartily approve – so many people read The Tribune these days. It's so good of your man Quaid to give me the space, Emmaline. And for no cost. Very generous."

"Of course, Father. Mr Quaid was very agreeable to the idea."

A fly on the wall during that negotiation would have no doubt been highly entertained.

"Sit down, Emmaline. Please...."

"I think I might have intruded." She edges towards the door.

Nugent ushers her to a chair. "This won't hurt a bit. Coffee?"

"No, thank you, Father. I've just eaten supper."

"Well, let's get down to business then. The lad here is ready for full initiation..."

Her glance bolts across the table and connects with his. He shrugs. She rolls her eyes and returns to Nugent.

"Easter Sunday is not far away. He'll be ready. Perfect timing."

"Yes, I agree," she says. "But are you *sure* he's ready?"

Nugent chuckles. "Quite sure. Well, go on, lad, ask her now."

He can't bear the sound of her big fat 'no' and how it will make him feel. Committed Catholics everywhere probably consider this sponsorship a life-binding state. Even with the progress they're making, she'll run a mile before she'd consider commitment.

He scraps back his chair. "You know, Father, I just remembered there is something I had left to do at the jail…"

Emma's eyes go round with surprise.

Nugent considers him with that well-practiced look of priestly disappointment. "Never pegged you for a coward, lad."

"I need time to think about the wisdom of this, Father."

"Wisdom of what?" Emma chimes in. "What are y'all saying?"

He lifts his hat from the table. "I'll talk to you later, Father. Good night, Emma."

"You're leaving?" she gasps, heartwarmingly disappointed.

Nugent waves his hands about. "Hold your horses. Hold them right there. You're not asking the girl to marry you…"

Awkward pause. His collar feels so tight it's strangling him.

"Heavens to Betsy, Cliff Ryan, what *are* you asking me to do?"

"Nothing, Emma," he croaks, scraping together what's left of his dignity. "There's sure to be a kind volunteer once Father asks around. Don't let me hold up your business any longer. 'Night."

In hasty retreat he takes himself off home, confident he has foiled Nugent's intention to have Emma be his sponsor. He walks quickly in the cold, his thoughts matching his strides, and those thoughts come to order after the muddle in Nugent's kitchen.

Strange as it seems, he has a feeling the heavenly powers don't want him to choose Emma for this role; a sponsor should focus a candidate's thoughts, shouldn't they? Emma is the love of his life, and the biggest distraction he's ever encountered. She had opened the door and shown him in, yes, but the role of sponsor isn't hers.

The insight keeps him busy for a time; as he turns up the lamps in the house; strips off his suit and pulls on his jeans and favorite shirt; lights a fire, gets the house warm; …

He's giving the fire a good prod when he hears his front door closing and noise in the hall.

He turns around to see Emma adorning *his* parlor doorway this time, very pale and somewhat forlorn. What happened to his rose?

"Emma..."

She rocks on her feet; before she swoons he leaps across the room and locks her up in his arms.

"What happened? You're hurt?"

"I fell, down the road from the church."

"Are you broken?"

"I walked... my knee ..."

"You want me to look?"

She nods and then collapses onto his shoulder. With a sniff.

In spite of her injury, he can feel her robustness and her uprightness and a tremulous energy that makes her who she is. He can't ever imagine a day that he wouldn't worry about her.

"Just hold me a moment."

"Holding you very tight, see?"

"You took off so fast..."

"I'm sorry."

"You didn't go the jail."

"I lied."

"To a priest?"

"He knew I was lying; it doesn't count."

"What happened? I don't understand."

"Don't worry about that now."

"What are you supposed to ask me?"

"Nugent wants me to ask you to be my sponsor at Easter."

Her head comes up; an interesting look for her – a smudged face; she must have collected some dirt with that fall.

"You don't want me?"

"Oh, Emma, in so many ways," he says, thumbing the dirt from her cheek, "but that's not one of them."

A look of excruciation grips her. "I'm in too much agony to show you just exactly how indignant I am."

The melodic 'southern' generates a pulse of euphoric delirium inside of him that surpasses the one he had when he saw her standing there.

"I know, I know. I'm a Yankee dog."

"Don't put words in my mouth."

"Well, hold that thought and come over to the fire."

As she puts pressure on her knee to walk, she lets out a tiny squeal. He holds her fast to him again.

"You can't walk?"

"I just need a moment. I can walk…"

"I know the thought of being a helpless female offends your sensibilities, but I could carry you to the sofa and the fire …"

And here he was thinking the evening was going to be long and tedious.

"I walked here," she chatters on, "I should be able to get to your sofa."

"Sometimes the final hurdle is the hardest."

"So it is," she concurs, and then grimaces.

"Maybe I should fetch Jennifer."

"At this hour?"

"It's not that late."

"You know what I mean."

He knows. Unspoken code of decency. Don't disturb the newly-weds.

"And not Dr Prewitt either; he'll think I'm accident prone."

"Not accident prone. More like operating precariously outside the parameters of average female activity."

"Ashcliff," she sighs impatiently. "Just you."

"Well, if you're sure you trust me…" He scoops her up, his arms gently enfolding what has become most precious to him, carrying her to the sofa in front of the fire, where she sighs again, this time with relief. He unlaces her boots, removes them and arranges them near the hearth to dry out and warm up. Then he grabs the footstool and gingerly elevates her injured leg, her right one. All the while she looks far too pale for his liking.

"Now what?" he asks.

Impatient with his apparent stupidity, gritting her teeth, she reaches forward and carefully draws her dress up to her knee to reveal a black and white striped petticoat. Truth be known, he has a weakness for black and white striped petticoats, and on her his weakness is fast becoming a slide into something worse. That she is his living breathing petticoat fantasy is making him more than a little crazy. Combined with her rust colored dress and her hair the shade of honey, the whole image is French, inviting and something he wants to gather up into his arms and never let go of.

She peels back the petticoat, the soft deep-ruffled hem piling up about her knee like temptation's welcome mat.

He clears his throat to tackle the next discovery...

"Are those long handles?" he asks.

"You were expecting muslin and lace? A body has to stay warm in this atrocious climate. Some days I wear two pairs."

"I had no idea."

"Should hope not. My undergarments are not your business."

"At this point, I beg to differ." But his freshness is ignored.

Gingerly, as if she can't bear to look, she inches up the wool flannel long handle leg to a fraction above her knee to reveal the brightest colored stocking he's ever seen in his life.

"What color do you call that?" he asks, fascinated to his bones and vaguely managing to keep his hands off her and focus on what matters – she's injured.

"I would have thought it was obvious."

"Of course. Chartreuse."

"Mustard yellow."

"I always get them mixed up for some reason."

Trying not to laugh, sucking in her breath, she eases the stocking down in delicate folds until it droops about her lower calf, exposing a section of one elegantly shaped white leg... topped with one unfortunately swollen red knee, although how it got so injured with all the garments it has to pad it is a mystery. But that's Emma. A bewitching mystery. In feller's underwear and striped petticoat.

She inspects her injury more closely and groans. "Look at it. It's hideously swollen."

"Hideous is kinda strong," he mutters.

"How would you describe it then?"

"That is one good-looking limb, Miss Roberts... what I can see of it."

"Oh, for goodness sake, be serious."

"I wouldn't joke about a thing like that."

"Now what?"

"Ice."

"Ice?"

"Mm." He could use some himself. "Heaps of it near the back porch. Wrap it up in cloth. Ice compress. Seen Jennifer do it."

"Honestly?"

"Mm. Ice shrinks things… I'll be back."

He makes her compress from a kitchen towel and returns to the fire; she's dozing by the look of her, the firelight dancing over her pale skin, and the exposed limb.

"Emma?"

"I'm awake, just trying not to think about the pain."

"This will help." He eases the compress onto her knee.

"Ouch, ouch…"

"Easy…"

The compress is on.

"I'm pouring you a brandy…"

"Who'd have thought ice would be my friend."

"A friend in need…" He puts a small brandy in her hands. "Sip this. I'll look after the compress. Sit back…"

That's when her hands start to shake.

A long quiet moment passes wherein she sips and he keeps an eye on her. The brandy needs a minute to do its work. And when it's done, he takes the glass away.

"Better?"

"Much. Thank you."

"You're welcome," he smiles as he sits down beside her, their shoulders touching, yet careful not to disturb the compress or bump her knee.

She glances at him and then smoothes the front of her dress.

"My sponsor was my cousin Louisa. She is ten years older than I. At the time of my confirmation she was engaged to be married to Some Yankee. They married and moved to Pennsylvania or Maine or maybe it was Buffalo, New York. I can't remember, it just sounded cold to me and a long way away. A fine weddin' though."

"Some Yankee? Good grief, Emma…"

"Well, that's what the rest of the family called him. He was the 'some Yankee' that cousin Louisa married. The point I am trying to make is…"

"The feller must've had a name."

"The point is I never saw her again."

"Oh," he frowns.

"Every Christmas she sends the family a card though, from Maine or Buffalo or wherever, and Mama sends one to her."

"That's nice."

"She's family."

"You sure? She did marry a Yankee."

"We… you and I would have no call to send a card every Christmas. I mean, if I was your sponsor, I wouldn't expect it, would you?"

"From you, no. You'd be scared I'd take it the wrong way. And I wouldn't dare send you one in case I made you think I was still in love with you. We should have some consideration for poor future wife."

"Oh, her."

"Mm. Poor future wife. The consolation prize."

"You shouldn't speak of her that way."

"You're right. She deserves respect, whoever she is."

"I should never have danced with you at the weddin'. That's what started all this…"

"Mm. All this. Why *did* you dance with me?"

"Poor future wife shouldn't have pieces of you I can't."

"She's already destined to have those pieces of me."

She gasps. "I didn't mean… you always twist my w…"

"Besides, the only person stopping you from having them is *you*. And yet when you danced with me, knowing that a thousand dances with poor future wife won't come close to just one with you, you robbed her of my heart, which you will always possess, even though *she*, as lovely as I'm sure she will be, will have my physical and material devotion and I hers. Fascinating…"

"There is nothing fascinating about it. And this conversation is unseemly, I can't believe we are having it, and may we please change the subject."

He starts laughing. "Unseemly… *you* are quaint."

"I am not. I'm well brought up, and raised right by a good southern woman." She gives a small cough into her hand. "Excuse me. The cold air."

"Why do you spend so much time gallivanting around in it?"

"My job. Your job…"

"*My* job? I should stay indoors to keep you warm all day."

"To be where you are I have to be cold."

"I don't like being apart from you either."

"You're doing it again… twisting my words… I wish you w…"

"*O you whom I often and silently come where you are that I may be with you, as I walk by your side or sit near, or remain in the same room with you, little you know the subtle electric fire that for your sake is playing within me.*"

She looks a little sheepish as she says, "You know it then?"

"I do now. Walt Whitman."

She smiles. "You guessed?"

"*Subtle electric fire…* who else would use such a phrase? Later I checked my copy of *Leaves of Grass*. And there it was." He gives her a sidelong glance. "What does your good southern mama think about you reading Walt Whitman?"

"Do I seem like the kind of person who worries about my mama's opinion of what I read?"

"She doesn't know, does she?"

"Not a clue."

"And how is *Leaves of Grass* not 'unseemly'?"

"It's elegant. Eloquent. Yes, it startles you at first, but you feel the inevitable truth of it. And in a world where so many things are taboo, constrained and frowned upon, in my opinion it's freeing, at least when you pick up the book and you are alone with your thoughts and the words on the page. And then your soul gives a cheer for free thought and freedom of speech.

"How dreary not to be able to read. I don't mean that in an arrogant way; I'm grateful. I thank God that I can read every day of my life. Even He couldn't disapprove of *Leaves of Grass*. The content of it expresses the fundamental nature and temperament of His creation. So, in my opinion, a person either surrenders to its persuasion or tosses the book away and continues as they did previously. Although I wonder at anyone not being affected even a little by reading it."

Thwang. Like an arrow. Straight into his heart. He could listen to her express her opinion for hours. Yes, her accent stokes the subtle and not so subtle electric fire inside him, but ever since he's known her so have her words.

He shifts his position on the sofa so he can look at her squarely.

She's biting her bottom lip.

"What's that for?" he asks.

"I talk too much."

"With me? That's never going to happen."

"Never?"

"I can guarantee it." He takes one of her hands holds it captive in both of his. "Recite it for me?"

"*O you whom I often and silently come?*"

"Mm."

"*O you* whom I often and silently come where you are that I may be with you, as I walk by your side or sit near, or remain in the same room with you, little you know the subtle electric fire that for your sake is playing within me."

And within him. Not so subtle. "If old Walt had an inkling of how electric his words could sound on the lips of a well-brought up and raised right southern girl I think he'd be very, *very* pleased."

"Oh, Ashcliff," she says, as though lamenting something.

"What?"

"If only you were a gentleman."

If only she realized how much effort he was exerting to be one! Or maybe she does… He starts to chuckle.

"Beg pardon, Ma'am, but I happen to think you like me just the way I am."

Her eyes flash a warning he suspects southern girls have raised to the level of art; he considers it a privilege and a triumph to be on the receiving end. Meanwhile the melting compress slides off her knee and onto the rug.

"I'll fix it. Stay there and don't move."

Emmaline

I think you are really getting the hang of it.

Hang of what, Celie?

Setting up yourself and that extraordinary man for complete and utter heartbreak. Do you have any idea of how much it's going to hurt, Emmie? It will feel unbearable.

Stop it, Celie. And why aren't you asleep?

I'm serious, Em. He adores you. When you walk away, what do you think is going to happen to him?

He'll get over it.

Wrong answer. And what about you?

I'll get over it as well... far away from here...

Second wrong answer.

Celie, you know it's not that simple...

You are making it complicated, Emmie. It doesn't need to be.

Can we not talk about this?

What the two of you have happens once in lifetime. Trust it. For once in your life quit focusing on Papa and Mama and their topsy-turvy, muddled-up marriage. You are not them! And neither is your Ashcliff.

Celie, stop...

This is it, Emmie; don't turn your back on it. Stop fussing about the future which is out of your control and grasp the glorious here and now...

I'm blocking you, Celie. We are not speaking from this moment on....

There is movement and Ashcliff's voice breaks through.

"Where were you just then?"

"Pardon me?"

"When I came in from the kitchen just now, you didn't hear me talking to you, and you seemed miles away..." Ashcliff resumes his position beside her on the sofa. "Emma, you're crying... your knee..."

"I... I got something in my eye."

"Both of them?"

"You know how it is... once one eye waters the other one does too..." She dabs at the corner of one with her handkerchief. "See. All better now."

He looks unsure.

"I was standing in the kitchen," he says, "and I was thinking that..."

"Ashcliff..."

Her interruption confuses him but momentarily. "Yes, Emma?"

"When... when I leave and return home, what will happen then?" There. The dreaded question.

A look comes over his face she cannot read. Then, abruptly, he sits back and folds his arms. "I don't think about that anymore."

"You don't?"

"I suppose I'll think of a way to get over you, *before* Christmas if possible."

"You'll be over me by Christmas?"

"Definitely by next Easter. A year should do it. All we have – let's face it, all any of us has – is the here and now. Did you know it's a known fact that people who live in the minute are a hundred and twenty-five times happier than people who over plan their future? I read that the other day."

"You wouldn't come after me?"

"I suppose there's a difference between planning in precise detail and having an overarching direction for your life. I want my life to be headed in a purposeful direction."

She gulps down his sarcasm. "So... so you wouldn't come after me?"

He turns back to her, deadly serious this time. "Is this a test?"

"No..."

"Because I don't know how to answer the question without you stomping all over my heart when you check my answer..."

"I..."

"What just happened, Emma?"

She looks at her hands but then decides to have enough courage to look him in the eye. "I've capitulated. I wasn't supposed to but I wasn't strong enough. I should not have danced with you. And now… Celina is right. It's entirely my fault. You speak about the future. What have I done to it…?"

He seems to have forgotten her knee because he hauls her into his arms and holds her tight to his chest. Their faces are barely two inches apart, their eyes level. His remind her of blue-green flames.

"I don't know what advice your sister has given you, but it's *our* romance and no one is going to tell me, or you, how to run it, and that includes telling you what or how to feel. If you intend to break my heart, Emma, and I think you do, then it's my right and my job to change your mind. I will fight to stop it from happening, do you understand?"

She nods fast.

"To me you are perfect the way you are. And you capitulated because what's going on between us is powerful and strong. Plus I've used every strategy I could think of, whatever I had to hand, every opportunity you've ever given me, and then some. But that doesn't mean the war is over. This is one day at a time, hand to hand at close quarters combat and I will keep on fighting you, Emma. I swear I will…"

Beneath her hands the warmth of his skin penetrates the fabric of his favorite old shirt, and she can feel his heart pounding. He is so wonderful she wants to clap. She gazes into those fiery eyes, feeling strangely triumphant for someone who's just admitted a defeat (of sorts).

Except there is another feeling overtaking it.

One not subtle at all.

She considers the shape of his mouth; generous, like his heart; strong, like everything about him, and soft, like it was made for her.

"James," she whispers, "stop talking now."

FOUR

Awake! Arise! The hour is late!
Angels are knocking at thy door!

Henry Wadsworth Longfellow
A Fragment

Caroline

Thursday, Day Four of Testimony

"Mrs Taylor, we have heard, along the course of testimony during this trial, how you came to be on the train bound for Cheyenne with Luke Taylor, your nephew. When was the last time you saw each other on the train?"

"The last time we saw each other was when he got up to find out what happened to the blonde girl Cadie McClements."

"What happened to you after this?"

"Nothing for a while. However, we'd seen Mr Donnelly on the train and if he should find me, well, I was scared for my life. But I was also concerned for Luke. Nevertheless, I stayed where I was, hoping Luke would return."

"But he didn't return, did he?"

"No. The train came to a stop. A sheriff and his deputy got on the train. They both had silver stars and pistols and one had a rifle. They came towards me and the sheriff asked me who the passenger was who was sitting next to me and were we traveling together."

"And what did you tell the sheriff, Mrs Taylor?"

"I told the sheriff I didn't know who the passenger was and that we were not traveling together. The sheriff identified himself – Ralph Walker of Lincoln County. He informed me there was an accident on the train and asked if I saw Luke talking to a young blonde girl. I told him I'd been reading most of the time. He asked if Luke had any luggage. I said I wouldn't know."

"Did Sheriff Walker offer any further information?"

"Yes. He had Luke in custody and the train would be held up

for a couple of hours while they investigated the accident. I was to stay on the train and call him if I thought of anything."

"Weren't you scared?"

"Yes, terrified. But my nephew and I vowed we would do whatever we needed to do to get the information about Mr Bodecker and Mr Donnelly to Cheyenne. I kept my vow to him because the lives of our family members depended upon it. If Luke was willing to sacrifice himself, the least I could do was honor my part."

"So, Mrs Taylor, what happened next?"

"The train got to Cheyenne and I walked in the early hours of the morning to the sheriff's office on 16th Street. I rang the bell for someone to come. A man named Clary came out and I told him I needed to speak to the sheriff. He gave me hot coffee and then fetched the sheriff. About twenty minutes later Mr Ryan appeared. I said I had a long story to tell him. He sent for his deputy Mac. I told Mr Ryan all the information about Mr Bodecker and Mr Donnelly conspiring to bring down the Alliance. And I told him what had happened to Luke on the train; that Sheriff Walker had taken him into custody."

"Thank you, Mrs Taylor."

"Mr Sturrock, do you wish to cross-examine the witness?"

"Yes, Your Honor. Now, Mrs Taylor, you yourself never heard Mr Donnelly and Mr Bodecker conspiring to bring down the Alliance, did you not?"

"No."

"You told Mr Ryan what Mr Taylor rehearsed you to say."

"We didn't rehearse, Mr Sturrock."

"Oh, really? Then how would you describe it?"

"Mr Taylor returned to my hotel after undertaking his investigations and related what had happened. I was his agent, Mr Sturrock, not his mouthpiece. He is my nephew and we are family. Neither of us had any intention of..."

"But is it not true that your *family*, in particular your husband Richard, has a long-standing, generational hatred for your nephew's family?"

"Yes."

"And your nephew, Luke Taylor, has a bitter attitude towards your husband, at least at the time of this alleged conspiracy."

"Yes."

"Then why should we be expected to believe that your nephew would be the least bit motivated to help you without self-interest?"

"I asked myself that question at first, but then as I got to know him better I realized what kind of man he is; he is able to separate and distinguish which people in this world are good-hearted and those that are not. He didn't hold my husband's dislike against me, and he has a great affection for my daughter, his cousin. I think she was able to show him, make him see, that we are decent people."

"I see. And what was the nature of the feud between your husband and your nephew?"

"Actually, the feud wasn't between them at all. The situation arose much long ago between Richard, my husband, and Morgan, his brother and Luke's father. There was a great deal of rivalry between the brothers. Their father appeared to favor Morgan a little more because they had the same interests. And then Morgan went to live in Texas, got himself a Texan ranching partner, Ethan Benchley. The pair went off to fight for the South in the war.

"Richard, a Union man, thought their choice despicable. He cut loose Morgan and his family. During the war Morgan's family suffered when Morgan and Ethan were captured and held in prison for a long time. My sister-in-law Sara asked for Richard's help. He wouldn't give it. Then later, when Morgan died, Sara wrote and told us about his death; again she asked for some assistance and support, Richard again refused it."

"Mrs Taylor, as touching as all that is, you realize, do you not, that it is impossible for the court to believe that after all this, your nephew would want to help you without being motivated by an undisclosed self-interest such as using you to deliver a slanderous falsehood about my clients."

"That's absurd."

"Mrs Taylor, your nephew is quite capable of deceiving a great many people. His marriage would still be a secret today if not disclosed in this very courtroom two days ago. His interests can be most self-serving when he wishes it."

"Objection, Your Honor. Counsel is leading the witness into some sort of character assassination of her own nephew. The feud was not of his making; his marriage was not made public as it was considered a private matter; and Mr Taylor helped his aunt because, as she testified, she was in grave danger, her children in peril, and it was within his capability to effect help."

"Objection sustained. Next question, Mr Sturrock."

"Yes, Your Honor. Mrs Taylor, you lied to a law enforcement officer on the train that day, you lied to Sheriff Walker's face; you are aware that you could be charged with hindering an investigation, are you not?"

"Oh, don't think so."

"You lied to a sheriff, Mrs Taylor, how do we know that you are not lying now, that you and your nephew didn't make the whole thing up?"

"What would be gained by that? The point was to stop the imminent destruction of the Alliance, Mr Sturrock. The Alliance is our family."

"So, Mrs Taylor, when Sheriff Walker informed you that your nephew had been taken into custody regarding an incident on the train, although you didn't know what it was at the time, did you believe that he had done what it was he was arrested for?"

"Objection..."

"Your Honor..."

"The witness will answer."

"Your Honor, Mrs Taylor had only just met Mr Taylor. She thought him a good man and she trusted him. I don't see what else she could possibly say..."

"We will see, Mr Faraday. Ask the witness the question again, Mr Sturrock."

"Yes, Your Honor. Mrs Taylor, did you believe that your nephew had done what it was he was arrested for? In other words, did you believe him capable of a criminal act?"

"Objection..."

"Your Honor, why won't my learned colleague allow this witness to answer?"

"Again, Your Honor, Luke Taylor is not the one on trial and

furthermore what Mrs Taylor considers him capable of has no bearing on this case. He might or might not be capable of any number of things, where is the relevance?"

"Your Honor, Mrs Taylor's nephew is quite capable of committing a criminal act. This court would be aware that last year Luke Taylor created a standoff between a US marshal and himself, holding up the extradition of the prisoner Wilson Cutter for his own ends."

"Your Honor, Mr Sturrock..."

"Mr Faraday, I will allow Mr Sturrock to continue with this line of questioning. Objection overruled. Proceed, Mr Sturrock."

"Yes, Your Honor. Mrs Taylor, in the previous incident I have just mentioned your nephew used a rifle and had it pointed at the prisoner's head for hours until he got what he wanted..."

"Objection. Your Honor, Mr Taylor was acquitted by the governor himself of any wrongdoing when it was discovered that the prisoner had concealed weapons and intended to use them during his extradition in order to escape. This prisoner was a convicted killer, the man who murdered Mart Keaton. Mr Taylor did everyone a service and saved the Alliance from further brutality."

"Your Honor, the question is everything to do with capability, not motivation and regardless of the outcome."

"Your Honor, it has everything to do with motivation and outcome. And Mrs Taylor has testified to the character of her nephew."

"Your Honor?"

"Why, yes, Mrs Taylor?"

"I might be new at this, but I think an individual's capability is tempered or driven by their motivation. My nephew's motivation comes from an honorable place. He wants to do good. I recognized that in him from the first moment."

"Thank you, Mrs Taylor. Gentlemen, the witness has answered the question, it is time to move along, Mr Sturrock."

"I have no more questions for this witness, Your Honor."

"The witness may step down."

Emmaline

Nan Morris' guesthouse

Emmaline reaches for her shawl draped on the end of her bed, wraps it around her shoulders and, yawning, decides to check her knee. Upon prodding the red lump and ugly bruise on her kneecap, she utters an involuntary *ouch*.

Then she smiles.

Keeping Celina blocked, she daydreams.

The smile spreads to every corner of her body and warms it like golden summer sunshine.

But her thoughts drift…

And encounter a place as dark as the bruise on her knee.

"Oh…"

Before her thoughts can work out where to go next, there is a knock on her door.

The time… what is the time?

She checks the clock on her nightstand. Late doesn't begin to describe the hour…

Again, the knock.

"Emmaline… it's Jennifer Sullivan.""

Jennifer?

"And I have Tressa and Adam with me, too. May we come in?"

She covers her knee and adjusts her shawl. Vaguely recalls locking her door last night. "One moment."

Her knee is not happy about her standing on it, or walking to the windows and raising the blinds (which unveils a dull morning).

A glance in her mirror. Oh dear.

All she can do is push her hair back from her face.

You would get yourself into these scrapes.

How did you get back in? I'm not speaking to you, Celie.

Well, good for you, little sis, bless your—

That'll be enough of that.

Once she's tightened her shawl, she turns the key and opens her door on their gentle, bright faces and that delightful little man on Tressa's hip. They say their good mornings and she stands back to invite them in.

"Have no fear, this is only a small invasion," Tressa says, setting Adam down on the bed.

"I don't mind at all, but I'm not sure what…"

"House call," Jennifer says, "for a patient with a bumped knee, and now I've seen you limping, my informant was correct."

"Informant?"

"I think you know the one I mean," she smiles. "May I look at your knee and make a professional assessment?"

"That's probably a good idea," she admits.

Adam is beckoning to her with his toy horse.

She limps over to him and strokes his cheek. "He's so beautiful. I think he knows me…"

"He has the Taylor memory," Tressa says. "He knows you."

"Would you sit back against your pillows, Emmaline?" Jennifer asks. "I need to examine you."

"Only my knee, right?"

"Well, I would like to be a little more thorough…"

"I didn't hit my head and I don't hurt anywhere else."

"That's good. Let's start with your knee…"

"Honestly, I don't need much more than a compress…"

"Amy is making you one as we speak," Tressa tells her, "and she will be here very soon. Full of herbs and very good for you."

"You look a little pale, Emmaline."

"I always look like this first thing in the morning."

"I wish I looked like you first thing in the morning," Tressa says. "You look like a flower. One I would paint. If I could do you justice, that is."

Emmaline shakes her head. "This coming from someone who

resembles the favorite subject of a French master... besides, you paint beautifully."

Adam jiggles his arms about, vocalizing his agreement.

"That's enough, you three, exam time... and then I'm afraid I will have to go. Luke is in court and he really likes me to be there."

Emmaline catches her eye.

"Not another word," Jennifer says, her green eyes smiling.

"Sorry," she whispers, clamps her mouth shut, unveils her knee and sits back.

Jennifer inspects it closely, saying, "And you did this how?"

"I fell, down the street from St John's Church."

"Mm, I remember there is a patch of uneven, rocky ground in that street. Twice as dangerous if it's dark."

"It was, and I was rushing."

"I see. How bad is the pain?"

"Last night it was very sore. It... er, it got an ice compress applied to it, for the swelling I was told. And the pain died down."

Jennifer gives a discreet smile. "Perfect."

"Now it throbs; it's a little uncomfortable."

Jennifer gives her a thorough test, bending, prodding, turning, toe wriggling... the examination aggravates the pain.

"It's a little sprained and badly bumped; you will have to take care of it. Reduce the swelling. Watch that bruise. Amy's compress will take care of that. And it will be fine." Jennifer reaches into her satchel and extracts a stethoscope.

"Why would you be needing that?"

"You've seen one of these before?"

"Once or twice."

"I want to listen to your heart and your lungs..."

"But I..."

"As I said, you look a little pale. Humor me, I'm a doctor. Remove your shawl for me?"

She cooperates without further delay. After a few minutes, heartbeats and breath sounds duly noted, Jennifer straightens up and stares at her with a critical eye. "Tongue out and say *ah*."

"Really?"

"Mm, really."

She complies and Adam mimics her, drawing out her simple *ah* into a long babbling sentence that puts smiles on their faces, even as the sides of her neck are being gently palpated by Jennifer's fingertips.

"So while your mouth is open let's pop a thermometer under your tongue..." Jennifer whips out a thin silver cylinder from her satchel and from it tips a slim glass tube. "Open, and... close. That's perfect, thank you."

Emmaline now has a thermometer under her tongue and sticking out of her mouth. Immobilized and silenced, she folds her arms and waits it out.

Tressa is grinning at her. "You're a better patient than I thought you would be."

Since it's impossible to smile with a glass rod under your tongue and not look ludicrous, she rolls her eyes instead.

Jennifer, meanwhile, returns her stethoscope to her satchel, where she has a bit of a rummage around. Now what?

Adam decides to crawl closer to her; his gaze becomes fixed on the thermometer.

"Da..." he says.

"Yes, you've seen one of those before," Jennifer says, stroking his soft blond thatch. "You are a perfectly healthy little boy..."

"Da..."

He mesmerizes them in those soft idle moments before Jennifer removes the thermometer, inspects it and announces...

"Everything *seems* fine."

"Of course. I only bumped my knee."

"I know," she says, "but a pale face where last week there was a rosy-cheeked one bears investigation. However, a bumped knee is all I can find and more than enough to be getting on with."

Even so, Jennifer looks unconvinced, and with a tiny frown she returns her thermometer to its case and the case to her satchel; in its stead she pulls out a small pill bottle. "A positive outlook in a patient is important and you certainly have that. I would like you to take two of these now as they will help reduce the inflammation and take the edge off your discomfort, and two more at lunch time, and then supper. Bedtime as well if you need it."

Emmaline takes the bottle and attempts to read the label. "What are they?"

"In its original form, and in Amy's world of herbs and natural remedies, it's called willow bark. In the medical world we call it salicylic acid. It reduces pain, fever and inflammation. Will it be a problem for you to take it?"

"No. I've taken it before."

Jennifer's scrutiny is more uncomfortable than a banged up knee. "May I ask what for?"

"I've had fever before. Hasn't everyone?"

"Mm…"

"Thank you so much for coming. I've never been attended to by a female doctor before. It's nice."

"Nicer than having old Doc Prewitt peer at you over his spectacles?"

"You might be interested to know that you both peer… in your own fashion."

Smiling, Jennifer straightens and shoulders her satchel. "I'll check back later. But if you need me, send for me. Stay off it for today, Emmaline, and rest. The whole day, yes?"

"Yes. I surely will."

When Jennifer has gone, she finds herself sighing.

"Are you sure you're all right, Emmaline?" asks Tressa.

"I will be. Doctor's examinations make me a touch nervous is all."

"I know what you mean."

"I'm glad of your visit though."

"Think nothing of it. I remember the first time I met Jennifer. I was very unwell expecting Adam. Luke brought me to her. I thought I had never met anyone so kind. That Luke fell in love with her was never a surprise to me. And not many people realize how kind he is as well. I'm glad they're married. They deserve to be happy. I know they will have their challenges because they are very different in so many ways, but deep down they have the same soul. Kind, compassionate and just. And he draws and she plays music, they have an encouraging heart for each other's talent, and their generous, artistic nature connects their souls in a profound way.

Like a river of peace flowing between them; even in their darkest hour, they are always connected and reassured. How both gentle and fierce they are, as strange as that sounds. But then I suppose love is fierce. It never gives up and it will fight to survive."

It's a full moment before Emmaline can speak. And then she doesn't know if she should.

Tressa sees her hesitation. "I said too much..."

She shakes her head. "Tress, that was magical."

"How so?"

"You stopped speaking but I wished you'd kept on going."

"Oh," she smiles shyly. "Luke would laugh at me waxing lyrical about them." But she raises her eyes again and asks, "Is there anything I can do for you, actually it'll be Tip who does it, but..."

"Well, I need to get some copy to Mr Quaid. I promised Father Nugent... and if Tip could explain why I'm not at work."

"I think the explanations have already been taken care of, but as for the rest, Tip awaits downstairs at your command. Hand over the copy and I will see that it is done."

She directs Tressa to where she left Father Nugent's copy on her desk. "And I don't think Luke would laugh at you. I think he would be decidedly touched and moved, like me."

"Now who's being kind. Watch Adam for me?"

"With pleasure. Come here, baby..."

While Tressa leaves, she sits Adam happily beside her, gallops his horse across the bed covers and observes the little boy's sweet face light up. He claps his hands together and laughs.

"Life is simple now, little friend, enjoy every minute of it."

When Tressa returns Amy Keaton is with her.

Treatment begins.

"Now, this here is a poultice of common comfrey and hyssop. Let's get it on your knee while it's hot." Amy bandages the pungent concoction to her knee, reassuring her that it's good for the bruise.

"How long does it stay on for?"

"Let it cool down on your knee. There's at least two more applications in this poultice so I will come back later and reapply it, if that's all right with you of course."

"Yes, but I'm putting you to so much trouble."

"Emmaline, this is what I love. It's what I do, and I am happy to have someone to attend to. I wish I could bring Signora Severini with me though. She's most interested, but I don't think Mr Faraday or Mr Ryan would be very happy about it. How does it feel?"

"Soothing."

"Excellent. There are so many benefits to herbal medicine. It is soothing and the various smells seem so natural to me. Remedies from the good earth itself. Of course, Jennifer might not totally agree, but she is very receptive. I think she is always ready to look at anything that might help heal. She came to me and said, 'I have a patient for you and that St John's Wort oil you swear by.'"

"I thought this was comfrey and…"

"Hyssop… yes, it is, but once the poultice is finished we'll apply some St John's Wort. And in this basin here is a cold compress of witch-hazel and wintergreen. You should apply that on and off throughout the day…"

They chat about the picketers outside the courthouse.

"Poor things," Tressa sighs. "Day after day."

"They want everything back the way it was," says Amy.

"That can never be I think."

"Although change in this circumstance should be welcome."

Emmaline says, "They are hoping someone will pay attention to their plight. They've been locked out and laid off, you know."

"We know. We read your story. Who is going to care about a strike at one of Bodecker's collieries?"

"We all should. They are hard-working people, same as us, who happened to be in the employ of the wrong person."

"Mm… Well, coal is coal and someday soon someone will be demanding it, so they shouldn't lose heart."

Nan Morris appears then with one of her superior breakfast trays; Amy declares it's time to remove the cooled poultice and gently applies the oil and a light bandage.

"I'm very happy with that," is Amy's pronouncement.

They all take their leave and this small space called home seems lonesome for a time with the echoes of their merry voices.

Eating breakfast, what she can of it, makes her weary, so she puts the tray to one side and pulls her bed covers to her chin, very soon drifting off to sleep.

When she wakes, sunshine is pouring into her room, reminiscent of what the sun can actually do – warm things. And when she wakes to that sunshine she has a cough that no genteel hand over mouth or polite *excuse me* will mask. And even that willing sun cannot warm the cold feeling inside her then.

Faraday

Faraday calls his next witness – Luke – and then begins a series of questions whose sole purpose is to guide the jury through the weight of Luke's testimony. Soon the jury hears the circumstances of Luke's arrest by Ralph Walker, how Walker refuses to defer to Cheyenne when Luke urges him and that Luke is manacled and sent to the lockup.

"Only you never make it to the lockup, do you, Mr Taylor?"

Luke describes how the deputy escorting him to the lockup is bashed and falls at his feet. He tries to protect himself but comes face to face with Donnelly who threatens him by saying *try something and you will never see that doctor of yours again.*

"I wonder how he knows about Jennifer. And I'm not about to let anything happen to her so I have to do what he says. He punches me hard in the gut, pulls me outside, punches me again, and then pushes me through the freezing cold with a colt pressed into my side until we reach a house on the edge of town. There is a strange, potent smell. A small man called Porterfield comes forward and asks *what's the story?*"

"Mr Taylor, please tell the court how well it appeared to you that Dr Porterfield and Mr Donnelly knew one another?"

"Very well. There was no small talk though. It was clear to me these men were partners of some kind. Like I wasn't the first unfortunate soul to get myself in this predicament."

"How did they seem to you?"

"They were both very pleased with themselves. Donnelly because he'd caught me and knew I was in for something bad; and

Porterfield because he couldn't wait to start experimenting on me. He was rubbing his hands together like I was a prize turkey at Thanksgiving."

"So were you expected?"

"It felt that way."

"What explanation did Mr Donnelly give Dr Porterfield for your arrival?"

"Donnelly told Porterfield that I had done what he himself had done: murdered Miss McClements on the train, and bashed the deputy and escaped."

"What did they do with you?"

"They imprisoned me in the basement of the house and Porterfield drugged me, making me helpless and unable to escape."

"Tell the court, Mr Taylor, what being drugged was like."

"I remember waking up from the first round thinking there was a snake about to attack me and I'm trapped. The smell is in my nose. And I feel like I'm going to vomit. I remember Ethan telling me he'd seen men drown in their own vomit, so I struggle to control it. This is the only time I can. I vomit constantly after that."

"And what is it like in the basement?"

"Dark, all around, pitch black. A voice says, 'how did you enjoy your first experience?' I was scared. He tells me that it gets better, more pleasant. I struggle to get away, but I can't move. Porterfield tells me that I can't escape because my body is almost separate from my brain and that if he keeps this up for long enough he can alter my personality or make me an addict but that won't happen for some time yet."

"Are you given food and water?"

"No. Porterfield always gives me this... this soup; it has the stuff in it. I always dream after the soup and after the dream I vomit. I feel weak all the time. He keeps sticking my arms with needles."

"What is it like during those long hours?"

"I dream about Ethan coming to save me. And I dream mostly about Jennifer. This cycle of dreaming and being sick goes on for so long I lose track of time. Eventually I wake up and I can't distinguish if I'm in utter darkness or if I'm blind. I find out later that I am blind. I can't control my body. All around me is evidence of it. I think of my friend Mart who used to say the only way to get to the end of anything is one step at a time. The worst part now is the darkness and I'm not sure when I'm dreaming and when I'm awake."

"What do you do?"

"I throw myself off the cot and onto the floor. Pain drills my body and I nearly pass out, but I smell dirt, earth, so I reckon if I can crawl maybe I can get away. So I start to try, spitting dirt and God knows what out of my mouth.

"Then the next thing I know is I'm waking up and lying face down inches from my own vomit. I haven't moved for so long I'm frozen to the floor. I hurt all over, I'm so cold and I'm shivering, but my skin is burning up. I can't see. I can't move. I feel helpless and start to despair. My hearing, my speech and sight are all gone. It occurs to me I'm dying."

"You *truly* think you are dying?"

"I do not think I am long for this world. I've wondered what it could be like, ever since I saw my two best friends die..."

"Mart Keaton at the hands of Wilson Cutter and Ed Parsons, and his sister, Miss Kelley Keaton, at the hands of Maverick?"

"Yes, that's them. They died honorable and innocent. But I didn't want to go this way, not able to fight, on my stomach in the dirt like worm, not if I could help it."

"And then what happens?"

"I feel someone pulling me. There is the sharp prick in my arm – the needle. Everything goes away again. The hell goes away.

"Later I feel Porterfield pouring that soup of his down my throat, I try to resist swallowing it but he holds my mouth so hard I have to swallow it. Exactly how often he repeats this I don't know because I lose consciousness and dream and prefer to stay that way."

"And did the blackness return?"

"Yes, the drugs begin to wane again. I smell things. A voice tells me to *take it easy*. I recognize the voice but believe it is the drugs causing me to hallucinate. Still, I find my tongue and try to speak his name."

"And who does that voice belong to?"

"Sheriff Ryan."

"And what does he do?"

"From that moment on he takes over what happens to me. No more drugs. He puts me in a warm bath and goes for a doctor. Doc Kincaid."

"Dr Arthur Kincaid of Dewey Street, North Platte, whose medical report we heard in court yesterday?"

"That's right. He knows what to do and takes care of me as well. He reassures me that the blindness will pass, that the withdrawal will be bad but to think of every discomfort bringing me one step closer to being free of the drug. I clung to that for a long time."

"What symptoms do you experience?"

"Vomiting, sweating that never stops, fever. And pain, bad pain. It hurts if anyone touches me. I'm restless; and real anxious; I fall asleep then jerk awake. Then the doc makes me this peppermint tea and when I start to keep it down it helps."

"Do you ever feel hopeless about recovering?"

"I admit at one point I lose hope. I need to believe there is an end and the Doc and Sheriff Ryan help me see it. Sheriff Ryan starts to tell me what has been going on back in Cheyenne, how he's given important information to Miss Roberts to take to Laramie and Dave Ransford, the Albany County Sheriff. He would see to the protection of the Alliance. I feel grateful but not completely certain. I know I have to get back to Ethan and the others."

"And then what happens?"

"The blindness lifts and I feel that a chance to help them might come. I manage to get some sleep, real sleep. On the morning of the third day, Sheriff Ryan tells me that we have company. His name is Fulbright. He's a messenger from Donnelly, come to see if I'm dead or not. Sheriff Ryan does what he has to do to ensure our escape and deal with the Donnelly situation. He can't tell me much at this time and we have to move fast, something which is not easy to do in my condition."

"How do you and Sheriff Ryan leave North Platte?"

"Sheriff Ryan gets us on a westbound UP, in the livestock car, with three horses and lots of hay. How good does the hay feel. How clean and fresh. But I'm so sick, in pain and shivering. I can't sleep. We have some supplies; I mostly drink the peppermint tea the Doc gave us. Sheriff Ryan gives me details about Maverick, about all that has happened in Cheyenne, and that he has Miss Keaton's killer in his lockup..."

"An important moment for you."

"Yes. It was."

"Continue, Mr Taylor."

"In my gut I have a strong feeling that Ethan and the others are in grave trouble and that I have to get to them. This is my family.

"In the early hours of the next morning the train is stopped on the border and searched. Sheriff Ryan buries us in the hay, but the livestock car escapes a search. When we make it to Cheyenne I tell Sheriff Ryan I'm not getting off. He stays with me all the way to Laramie where Deputy Mason tells us what Sheriff Ransford has planned to help the Alliance. We also find out that Miss Roberts, who brought Sheriff Ransford the information, has gone with him to Bright River. Sheriff Ryan discovers that Donnelly has got ahead of us. We proceed to Dickson on horseback. It becomes imperative now that we get there, and fast."

"How do you manage in your condition to ride for so long?"

"I'm convinced my family is in serious trouble. It's all I can focus on, think about. Getting back to Ethan and the others. So what if riding hurts and I nearly fall off a few times, I just get through it because I have to. We get into Bright River and then to the valley where we live. I sense we need to go straight to the Diamond-T. "

"And what do you find on your way there?"

"Ethan and Ben, my cousin, are pinned down in the snow by a couple of Mavericks. There is a gunfight in progress. Sheriff Ryan and I split up and deal with the mavericks who have started to fire on us. It's done and all goes quiet at last. Unfortunately, Sheriff Dave Ransford is dead, killed defending Ethan and Ben."

"And then?"

"Ben is cold but fine, but Ethan has been shot, his shoulder is bleeding. I collapse after that. And then they take me home, to the Diamond-T. I've never been so glad to be home in all my life.

Deputy Deloight is there; he has defended the Diamond-T from the maverick Tyner who he caught and tied up.

"And who else is at the Diamond-T?"

"Tip and Miss Roberts."

"And what did you do after this, Mr Taylor?"

"We licked our wounds and got our strength back, me included."

"That's all at present, Your Honor. I will be recalling this witness later."

"We will have a ten minute recess, Mr Buchanan, Mr Sturrock. Do you have any objections?"

"None, Your Honor."

"All rise."

Buchanan

Courtroom

"So, Buchanan, what are your plans for the melodramatic, delusional prick this time?"

"With Taylor on the stand, Loren, we require patience," he says, forcing patience from himself. "Taylor has a weakness, we'll find it. Sit tight. I need to confer with Sturrock."

He indicates to Sturrock to join him away from the defense table so Loren is out of earshot – but now alone at the table with Donnelly. With Sturrock up, only one chair separates the one-time partners; now their acrimonious dislike for one another could threaten their case.

He leans across to Loren. "Do not speak to Donnelly under any circumstances."

Loren kills him with a look and turns away.

Meeting his colleague in a quiet spot between their table and the bench, he asks, "Your thoughts?"

"In my estimation, Buchanan, there isn't one of Faraday's witnesses who hasn't done something illegal or at best questionable," Sturrock offers. "I believe we could convince the jury all their actions are suspect and unlawful."

He shifts his feet. "Then it comes down to motivation. Who considers being altruistically motivated to carry out something unlawful acceptable, or at least mitigating?"

"Who is to say that the jury is a pack of altruists?" Sturrock refutes. "I say they prefer their financial security to supporting someone who put himself in tight spot for the sake of someone else."

He adjusts his shirt cuffs. "Protecting your bank account is a higher calling than backing a do-gooder?"

"One plays to their sense of duty, the other to their fear of the future. One is moral and one is not."

"Let's find out, shall we, if the jury can be persuaded to negate Taylor's morality in the face of his divergent attitude to law and order?"

The bailiff announces the re-adjournment.

They stroll back to their table. He sips some water and observes the jury filing into their places. Sturrock sidles up to him and slides his hands into his pockets.

"Juror Four was crying during Taylor's testimony. Be careful."

"I saw. I will."

The Judge calls order. "You may begin, Mr Buchanan."

"Mr Taylor, when you left North Platte you were as good as escaping custody, weren't you?"

"I'd been reefed out of custody by Mr Donnelly. When I left North Platte I was escaping with my life to help keep the lives of my family safe."

"Very noble sentiments and I'm sure we all agree that sometimes in life the shortage of time can be against us. But the fact remains, Mr Taylor, that you should have gone to Sheriff Walker with Mr Ryan and got yourself cleared before returning home."

"Walker would not have listened."

"What you did, Mr Taylor, was unlawful..."

"Objection..."

"Overruled."

"What you did, Mr Taylor, was unlawful, wasn't it?"

"What Donnelly did was unlawful."

"Mr Taylor, no one saw Mr Donnelly do anything. You say he bashed the deputy in North Platte and took you to Porterfield's. But the deputy was hit so hard he doesn't remember anything to do with the incident, so we have no witnesses that it was Mr Donnelly, only you."

"Objection."

"Mr Faraday?"

"Your Honor, Mr Buchanan just stated that *the deputy was hit so hard he doesn't remember anything to do with the incident.* Where is the evidence supporting this?"

"Mr Buchanan?"

"As I do not have the deputy's medical report at this time, Your Honor, I withdraw the statement."

"The jury will disregard it. Proceed, Mr Buchanan."

"Thank you, Your Honor. Now, Mr Taylor, isn't it true that the Alliance, comprising you, Mr Benchley and the Keatons, is not a friend of the cattle barons?"

"I don't know where you get your information, Mr Buchanan, but the Alliance has no problem with the cattle barons, tycoons or anyone else."

"I wonder if you are familiar with the role of the cattle barons and the mine owners in this territory, Mr Taylor. Their extensive finances, their enterprise, keep it functioning – and growing. My clients are such men, Mr Taylor. They have too much to do contributing to the wealth of this territory to be wasting their time abducting you!"

Murmurs fly around the courtroom. The Judge cracks his gavel. "Order..."

"No one witnessed the defendants do anything unlawful when you were arrested, Mr Taylor; but you, on the other hand, have admitted to committing an unlawful act. You escaped lawful custody. Who are we to believe, Mr Taylor, my clients who are two of the major cogs in the wheels of business in this territory, who keep money rolling into our pockets and our bank accounts, or you – small independent rancher with a small and bitter ideology? Who, Mr Taylor?"

Taylor looks for a long moment as though he wants to vomit his indignation and justify his very existence, and then...

"Me."

"You!" *Blink, you sonofabitch.* "You..." He eyes the jury. Jurors seven, nine and ten are thoughtful; the rest still seem as wide-eyed as they did at the start of the trial. "You sneak out of town, hide away on a train, coerce Sheriff Ryan to take you to your ranch and not get off the train in Cheyenne where he had intended to take you because he considered you so important to this trial. You behave like an outlaw, Mr Taylor. It's all about *you*. And *your* wishes and *your* demands. You do what *you* want, what *you* think is important. Now isn't that so?"

"No."

"You are reckless. You behave like an outlaw. You try to have us feel sorry for you, for your problem with drugs, how dreadful the experience was, but in actual fact you acted unlawfully, didn't you? – and you only have yourself to blame!"

Taylor doesn't answer. He thinks, this one. That's the problem. You can rant and rave at him but he listens carefully to each question and doesn't answer impulsively.

"Let me ask this another way, as it appears as if you are having trouble with a simple question. You knew an outlaw named Wilson Cutter, correct?"

"I did."

"And this outlaw, you deemed him dangerous and went after him yourself, didn't you?"

"He was dangerous because he murdered my friend Mart Keaton and eventually hanged for it. But I did track down Wilson Cutter, yes, with the intention of bringing him into Cheyenne."

"You took the law into your own hands, correct?"

"I don't see it that way."

"No, of course, you don't. You knew that Sheriff Ryan and his deputies were actively looking for him, now isn't *that* correct as well?"

"Yes."

"Yes, it is. And not only did you go after this outlaw but you found him and you shot him, isn't that *also* correct?"

"Yes, and he shot me."

"And he shot you... Mr Taylor, you seem to think that makes it all right, that it mitigates your guilt. You shot a man. Anyone can see, everyone in this courtroom can see, that you have a propensity for taking the law into your own hands. And you have a whole set of excuses for why we should all look the other way. You have all the answers, don't you? You sound like a ten year old boy. Only you are a much older, more cunning and far more dangerous man. You have men such as Sheriff Ryan bending over backwards to help and yet you still behave like a reckless outlaw, outside the law, Mr Taylor, outside the law. In fact, Mr Taylor, you are more like a maverick than the so-called Mavericks, aren't you? You are divergent, you are self-motivated and *you* are maverick."

Silence… punctuated with coughs from the gallery.

Taylor is stony-faced.

No objection from Faraday?

"Your Honor, it seems to me that if Mr Taylor feels he will incriminate himself by answering yes or no to a simple question, then I already have my answer. I am done with this witness. No further questions."

"This court is adjourned for lunch."

"All rise."

Faraday

"That, my friend, was being pummeled."

Luke is standing by the window, staring out at the street but seeing nothing. His agitation is palpable and some fast talking will be required to assuage it.

"And we let Buchanan get away with it because?"

"Because it was inevitable and it's better to get it over with and move on with the evidence and testimony that genuinely counts."

"Do I really sound like a ten year old?"

"Luke, you have to understand what…"

"And what the hell is divergent?"

"In context, essentially another word for maverick."

"Do you think the jury knows that? – cause it don't sound right, like there's something wrong with me, and I don't want folks thinking I'm some kind of…"

"No, no, that's not going to happen."

"Are you sure?"

"Luke, as I said before, let's move on with the evidence that counts. I'm impressed that you knew what to do; and that is to your credit. The jury will have taken your honesty into account. You wouldn't have achieved anything by retaliating and that includes making yourself feel better. You wouldn't have, believe me. And it showed the jury there is a bigger picture and that is all you are concerned about. Luke, you can't feel bad about this. Likely it is going to get worse before it gets better…"

"Cliff."

"Precisely. But Cliff knows what to do, too. Clearly, Buchanan's strategy is to make you all look like law-breakers, but particularly you. Fighting back, fighting for survival, can present that way if the view of such perilous activity is skewed so that natural justice is ignored. But the weight of evidence against Bodecker and Donnelly will win out in the end. We just have to keep the jury's eyes fixed on who are the real criminals. The black suits will not be so cocky then."

With a great sigh, Luke mutters, "If you say so, Cam. Just a battle, right, not the war?"

"Have you been speaking with Meg?"

Emmaline

Emmaline limps across to her coat, the one she was wearing yesterday. With it hanging from a row of coat and hat hooks on the wall next to her door, access to the pockets is easy, and it takes a second to find what she wants.

The silk petals look a little creased, but the pink is still vibrant.

It's pretty, like you.

Her cheeks do have a tendency to color up, probably this shade of pink, too. Probably coloring up now.

Has he noticed yet that it's missing? When he wasn't looking, when he was checking the outer office, she snatched it from his desk and slid it into her pocket. The memory pulls her mouth into a smile.

She limps back to bed and makes herself comfortable, sighing out of gratitude for this cozy, warm and safe place to rest.

Twirling the rose between her fingers, she follows her thoughts here and there until they decide they would like to focus on the exact moment she *realized* she had capitulated. His unrelenting resolve was an obstacle in the battle to master herself, or so she thought. But then the realization happened.

No, the moment of realization wasn't the dance.

Or him reading to her.

Or the ardent, melting kiss that followed him reading to her.

All right! The kiss was unforgettable. And it should have been the moment. To give it its due, it did prepare the way.

And although the dance should have been the moment, she

remained under the illusion she hadn't capitulated. In hindsight, it made sense that if she hadn't already acquiesced she wouldn't have danced with him.

But the moment of true realization began to dawn when she couldn't resist the urge to show him her hat in Mae's window. What woman does that with a man she is trying to discourage? For all its spontaneity, it was a moment of intimacy, and a natural one; after all, the hat had personal significance to them and them alone. She had no desire to show another living person that silly old hat.

Then, when he looked at her, she knew the expression in his soft sparkly eyes mirrored powerful words he was holding in; kept back out of respect because she'd told him he was not to say them. She stumbled but regained her footing.

It wasn't to last long.

On that dreary, unromantic walkway, with the cold wind whistling and the gallows in plain sight, he did something that pulled the proverbial rug from under her and she didn't get up.

Would you hang a man for the color of his skin, James?

No, Emma, I would not.

Neither would I, but I have.

Then so have I.

Whether he knew what he saying, really knew, it mattered little. He was prepared to take on something unspeakable for her sake, share the burden he'd perceived she carried because of a shared humanity. He definitely knew that. And he chose it.

She couldn't let him do it. *No, James. You haven't.*

She wanted to embrace him and say he was far too noble for her to allow such darkness to blacken his soul. But Sergeant Meyers came along and she had to check herself.

Perhaps it was the starkness of the setting that wrought the even starker realization: she hadn't been fighting herself or him; she'd been *fooling* herself and not fooling him at all. He knew she had capitulated when she danced with him; he was waiting for her eyes to open, while piling on a huge helping of romance.

She tried to get up. Gave it one last chance.

On entering his office, there was the rose. She could make fun of it, accuse him of this and that... but he was having none of it.

Actually, she could've just asked him some questions for the so-called exclusive, but clear thought had deserted her.

In utter desperation she begged him to choose anyone but her, cried all over his shirt, even got an apology out of him, but it was too late.

And all that sweet talk...

Seeing you is the best part of my day.

This tugs her smile wider.

The rose comes back into sharp focus; drops of moisture from somewhere have splashed onto its petals and those drops she is shocked to discover are falling from her eyes. Her desperate, open eyes.

Faraday

After the lunch recess, Faraday has in mind a slight change of direction.

First up is Donnelly's neighbor – Freida Lukas – from Laramie.

Mrs Lukas tells the court that she became aware of Mr Bodecker staying with Mr Donnelly over the summer, confirming that Bodecker was there inclusive of those dates of Ed Parsons' trial. She never spoke at length to him, only to bid the man good day or comment on the weather.

Under cross-examination, she stated that she never witnessed either man behave or speak in an unusual manner or in such a way as to cause suspicion.

Next, he calls to the stand Mr Bodecker's secretary, Harvey Wallace, who he had subpoenaed as a witness for the prosecution before the black suits could get their hands on him – a sore point with the black suits and a situation which incurred Bodecker's wrath and consequently the Bugle's, resulting in a scathing editorial railing against the tactics of the prosecution.

Wallace is sworn in; he's a scholarly looking man in his late forties, with spectacles, a gold fob chain reaching across his vest, thinning hair on top but substantial, graying side whiskers.

"Now, Mr Wallace, could you please confirm for the court that Mr Bodecker was absent from Cheyenne during the trial of Ed Parsons?"

"Yes, sir, he was."

"For what reason?"

"He went to Laramie on business."

"His business in Laramie lasted the entire length of the summer and part of Fall?"

"It would seem so."

"Indeed. Why did Mr Bodecker return to Cheyenne in the closing days of the Parsons' trial? Why not before, or after the trial?"

"I have no idea."

"You're his secretary. Surely you are called to know these things."

"Not always."

"Did Mr Bodecker often go on these lengthy business trips?"

"Sometimes."

"What is the longest?"

"I don't remember."

"Please try, Mr Wallace."

"I really don't remember."

"Mr Bodecker has large offices in Omaha, I understand."

"Yes."

"How often does he usually spend there?"

"A couple of weeks."

"And yet he went there early this year and didn't come back?"

"Er, no."

"He didn't come back to Cheyenne?"

"No."

"Where did he go after Omaha, while the Alliance was fighting for its survival and good men like Sheriff Dave Ransford and Deputy Jim Crogan were being killed?"

"He... he went to Denver."

"Denver! The word was that he went south for his health. But are you telling the court that isn't true?"

"He went to stay at his Club in Denver."

"I can't think of one person who would go to Denver in winter to improve their health, can you?"

"Er, no... no."

"But Mr Bodecker did, telling all his investors not to panic. Denver is where he was arrested, correct?"

"Yes."

"And what kind of correspondence did you receive from Mr Bodecker during his absence, first in Omaha, while the plot against the Alliance was being unleashed, and later on from Denver?"

"Er... There were the usual business matters. Day to day things."

"Did he send instructions?"

"Yes, he usually does when he is away."

"And the same volume of instructions came to you when he was holed up in Denver for so-called health reasons?"

"Yes."

"So when he was absent for most of last summer in Laramie there must have been a great deal of correspondence between yourself and your employer."

"Sure."

"Did you travel back and forth between Cheyenne and Laramie yourself?"

"Yes, I did."

"And was Mr Bodecker staying with Mr Donnelly at his house in Laramie all summer?"

"Yes, he was."

"Mr Bodecker must be an excellent houseguest to be invited to stay so long."

"Well, Mr Donnelly wasn't there all the time."

"Oh no? Where was Mr Donnelly?"

"Oh... er, he had his own business matters to attend to."

"What were those, Mr Wallace?"

"I really couldn't say.

"Mm. Do you do any work for Mr Donnelly yourself, Mr Wallace?"

"Er... sometimes."

"What is the nature of this work you sometimes do for Mr Donnelly?"

"Sometimes there are business contracts he needs drawing up."

"So Mr Bodecker lends you out to Mr Donnelly because you are proficient at drawing up contracts along with Mr Dillon Kerr, Mr Bodecker's attorney?"

"Yes, you could say that."

"When Mr Bodecker is in Omaha or Denver on business, how often is he accompanied or joined by Mr Donnelly..."

"Well, I really couldn't say exactly."

"I'm sure a secretary as efficient as you has a good idea of these things. How often, Mr Wallace?"

"Mr Donnelly usually joins Mr Bodecker when he is out of town."

"And I'm sure the bills start coming in?"

"Yes, they do."

"What kind of bills?"

"Food, wine, entertainment."

"Women?"

"I guess so."

"And written on those bills for entertaining women, would you be likely to see payment for Mr Bodecker's women *and* Mr Donnelly's women?"

"Together on the one bill you mean?"

"That's correct."

"Sometimes."

"They have an account with their favorite brothel in both Omaha and Denver, isn't that true?"

"Yes."

"And Mr Bodecker pays for both of them."

"Mr Bodecker is a very generous man, but I think Mr Donnelly pays his way mostly."

"Was Miss Cadie McClements one of the workers in the Omaha brothel favored by Mr Bodecker?"

"She could have been. I don't know."

"Well, I know, Mr Wallace. Here, sir, is a list of the women who have worked in the Omaha brothel favored by Mr Bodecker over the past three months. Read down the list, please, and tell the court if Miss McClements' name is on it."

"... Yes, Miss McClements' name is... is on this list."

"Your Honor, People's exhibit 6: the list of the women who have worked in the Orchid Palace, operated by Jenny Mayfield. The list is written in Miss Mayfield's own handwriting and was obtained by Marshal Dan Hummer."

"Thank you, Mr Faraday. Proceed."

"Mr Wallace, you pay the bills regularly? A retainer, if you prefer, correct?"

"Yes."

"Mr Bodecker got first pick, didn't he, for his generous retainer?"

"Yes."

"And Mr Donnelly did pretty well out of the arrangement, didn't he?"

"Yes."

"Second pick, after Mr Bodecker?"

"Yes."

"How young are these women preferred by Mr Bodecker and Mr Donnelly? What are their ages?"

"Sixteen and seventeen."

"Babies, innocents, wouldn't you say?"

"Some might say so."

"Yes, indeed. In fact, in the eyes of the law they are minors."

"Objection! Mr Faraday is behaving like a moral crusader. A great many businessmen frequent brothels and they are full of young girls trying to make a living."

"Thank you for that insight, Mr Sturrock. Overruled."

"And you, Mr Wallace, pay the retainer month after month?"

"Yes."

"For businessmen respected for their wealth and their power, while they are in the business of corrupting young girls."

"Objection. Your Honor…"

"Your Honor, these despicable habits of the accused are in plain sight for all to see and therefore open for judgment, surely?

"Your Honor, they have no bearing on the case."

"They go to character, Your Honor. Surely upstanding citizens would work to relieve society of vice and corruption, not enhance it."

"I appreciate that, Mr Faraday, but your comment regarding the defendants being in the business of corrupting young girls is generalized and unsupported and I am going to sustain Mr Sturrock's objection, and the jury will disregard it."

"Very well, Your Honor. Now, Mr Wallace, Miss McClements disappeared the day after she spent the evening with Mr Bodecker. Did Mr Bodecker give these girls a generous payment for their services?"

"Yes."

"Enough to pay for a train ticket from Omaha to Cheyenne and eventually on to Bright River?"

"Well, yes... I suppose so."

"You keep track of these things, Mr Wallace..."

"Yes. Miss McClements would have been well paid."

"The court has heard Mr Taylor testify that on the train from Omaha to North Platte he saw Mr Donnelly tapping Miss McClements on the shoulder and indicating that she should join him in another place on the train. Have you any idea why Mr Donnelly would be on the train, Mr Wallace?"

"No."

"I see. Do you have frequent dealings with Mr Donnelly's staff in Laramie, Mr Wallace?"

"He doesn't have many staff."

"He relies on you a great deal more than you are letting on, doesn't he?"

"Well, I don't like to brag."

"How many staff does Mr Donnelly have, Mr Wallace?"

"He has a man, you know, who keeps his house. And a cook when he's at home..."

"And you to draw up his contracts, write his letters, see to his business matters?"

"That's correct."

"Mr Bodecker shares you with Mr Donnelly?"

"Yes."

"That must keep you extremely busy."

"Mr Donnelly's business is a lot simpler than Mr Bodecker's. I find it busy but not overly demanding."

"You know, I'm confused. Would you say that Mr Bodecker and Mr Donnelly are business partners and associates rather than colleagues?"

"Objection!"

"Overruled, Mr Sturrock. The witness will answer."

"Sometimes."

"Sometimes? They are or they are not. Which is it?"

"Well…"

"Going on the work you do for Mr Donnelly, the number of times Mr Kerr helps him with legal matters, the length of time they spend together away from their offices, the entertainments and interests they share, what conclusion are you to come to, Mr Wallace?"

"I don't know."

"Let me give you an example. Mr Sturrock and I are both attorneys, we are colleagues; you may hear us refer to one another as my learned colleague. It indicates we are in the same profession. But we will never say my associate, my partner. We would have to work on the same team for that. So, using that as an example, how would you describe the relationship between Mr Bodecker and Mr Donnelly – partner and associate or colleague?"

"I… I guess it would be the first."

"Partner and associate?"

"Yes."

"And yet the public and the investors are lead to believe that this is not the case, and, in fact, up till now were unaware."

"No. It wasn't common knowledge."

"No, it wasn't, Mr Wallace, you are right. It wasn't common knowledge about the close partnership and association between the accused. And finally, Mr Wallace, did you ever do any work for Ed Parsons of Bright River, who is now serving a life sentence for conspiring to murder Mart Keaton?"

"No, I never did. Why would I?"

"Think carefully, Mr Wallace."

"No."

"Did the accused ever mention Mr Parsons to you?"

"I don't believe so…"

"You are under oath, Mr Wallace. You cannot lie or fudge the truth. Let me repeat the question in case you misheard it: did the accused sitting over there on my left ever speak to you regarding Mr Parsons?"

"Mr Parsons was an association member and occasionally I would be asked to send him correspondence, likewise other association members, if that's what you mean."

"Well, that's very interesting because not a single piece of correspondence from the accused to Mr Parsons was ever found in his records or in his home anywhere."

"That's not my concern. I only send the letters."

"And yet when Sheriff Ryan went to your office to investigate any letters you may have sent to Mr Parsons, there were no copies of them kept by you or by anyone else to be found in Mr Bodecker's or Mr Donnelly's folios or records."

"The gentlemen are not the type to keep records of correspondence."

"That's not strictly true, is it, Mr Wallace? You have copies of all sorts of correspondence in your filing drawers, don't you?"

"Well, yes, I do have some, I guess."

"So, what kind of correspondence do Mr Bodecker and Mr Donnelly not keep copies of… which particular kind?"

"They…they always ask me not to make any copies of letters and such to association members."

"And why is that?"

"Communication between members is strictly confidential."

"So all manner of communication goes on between the accused and members of their association and it is all secret."

"That's correct."

"So you have no idea of any special relationship that Mr Bodecker, Mr Donnelly and Mr Parsons might have had, particularly in dealing with the Alliance?"

"Objection…"

"Overruled. The witness will answer."

"I…I know they all knew one another, of course."

"Were all three business partners?"

"I don't think so."

"Come on, Mr Wallace, you would know this. You dispense the secrets of the association."

"I do not pay attention to content, Mr Faraday. There is a lot of it and it is not my job to retain the information."

"Mr Wallace, you must answer the question or I will ask the Judge's permission to treat you as a hostile witness and there will be consequences…"

"Your Honor, it seems to me that my learned colleague is already treating this witness as hostile, with one leading question after another…"

"Your Honor, I do not believe I have done so. Perhaps Mr Sturrock is miffed because over the course of this witness's testimony a clear picture of the strong connection between his clients is emerging."

"Your Honor, this is outrageous…"

"Your Honor, if Mr Wallace would answer my question I am sure we can settle ourselves down and move along."

"Ask the witness the question again, Mr Faraday. Mr Wallace?"

"Yes, Your Honor?"

"You must answer yes or no, do you understand?"

"Yes, Your Honor."

"The question, Mr Faraday."

"Mr Wallace, were Mr Bodecker, Mr Donnelly and Mr Parsons business partners and associates, all three?"

"I…I…"

"Order, order…"

"Permission to treat this witness as hostile, Your Honor."

"Permission is granted."

"Mr Wallace, if you do not answer yes or no to my questions you will be held in contempt of court and you will be penalized. Do we understand one another?"

"Yes."

"Once again, Mr Wallace, were Mr Bodecker, Mr Donnelly and Mr Parsons business partners and associates, all three?"

"Y…yes."

"And they corresponded regularly, did they not?"

"Yes."

"And this correspondence was about the Alliance, was it not?"

"Yes."

"And you saw the words that plotted and schemed and connived to destroy the Alliance, did you not?"

"Y…yes."

"And those words also outlined what to do with their land once they were gone, did they not?"

"Yes."

"And what were those words, Mr Wallace?"

"I…I don't remember exactly."

"Come, Mr Wallace, you wrote them, did you not?"

"Yes."

"You were enthralled by every detail, weren't you?"

"I…"

"Yes or no, Mr Wallace."

"Yes, I…

"These were letters and correspondence without copies, not telegrams which would have exposed their schemes to the public, isn't that so, Mr Wallace?"

"Yes."

"So have you thought of any of those phrases yet, Mr Wallace?"

"No, I… I can't thnk."

"Then allow me to help you. Did they write things such as *let's form a consortium with the goal of acquiring the ranch lands of the Taylors, Benchleys and Keatons*?"

"I seem to remember things along those lines."

"And they wrote phrases such as *nothing could be allowed to stop them*, did they not? Things such as *no one will get in their way*?"

"Yes."

"Things such as *we will stop at nothing to get what we want*?"

"Yes."

"And Mr Donnelly wrote that he has a bunch of sharpshooters he called Maverick who can deal with anyone who does get in their way, did he not?"

"Yes."

"And he wrote about the victims of the Maverick attacks, his successes and his failures and where he would try again, did he not?"

"Yes."

"And their correspondence changed significantly in tone after the murder of Miss Keaton, didn't it? They wrote they needed to be more careful because Sheriff Ryan had begun a slow and painstaking investigation of Mr Bodecker, am I right?"

"Yes, you are right."

"Yes, I am, Mr Wallace."

There is undeniable frustration in not being able to produce the correspondence as evidence; and no doubt the black suits are relieved, although they give nothing away.

Well, you don't build a wall out of one brick, but hundreds, with steady progress and consistency, a measure of skill and a dose of integrity; and when it's built it is solid. Besides, he has a surprise to two up his sleeve which will shore up Harvey Wallace's testimony.

Emmaline

Amy Keaton returns at that time of the day when lunch is over, the afternoon is still young and more rest for the afflicted is inevitable.

"Oh, you are a welcome distraction, Amy Keaton!"

"And why is that?" Amy smiles.

"This is my least favorite hour of the day. It feels... feverish."

"Mm. You are used to people, Emmaline." Amy lays out her treatments on the night stand. "The more the better, I'd say."

"I can't say you're wrong, but I like peace and quiet, too."

"This room reflects too much activity to be my idea of peace and quiet, but each to her own. Now, let's see that knee..."

Emmaline turns back the quilt. "No Tressa and Adam?"

"Adam was reluctant about taking his nap. You don't come to supper nearly often enough. Come tomorrow if you feel up to it."

"Thank you. I will."

Amy unrolls the bandage and makes her inspection. "How well that's looking, even after such a short time." She looks this way and that. "The bruise will take its own sweet time, but the swelling is definitely reduced already. You'll be walking with ease in no time. So, here is our warm comfrey and hyssop compress. Let's allow it to cool down on your knee and after we will apply the witch-hazel and wintergreen cold compress. And finish with the St John's Wort oil. Same regimen as this morning."

While they do all this, Amy talks a great deal about Adam, finishing with, "Being that child's grandma is the finest thing in my life. I'm so blessed to have him."

Now who would dare to refute it?

Faraday

"The witness has previously given testimony and is therefore already sworn in, Your Honor."

"Thank you, Mr Faraday. Proceed with Mr Ryan's testimony for today."

"Yes, Your Honor. Now, Mr Ryan, how was it that you came to be on the train to Laramie on Monday morning six weeks ago?"

"Well, it started liked this. Caroline Taylor came into town in the early hours of the morning. She had several very important things to tell me. First, Sheriff Ralph Walker had taken Luke into custody on the train at North Platte.

"Secondly, she had promised to deliver information from Luke regarding a meeting he had witnessed between Mr Bodecker and Mr Donnelly in which both men discussed the progress of their plans to bring down the Alliance through the Maverick operation.

"Thirdly, Caroline Taylor was frightened for her children, her daughter Mrs Tressa Keaton and grandson Adam, and her son Ben Taylor. Mr Donnelly had threatened her in her own home. Also, she didn't know the whereabouts or the condition of her husband who had gone missing and had been absent from home for some days."

"And what confirmation did you receive about Luke Taylor's fate?"

"Later that morning I received a telegram from Ralph Walker telling me he had been holding Luke Taylor in custody on suspicion of murder, but he had assaulted a deputy and escaped and still had not been found. The telegram also said Luke had named Donnelly as the murderer."

"Your Honor, People's exhibit 7: the telegram from Sheriff Ralph Walker in North Platte to Sheriff Ryan."

"Thank you, Mr Faraday. Proceed."

"Sheriff Ryan, did you believe that Mr Taylor had done the things Sheriff Walker was accusing him of?"

"No. Mac and I believed it was very likely that the accused Mr Donnelly had picked up Luke, which meant he was in danger. The situation was grave by this time. The Alliance was under threat from Maverick, Luke had fallen into Donnelly's clutches, and we were here in Cheyenne with the telegraph wire down between Dickson and Bright River due to a snow storm. We had no way of warning the Alliance to prepare to defend itself."

"An attack from Maverick was imminent?"

"Yes."

"Did you respond to Sheriff Walker's telegram?"

"No. Not knowing the situation in North Platte and what had really happened to Luke we decided to keep our advantage over Donnelly, that is, we knew what he was about to do to the Alliance, but he didn't know that we knew. We had the advantage and thought that alerting Sheriff Walker might also alert Donnelly."

"You did not consider Sheriff Walker trustworthy?"

"No, I did not."

"But you left Mr Taylor to whatever fate had befallen him in North Platte to attend to the Alliance and Maverick?"

"It wasn't an easy decision, but I believed that is what Luke would have wanted – to take care of his family and the Alliance. Any extrication of Luke from North Platte would have to be done in secret for fear of alerting Donnelly in some way."

"And so you boarded the morning train for Laramie."

"I did. With the aim to ensure all the relevant information got to Sheriff Dave Ransford in Laramie and he had someone on hand with expertise in how Maverick operated."

"You didn't feel concerned about leaving Cheyenne at this time?"

"Not so much. Mac is a lawman more capable than most. He's been acting sheriff, more recently when I was a deputy US marshal. It was a natural division of labor. That's how we work together and always have. I know, as does everyone, that Cheyenne and Laramie County are in good hands with Mac. He and I spoke about ensuring Caroline Taylor's secrecy and safety, and I asked him to get in touch with Dan Hummer. I didn't think it would be long before we would need a US Marshal."

Emmaline

About an hour after Amy Keaton leaves, Jennifer arrives – with Nan Morris and a silver tea tray holding teapot, matching cups, creamer and sugar bowl; these are not Nan's every day dishes; this set with the pink roses she keeps for company. To top it all off is a cake plate of shiny pink French fancies.

"Oh my," Emmaline breathes as Nan crosses to the desk with a triumphant air about her. The tray is rested on top of two piles of her books, which seem to serve as table legs.

"These are your favorites, Emmaline, eat up now! Always a pleasure to see you, Dr Sullivan. I enjoyed our chat while we made the tea."

"As did I, Mrs Morris. And thank you for the tea," Jennifer says with such natural charm Nan leaves the room beaming.

"She's right," Emmaline says to the back of the door after Nan has left, "they are my favorites, I didn't know it until I came here and ate them, but it's true. Although I do prefer my tea iced and sweet, in a pitcher and on a porch."

Jennifer sits by her on the bed, chuckling softly. "Not expecting a tea party?"

"So kind of her... and I was so shocked I didn't even thank her."

"I wouldn't worry. She liked the expression on your face and you forgetting your impeccable southern manners much more than any perfunctory expression of gratitude."

"I guess. I don't think we should tell Amy Keaton we got tea and French fancies, do you?"

"Not when Amy is doing all the hard work, no!"

"Anyone would think Nan wanted you and me to be friends."

"It looks that way. All my friends were born above the Mason-Dixon Line."

"And all mine below!"

"Although my lately acquired husband was born in Texas. Does that count?"

"Texas? Texas just wants to be Texas."

"Well, pardon me. I am only a Yankee after all."

"A New England Yankee, the genuine article."

"Really?"

"Mm. So I understand."

"Not so long ago I discovered I am a blue belly as well."

"Same as a Yankee. There's a whole bunch of names in fact."

Jennifer gives another of those gentile chuckles. Then, looking around her, she says, "Look at this room. It's as though you have lived a hundred days in one morning. Are you sure you rested?"

"Barely left the bed."

"Remarkable."

"I don't like things too neat; neatness can kill your ideas stone dead."

"That's definitely a fresh perspective. And it may explain my new husband. Oh, that silk rose is pretty. That reminds me..." Jennifer reaches into her dress pocket. "I was asked to give you this..." She holds out a white envelope which has LARAMIE COUNTY SHERIFF'S DEPARTMENT stamped in the top left hand corner. "When I teased the handsome bearer that I was honored to be elevated to the role of go-between, I was told not to forget or I will be demoted to the status of *you will never be asked again*. Of course, I was trembling in my boots..."

Emmaline stares at it with a curious sensation starting in her midsection that quickly shoots off to all parts of her body while closing in on her brain, but before she can actually name it, Jennifer interrupts...

"I understand how you are feeling, Emmaline."

"You do... I mean... what exactly are you speaking of?"

"Men." Jennifer lays the envelope gently on the quilt within easy reach. And her eyes rest upon it as she speaks. "My... my childhood was not the most conventional. I had only one person I could really count on..."

"Your brother Frank?"

"Yes," she smiles and looks up; her grin is infectious. "How like you to guess. Frank was the best person I knew, until I met Cam."

"You've known Mr Faraday a long time, haven't you?"

"Cam and I go back a long way. Really, he's like another brother, although I did have a crush on him for about six months when I was thirteen."

"Totally understandable. A real gentleman is Mr Faraday."

"Yes, he is. Boston born and bred we three. As I got older I realized they were the best men I knew. And to have two such men in my life and all that came with them, including Jeanne and Meg, made my life rich and made me very grateful.

"And then along came Luke; he was *so* different compared to them. It was confusing at first. Despite all that I had and knew and did, knowing Luke revealed to me how narrow my existence was. A life of promise far beyond friendships and family and even professional satisfaction flooded my mind and visions of the richest life possible simply refused to go away."

"Sounds like he sent a shockwave through your thinking."

"Precisely. This was happiness, real and worth fighting for. I realized I didn't want to live without it, without him. And because his sympathies for my intellect are so natural and generous, there is no conflict. One of the conditions of his marriage proposal was that I was to become the best doctor I could be. Where would I ever encounter such a man again anywhere in the world? He doesn't see life with constraints. Duty and honor, absolutely; justice and integrity, without question; family and friends, unequivocal love and loyalty. For me, these unshakable qualities are like the cornerstone of my life."

"He is an endearing soul, in his own way. And very brave."

"I think he's had to learn to accept people seeing him that way. Our perception of ourselves can change, I believe, as we learn and accept how others see us. Emmaline, let's look at your knee..."

Emmaline turns back the quilt with a recollection that doctors sometimes like to talk while they work. "I think you will find it a good deal improved."

Jennifer begins her examination. "And with Luke came Ethan. When Ethan pats my cheek and tells me everything's all right, I know it to the core of my being. That is more precious than gold..."

Her knee goes this way and that under Jennifer's light touch. Any twinges of pain are slight, a good sign in anyone's book.

"...so I have my Boston boys and my Texas men. Good strong men I can count on, who love me and whose friendship I know I will have all my life." She returns the quilt to rights and looks up with an enigmatic doctor smile. "You're right. It is much improved. Amy has done well. Time for tea?"

"Yes..."

"I'll pour if you like. You should continue resting."

"Pouring tea in my nightgown is not my strongest attribute. I'd be pleased if you would."

Jennifer's eyes sparkle. She continues a gentle, charming patter about her men while she arranges napkins and side plates, pours tea, sugars it, asks about cream, and offers the French fancies, all accomplished with mesmerizing grace.

"So I went from having only Frank to a whole list! And now I have *five* of them."

Before she knows it, Emmaline has everything she could wish for, including two little delectable cakes on her plate. "Indeed, they are very fine men," she murmurs, and frowns. "*Five?*"

"There are five."

Light dawns. "Oh..."

"Mm. Cliff had my back the moment I arrived in Cheyenne. He has been my friend, my protector and my confidante."

"For me, too," she admits.

And they sip their tea.

The admission seems to have taken the wind out of Jennifer's sails momentarily, although more than a pot of tea and a plate of French fancies will be needed to steer the rest of this conversation away from its present path.

So Emmaline lifts that pink delight to her mouth and revels in the bliss of that first mouthful... the divine combination of sponge, butter cream, marzipan and sweet fondant drizzled with chocolate.

"This is delicious," Jennifer enthuses meanwhile. "I'm glad Luke's not here. Our plate of little cakes would have been devoured already."

Nan Morris may have orchestrated this tea party with a view to nudging two like-minded women into friendship, but now, sipping her tea, Emmaline seriously considers it. Celina has always and forever been her closest friend but after the telling Celie gave her last night they're not on speaking terms for the time being. Mama always said it's not quantity but quality that's important, particularly with friends. *You be cautious about which Yankee friends you make when you're away from home, Emmie.* She assured Mama there was nothing to worry about. But Mama wouldn't quite know what to make of Jennifer... surely she should come with a warning: New England Yankee and female doctor. She can hear Mama now... *what is the world coming to, Emmie, I ask you?*

Maybe the world is coming to a place where a woman's participation can be considered of equal value to a man's. Maybe Jennifer believes this is how it should be, same as Emmaline. Maybe they are both making a contribution. So just maybe, with so much in common, they should be friends, not just acquaintances...

Jennifer rests her cup on its saucer. "What I said before about Luke, the same goes for Cliff. I've worked out that what men like Luke and Cliff think about unconventional women like us is that what we do is integral to who we are. And they like it. I think they are really rare."

But what is Jennifer's motivation? The list for *that* is surely at least as long as the good doctor's list of men she can trust. And what made Jennifer so distrustful of men in the first place? Celina doesn't have to be in her ear for her to know what she would say... *Papa made you distrustful, and he wasn't even trying...* The thought freshens her deep pain regarding her father; she buries it in the prospect of more French fancies... and camaraderie with Jennifer.

"Emmaline?"

"Mm? Pardon?"

Jennifer gives a lopsided smile. "I've lost you."

"No. Truly you haven't…"

"I can see you don't want to talk about Cliff."

"I wasn't thinking about him."

"Emmaline, I know the stage where you don't have to be actually thinking about them in order to be thinking about them."

Is she at that stage?

"So before I have to go…"

"Go? More tea, cakes… we haven't eaten them all…"

Jennifer's grin this time is decidedly more knowing. "There *is* something I wanted to say. Luke told me in detail everything you did for the Alliance; that without you he wouldn't be alive…"

So here it is; the reason above all others for friendship between them.

"Luke says you are one of us and by that he means the Alliance family, and I agree with him. You are family."

There! The fullest of explanations.

And the unmasking of the real architect of their tea party.

"I know Cliff saved him but without what you did he wouldn't have had the chance. You and Cliff have my undying gratitude. I will never forget it. And don't say you were only being a reporter and doing your job because I know if that were true Cliff wouldn't have trusted you to do the remarkable job you did."

Ashcliff knows why she did it; for him. Yes, she wanted someone to save Luke, and the Alliance, but that came second. And the story she'd get came a close third. But she has examined her motives a hundred times since that moment on the train and it all came down to one thing; she couldn't bear for Ashcliff to feel distraught and guilty for the rest of his life about not saving his friend. And when he pressed his silver star in the palm of her hand, throbbing as if it was his heart she held there, she felt every ounce of trust he had in her, and she thought she would burst with the emotion it caused. But that emotion strengthened her for the grueling task which followed. Instead of sagging under the weight of cold weariness and the grim unknown, it caused her to look up at the sky and marvel at the stars that lit her way, and be thankful and confident that together they had made the right decision.

A light clatter of china on tray brings her out of her thoughts.

"And one other thing… the story you wrote for the paper about Luke and me… you wrote it so well, with such honesty and genuine feeling. I felt like a heroine from the classics it was so beautiful. I will always treasure it. And I also know what you did to keep our wedding from the prying eyes of that Bugle reporter and I want to thank you for that as well, with all my heart. Now you are my patient and I'm able to impart some of the tender loving care you deserve. You are an extraordinary person, Emmaline, and I'm so glad I know you."

"Well, I… Honestly, Jennifer, I feel privileged to know *you*."

"Friends?"

"Friends. Always. And thank you for the tea party. I've l…"

There's a knock on the door. It opens slightly and a flushed face appears. "Am I too late?"

"Tressa!"

Atoms of delight agitate the room anew as Jennifer welcomes Tressa, declaring, "Behold my accomplice!" and guiding her into their tea party sanctum. Tressa is too young and beautiful to be wearing black all the time, and yet the contrast between the mourning clothes she wears and her beauty does serve to highlight and dignify her loveliest features.

"Adam went to sleep at last, but then I had to wait for Tip." Tressa's embrace still carries the hum of Cheyenne's busy streets, and is sweet with shy affection. "How cozy it is in here. I love this room, with all your things, Emmaline. And the afternoon sun through your window."

"Tea?" Jennifer says. "It's still hot."

"Yes, please."

"I think I should ask Mrs Morris to freshen the pot…"

"I didn't even notice there were three cups…"

"Emmaline, until you read that letter I'm not sure you will notice much of anything…"

"You didn't tell me Tressa was coming…"

"I wasn't sure I could make it…"

"French fancy?"

"Thank you. Oh, they look so good… Now, do tell, what have I missed?"

When the afternoon sun is inclining its weary head toward the horizon...

OFFICE OF LARAMIE COUNTY SHERIFF
Ferguson Street, Cheyenne
Wyoming Territory

O Captain! my Captain! My Emma!

I seem to be missing a certain item from my desk. I feel sure you know the item of which I speak.

I miss you, Emma. I hope your knee is healing well. Between Amy Keaton and Jennifer I pray that beautiful limb is back to its best because if you are not following me around at least some part of tomorrow or ambushing me outside the courthouse I don't know what I will do.

I know you needed today to be warm and safe and comfortable, to leave the world outside for a day and rest. And I know you have a spirit in you that needs to soar. You are the evening star that rises to blaze a trail across the night sky; you are the quiet dawn where the best peace of any day is to be found and treasured and held. I would follow you wherever you lead; I would lay down my body next to yours wherever you rest.

Emma, on the 27th January I looked into your golden eyes and the world stopped. And when I looked away again, the world had changed. Don't you know, Emma, that's all it took? And now we need to work out what to do about it.

I am due in court and so cannot write more. J.

Cliff

"You weren't the only one on the train that morning headed for Laramie regarding Mr Donnelly?"

This isn't going to be easy, giving testimony about Emma, talking about her without thinking about her, without divulging his feelings and yet always telling the truth. He has to rely on Cam's direct questions until the narrative moves beyond his time with her on the train to Laramie. Here goes…

"No, I wasn't."

"Miss Emmaline Roberts of the Tribune was also on the train, on assignment with her paper?"

"Correct."

"You ended up seated next to one another."

"Yes. I found Miss Roberts in the aisle surrounded by a number of ladies from the town protesting about her articles regarding Mr Bodecker. I helped her find a seat and we ended up sitting together."

"What did you talk about?"

"Small talk at first, then she got around to telling me why she was going to Laramie."

"And why was that?"

"Miss Roberts was going to Laramie to investigate Mr Donnelly."

"And at that time did Miss Roberts know about what had befallen Luke Taylor?"

"She did. Her newspaper editor, Charlie Quaid of the Tribune, had received a telegram from a source in North Platte telling him

Luke Taylor had been arrested for murder and had escaped. He passed that information onto her."

"Did she ask you if Mr Taylor had murdered someone on the train?"

"She asked. I told her Luke wasn't a murderer and that Mr Donnelly was the suspect."

"And she agreed with that?"

"She did. Without me saying anything else, she quickly calculated the likelihood that Mr Donnelly had abducted Luke and that Mr Donnelly was Maverick. That he was planning an assault on the Alliance and likely Luke was the bargaining chip."

"You yourself had already come to this conclusion?"

"I had."

"Were you not concerned for her safety?"

"Indeed I was. There had been two attempts on her life already."

"What did you do then?"

"I told her everything we knew, except of course about Caroline Taylor."

"What did you hope to achieve by telling her the whole story about Mr Donnelly and Mr Bodecker?"

"Two reasons. First, I figured I could not stop her from going to Laramie, so that knowing the danger she could stay out of its way, or at least not be blind-sided by it. And secondly, she is a responsible journalist and to have someone recording the events would be a useful thing."

"You believed Miss Roberts to be a trustworthy person?"

"Correct."

"She is not interested in scandal or sensationalism?"

"No. This is unusual in a reporter, so she stood out in this regard."

"And now we come to your dilemma, Mr Ryan? Would you explain this to the court?"

"As a result of our conversation, Miss Roberts recognized that I had a dilemma. I needed to go to Laramie to do what Luke would want me to do, when really I wanted to find Luke in North Platte.

"And then?"

"Then she offered to help me. She offered to take the information to Dave Ransford in Laramie, which would leave me to help Luke."

"How did you react to this extraordinary offer of help?"

"I was shocked. I said I would have to deputize her so that Dave Ransford would know she has the authority. And I said no, of course. It was dangerous."

"But she didn't let it go at that?"

"No. She promised she could do the job. She knew the story, precisely understood the information, had first-hand knowledge of the Maverick operation…"

"Having had two mavericks make two attempts on her life?"

"Yes. It seemed to qualify her for the job, better than anyone else in fact. Still I said no. She claimed it was because she was a woman. Again, I said it was dangerous."

"And did the danger element bother her?"

"No. She said she was already planning to investigate Mr Donnelly and interview the Keatons for the Tribune, so the situation was not so removed from her plans. In other words, these things she'd planned already carried an element of risk."

"And you still said no?"

"And she still insisted she could do it. Our discussion went back and forth until the train moved towards Watt's Landing, my last chance to get off if I wanted to change my plans."

"The dilemma."

"That's right. I knew Luke needed my help. I knew Miss Roberts was extremely capable and reliable. I knew what losing Luke would do to the Alliance. I knew how capable Dave Ransford was and how dedicated to the people of Albany County. I believed that the Alliance was getting a good deal. I believed Luke would get no deal, no mercy at all. The decision became clear."

"And what did you do in that moment of clarity?"

"I gave Miss Roberts my star and deputized her. She promised me she wouldn't fail and I believed her. We parted company and I got off the train."

"Can you again explain for the court how you could leave the fate of the Alliance in the hands of a young female reporter?"

"As a lawman you develop a sense about people, who you can trust and who you can't, who is capable and intelligent and who you couldn't rely upon to fetch you a cup of coffee. Part of the job is knowing people and developing a sense about them."

"And you had a sense about Miss Roberts?"

"I did. Due to the Maverick threat and those attempts on her life, I had spent time guarding her and got a sense of the type of person she is."

"Are you in the habit of giving important jobs to just anyone?"

"No. They have to prove themselves to me. Miss Roberts had already done this."

"You had confidence in her ability."

"Yes. And in my ability to judge her character."

"And confidence in your decision?"

"Definitely. It was the right decision."

"What did you do when you left the train in Watts Landing?"

"I commandeered a horse from the livery and followed the rail line on horseback until I found a town expecting an east-bound UP to North Platte. About half a day's ride. It was a sleeper train estimated to arrive in North Platte in the morning around breakfast.

"On arrival in North Platte the temperature is freezing cold and I am concerned for Luke. I decide the best way to find Luke is to go undercover and listen to loose talk around town; an escaped murderer in town would be the main topic of conversation. Sure enough, it is. I ask the waitress at the popular restaurant Nebraska Bite if her customers have noticed any suspicious characters about.

"The waitress tells me people aren't suspicious in North Platte; they have their odd folk but everyone knows who they are. One thing I've learned in my job, the folk in town that people call odd are usually the ones that know everything about everyone. I find out from the general store owner who the odd folk in town are, and more importantly who in town might be buying more supplies than usual, as if they have visitors staying with them. I make a list of all these people and set about visiting them one by one."

"And who are these people?"

"A farmer, a rancher, a widow, a bank teller, two saloon girls, a scientist, an artist, and two homeless women who exist on the margin of society. Ten in all. Easy to remember. I begin to eliminate them from suspicion. The saloon girls are too obvious for a cover. Farmers and ranchers live too far out of town and Ralph Walker would have already searched there himself. So I look into the others. One by one, I find a perfectly acceptable reason for their extra supplies. Even the homeless women. All except the scientist. He is unfriendly and behaves suspiciously when I talk with him.

"My suspicion regarding the scientist, whose name is Dr Louis Porterfield, grows into a hunch and that grows into a healthy need to investigate him.

"His house is on the edge of town in a street with several other houses, but his is the last, surrounded by extensive grounds. There is a basement around the back, padlocked and under heavy snow. To gain access I knock on the door and impersonate someone bringing him a parcel of vegetables he left in the store, who has just found out that Porterfield manufactures chemicals in his laboratory and that I have a cousin who is in the same profession. I talk my way in, asking if I could see the laboratory. He tries to get rid of me. We get to the kitchen; there's coffee on the range and a boiler full of vegetable soup steaming away. Extra vegetables are Louis Porterfield's extra supplies and what got him onto my list in the first place.

"I question him about the huge pot of soup, does he have a visitor? A clock chimes the hour and he looks panicky and tries to make me leave by telling me he has an experiment he needs to attend to. He pulls a pistol out of a drawer and tells me it's loaded and if I don't leave he'll shoot me. However, I draw mine from beneath my coat. He allows me to take his pistol from him. And I tell him to take me to his experiment.

"We get to his laboratory; it's dark, full of hissing, bubbling sounds and intense smells. There are doors, one of which clearly leads to the basement I'd seen from outside. I instruct Dr Porterfield to open the basement door. The smell hits me, a rank smell that makes me wilt. I grab a lantern and shove Porterfield through the basement door. We descend a flight of wooden steps. The smell is overpowering. Human waste and putrid air and it's hard to breathe. We light another lantern. This lantern reveals something. The very thing I came for. Luke is lying on a cot surrounded by filth, in such a state. Unconscious. Almost dead, I thought."

A lump swells quickly in his throat and he gulps, unable to help it; a couple of groans from the jurors alert him to the depth of the jury's attention, but Cam distracts him.

"What did you do, Mr Ryan?"

"I admit, my anger and revulsion got the better of me. What Porterfield had done... I was outraged. I punched Louis Porterfield in the face, and he fell to the ground."

Tentatively, he looks over at the jury. The face of juror number four is awash with tears. His throat constricts again. The rest of the members wear looks of intense revulsion. They stare at him and he at them for several long moments.

Cam says, "Your Honor, People's exhibit 8.... the photographs of Louis Porterfield's house and laboratory taken by North Platte photographer Bernard W. Brown at Sheriff Ryan's request. These were shot on Sheriff Ryan's second trip to North Platte when he finally arrested Dr Porterfield. I offer them into evidence. Mr Ryan, please inform the court, had the conditions in the house changed in any way from the first to the second visit?"

He clears his throat. "No. Nothing had changed."

"These photographs, Your Honor, which the People would like the members of the jury to view now, reveal exactly the conditions in which the events as told today by Sheriff Ryan took place."

"Thank you, Mr Faraday. Proceed."

One by one, the photographs Bernard Brown and his assistant John Frasier took so much care shooting are handed to the jury and passed along. The men study the pictures, some wide-eyed and pale, others squinting in revulsion. In the rest of the courtroom an odd silence prevails. Morose, as if Luke actually died. The pictures are collected by the bailiff and placed on the evidence table.

"Your Honor, I ask for an adjournment until tomorrow morning for the court to hear the second half of Sheriff Ryan's testimony regarding the events in North Platte."

"So granted. Court is adjourned until ten o'clock tomorrow morning."

Luke

They eat supper and it's good. Very good. Jennifer cooked it. He never imagined she could cook as well as she does, although considering she conquers practically everything she turns her hand to, it should be no surprise.

She lifts a brow at him. "Stop looking as though you thought it would taste like pig swill."

"Pig swill? How agricultural!'

"How long have we been married?"

"A week."

"And how many times have I cooked?"

"All right. It's good. Happy?"

"You can wash the dishes for that."

"Coffee?"

She shakes her head. She drinks lots of water. And milk. Her skin is clear and smooth and glowing. Eyes star-bright. Hair so shiny his hands slip through it. Although he holds her in his arms like his most cherished possession every night, he still can't detect any changes in her body; she assures him they are happening.

Occasionally she seems light-headed. He can see her tire when normally she would press on. She doesn't complain of nausea but he thinks she must be feeling off-color when she mentions she needs to rest a spell.

"Leave the dishes," he says and reaches for her hand.

"We left them last night," she laughs. "And the night before that..."

"And wasn't it a good idea?" He pulls her to her feet.

"Mm, except for the part when you go off to court first thing and I wash them."

He wraps her up in his arms. "I promise I will do them. Cliff is first up."

"Mm, better…" she says, fiddling with his shirt collar.

"Although, why I would want to waste a perfectly good morning in bed with you to wash dishes…"

"Oh, so unfair to be on honeymoon and on trial at the same time," she teases.

"For some of us. Do you ever see Ben and Raina?"

She laughs. "They're still in town?"

"Last I heard," he grins. He dives into her bright green eyes. "Leave the dishes."

Emmaline

Emmie, are you speaking to me again?

Lord have mercy, Celie. Are you still at it? This is my life, no matter what you think of it. I don't want to know whatever it is you think I need to hear. So, no, we are not speaking.

But there is something you need to know...

Well, whatever it is and whenever it happens then I will deal with it.

With her shawl exchanged for her blue robe prior to Nan Morris bringing her supper on a tray, Emmaline has been doing her best these past few hours to feel less like a patient and more like an ordinary person, preparing for bed and recalling tomorrow's schedule. She continues brushing her hair sitting at her dressing table, finding herself interrupted at her task every so often and fingering her brush instead. Interrupted by sobering thoughts.

In the semi-darkness of her cozy room, the lamp glows low beside the mirror. Behind her, around the bed, over her desk, by her window, about the door, throughout her things, hover the echoes of a day that seems longer than most, filled with mixed emotions.

She places the brush on the table and draws half of her hair forward. As she braids it, those sobering thoughts and mixed emotions arouse tears in her eyes.

Seeing you is the best part of my day.

Not this day.

Oh, dear. There will be a whole lifetime of days without even a glimpse. Just memories. With the only hope they will fade in time.

With her right braid done, she ties the white ribbon into a bow.

She would never concede anything about her is beautiful

except for her hair; she would admit she has good hair. It shines and curls just right and behaves itself. And the color is pretty. Yes, she would change many frustrating things about herself if she could, but she would keep her hair...

She picks up the brush and has it up to the other half of her hair when it's almost startled out of her hand by a calamitous noise at her window.

Since the days of the mavericks any disturbance of a sudden nature tends to cause her heart to stop and her body to seize up. Dreading what she might see but compelled to look, she slowly turns her head in the direction of the window...

...brush raised, breathing withheld.

More movement and cracking of branches in the leafless climbing plant outside her window. And then *tap tap tap* on the windowpane. She flinches. The lower sash is raised with a *swish*.

She wants to scream but there's something about the figure in the window which causes her scream to dry up.

A familiar voice says, "That'll make for an interesting headline. Sheriff knocked off lattice by flying brush."

Speech still eludes her.

Then something cracks, there's a slippage of some kind and the figure in the window noisily grasps the window ledge, before hoisting himself up and climbing through the opening to land with more noise on the floor of her room.

He gains some composure and sits up, looking straight at her.

"My life is complete," he grins. "*You* are lost for words."

"Ashcliff?"

"You were expecting someone else?"

Her next attempt at speech comes out as a line of stammered 'w's.

He catches on. "What am I doing here?"

She nods, or think she does.

He smiles. So beautifully her stomach cartwheels. "Seeing you is the best part of my day. I hadn't had the best part, till now."

The Sheriff of Laramie County has just climbed in her window. No one would believe it. "You...you...you are a very bad boy."

"Are you going to lecture me?" he asks, his tone arched.

She tries a laugh but it comes out like a croak.

"You want to stick that brush back in its holster?"

"Mm."

"Emma?"

"Mm..." She stares, lost in a mixed state of shock and intense pleasure. Is there no limit to his ingenious designs to win her over?

Rap rap rap! On her door this time. The further jolt to her nerves causes her to drop the brush on the floor.

"Emmaline, my dear..." Nan Morris.

The thought occurs to her that once Ashcliff must've been a *very* naughty boy. He's certainly wearing the look of one as he considers her predicament. Such flagrant attention is very flattering.

More tapping, gentler this time. She blinks; comes to her senses at last. His sweeping romantic gesture could have disabled her sense of reality. Then where would she be?

She limps to her door, opens it wide enough to be polite and no more, and comes face to face with a worried looking Nan.

"Mrs Morris..." She starts making her other braid.

"Oh my dear, I can see you are preparing for bed. I'm sorry to disturb you, but I heard thumping, and perhaps some crashing, coming from your room..."

"Oh." She stops braiding. "After all the rest I've had today I couldn't sleep. I knocked some books off my desk, then I didn't have the lamp turned up and I crashed a chair on the floor... I'm so sorry I disturbed you or caused you concern."

"No harm done?"

"Not a bit. Nothing broken or smashed or anything."

"I meant you, dearie. How is your knee and is there anything I can help you with?"

"I think my knee is very nearly healed, and there is nothing at all. But I'm glad you knocked, so I can thank you again for today. I'm ever so obliged, I truly am."

"Oh, think nothing of it. I enjoyed all that female company, and I wager you did, too."

"I did. They are lovely women and I'm very blessed."

"Well said. So, I'll leave you now. The house is all gone to bed. Myself included. I'll say goodnight, my dear."

"Good night, Mrs Morris."

Nan turns away, softly smiling; Emmaline closes the door.

She turns around and lets out a long breath.

She's never going to make amends for that fib; no hat to buy or reparation to pay. She'll have to live with it for the rest of her life.

Across the room Ashcliff is still on the floor where she left him, his forearms resting on his drawn up knees, watching her.

The window is now closed. Shade down. Curtain in place.

She limps back to her chair, sighs again, returns his irresistible gaze and wonders how on earth she is going to get to the end of the trial without doing something foolish that will cause lasting regret. Sometimes love isn't about holding on; it's about letting go...

But for now, love is about whispers.

"Ashcliff..."

"I'm listening."

"I had the most extraordinary day, captured in this room, unable to leave..."

"I thought about you... *This lime-tree bower my prison.*"

"Samuel Taylor Coleridge," she smiles.

He returns it, with a nod.

"I confess I didn't visualize you walking on *springy heath* or *beneath the wide wide Heaven* where I could not go... or even follow my visitors in my mind's eye as they strolled down 19th street or jostled along 16th. I stayed here, all day, both in mind and body, and it seemed to me that the whole world and all of time happened in here, and there was no outside world at all. And all my visitors were angels, with gifts of healing and friendship."

"Then, you were happy in your *stately pleasure-dome.*"

"*It was a miracle of rare device.*"

He chuckles very softly. "Do you know every line of every poem ever written, Emma?"

"Of course," she laughs. "Don't you?"

"Truth is I've loved literature all my life but I've never had a kindred soul to share it with, until now. Sharing it the way we do makes me see things in a way I never have before; we create an energy that brings it to life, I guess. I started out shamelessly using it to get your attention and as a means of persuasion, but now..."

"You like it."

"Mm. For the joy of it, and because it's a symptom of what draws us together. I could drown in that thought alone and never want to be saved."

If it is a symptom, are they too far gone to be saved?

"Right now, for example, I only know I'm with you. There is no other place."

No, there isn't. And that's what worries her. *The Good-Morrow* by English poet John Donne springs to mind but enough poetry for one night and one poet per night is enough.

The next move is hers.

She extends her hand, her fingertips tingling as though they possess the heady power of a sorceress to summon at will.

For a man who looked content to sit by a window and discuss poetry all night, he moves like a flash of light. He's on his knees before her, his hands on her waist, his lips on her forehead, her brow, the side of her face, and her cheek... and, yes, there is magic between them. She puts her hands around his face and stills him. Beneath her fingers and their tips she feels the day's stubble on his cheeks; his eyes tell her he's not eaten supper and that he's worked too hard... apart from the trial, there's the regulation barroom brawls on 15th Street and at least a dozen other law and order matters he attends to before he calls it a day... and yet he climbed a plant to get to her. She closes her eyes; maybe if she can't look upon him she will feel less.

"Intense, isn't it?" he murmurs against her mouth.

"It is," she agrees, her lips touching his.

"Emma, my heart breaks just for looking at you."

"Don't look, James. See, my eyes are shut."

She feels the breath of his gentle laugh on her mouth.

"My whole being is a pair of eyes."

She blinks hers open and grins. "You read too much poetry."

"You, Emma mine, are the poetry in my soul. I speak it to you and only to you. And you hear it because it was meant for you and no one else."

Her heart starts to beat very fast. "What about poor future wife, won't you speak it to her?"

"Maybe. If I'm very lucky. Emma, if you want to talk about the future then you have to listen to what I need to tell you."

"No... I'm sorry. I didn't mean to bring it up. Last night I said I wouldn't and I meant it. I don't know why I forgot."

His eyes start to sparkle, like he knows. His hands leave her waist and reach for her hair, which he releases from the half-hearted braid she began for Nan Morris' benefit; he seems quite intent on his task, particularly when he starts on sliding the bow from her completed braid, releasing all the strands and loosening them.

When his gaze slides back to her face, stopping her heart in its tracks, she knows why, too.

The magic at work is beyond her power to control.

Eventually he will break down her resistance.

And he will use whatever means necessary to do it.

Sooner or later, she will hear the one thing she refuses to know.

His hands lose themselves in her hair and he kisses her mouth with slow, deliberate, deepening confidence. Surely only a very bad boy kisses a woman alone in her bedroom; or maybe a very good man with a ruthless streak fighting for what he believes in. Either way, she is the willing receiver and when he stops she knows the question has been asked - again.

She manages a breathless, "No."

"No? After that?" he whispers.

Perhaps a challenge issued with less confidence and more humility may have persuaded her, at least that's what she's telling herself.

"Not everything you want is within your grasp, James."

"I don't believe that, Emma, I never have."

"So when... so the one time you don't get what you want how will you bear it?"

"I don't think about that; that's called failure. I remain focused on what I must do next to get what I want. That way everything I want is within my grasp."

His words tear through her like a summer wind, rattling the windows of her resolve, buffeting the veils that mask what she hides from him.

"What is it, Emma?"

"It's... nothing."

There is silence between them for a long moment. Some of the heat cools. While he looks a little thoughtful, she recovers her composure; she needs to, to stay one step ahead of him.

"Then may I have *one* thing I want?" he asks.

"A polite request? I was under the impression you come like a thief in the night."

"Amusing."

"James... what one thing?"

"See me tomorrow?"

"Of course. I'll be back at the paper and..."

"No, I mean outside of work. Something we arrange ahead of time. Where you don't stumble into my house injured and I don't climb into yours like a thief in the night."

"I do understand the concept, you know."

His eyes twinkling, he smiles with such radiant charm a ribbon of delight wraps itself around her insides and ties itself into a bow of anticipation.

"What do you say?" he murmurs.

"I will think about it. And I will let you know."

"Mm. That sounds long."

"Considered."

"Unnecessarily cautious."

"Reasonable."

"Then I will make sure we stumble upon one another so I receive an answer."

And if it's not the kind of answer he wants?

"Now I have a question for you," she says.

"Mm?"

"How are you fixin' to get out of here? You can't climb back down; you'll kill yourself and, even worse, get me into trouble."

"Are you kicking me out already?"

"Well, I need to think about your one thing, and you need to eat supper and gets some rest."

Moments tick by.

He breaks his gaze, directing it towards the door.

The liquid expression in his eyes hardens ever so slightly.

"You never had a getaway plan, did you?" she murmurs.

He looks back at her, grinning. "If I worried how I was to get out of something I'd never go in – you're the same, I've seen you work."

"I guess," she murmurs, sliding her finger along his jawline and stopping at his chin.

"Something tells me you'd prefer I stay."

"No, no," she says smoothly, "I'd rather you left."

"Mm. Before you leave town you will have become the consummate fibber."

"Sounds as though I finally have your blessing to leave."

His eyes flash.

"No, Emma," he says, suddenly serious, "you don't."

With that, he gets to his feet.

Slowly, she lifts her gaze to meet his. She may not like what she sees, but she recognizes his right to look that way. They established that last night.

"Not till you hear me out."

There are two things she refuses to do: tell him she loves him, and hear what it is he wants her to know. Her goal is to get to the end of the trial. She needs a way to do it. And she can't think straight with him standing in her room.

She turns to face the mirror, draws her hair over one shoulder and begins to divide it for braiding. "Have you thought of an escape plan?"

"Have *you*?" he shoots back.

Their eyes meet in the mirror.

Her body flushes hot and cold in guilty silence.

"I love you, Emma, and I promise you I will as long as I live."

"You can't promise that."

"I just did. And all I need from you in return is a willing ear."

She breaks eye contact, gulps back her feelings and strengthens her resolve against his latest onslaught. She can be flinty, too. "I think you should go, before we wake the house…"

Suddenly he is squatting beside her, taking her chin in his hand and turning her face to his. His gaze dances over her then settles on her eyes. "Emma," he whispers, "I believe in this with all my heart."

By sheer force of will her emotions stay put. "Oh, James, it doesn't matter what you believe."

His eyes register the hit; they stare hard at her for a delayed moment. Then, "Well, Emma darling, I don't believe *that*, not even for a minute."

He plants a hard kiss on her lips, as if stuffing the last trinket of value into his burglar's rucksack, and, without looking back, takes off across her room and out her door into what she hopes for both their sakes is a deserted house in total darkness.

Her thief in the night.

She scoops her brush off the floor and slams it on her dressing table without a care for who hears it. "And I am not your Emma darling," she mutters, long after the moment for having the last word has passed her by.

Luke

They have been asleep for some time when he finds himself in Porterfield's basement.

All around him is the blackness.

He's burning. His skin is on fire.

Jennifer is coming. He shouts her name. She doesn't respond; she walks on by.

His heart pounds wildly as panic seizes him.

No, no, not again.

Come back. *Jennifer. Jennifer.*

Come back. Don't leave. Please, please, don't leave.

He's so hot; drowning in sweat. It rises up all around him, like floodwaters. He can't breathe. His lungs fill with water.

No, not water. Filthy, stale air, clogging his airway, causing pain when he takes a breath.

Something is pulling him; hands pressing him.

Don't. Hurts. He's gasping, searching for clean air.

Someone is saying his name.

"Luke, Luke, wake up…"

Can't wake from this. It goes on and on. There is no awake.

"Luke, wake up."

The pressing and prodding hands stop.

Cool hands now, soothing his brow…

"Wake up, my blue-eyed boy, wake up now. It's just a dream."

Jennifer. She came back? Where? Where is she? Can't see…

"Jennifer…" he chokes.

"Yes. That's it. Come on, open your eyes."

"Blind."

"No. Wake up, come on. I'm right here. See for yourself."

His eyelids are so heavy.

"Open your eyes and see."

He hears a clock ticking.

Moonlight seeps through the darkness.

"Awake?"

"I think so."

"I'm fetching a wet cloth. I'm coming back to you."

The bedcovers move as she leaves him. He sits up with sweat like a thick film across his skin. The basement lingers before his eyes for several moments and then... Their bedroom. Their home.

Jennifer returns. Using gentle strokes, she bathes his face and his shoulders with a shudderingly cold wet cloth.

His body sighs and trembles.

"Just a bad dream," she whispers. "I'll never leave you."

Beautiful, soft, fragrant Jennifer.

His sweetheart, his darling, his love.

He reaches for her; puts his lips to her shoulder, her throat, her cheek, her mouth, holds her tight and centers his world.

FIVE

A moment only, and the light and glory
Faded away, and the disconsolate shore
Stood lonely as before...

Henry Wadsworth Longfellow
Palingenesis

Emmaline

The next morning

Sunshine catches her eye as she closes the front door behind her. From the edge of the porch she looks up into a stunning cerulean sky. And yet it's so cold. If it weren't for her pampered invalid's holiday yesterday and the hot bath she had this morning (Nan Morris insisted on adding her homemade bath salts enriched with lavender oil and dried rose petals), this climate with its unrelenting grip on frigidity could drive her back inside for good.

Her knee feels quite steady as she descends the small stoop down to the garden path. Amy Keaton's final treatment after supper last night did the trick. Nan served them hot cocoa and cookies, for which Emmaline was very grateful, and over the sipping and munching Amy chattered about Signora's Italian recipes.

"You know, the continental emigrants have brought so many culinary delights to this country."

She wasn't going to get any argument about that.

All this happened before her thief.

At the gate Emmaline looks up. If she's not mistaken, a taxi cab is waiting at the sidewalk and the driver is tipping his hat at her.

"Mornin' to you, miss," he says and holds the gate for her.

He's a man of color, a fine looking one, and a gentleman.

"Good morning," she replies.

"Where can I take you?"

"Pardon me?"

"Where would you like to go?"

"But I didn't order a taxi cab…"

"No, Ma'am. Doc Sullivan did. She says she doesn't want you walking into town on that knee, and that she's the doctor. I've been expecting you. Cold this morning for such a pretty day." By now he's holding the door of his taxi, waiting to help her.

Because she didn't come by her suspicious nature by accident, she hesitates.

The driver chuckles. "My name's Clive... Clive Aiken."

"Emmaline Roberts."

"I know who you are, Miss Roberts. Everybody does. And it would make my day to drive you to your newspaper or wherever you need to go this fine morning."

She approaches the taxi, aware of the honor his words do her.

"Anybody who's a friend of Doc Sullivan is a friend o' mine."

"I don't quite know what to say," she murmurs as he hands her into his taxi cab and she takes it steady on her knee.

He chuckles and gives her a blanket. "Your destination is all I need to hear..."

"Where are you from, Mr Aiken?"

"I'm southern born, like you, Miss Roberts."

"We've both come a long way then."

"Yes, Ma'am. A mighty long way."

She's been writing at her desk for about half an hour, still feeling the warmth of her work colleagues' *welcome back* after their expressions of affection and concern for her health, when a familiar figure walks by. His destination is clearly Mr Quaid's office. Well, that's odd; probably no less odd than that her heart is racing at the sight of him, but puzzling nonetheless. What business would he have with Mr Quaid? What Ashcliff does in his own time is no business of hers, and she ought to get used to it. Nevertheless, she finds herself making fancy swirls on her copy page and daydreaming and wondering if Nan Morris has noticed that her climbing plant has some branches missing...

Mr Quaid appears and barks, "Roberts. You're smiling. Stop enjoying your job and get in my office. Sheriff wants to talk to you. Take your notebook. Whatever you did wrong, I still want copy."

Cliff

Maybe Cliff had gone too far threatening Charlie Quaid with a fire ordinance check on the building if he didn't give him ten minutes with the Tribune's ace investigative reporter; Emma was bound to feel the effect. But Charlie didn't want to cooperate, thinking he was protecting his best reporter from whatever scrape he thought she'd got herself into. Sooner or later the penny was bound to drop with Charlie; it was only a matter of time now.

He needn't have worried about Emma at least. Her expression as she walks in and makes eye contact with him reads like it did last night; she has everyone in her life under her thumb except him.

Perfect. Or it would be if the same didn't go for him, vice versa.

She closes the door and leans back on it, her arms loosely wrapped around her notebook and a pencil tucked behind her ear. She wears a cadet-blue woolen dress that's trimmed at her throat and cuffs and along the bottom of its buttoned jacket and pleated skirt with black velvet. Her hair is swept back off her face in a simple style, as though she doesn't want anyone to notice she is in possession of the most beautiful hair he has ever seen, but that doesn't stop him from recalling how it looks, or feels, when flowing around her shoulders and down her back.

If only he had Bernard Brown here now, to take her picture. She's beautiful wherever she is, but here at the paper she loves and where her talent shines, she is luminous, her best self, and she takes his breath away.

Quaid granted him ten minutes; they don't speak for the first two of them.

Her expression begins to shimmer, like the crystal beads in her oval-shaped blue and silver earrings. "You summoned?"

He shakes the lead out of his boots and goes to her. Those golden velvety eyes look up at him with both challenge and surrender. This is the face of a woman who wants to be kissed by the man she's in love with. He almost can't bear it. He gently peels her off the door and into his arms. Tight and whisper close. Face touching face. Her notebook has slipped to the floor. Her sweet softness, her fragrance, sends him reeling.

"You slept on a bed of roses, my Emma?"

War can be a cruel master; you have to win the battle before you can plunder the spoils. Another battle is about to begin and the outcome is anyone's guess.

While her silent entreaty and his desire to grant her wish have overtaken him body and soul, he is able to remove her pencil and put it where it can do the least damage – his coat pocket.

"I'm not your Emma," she says, her voice as light as breath.

His gaze locks onto the rosy, melting curves of her mouth. He knows those curves, their give, and take. "Always my Emma."

"Not now. James, not…"

He kisses her once, twice. "Definitely here." Their separateness blurs, swirling into delirious patterns. He is lost in her. Quaid could walk in, clear out the furniture and tear down the walls and he wouldn't notice a thing because all that exists is Emma and loving her is the sole reason he lives. Yet all too soon he senses her gentle retreat and not long after a thin veil of air divides them; he rallies, quickly gathering her face between his hands, keeping her attention before him. Her earrings tickle the back of his hands.

"Emma," he whispers, "hear me out?"

"Why do you ask, why don't you just say it?"

"Because it will change things and you have to choose it. I need you to trust… will you trust me…"

She is shaking her head inside his hands, earrings flashing. "It won't change anything, James."

"Ah, I think it will. When you know you will understand…"

"There's no point. Besides, I don't want anything to change. This how it is; will always be. Nothing more. And nothing less."

"I don't believe you… or that you mean it…"

"It will fade after we part."

"No, it won't. It's going to hurt, Emma, for a very long time."

"Maybe for a while, but in the end it will work out for the best. I am sticking with my decision…"

"Emma…"

"So life may proceed as it should for you, and have me return to mine."

"Emma, can't you imagine for even one second that our lives are not meant to be separate?"

"Be pragmatic, James, not romantic. We are *very* separate. We are *worlds* apart. I am from the south. You are from the north. Our worlds are worlds apart."

In that very instant her mind opens up to him.

Cousin Louisa married Some Yankee and ended up in the frozen wilderness with only a card at Christmas…

Then there was their conversation outside the jail which gave him that strange feeling in his gut and for her brought on a restless discomfort he had never seen before…

"Have you seen anyone hanged, Emma?"

"I live in the south. You wouldn't believe the things I've seen."

A chill ran along his veins – for God's sake, what had she seen?

"I've seen innocence hanged on a tree, justice hanged, the constitution of a free people hanged, I've seen fruit on a tree that had no business being there. Time we stopped hanging folks…" She was in pain, real and deep. *"Would you hang a man for the color of his skin, James?"*

"No, Emma, I would not."

"Neither would I, but I have."

"Then so have I." If she hurt, then so did he; there was no escaping it now, not ever…

"No, James. You haven't."

And he is all at once struck.

She is protecting him.

Oh, Emma!

So principled is she that she fears exposing his principles (which happen to be close to hers, inherently connecting them) to the battles and bombardments hers suffer every day.

That's one way of conveying that you love, admire and respect someone way more than you're letting on without actually saying the words.

"You're thinking something…" she murmurs.

"I am. And it might surprise you."

"What is it?"

"I will learn to understand your world, Emma."

For a long moment she gazes up at him, her golden eyes aglow with feeling. "I thank you for saying that."

He's misjudged her somewhat, but the labyrinth of issues she's constructed to keep him at arm's length hasn't been easy to navigate. She'd started with the obvious and circumstantial, moved on to the painful and the poignant, and even resorted to invention, until they'd got to this point. The deep heart.

Now to find their way out…

"But I hope what I have in mind will help you understand all that you need to. Your one thing, James. To meet outside of work?"

"So how do you want to meet, Emma?"

"Sometime today you will buy me a book and I will buy you one. Or perhaps we each have one already that we could give one another. And I don't mean Emma by Jane Austen. That is not what this is about. Then, at five o'clock this afternoon we will meet in that hot chocolate place of Mrs Landers and we will swap our books."

"The Fancy Boots Café at five for a book swap?! How will that help?" His tone is involuntarily sharp and he regrets it at once. Frustration has got a rise out of him and he needs to ditch it fast.

"You'll see." Even so, it appears from the look on her face that his skepticism has made her unsure, whether of him or the idea he can't tell. She takes his hands down from her face and holds them tightly instead, probably in an attempt to reverse what he just saw – uncertainty.

"Then, in the meantime," he says, careful to soften his tone, "will you think about something?"

"I guess that depends."

He gently squeezes her hands. "Imagine, Emma, if you will, there is no north or south, no conflict of duty or job, no parental blunders, nothing to divide us…" He has to swallow before he can go on. Oh, she is breaking his heart all right. "When you strip away where a person lives, their occupation in life, and all the trappings of their life, what are you left with?"

She shrugs.

"It's easy, Emma. Just *them*. And if you take everything about us away, we are left with just us."

"It's only a notion, James. People aren't like that. Plain, uncomplicated, unencumbered by the circumstances of their lives."

"When they love, they are exactly that. *We* are exactly that."

Moisture forms a glistening rim around her eyes.

Abruptly, then, she pulls away from him a little. She drops his hand and then coughs into the side of her fist.

"What's that?" he asks when she stops.

"What's what?"

"That cough," he frowns.

"It's just a cough."

"You didn't have it before. Not like that anyway…"

"James," she murmurs, ignoring his remark, her gaze bright and intense. "I will be in Fancy Boots Café at five. And I will have a book for you. It will help you to understand. At least I hope so. And… and if there was such a world as you just described, how could I not be in it with you. But it's not real. This is the time we have, only so many days. I will share them with you and then I have to go home."

Her eyes glisten with feeling. His insides cave.

She kisses his cheek. Steps away. Holds up the pencil she has without him knowing lifted from his pocket and grins.

He smiles back, even though his heart is sinking, and retrieves her notebook from the floor. As he hands it to her, a flash of recall brings to life the moment they ran into each other outside Quaid's office the day they met and he knocked her papers out of her hands; he picked them up and was determined she would see more in him than the boorish frontier sheriff he'd become.

Softly, he recites, "*The heart hath its own memory, like the mind, and in it are enshrined the precious keepsakes, into which is wrought the giver's loving thought.*"

"Longfellow. And you were remembering… a memory of us?"

He nods, conceding this round is hers, as is the last word.

"I must go back to work," she says. "I shall see you later. I can't wait to see what you bring me."

She turns for the door, opens it and is gone before he can gather his wits.

Unfortunately, only seconds elapse before a bothered Charlie Quaid replaces her.

"Finished, Ryan?"

He pulls himself together. "Ten minutes, as we agreed."

"What did you say to her?"

"Why do you ask?"

Quaid grunts. "She looked upset."

"She did?" That was some brave face she was putting on then.

"You got no call upsetting my best reporter."

"*Me* upset her? You fired her a few days ago, now she's your best reporter?"

"I'm doing her a favor, Ryan. What are you doing for her?"

And they stare at one another. The seconds pass.

He has a pretty good poker face; exactly how good when it comes to Emma is suspect; still he uses it. "Thanks for the loan of your office."

He clears off while he assumes the proverbial penny is beginning its slow descent.

Faraday

Friday, Day Five of Testimony

Faraday waits with Cliff in a discreet spot outside the courtroom where Judge Callaghan flies past them having forgotten, as usual, his spectacles; why his clerk can't remember them for him should be grounds for discipline in Faraday's book.

"Five minutes, gentlemen!" The Judge disappears around the corner, muttering about the 'pesky mob' out front of the courthouse.

People traffic into the public gallery, filling it up by the look.

"Are you sure you're all right?" Faraday asks again.

"Fine."

"You don't look fine."

Cliff doesn't reply.

Faraday sighs his sympathy. "You haven't told her."

"No." Cliff tunnels his hands into his pockets.

"You have to tell her sometime."

"It might sound lame to say this but I *cannot* get her to listen to me, or even want to... you're laughing... Cam, truly it's not funny."

"It sort of is when you think about it. She's just a young woman."

"Cam. You know her. *Just* a young woman?"

"Who has you in the grip of some southern enchantment."

"Spare me the poetic whimsy, Cam. She is determined to have her own way."

"And you are unaccustomed to not having yours. Interesting."

"If you say so. We were making good progress, so I thought... and this morning..." The shrug says it all.

"Want some advice?"

"No." And he clears this throat. "Thank you."

"Good, because I don't have any. At least not right now."

A trace of a smile appears on Cliff's face.

"Is that a smile? You're supposed to be frustrated and out of ideas."

"I am. This is something else. I've been meaning to tell you."

"Oh?"

"Between you and me, Cam, I'm becoming a Catholic on Easter Sunday… yes, a Roman Catholic. Huh, you're not laughing now."

Faraday lifts his jaw off the floor. "For Emmaline?"

"No, not for… for *me*."

"I'm impressed."

"Why should you be impressed?"

"Because it's bold. And it's part of something bigger."

"You think so?"

"I do. D'you mind if I ask why you would become a Catholic?"

"I've asked myself that a lot. It hit me one day that it contains a mystery I'll never solve, but which is tantalizing enough to make me want to keep on trying, because even while I'm thinking it's not possible to believe it, I do. That's a fascinating contradiction, right?"

"Most people just say they got religion. Plain and simple."

"Plain and simple, Cam, when I walk into the church I feel a sense of peace I don't get anywhere else."

Watching the last person make their way inside, Faraday finds himself voicing what is half question and half conclusion, "You're resigning after the trial."

After a pause comes a quiet, "Yes."

Faraday sighs. "I'd be lying if I said this is unexpected."

Cliff rubs that favored spot over his eye.

"Emmaline shook you loose of this town."

"If nothing else, without her I would've never realized it was time to move on."

"Where will you go?"

"I've decided I'm returning to Chicago."

"Good for you. And, I'm happy for you. You're bound for great things, I'm sure of it."

Cliff lets out a laugh. "Greater than this?"

"Who knows?"

"Well, it's the right thing to do."

"But will you be returning alone?"

"That's the burning question, isn't it?"

"A man like you, you should be more positive."

"Not if I can't get her to listen to me."

"Mm. There *is* someone who is going to miss you."

"You mean Luke."

"We *all* will. But you did what I could not. You filled the space left by Mart Keaton, and if you hadn't done that, Cliff, we wouldn't be here now…"

The bailiff appears, looking stern. "Gentlemen?"

"One moment, Owens," Faraday murmurs.

Owens obliges and returns to the courtroom.

"As for Emmaline," he continues.

"Who fills her space?" Cliff says, with a lift of his brow.

"I don't know. I… that I do not know… but I don't want you giving up. You are *not* to give up."

A fleeting wry smile is all the reply he receives; followed by the resigned observation, "Well, let's get this done. No one is going anywhere until it's over."

Faraday's frustrated and lovelorn witness gives an excellent performance on the witness stand. Whenever he begins with the words 'the circumstances were these', every jury member sits up and listens intently. When he talks about Luke, they practically weep. When he tells them about Doc Kincaid, they sigh with relief.

And when he reveals what happened when a man called Larry Fulbright comes to Porterfield's door they are perched on the edge of their seats.

"Fulbright says, 'You remember me, Porterfield – Larry Fulbright. Donnelly said you'd be expecting me. He said it's time to start bargaining with Taylor. He capitulates or Maverick will start picking off his family and friends one at a time. His boys are in the area right now'.

"I question him regarding the code words for the telegram he is meant to send to Donnelly. MAVERICK NIGHTHAWK LULLABY ROUND UP AND DRIVE, or MAVERICK NIGHTHAWK LULLABY BEGIN."

"What do each of these mean?" Faraday asks.

"In essence either message would bring the same result. Maverick was to kill off the Alliance. This was a powerful game to Donnelly. The coded messages, the set up. It made him feel important, empowered and in control because Mr Bodecker usually told him what to do."

"Objection, Your honor, Mr Ryan cannot presume to know how my client feels. I move these remarks be stricken from the record."

"Your Honor, the witness knows what the messages mean."

"Gentlemen, the meaning of the messages may remain; Mr Buchanan's objection to Mr Ryan's interpretation of the defendant's feelings is sustained and the remarks will be stricken."

"If I may be permitted to rephrase the question, Your Honor?"

"Very well, Mr Faraday. You may rephrase. The witness will answer without personal opinion."

"Thank you, Your Honor. Mr Ryan, what are MAVERICK NIGHTHAWK LULLABY ROUND UP AND DRIVE and MAVERICK NIGHTHAWK LULLABY BEGIN designed to do?"

"They are the signal for Maverick to begin killing off the Alliance in Bright River. Although they are two different messages, sending either one is the trigger for the final fatal attack."

"Then what is the essential difference?"

"The first indicates Luke has surrendered and is therefore alive, and the second he refused to yield and is dead. It would have made no difference to Luke either way. If I hadn't found him, he would have died as a consequence of Dr Porterfield's treatment at Mr Donnelly's request."

"Order... order..."

"So Mr Fulbright is supposed to send one of these messages, depending upon what he is told by Dr Porterfield regarding Luke."

"That's correct."

"To your knowledge did Dr Porterfield ever ask Luke Taylor if he would give in and surrender the Diamond-T to Mr Donnelly if Mr Donnelly called off a maverick attack on the Alliance?"

"Not to my knowledge. Luke has never mentioned it to me; neither did Dr Porterfield. Luke was either too ill to know what was being asked of him, or Porterfield just didn't bother."

"So if the question of capitulation was never put to Luke Taylor, or if, as it appears, it was of no consequence, what was all this coded message business really about?"

"Objection. Your Honor, this calls for the witness to speculate."

"Your Honor, I don't believe it does. I believe it is clear to the court that Mr Ryan is in the position of being an expert on Mr Donnelly's Maverick operation. He should be allowed to answer."

"Your Honor, Mr Faraday has willfully led us round in circles."

"Then it's been a very informative circle. Objection overruled. The witness will answer the question."

"I will ask it again, Your Honor. Mr Ryan, as an expert on Maverick, what was this coded message business really about?"

"Mr Donnelly is a cruel and calculating man. He has no regard for human life whatsoever…"

"Order…"

"To him, Nighthawk Lullaby, the coded messages, was all a game, a deadly one which excited him, and one that affected him with a sense of power and control."

"Objection…"

"Order! Order!"

"Your Honor…"

"Order! Objection overruled. Continue, Mr Faraday."

"Your Honor…"

"Sit down, Mr Buchanan. Mr Faraday."

"Thank you, Your Honor. Mr Ryan, back in North Platte, does Mr Fulbright ever send a telegram?"

"No. I do. I send it because Fulbright explained that if Mr Donnelly did not receive a telegram he would become suspicious. We have to keep the element of surprise. He can't know we know."

"Which did you send?"

"The first. MAVERICK NIGHTHAWK LULLABY ROUND UP AND DRIVE. I wanted Donnelly to believe Luke was alive and planned to stay that way. If he thought Luke had capitulated it was neither here nor there at this stage."

"Wouldn't it have been better *not* to send the telegram?"

"It might seem that way at first, but the Mavericks were going to shoot their victims regardless. It's what Donnelly wanted. At this point it was critical Donnelly be drawn out and caught. As hard as this is, it had to play out or all of it would have been for nothing."

"Did Mr Fulbright try and stop you?"

"No. I tied him up with Dr Porterfield in the basement."

"Did Mr Fulbright offer any explanation as to why the accused Mr Donnelly was unleashing his mavericks on the Alliance in this catastrophic way?"

"Objection, Your Honor. Any response constitutes hearsay."

"Overruled. I will allow the witness to answer."

"Mr Ryan?"

"Mr Fulbright was under the impression that Mr Donnelly was trying to make amends for mistakes he'd made in Cheyenne."

"And what, in your expert opinion as Laramie County sheriff, are those mistakes, Mr Ryan?"

"The two failed attempts on Miss Roberts' life. She'd stirred up a lot of mud which was beginning to stick to Mr Bodecker, and we had two mavericks in jail, one of whom had spilt the beans on the Maverick operation. Fulbright was under the impression that Mr Donnelly's boss was not happy about any of it."

"Objection. Your Honor, the witness is attempting to associate my client with this person he calls Mr Donnelly's boss. There is no evidence in the testimony to substantiate this at all."

"You are correct, Mr Buchanan; however, I did not hear Mr Ryan attempt what you just described. I believe he was relating Mr Fulbright's impressions. Objection overruled."

Buchanan favors Cliff with a long, disgruntled look before he resumes his seat.

The jury, meanwhile, are ready to hear more.

Their sheriff tells them how he manacled Porterfield and Fulbright to shelves in the laboratory; then he and Luke escaped into town.

Tells them how he took Luke to the depot and they boarded a westbound Union Pacific, stowing away with the horses. That the hay and the horses seemed to ease Luke's distress and suffering.

That the train was stopped and searched at the border but the two of them escaped detection, and stayed on the train until Laramie.

How they rode night and day until they came upon Ethan and Ben Taylor out of ammunition and pinned down in the snow by the mavericks. That Sheriff Ransford had died after being mortally wounded by one of the mavericks, who Ethan had killed in self-defense as a result. That he and Luke shot the remaining maverick, which saved Ethan and Ben, although Ethan had been wounded.

How Ethan then related the previous days' events at the Keaton Ranch, where Sheriff Ransford and the Alliance caught Donnelly in the Keaton ranch house and had engaged in a gunfight with the maverick Erastus Cole, who was apprehended by Sheriff Ransford. That they then rode to the Diamond-T to find that the maverick Jedidiah Tyner was already apprehended by Deputy Chase Deloight, with the aid of Tip Benchley and Miss Roberts.

"Then what did you do, Mr Ryan?"

"I telegraphed Cheyenne to let yourself and Mac know we had been successful and I asked for United States Marshal Dan Hummer to be dispatched to Bright River."

"And when Marshal Hummer arrived?"

"He took charge of the prisoners, Donnelly, Cole and Tyner, and the bodies of Sheriff Dave Ransford, Deputy Jim Crogan, and the two deceased mavericks, who were later identified as Eugene Stevens and John Banning."

"What is the average age of the mavericks, Mr Ryan, and what are their circumstances?"

"The average age is nineteen. They all come from difficult family circumstances. They need money. Combined with a reckless disregard for what they might have to do to get it and their talent for sharpshooting, they were ripe for exploitation."

"Were these young men aware of the risk to their own lives as a consequence of this attack on the Alliance?"

"No. They were led to believe that all they would have to do was shoot their targets. You have to understand that at Bright River the mavericks didn't know their victims had forewarning of them, so a gunfight was not something they would have expected or trained for. They were sharpshooters, crack shots, who once they lost the high ground or predetermined strategic positions were vulnerable."

"Thank you. Now, if we could return to the arrival of Marshal Hummer. What did he do after he took charge of the prisoners?"

"Marshal Hummer informed me I'd been given jurisdiction as town sheriff of Bright River for a few days; McCurdy's old job. I thought it was to cover the time I'd spent there waiting for him and guarding the prisoners, but he had other ideas as well."

"And those were?"

"To determine if there was a remaining Maverick threat, and investigate the mavericks' time in Bright River, where they met, waited, and so on. So he requested I stay on at the Diamond-T for the rest of the week."

"Did he carry search warrants for the task?"

"No, he didn't."

"Did that seem strange to you at the time?"

"Not really. The whole operation had been kept under wraps and happened quickly. The situation could not have been well understood by those in Cheyenne at this time due to distance and difficulty with communication. Telegrams had to be sent and received from Dickson due to a downed telegraph wire."

"So then what did you do over the next few days?"

"Now that I was free from guarding the prisoners – and I also saw the need for investigating the mavericks as clearly as Marshal Hummer – I went out and took a look around. Although I didn't have search warrants, I did have probable cause for anything to do with Maverick. Also, because of her skill as an investigator, I asked Miss Roberts to accompany me."

"And where did you go?"

"Our first stop was the Parsons ranch house. Because Mr Bodecker had acquired ownership of it after Parsons' incarceration, I needed to rule out any maverick threat or if the mavericks had used the ranch house as a base of operation."

"And this was your probable cause?"

"That's correct."

"And was there any sign of Maverick in the house?"

"No. The place was deserted."

"There were no signs anyone had been there recently?"

"No. So as a maverick den it was ruled out."

"Did you and Miss Roberts find anything of interest in Ed Parsons' ranch house?"

"Objection! Sheriff Ryan had no warrant for such discovery."

"Your Honor, Mr Ryan and Miss Roberts have eyes in their heads. Miss Roberts can corroborate Mr Ryan's observations."

"I will allow it. Overruled. The witness will answer."

"Yes, in fact, we did find something of interest. The object was unrelated to the maverick attack but it provided valuable insight."

"We will come to that insight, Mr Ryan. First, what was the object you saw which provided the insight?"

"On the wall of Ed Parsons' study were several huge wall maps. One of them was a map of the local area. All the ranches and homesteads were marked. Another was of the Territory rail network, every station, siding and water tower, and it had a key of colored dots indicating the approximate population of each town, stars showed how many passengers, markers indicated what type of freight or consignments. Every coal mine, gold mine and silver mine. But it was the final map of southeast Wyoming, including Albany and Laramie Counties, which stood out. Written in the corner were the words *The Empire of P D B*."

"P D B?" Faraday asks. "What did these letters mean to you?"

"Parsons. Donnelly. Bodecker."

"Objection. This is a broad and prejudicial assumption, Your Honor. These names appear nowhere on the map."

"Let's look for ourselves," Faraday declares. "Your Honor, People's exhibits 9a, 9b and 9c: the maps from the study of Ed Parsons. If they could be brought into court now."

"Bailiff, call for Mr Deloight and have the evidence brought into court."

Delighted, Faraday watches Cliff's face as they are brought in. Their sheriff's jaw has dropped.

"Your Honor, People's exhibit 9a: map of the location in Albany, Laramie and Carbon Counties of all mountains, rivers and natural landforms, including roads leading to ranches and homesteads; exhibit 9b, detailed map of the railroad network in those same counties; and exhibit 9c, detailed map of the south east quadrant of Wyoming Territory. I offer these maps into evidence. They have been viewed by defense counsel."

"Thank you, Mr Faraday. No objections, Mr Buchanan, Mr Sturrock?"

"Not at this time, Your Honor."

Even so, the black suits do not look happy, not surprising since the Judge had refused their motion to have the maps ruled out and now here they are for all to see.

"Proceed, Mr Faraday."

"The maps have only recently arrived in Cheyenne. I had them brought here from Ed Parsons' study under warrant with the assistance of Deputy Chase Deloight."

The large maps set into wooden frames are placed upon the railings surrounding the Judge's bench for best possible viewing by the jury. Constant murmuring swirls around the courtroom and everyone is craning their necks to see. Meanwhile, the gentlemen of the jury are so far forward on their seats they look like they'll fall off them, and there is a sparkle in Cliff's eyes.

"Order... order..."

"Mr Ryan, you testified that you and Miss Roberts found these maps on the wall of Ed Parsons' study. Did you touch them?"

"No, we only looked at them. We had no warrant to touch or remove these. Although in my written report I mentioned them in some detail and suggested a warrant for their removal be obtained in order to ascertain their significance."

"And since that moment the significance of them for you has given you renewed impetus to doggedly continue in this case?"

"Correct."

"What did you understand from seeing these?"

"This was Bodecker, Donnelly and Parsons' empire, what motivated them to carry out all the acts of murder and terror and plunder, and the Alliance was in the middle of it, getting in their way, always trying to stop them. Miss Roberts and I wondered about such a scheme. The time it would take. What it would bring, the change it would require, political, social and economic. How many associates would be involved. Everything suddenly seemed so much bigger and more urgent even than before. This went beyond the Alliance. This was us, all of us, and our democracy."

There is silence in the courtroom; the murmuring has stopped.

Everyone is staring at the maps.

Contemplating.

Faraday watches as slowly the gaze of the jury drifts towards the defense table. The jurors stare at Bodecker and Donnelly with eyes that perhaps finally understand. He hopes so.

"Your Honor, I would ask that Bailiff Owens and Deputy Deloight turn the map of the south east quadrant around so that the back is facing the court."

The murmurs around the courtroom start up again; Judge Callaghan taps his gavel and they stop.

"Mr Ryan, you have not seen the back?"

"No, Mr Faraday, I have not."

"So you could not know that on the back of this map are these words... Your Honor, if Bailiff Owens could read the words on the back of the map for the court."

"Bailiff, if you please."

"Yes, Your Honor. The words say: *Ed, for your study wall to remind you of our goals and aspirations. With perseverance comes success. Loren.*"

The murmurs swell up; tapping follows.

Owens steps back into his normal position. His usually stony face is flushed and his eyes bright.

Meanwhile, Buchanan has stormed to his feet. "Objection! Your Honor, this is a gift to a friend. We cannot draw such dramatic and unfounded conclusions from a simple map. I strongly object to the prejudicial nature of it and Mr Faraday's questioning and Sheriff Ryan's testimony. A gift is a gift. Mr Faraday might as well have a pen and say this is the implement used to write the words on the front, words which are merely fanciful and nothing else. They prove nothing and mean nothing."

"Your Honor, this is cold, hard evidence of Mr Bodecker's associations and intentions."

"Your Honor, I fail to see it."

"There is no evidence more credible or concrete than a man's own handwriting and signature. Your Honor, I have witnesses that will testify that this handwriting and signature is the accused Loren Bodecker's."

"Thank you, gentlemen," says the Judge benignly. "Mr Buchanan, your objection is overruled."

In direct contrast, Buchanan's face is livid.

With his point won, Faraday takes Judge Callaghan's tone. "Your Honor, I have a few more questions to ask Sheriff Ryan."

"Continue, Mr Faraday."

"Mr Ryan, where did you go after leaving Ed Parsons' house?"

"The Stewarts' place. The Stewarts are next door neighbors of the Keatons."

"Why did you and Miss Roberts go there?"

"Because it was lying vacant. The Stewarts had moved away until such time as the trouble ceased. The mavericks had to be stationed somewhere close by. We decided to investigate there as a possibility."

"And what did you discover?"

"Clear signs of recent activity. Footprints everywhere... yard, barn, corrals, the backyard. We went from room to room. Littered with clothes, left over food, the beds slept in, the whole place was a pigsty."

"Couldn't the Stewarts have returned home?"

"A family doesn't usually live in their home this way. So, no, it did not seem that the Stewarts had returned, even at the outset."

"What conclusive evidence then have you that this was the maverick den?"

"In the pocket of one of the shirts lying about the place I found a piece of paper with the words of an intended telegram."

Faraday retrieves the paper from his table and holds it up. "Your Honor, People's exhibit 10: this is the intended telegram Mr Ryan found in the shirt pocket at the Stewarts' ranch house."

"Thank you, Mr Faraday. Proceed."

Owens places it on the evidence table with the other exhibits.

"And what did the words on the paper say? Do you need the telegram, Mr Ryan...?"

"No. I don't need it. Those words are firmly fixed in my mind, like all the others. It reads: MAVERICK. READY AND WAITING THE SIGN. NIGHTHAWK LULLABY."

"What is the significance of the intended telegram?"

"First, that it never got sent; the snowstorm prevented Banning, Stevens, Cole and Tyner, the young mavericks, from getting to Bright River to send it, which would have been impossible anyway due to the downed telegraph wire."

"And secondly?"

"Following on from this situation, they decided amongst themselves, and in the telegram they are Nighthawk Lullaby, to go ahead with the attack based on the schedule Donnelly, who is Maverick, worked out ahead of time, regardless of the final sign."

"What was the sign?"

"The arrival of Donnelly. Due to the snowstorm, the downed wire and confusion all over the district, the young mavericks couldn't determine Donnelly's progress, or even if he were coming at all, but he was on his way and of course did in fact arrive at the Keaton ranch house. They couldn't risk not proceeding with the plan and facing Donnelly's wrath, which they knew to be violent."

"Have you any further observations, Mr Ryan?"

"It was unusual for the mavericks to work together; previously they worked alone and didn't know one another. The change in tactics would indicate that this attack was meant to be the final blow for the Alliance. The discovery of this maverick den and this piece of evidence should convince anyone that what Luke did in Omaha and then in North Platte, giving Caroline Taylor the information, what Caroline Taylor did in bringing it to me, what Miss Roberts did in taking it to Dave Ransford and assisting him and his deputies Crogan and Deloight with the mavericks, my going to North Platte and Luke insisting on going straight home, were all critical actions in saving the Alliance from the evil schemes of the accused. Innocent people were going to die at the hands of Mr Donnelly's mavericks. But they didn't... Donnelly failed."

Faraday hears raw emotion fraying the edges of Cliff's normally smooth voice.

An inspection of the jury reveals some of the men gazing at the witness in awe and the rest looking a bit grim; perhaps they are imagining what it would be like to be forced to defend themselves against the mavericks. To stare death in the face. To win or perish.

Meanwhile, the Judge clears his throat; he's staring hard at Cliff and Faraday wishes he knew what their wily Judge Callaghan was thinking. Perhaps what he himself is thinking; that Cliff continues to play down his part in all this.

Faraday casts a glance at the table where Donnelly and Bodecker sit like granite statues. "I have no further questions for this witness for the present time, Your Honor."

"Thank you, Mr Faraday. The witness will step down. You get to cross after a fifteen minute recess, Mr Buchanan. Bailiff, secure those maps." The Judge taps his gavel.

Owens declares, "All rise."

Judge Callaghan leaves the courtroom. As does the public gallery in a tidy fashion. From the press gallery, Quaid and the Bugle's Obadiah Williams leave first in haste. The jury, meanwhile, files out for refreshments and a stretch.

And Cliff steps down from the witness stand.

They meet in the middle of the courtroom, conversing as they follow everyone else...

"Early birthday present?" Cliff grins.

"Well, you might not be here when it comes around."

"I'll take it when I can get it."

"Thought you might. Coffee?"

"Thanks, no. Fresh air. I need to think about Buchanan's next move."

"He won't be kind."

"I know. But honestly, Cam, he can go to hell."

"Are Catholic boys allowed to say that?"

"I have till Easter."

Outside in the hall, some small distance away, Emmaline and Quaid are talking. Seems Emmaline has found out about the maps; she is gesturing that she can't discuss the evidence with him, but Quaid regards her like a freshly opened bottle of expensive whiskey anyway.

Faraday glances at his companion. "Sure you won't have coffee?"

"No, I..."

"Ryan?"

They turn around. Deputy Deloight is coming towards them.

He and Cliff shake hands.

"Good to see you, Chase. How are things in Laramie?"

For several minutes they chat about the situation in Laramie with Dave Ransford gone, and then Deputy Deloight stops mid-sentence and does a double-take at something he sees out of the corner of his eye. "Is that Emmaline?"

"Yes, it is," Faraday tells him.

"Excuse me. I'd like to catch up with her."

"Then by all means..."

The deputy tips his hat and is off.

"Interesting," Faraday murmurs. He glances at Cliff to find him guardedly watching the meeting between Chase Deloight and Emmaline, who are obviously delighted to see one another once again.

"I'll be back in ten," Cliff says and takes off, making his way through the crowd and heading towards the exit.

Emmaline spots him and her gaze carefully, closely tracks him, despite her reunion with Chase Deloight, and despite Charlie Quaid's enthusiasm for the latest evidence which continues particularly now that the editor has met the deputy.

What they miss in their excitement is the look on her soft face that would tell them she wants to go after Cliff and is just barely holding herself in check.

There's something about Emmaline, something none of them truly understands, not even Cliff.

Outside his office is the figure of another young woman, one who is pacing and busily wringing her hands.

George.

"Oh, Cam, I'm so relieved you're out."

"What's happened?"

"Is Cliff not with you?"

"No, he had something to attend to. George, what is it?"

Intense worry clouds the usual luster of her bright green eyes.

"Come in here," he says, guiding her into his office.

"Luke is unwell. Ethan's with him now and I've called Gus Prewitt in for a second opinion."

"What's the matter with him?"

"It started with a nightmare last night. Porterfield's basement. He woke disorientated and drenched with perspiration. Since then, he's been pale and unwell, running a fever."

"What does Prewitt say it is?"

"He suspects as I do that Luke is reacting to dredging up the past."

"His testimony regarding the basement and Porterfield..."

"Yes, yes, all that. And then Sturrock's cross..."

"Do you want me to go to him... don't know what good I'll be. And we're due back in court in several minutes."

"Cliff too?"

"He's going under Buchanan's cross." Faraday takes her hands in his. "Look at me, George. No, stop that and really look at me."

Her worried eyes find his at last and stick.

"The old Doc can bring down the fever," he says gently. "But what Luke really needs is you."

"This is the first moment I've been away..."

"I don't mean that. He knows you're *real*. And you won't leave him to despair and suffering. Remind him of that every minute. If you panic, George, he'll think it's more serious than it is."

"It *is* serious."

"It is unexpected. And yet we should have seen it coming."

"Oh, will that trauma ever go away!"

"I know it's frustrating. But you and I know the passage of time and your life together will fix it."

"Yes, Cam."

"Who knows how many nightmares he had before you were married and he never told a soul? He didn't look well, so I'd say a great many. But already you have made the world of difference."

"I... yes, Cam."

"This is a test of his strength of character and his mind. He will want to defeat it with all he's got."

"Yes, I know, but..."

"Just help him." He leans forward and kisses her forehead. "It's all right, George. It's all right. You won't lose him." He hugs her tightly for a few moments and then sets her back. "You are the one dream that kept him going for so long; I don't think he has any intention of leaving you now. Cliff or I might be all right to have kicking around, but all Luke needs is you."

Luke

The Taylors' residence

"So, what's going on inside that ornery head of yours?"

"You think this is all in my head, Ethan?"

"Pretty much."

"How do you feel so sick from something in your head?"

"How should I know? Do I look like a doctor?"

Luke feels a grin somewhere. "Powerful thing, the mind."

"You said it. Taking those pills?"

"The fever ones, yes. She threatened to give me willow bark to gnaw on if I didn't take them. I think she had visions of me at five years old."

"I have visions of you at five years old, and ten and fifteen and…"

Jennifer appears in the door, wide-eyed and pale; he's scaring her, he knows he is, but it makes no difference what he says; he can't allay her fears.

"Where'd you get to?" he asks in a playful tone.

She sits by him on the bed squeezing a cloth into some watery concoction Amy made up for his fever.

"Jennifer, honey," Ethan says gently. "You okay?"

"I'm fine, Ethan," she says like it hurts to speak. She settles the cloth on his forehead and studies his face like she's looking down a microscope.

He catches Ethan's eye. Ethan is pointing to the door and mouthing *I'm goin' now*, leaving after giving Jennifer's shoulder a couple of pats.

"Bye, Ethan," she says distractedly.

Luke looks into his wife's eyes. Or tries to.

"Where did you go?"

"To see Cam."

"And what did he tell you?"

"Just things."

"Did they make any difference?"

A genteel shrug.

"He and Cliff are both in court," he says.

"Mm. Don't talk anymore. Just rest. Close your eyes and go to sleep."

"Lay with me."

"Some doctor I am," she mumbles, getting onto the bed beside him, "can't even cure my own husband of a trifling fever."

"You used to say fevers weren't to be trifled with. Besides it's almost gone."

She lays her head on his shoulder and places her arm around his middle. The peace that fills him in that moment is like he imagines heaven to be.

"Talk to me about the kid," he whispers.

"All right. What should we name him – or her?"

"You decide," he says, feeling tired. "You tell me your favorite names for boys. I'll tell you mine for girls."

"I didn't know you had favorite names."

"See, you doctors think you know everything."

She laughs softly and murmurs, "I love being in this room with you."

"Same. Now, the kid…"

"It feels strange to be talking about him – her…"

"Still thinking the future won't happen?"

"When I'm with you I always have the future."

He smiles against her chestnut hair.

She sighs and says, "I like Frederic."

"No. One day I will tell you why."

"Oh. Then, how about Aaron?"

"Better."

"Jonathon."

"No."

"Samuel."

"No… although Sam Adams was a Son of Liberty in Boston."

"Yes, I know all about the Sons of Liberty in old Boston," she humors him. "Alexander."

"Too long."

"Alex."

"Better."

"Donald… or, Ronald."

"No and no."

Before long, her delicate giggles start to tickle his ears and sing in his heart. She must be reciting every name she knows…

Sleep is approaching; he hears every second name now.

But he thinks the last, before sleep claims him, is Evan.

He wants to tell her *yes*, but his mouth is no longer awake.

Cliff

Courtroom

"You broke into the Parsons' ranch house and conducted a search, didn't you, Mr Ryan?"

"I had probable cause to search for mavericks and whatever evidence they left behind, Mr Buchanan. It wasn't the time to assume that just because four of them attacked there weren't others hiding out. This had to be determined once and for all. So I found an open window at Ed Parsons' ranch house, I went in and looked around to determine if this was the mavericks' den."

"And at the Stewarts' ranch house you conducted a search."

"The Stewarts gave John Keaton authority to keep an eye on their place. I asked Mr Keaton's permission to search the ranch and everything in it. He granted it and gave me the key."

"And the reporter Miss Roberts aided you on these searches?"

"Yes."

"And did Miss Roberts also climb in the window you found 'open'?"

"Order... order..."

"Yes."

"Remarkable."

Tap, tap...

"I see you are frowning, Mr Ryan; you don't think it remarkable?"

"Miss Roberts is a reporter. It's what reporters do, in my experience."

"I see. And it didn't bother you that she is a woman?"

"No. What is your point, counselor?"

"No point, Mr Ryan. I was just asking. However, I was always under the impression that it is highly unethical for a lawman and a member of the press to collude. Is that not the case, Mr Ryan?"

"Objection. Your Honor, just who is on trial here?"

"Overruled, Mr Faraday. The witness will answer."

"We weren't colluding, counselor. I needed help to carry out the search and Miss Roberts, being an expert on Maverick, was fit for the task."

"But you colluded on the train to Laramie, when you had your dilemma and Miss Roberts solved it for you. In fact, you were conspiring, the pair of you."

"No."

"It is clear from your testimony you intended to extricate Mr Taylor from North Platte no matter what it took. Now, on the train, you conspired with Miss Roberts with the aim of doing this."

"No."

"You have expressed a good opinion of Miss Roberts on more than one occasion, Mr Ryan, so that makes you and Miss Emmaline Roberts excellent partners for conspiracy. In fact, you pretended you were a reporter to gain access to those people in North Platte you suspected. You took your cover from Miss Roberts, didn't you? A reporter. She became you, a sheriff, and you became her, a reporter."

"It was a decision based on what needed to be done; there was no conspiracy."

"In a moment we will come to the matter of illegality. For now, let's go back further. Yesterday we heard you say that you didn't reply to Ralph Walker's telegram asking for confirmation about Mr Taylor and Mr Donnelly on that fateful Monday morning. You preferred to keep Sheriff Walker in the dark about the whole thing. Why was that?"

"Because we couldn't risk Mr Donnelly discovering from Sheriff Walker that we were onto him."

"Sheriff Walker is a respected lawman. Are you shifting yet more blame for your dubious actions, Mr Ryan?"

"No, I am not shifting blame, my actions were not dubious, and it is important to understand that where Mr Donnelly is involved, his ability to lie and deceive can create confusion and terror for those who don't know better. A man, even a respected one, might unknowingly think he's doing the right thing."

"Isn't it a fact, Mr Ryan, that you and Ralph Walker don't have a happy relationship?"

"Could you explain what you mean, counselor?"

"I mean, Mr Ryan, it is altogether possible you didn't wire a reply to Ralph Walker that morning because of the professional rivalry and personal animosity that exists between you. You didn't want him to get any of the credit for whatever might happen."

"Who gets the credit for what doesn't come into it. At the time I didn't want to risk Sheriff Walker encountering Mr Donnelly knowing what we knew. The success of what we needed to do, both in Bright River and in North Platte, depended upon secrecy."

"But Sheriff Walker could have helped you, being a colleague and the actual sheriff of the jurisdiction you invaded."

"No, I did not invade Sheriff Walker's jurisdiction. I was disguised and for good reason. Luke was an innocent man in serious trouble and needing help. And as for Sheriff Walker, he couldn't find Luke as the suspect in a crime; he would never have found him out of the goodness of his heart."

"But the fact remains that you went in *on the sly* into his jurisdiction and extricated a man he was holding for murder and assault. Where is the respect for the law? Of one lawman for another? You should have reported to Sheriff Walker on arrival and told him of your intentions. Instead you hindered the capture and arrest of a wanted man and perverted the course of justice. How can you expect us, any of us, as the citizens who elect you, to trust you ever again? Explain yourself, Mr Ryan!"

"I was rescuing an innocent man from certain death, not hindering the capture of a wanted man. Luke had not been charged with any crime; he was being detained by Sheriff Walker as a person of interest, and all the so-called evidence was circumstantial. Mr Donnelly and Dr Porterfield were the hinderers; the first kidnapped Luke and the second detained him against his will and deprived him of liberty, both with the intent to kill, a slow and painful death, poisoning with drugs. And the perversion was that which saw Luke in the hideous situation in which I found him, thanks again to Mr Donnelly and Dr Porterfield. Furthermore, I expect the citizens of Laramie County to trust that I would do whatever it takes to protect them from any threat big or small, including those they cannot perceive for themselves, or those that come from the least expected places."

"So you would break the law in order to uphold the law? Frankly, Sheriff Ryan, that is bizarre coming from a lawman."

"And it would be if I had said that, but that's *not* what I said. I've just explained, counselor, and I'm pretty sure every man and woman in this courtroom heard it; I was rescuing an innocent man from certain death. Not breaking the law."

"Mr Ryan, you want this jury to find the accused guilty of serious crimes when you yourself are guilty of breaking and entering and suspect searches, willful dereliction of your position as sheriff, colluding and conspiring with a member of the press, undermining the capture and arrest of a wanted man and perverting the course of justice. How can you sit there and expect these citizens, the people you serve, to choose *you*, to believe *you*, over men who further the progress of this territory with their tremendous enterprise and overwhelming pecuniary commitment and contribution?"

"First, counselor, I didn't do those things you just accused me of and if I had I would be exercising my rights under the Fifth Amendment, which I'm not; if it is your aim to bully me into doing that, you will not succeed because I have done nothing wrong.

"And secondly, where the accused are concerned, I don't see murder and conspiracy to murder as furthering the progress of this territory, nor do I see murder and conspiracy to murder as enterprise, although Mr Donnelly and Mr Bodecker have shown extraordinary commitment to the destruction of the Alliance, small ranchers and homesteaders alike.

"Lastly, the ill-gotten personal gain of powerful and influential men is not the same as their pecuniary commitment."

"The fact remains, Mr Ryan, you sat on a train with a reporter and proceeded to divulge to her sensitive information; you handed over your star and your authority to this young woman to do what you yourself should have done. Deny that, Sheriff."

"I don't deny I deputized Miss Roberts to help Sheriff Ransford, but I was not derelict. I whole-heartedly believed that extricating Luke Taylor from North Platte and out of Donnelly's clutches was the correct course of action."

"You can be very smug about it now, now that it has turned out the way you wanted. The fact is two good men died, Mr Ryan, because you gave your job to Miss Roberts and left Sheriff Ransford and his deputies to go it alone."

"You are the only person I know of, counselor, who holds such little regard for the capabilities of Dave Ransford."

"Mr Ryan, could Miss Roberts pick up a rifle and shoot?"

"You would have to ask her that."

"So, not knowing what she was capable of, you sent her off to Laramie and then you went the other way?"

"I knew Miss Roberts capable of delivering the information and then having important knowledge about maverick. These were the critical needs. Again, let me remind you that Dave Ransford and his deputies were extremely capable. Proven and renowned, in fact."

"So sure were you?"

"Yes."

"And yet Dave Ransford and Jim Crogan died. I believe, Mr Ryan, that you should accept responsibility for their deaths…"

"Objection. Move to strike Mr Buchanan's last two statements, Your Honor."

"Sustained. Motion to strike granted."

"That you should have been there for them…"

"Your Honor, Mr Ryan is not the one on trial here…"

"That you sent a *woman* to do *your* job… why, it's outrageous!"

"Objection…"

"Mr Buchanan…"

"And now we are expected to *trust* you, *believe* you?"

"Mr Buchanan, you are out of order!"

"Trust you with the future of these defendants who you accuse of what, Mr Ryan?"

"Mr Buchanan!"

"Of murder! And what did you do to Dave Ransford and Jim Crogan? You left them to die!"

"Move to strike, Your Honor."

"Motion granted. Mr Buchanan, desist or I will hold you in contempt!"

"Yes, Your Honor. Nothing further for this witness."

Lunch recess

"Strange how so many events can bring you to a single decision. They all play out, leaving you with one simple thought."

"So you got pummeled, Cliff, join the club. Don't think we'll find you in bed with a fever over it."

"Luke, you're supposed to ask, what one thought, what single decision?"

"I don't want to. There won't be answer I want to hear."

Cliff turns from the window. "There's more than this, you know."

Luke sticks his finger and thumb into his feverish eyes. "Drop it, Cliff."

"Sorry. Jennifer okay?"

"She will be, when I get out of this bed, which will be when they stop ordering me to stay in it."

"Which will be?"

"Tomorrow morning, whether they like it or not. I'm only in it now for Jennifer's sake. I told you, didn't I, remember?"

He nods and manages a smile. "I remember."

"Well, it won't be happening again. Now I know what dredging it all up does, I will find a way to control it."

"We might not come out of this looking too good."

"Do you care?"

"Do you?"

"I asked first."

"A little. I don't really want to be known as the sheriff who deserted his duty and gave his job to a woman, even if it is Emma."

"Maybe you *should* think about exercising the fifth."

"No, that would spell out in big letters for the jury that I broke the law. I refuse to do it. Anyway, we can't be speaking about this. And there's something I have to do…"

"Sure, Cliff."

"Get some rest."

He hurries along to the bookstore. Walking along the shelves, the books all merge into one long blur. His heart truly isn't in this. Not even close. But he's got to make some kind of an effort.

And meeting Emma in a public place seems unwise at this point. He should be staying away from her. They should stay away from each other. Exactly the opposite of his *one thing;* to meet outside of work. The ideal way for their romance not to become public and therefore fodder for the black suits is for one of them to leave town. Maybe this is the excuse Emma has needed all along.

And on that gloomy thought, a book spine comes into focus…

Back at his desk, he writes a letter for Emma to accompany the book; as he thinks and writes he munches on the reviving roast beef and pickle sandwich that was on his desk.

Mac appears as he's manipulating the note into an envelope.

"Thanks for lunch, Mac."

"Anytime."

"You're not feeling sorry for me, are you?"

"You? Not on your life. You got it too easy to feel sorry for. I'm the one that's gotta keep this place running. You know, you shouldn't be letting that black suit talk to you the way he does."

"You were there?"

"I stuck my head in."

"It's his cross, Mac."

"Is he done?"

"For now. Mac, I appreciate everything you're doing."

"Forget it. What's that you got there?"

"Something for Roberts. Gotta go deliver it. I'll head back to court. See you later, Mac."

"You could try the fifth…"

Emma isn't at her desk. In fact, the shop floor of the Tribune is deserted. He rather put the book in her hand and explain, but settles for depositing the parcel, with the letter slipped under the string, on her chair. It will have to do for now.

With lunch recess all but over, he departs for court.

Standing at the back of the courtroom, he observes the activity involved in preparing for the afternoon session. Mac's prison guards shuffle Bodecker and Donnelly into their seats and stand guard while Buchanan and Sturrock and their seconds, still immaculate in their black suits, enter and hover around their table, talking.

Cam is speaking with Josh at the prosecution's table, Josh nodding a great deal. He is Cam's detail man. There wouldn't be many facts or figures that Josh didn't have at his disposal for this trial. He hands Cam a folder pages thick. Witness statements.

Journalists, meanwhile, move into their favored positions in the press gallery.

Quaid sidles up to him.

"On or off the record, Buchanan got to you, Ryan."

"Can't find a seat, Quaid?"

"Roberts got excited over those maps. She said you wanted them at the time but you didn't touch them. She said that's where she got the name for her story, while you two were discussing what the maps could mean."

Chase Deloight and Bailiff Owens are moving the maps back into position along the railing.

"Nice feller that Deloight," Quaid remarks. "His ride with Roberts from Laramie to the Diamond-T should make exciting reading, don't you think?"

Cliff is not in the mood to be baited by Quaid; he agrees curtly and then continues his perusal of the courtroom with the public filing in to watch the afternoon session. A young rancher walks by with his sidearm tucked into his belt. Cliff moves away and tells the rancher to check his colt with the clerk outside or stay out of the courthouse. The rancher leaves.

Meanwhile, Quaid dogs him. "What would it take to put you off your guard, Ryan? – I wonder…"

Cliff sticks his head out of the courtroom door and watches as the young rancher checks his sidearm. That's when he spies Emma in the corridor, seated on the long bench, writing in her notebook with people milling around her. She coughs into her hand and resumes writing. His first instinct is to go to her and tell her about the book. But meeting with her in Quaid's presence would give the game away before she is ready and embarrass her completely.

Quaid says in his ear, "You know, Ryan, I think guarding Roberts is a habit you're finding hard to break."

The young rancher comes back to him. "Sheriff, the clerk told me to tell you I'm the first to check in this afternoon."

Ignoring Quaid, Cliff makes a general announcement to the whole room. "Weapons of any kind and sidearms are banned from the courtroom. Check them outside or leave the building."

About half the room clears, to the sounds of grumbling, and a queue forms out front.

Cliff folds his arms, watching the lineup; his glance makes contact with Quaid's gaze.

Quaid smirks and says, "You'll keep, Ryan."

Chase

"Please state your name, place of residence and occupation for the court."

"Chase Deloight, I live in Laramie City, and I'm a deputy for Albany County, Wyoming."

"Please tell the court, Deputy, what transpired in the Albany County Sheriff's office on Monday afternoon five weeks ago."

"Yes, Mr Faraday. Young woman by the name of Miss Emmaline Roberts came to see the late Sheriff Dave Ransford. She said she had vital information for the defense of the Alliance. She related that information. When Dave asked her where she got it, she said Sheriff Cliff Ryan of Cheyenne had deputized her to bring him the information and give any assistance in understanding the Maverick operation. She said two attempts had been made on her life; she knew how Maverick worked and had extensive knowledge about the whole matter."

"What did Sheriff Ransford do?"

"Even though Miss Roberts had Sheriff Ryan's star in her hand, Dave wired Cheyenne right away for confirmation of her story."

"And was that confirmation given?"

"Yes. Mac, that is Deputy McNamara, wired back that he and yourself, Mr Faraday, could vouch for Miss Roberts and that we were to proceed with Sheriff Ryan's instructions to defend the Alliance from the mavericks."

"Can you recall the nature of the information Miss Roberts gave to Sheriff Ransford?"

"Miss Roberts gave specific information about the mavericks, that they were snipers, they got clear instructions via the telegraph from Maverick, who was Mr Donnelly, they usually worked alone 'til they got the job done, they knew their victims – they had a description, they stalked and they watched."

"And what did Sheriff Ransford do after hearing this?"

"Dave set about planning the offensive. We got out a map of the area – in fact, the map we used is identical to that one there…"

"Your Honor, the witness is indicating the first of the three maps brought down from Ed Parsons' ranch marked exhibit 9a."

"Let the records show the witness is indicating exhibit 9a."

"Continue, Deputy."

"We consulted the map to find the fastest way to get there – we had to take into account there'd just occurred a serious snowstorm and all the passes were closed – but unfortunately we had to settle on the stage route."

"Why unfortunate?"

"Because it was dangerous; it meant we were exposed."

"Exposed to what exactly?"

"To the mavericks."

"So what was the plan?"

"Dave wanted complete secrecy while the operation was undertaken. Nothing got leaked to the papers. And stealth would give us an advantage over Mr Donnelly and the mavericks because they didn't know or hear us coming. The plan was that Deputy Jim Crogan would proceed to the Keatons, warn them and assist them against any attack. I was to go to the Diamond-T to do the same. Dave wanted me to go by the Stewarts' stock trail and cross the stream, taking cover in the forest. Dave would head out to the Parsons' place and check for mavericks and cover the middle ground between the two ranches. We were to take prisoners if it were possible."

"How was it that Miss Roberts accompanied you, Deputy?"

"Dave didn't want her along at first; it was going to be a long, hard mission. But Miss Roberts is a very confident young woman, and she convinced Dave a journalist was needed to record and later report back to the public. He saw her point of view. So, he chose the Diamond-T for her, which meant she would travel with me. Doug

Mason stayed behind in Laramie and held down the fort. We left town the next morning, steady and quiet, one at a time."

"Describe your ride to the Diamond-T, Deputy."

"Was a hard, cold ride, Mr Faraday. Miss Roberts proved to be a good rider, which was just as well, the journey being so long and cold. Only incident was I needed to change horses at Bright River. Took a while to find our bearings once we got into the valley; snow was thick and the landscape looked different to the map. So we got lost here and there.

"At last there was a faint light in the east, the moon had set, we came upon the Diamond-T ranch house in the gloom afore dawn. It was freezing cold. We stabled the horses, found the main house empty, and in the bunkhouse the boys were all sleeping. Whole place was quiet and still. We proceeded to the other house."

"And what was the situation there?"

"Tip Benchley let us in, lit a lantern, I told him to extinguish it 'til such time as I thought it was safe. I informed him that the Alliance was in trouble. Tip is alarmed at first; he informs me his father Ethan Benchley is at the Keaton place and Sara Taylor, Luke's mother, is in New York.

"I go back to the bunkhouse and tell the boys they have to stay inside. That we don't know how or when the attack from this sharpshooter or shooters might come. I tell them to keep their eyes peeled, but not to do anything without checking with me first. They agree."

"Very good, Deputy. What was your next move?"

"I decide to move Tip Benchley, Miss Roberts and myself to the Taylor house because it has a better view of the road, the stables and the yards. I put Miss Roberts on a watch at the back door. Tip on one upstairs window overlooking the front yard. And they both did just fine.

"For a long time we see nothing. Then Miss Roberts reports she saw a reflection she thinks might be off metal. I can't take any chances so I investigate; the reflection is fleeting – I see it myself once is all, but something or someone is on the move. I wonder, if a maverick is hiding in wait, is he wondering about the ranch not operating the way it should be and where everyone could be.

"I tell Tip and Miss Roberts our plan is we are going to wait for the maverick to make the first move. And we stay vigilant.

"We wait all that day and when darkness comes we position our lamps so we don't throw shadows. I feel sure something is going to happen, so I play to that hunch. Tip, Miss Roberts and I have specific positions in the house. We leave the back door unlocked. Sure enough, the young maverick enters the house and creeps into the hall. Tip appears and distracts him. The maverick has his back to me, I hold a rifle to him and demand he hand over his weapons, which he does. Then I put the bonds on him. We captured a maverick."

"And no one got hurt? No shots fired?"

"No one. And no shots. We kept the maverick locked up and securely bound. But 'til we knew if there were any more out there, even though this maverick told us there weren't, we kept our vigil."

"And what is the name of this maverick, Deputy."

"His name is Jedidiah Tyner."

"What were you thinking at this stage with regards to the fate of the others?"

"Figured Dave would come along eventually and tell us when it's over."

"Were you tempted to leave the Diamond-T?"

"Dave gave me strict orders to stay with the folks at the Diamond-T 'til I was told otherwise. I followed his orders."

"Did Sheriff Ransford come along eventually?"

"Not exactly… Late on the next day a party of riders came into the yard. They were Sheriff Ryan, Luke and Ben Taylor, and Ethan Benchley who had a gunshot wound to his shoulder, and they had Dave's body. Dave had been shot and killed by one of the mavericks. We found out Jim Crogan was also dead. And Donnelly and another maverick had been caught. Sheriff Ryan took our maverick to join Donnelly and the other maverick in the Bright River lockup; he collected the deceased mavericks and took them and Dave's body to the Bright River undertaker. I stayed on at the Diamond–T two more days 'til the situation settled down; Ethan was hurt and Luke was ill. Then Marshal Hummer arrived to take the prisoners away; I went back with him to Laramie to look after the bodies of Dave and Jim. Sheriff Ryan stayed behind to keep an eye on the Alliance 'til the end of the week. Dave and Jim were good men and they died doing their duty."

"Thank you, Deputy. No further questions, Your Honor."

"Mr Buchanan? Mr Sturrock?"

"I have some questions for this witness, Your Honor."

"Go ahead, Mr Sturrock."

"Deputy, who would Sheriff Dave Ransford have preferred to have along on this undertaking: Miss Roberts or Sheriff Ryan?"

"Objection. The question calls for the witness to speculate on the mind of Sheriff Ransford..."

"Sustained."

"I'll rephrase the question. Did Sheriff Ransford ever express to you his thoughts as to whether he would've preferred Sheriff Ryan's assistance to Miss Roberts'?"

"No."

"He didn't show any reservations regarding Miss Roberts' involvement?"

"Reservations?"

"She's a woman, for example."

"Objection. Your Honor..."

"Overruled. The witness will answer."

"Well, once he had confirmation from Cheyenne about Miss Roberts, Dave treated her like she was one of the team."

"And you, Deputy, who would *you* have rather had along on the so-called maverick operation – Miss Roberts or Sheriff Ryan? Mm?"

"Well... "

"Come, Deputy, this isn't such a difficult question...we're waiting for your answer."

"Well, I was going to say before you interrupted me, Mr Sturrock, it's like I said before, we had no problem at the Diamond-T. Not a shot fired. No one got hurt. We put our heads together and handled the situation pretty well, I reckon."

"So you say, but..."

"Objection. Your Honor, I believe the Deputy has answered the question. And as he cannot speak for the others, this line of questioning, which swings from trying to discredit Sheriff Ryan and Miss Roberts to blaming the Alliance for what happened, is just wasting the court's time. It is not relevant to the guilt or innocence of those men on trial. The maverick who shot Sheriff Ransford is dead; the men responsible for the planning and execution of the attack on the Alliance are the ones on trial – not Sheriff Ryan and not Miss Emmaline Roberts of the Tribune."

"Nothing further, Your Honor."

"Thank you, Mr Sturrock. The witness may step down."

Emmaline

When she spots Chase striding from the courtroom, Emmaline steps forward from her bench to meet him. He looks pleased to see her.

"Glad that's over," he says, combing his fingers through his blond mane and then taming it with his hat.

"You look concerned, Chase."

"Kinda tense in there." His blue eyes reveal the perceived tension as they look out from under the brim.

"How did it go?"

"Told the story. Answered Mr Faraday's questions. Sturrock tried to catch me out at the end. Can't say any more than that."

"Of course."

"Well, I'm done. Wanna grab some coffee?"

She can't help but feel odd about this.

But Chase grins, which she doesn't remember him doing often. "C'mon, Roberts, one cup of coffee. Pretend you're interviewing me or something."

"Martha's? It's closest."

"Sure."

They weave their way through the vexed crowd outside the courthouse and head down the street, her knee holding up well.

"Have you heard what's happening about the lockouts?" Chase asks, looking relieved to be clear of the courthouse.

"Someone has mentioned negotiation, so here's hoping."

"Think I'd be more scared of an angry mob than anything Bodecker might do to me."

"They'll move on later, perhaps to Bodecker's building…"

They reach Martha's and sit in the middle of the room; they sip their coffee, a brisk trade going on around them.

"So, how's our story coming along?" His hat comes off and at last he seems more relaxed.

"Our story?"

"Our moonlight ride to the Diamond-T," he intones rather whimsically. A teasing grin follows.

"It's done. Mr Quaid will publish it as a serial after the trial is over. Tell me, how are things in Laramie now that... er, without Mr Ransford and Mr Crogan?"

Chase puts on a brave face. "Rough. But seeing you again kinda cheered me up, Emmaline. That can happen, being cheerful, but then I remember they're no longer with us. You know?"

"I know. It's natural, a part of grief, Chase."

He shrugs his broad shoulders. "Doug Mason is a fine acting sheriff. Appointed two new deputies to replace Jim."

"A mark of respect for the work Mr Crogan was capable of."

"It's not the same. We miss them. Just getting on with it."

She nods, her sympathy acute. "What else can you do?"

"So," Chase says, brightening a little. "What's with you and Ryan?"

"Pardon me?"

"You and Ryan. I saw how you looked at him earlier."

"Looked at him? I don't know what you're talking about."

"You may be a reporter, but you're still a woman. You know what I'm talking about, Emmaline."

"I see. Well, I really don't have the time for that kind of thing."

Chase grins and almost seems likeable. "Not even with me."

She feels warmth in her cheeks. "Oh. No. Not even you... as...as charming as you are."

His face falls a bit, but he keeps up the good humor. "We make a good team, Roberts, though you tend to ask a lot of questions."

"A professional hazard that's become a lifelong habit, I regret to tell you," she murmurs and then plies herself with coffee.

A moment of silence falls between them and when she looks up from where she is hiding behind her coffee cup, Chase is studying her. She smiles politely at him, hoping to put an end to his personal interest. Ashcliff is decidedly more than enough as it is; having two men interested in her would be far more than she could endure regardless of the endless entertainment it might provide Celie...

"You look kinda pale, Roberts. Cheyenne not treating you well?"

"I... I was thinking, is it ever warm in these parts?"

"May surprise you to know summer can get real hot in these parts. In a canyon near Horse Creek in the Laramie Mountains I once fried me and Jim Crogan some eggs right there on the rocks."

"I've had my leg pulled before, Chase," she protests softly.

"Honest," he chuckles. "But this winter's been kinda harsh. Ain't good for the cattle."

"The cattle barons have mostly range cattle, don't they?"

"Mm. Been concerns of overcrowding for some time now; less feed for the cattle means skinny cattle and less income."

"That wouldn't be a problem for ranchers like Taylor, Benchley and Keaton, would it?"

He shakes his head. "Problem for them ain't feed; they grow their own and hand feed in winter. Their problem will come if the bottom falls out of the market. Lotta underfed and inferior quality cattle flood the abattoirs in cities like Chicago and prices drop."

"I see. If the range is overcrowded, then it is understandable why men like Bodecker and Donnelly would be interested in the Keaton ranch and the Diamond-T and the Stewarts and so many ranches like them."

"Mm. Best pasture, barns, hay farming all set up. Clean out the homesteaders and the sheep men. Keep the mines running, lotta money in them. Into the bargain, coal, silver, gold – even oil – might lie beneath these small ranches and homesteads. Why not? It wouldn't be the first time. And if you can't get to the land to find out, what do you do? What any self-respecting baron does – you take over the place?"

She catches her breath. That Donnelly and Bodecker had intentions of doing just that across the Bright River valley is staggering but entirely possible.

"Chase, you are a genius."

He gives a firm nod; his hair falls forward with boyish charm.

"So, then, how does anyone know where to look for coal, or silver and gold?" she asks.

"Don't have a clue. D'you think I'd be a humble deputy if I knew? But come to think of it, I reckon I ain't got the inclination to be a prospector anyway. I like being a lawman just fine. Besides, when it comes to prospecting you're better off if you employ one of those... I don't know, what d'you call them?"

"A geologist?"

"That's the one."

"I see. No offence, Chase, but how do y'all know about geologists?"

"Huh! That's a fair point. Just so happens a party of them, geologists and prospectors, came into town late last year."

"To Laramie?"

"Yep."

"Mm... That's Donnelly's domain. When was it exactly?"

"Come to think of it, it was twice. Once last summer..."

"The Parsons' trial was on last summer. Last summer Bodecker stayed with Donnelly."

"...and then again in December."

"Were these geologists and such together, like an organization or a company?"

"Think so."

"Who sent them, or hired them?"

"Don't know off hand. I'll wire Laramie this afternoon, Mason won't mind checking. Ask him to wire the information straight back."

"That's excellent. Thank you."

"You know, Roberts, you really do ask a lot of questions." Chase's eyes crinkle in the corners as he beams at her. "You're quite a girl, Emmaline. You sure there's nothing going on with us?"

"I'm sure," she says as politely as possible.

He laughs out loud. "Well, at least a feller knows where he stands."

She goes to explain – why would he want to be with her anyway – but he holds up a hand to stop her.

"You'll only make it worse," he chuckles.

"It will?"

He chuckles a little more. "Trust me. I still think Ryan's the man." He fishes out some coins for their coffee and tables them, while she decides to exercise the Fifth. "Guess I'd better get back to court. Who knows when those maps need a break from all that gawking?"

She follows him to her feet. "How long must you stay in town?"

"Mason told me to stay until Faraday said he didn't need me."

They steer themselves around several incoming patrons and head out into the slanting afternoon sunshine.

"Going back as well?"

"Mr Quaid likes me to hang about. I'm supposed to pick up all the side stories to the main trial while he covers the courtroom. I think what you just told me is a case in point."

"I guess. You're a witness for Faraday."

"Yes. But I haven't been asked to testify much as yet. Only once; the first day. I wonder about that."

"Do you? I heard Buchanan chewed up Ryan into little bits and spat him out before lunch recess."

"Oh?"

"Think your name might've come up, if you get my meaning."

"Giving me the information on the train," she deduces.

"Among other things," he says with an awkward glance in her direction. "Don't think Faraday fancies putting you on the stand again too soon."

"Oh?" Her heart seems to be skipping beats.

"They got you in their sights, Emmaline," he says, keeping his voice low since they are passing people on the sidewalk. "Surprised Quaid didn't tell you at lunch. No one likes to be blindsided."

"I…I was busy all lunchtime. I didn't see Mr Quaid or get back to the paper."

"Guess he'll fill you in later."

She's not sure she wants to be filled in later; Mr Quaid has been giving her strange looks since the moment she left his office this morning… after she and Ashcliff used it. The erratic heartbeats are becoming uncomfortable as they approach the courthouse.

"I'm sure Mr Faraday will advise me. I wonder who is on the stand now."

"Soon find out I guess."

They enter the courthouse building and part company.

She sits on her bench and coughs into her handkerchief while pulling out her notebook and pencil; she sets about making comprehensive notes from her coffee break with Chase, all the time wishing she'd been a fly on the wall during Buchanan's cross-examination of Ashcliff.

Faraday

"No further questions for Mr Keaton, Your Honor."

"Mr Buchanan, Mr Sturrock? Your witness."

"Thank you, Your Honor." Sturrock pushes back his chair, stands up at their table and slides his hands into his pockets. "John Keaton, you may or may not have noticed that Mr Donnelly has a slowly healing wound on his right hand."

"Yes."

"Which is it? You have noticed or you haven't?"

"Have."

"He sustained the wound when he was shot in your ranch house, did he not?"

"Yes."

"And the man who shot him was Ethan Benchley, was it not?"

"Yes."

"A man you have never met before comes to your house, passing through, looking for comfort on a cold morning, and you had Mr Benchley shoot him. Hardly what a stranger would expect from the famous Keaton hospitality is it?"

"As I said in my testimony, Mr Sturrock, Mr Donnelly went for his gun first; whipped it out and aimed to shoot at young Ben Taylor. Ethan beat him to it, saved young Ben's life. Sheriff Ransford backed up with his Winchester. Mr Donnelly was gonna run away but the sheriff fired his Winchester over Mr Donnelly's head and scared Mr Donnelly into staying put while the sheriff put bonds on him and settled him down."

"Had Mr Donnelly ever visited your ranch before, Mr Keaton?"

"No."

"He showed no interest in you or your ranch?"

"No."

"You have never had any association with Mr Donnelly before?"

"No."

"Apart from being a successful ranch, is there anything special about it?"

"No."

"Anything special about you?"

"Not to anyone but my wife and my horse."

"Order... order..."

"Your Honor, I have no more questions for this witness."

Faraday gets to his feet. "Your Honor, the People call Ethan Benchley to the stand..."

"Your Honor, before Mr Faraday proceeds, if I may draw the attention of the court to a serious matter. The wound in my client's hand is giving him a great deal of pain this afternoon. The conditions in Mr Ryan's lockup are far from satisfactory for an injured person. I request an adjournment until tomorrow morning so that my client can receive some attention for his injury."

"Objection. Your Honor, this is a delaying tactic and a blatant attempt to seek sympathy from the jury."

"Mr Faraday, while your suggestion is appreciated, your objection is overruled. Mr Sturrock, the defendant may receive medical attention and then I want the doctor's report on the medical condition of his hand on my desk first thing in the morning, and I trust there is something to report. Until then, we are adjourned."

Faraday sits down and watches the courtroom clear, including Cliff as he accompanies the prison guards escorting Bodecker and Donnelly back to the lockup.

If his book is clear, he'd like to take a few minutes to visit Luke.

Tomorrow is Saturday. Half-day court. He and Meg need to do something together and leave this trial behind for tomorrow evening. No doubt there are other things happening in this town apart from the trial. Has to be. Surely.

One can hope.

Quaid

"I have a promising lead," Roberts declares as he reaches her in the crowded corridor. She looks peaky, even by his standards.

"A lead, Roberts?" he says in a hushed tone, loosening his necktie, wondering what the hell can be the matter with her.

"Yes, something else about Donnelly and Bodecker. My source is looking into it. I'll know more later today or tomorrow I hope. I've made thorough notes…"

"Are you all right, Roberts?"

"Well, of course. Are you listening to me, Mr Quaid?"

"Hear every word you say, Roberts. Always do."

"Then what… Never mind. I see Ethan didn't make it onto the stand by the looks of things," she remarks as their gaze follows some of the Alliance group who are melting away into the crowd and looking none too pleased.

"No. Sturrock's playing games. Faraday looked ready to strangle a cat. Listen, I'm heading back to write up my copy."

"I'll come with you."

"Anything urgent in those notes of yours, Roberts?"

"Not until my source comes back to me, no. But you…"

"Good. It's been a long week. I want you to go home, put your feet up for a spell. A long one."

"I had a spell yesterday, remember? Mr Quaid, are *you* feeling all right?"

"Never better. Love the courtroom. Gets my juices going."

"For all the testifying I'm doing I might as well be in there with you."

"Cheer up, Roberts. Faraday knows what he's doing. Can't have you thrown to the wolves."

"What do you mean?"

"As if I need to explain that to you. C'mon, hand over your notebook. I'll see if there's anything I want."

"The last bit is the lead I just told you about."

"Don't worry; I'll take good care of it." He tugs it out of her hand and slots it under his arm. "Just how many of those notebooks have you filled since you got here?"

She shrugs daintily. Everything about her is dainty, except her spirit. That is tenacious. But now he's beginning to think something's out of kilter.

"There *is* something I have to do," she says. "Oh, I should head back and grab a handful of pencils from my desk though... I'm..."

"Here," he says, giving her his, plus extras from his pockets.

"...very low..."

"Have mine."

"Thank you. Well, I'll see you in the morning then."

"Sure thing. Get plenty of rest."

"Are you up to something, Mr Quaid?"

"What? No. Y'know, just because you're a reporter doesn't mean you have to be so suspicious of everyone all the time."

"Well, no, I'm ..."

"Adios, Roberts."

Emmaline

Emmaline stands in front of Nan Morris' hearth, absorbing the warmth of the fire and the benefits of the excellent soup they had for supper. She stares into the flames as if she will read in them what is happening to her life. Close to an hour she waited. In case something held him up. He didn't show. And she has no idea why. She thought they agreed...

Perhaps it's not too late to go knock on his door and ask him to explain, but terrifying feelings of foolishness are causing her untold internal agony. This turmoil is new to her. She's not even sure she would make it to his front gate without turning back; not even sure she can move her feet from the spot on which they now stand.

All the questions swirling around in her head need answers from him. She could create all the answers and the excuses for him to assuage her distress, then see him tomorrow and pretend it was nothing, but nothing about that is authentic, not who they are. What it is, however, is her way out.

She ought to be rejoicing that his failure to keep up his end has given her the opportunity she's been needing all this time. Maybe when the disappointment and hurt have worn off she will be able to use it to her advantage.

And all the while in her head the words of reason are streaming: it is unlike him to do something like this without explanation, you know him and you know it is...

Just then there is a loud knock on the door of the guesthouse. It's him, come to explain! It has to be. A king tide of hope washes over her only to be dragged out and swallowed up by the mother of all lowest ebbs – *doubt!* This will never do, living from one pathetic hope to the next...

"Emmaline, my dear, would you see to the door?" Nan Morris has sewing on her lap; she appears to be darning a dozen pairs of socks and several pairs of colored stockings at the same time.

The other residents are engaged in quiet conversation on the far side of the room.

She gathers her wits and heads for the door, proving her feet do move from their spot when required, at least out of respect for her elders.

Her hand grasps the doorknob and she remembers to breathe.

"Who is it, Emmaline?"

Emmaline

"Hope it's not too late to call."

"No… Come in, Chase."

"Have the information you wanted."

"Who is that, Emmaline?" Nan calls out.

Something she needs; a diversion.

"Deputy Chase Deloight. He has information for a story I'm working on. I'll show him into the dining room where we can talk in private."

"There's a pot of coffee in the kitchen. Help yourselves."

"Thank you."

She smiles up at Chase. "You can hang your hat and coat right here, if you want."

"Thanks. Don't mind if I do."

He pegs his hat on the functional hallstand that fills a good part of Nan Morris's entrance hall; it's a handsome piece of carved oak, with a large rectangular mirror and a bench seat.

"Won't stay long." And his coat stays on.

"This way." She leads the way into the dining room with him looking all around. Nan's impressive dining table and chairs are a good match for her hallstand. A small lace cloth set on the diagonal with a fruit bowl standing in the center adorns the table top.

"Nice place," he remarks, pulling a chair for her.

"The house is very comfortable. And warm. Nan's brother built it as a mansion for his family but he moved on and gave it to Nan; she turned it into this wonderful guesthouse. The rooms are large and well-appointed. It's a well-loved home. Coffee? Fruit?"

"Thanks, no," he grins.

She sits and waits for him to do the same. "So, is this good news?"

"Think you'll like it. Doug Mason wired that information you were after late this afternoon. Thought you'd be keen to know what he found."

"Certainly."

"One thing though. When I found out I felt it my duty to tell Ryan and I guess Faraday knows by now."

"Oh? Well, that's perfectly all right, Chase. You're a lawman, not a reporter. Main thing is we got some valuable information."

"Sure did. Gave you the credit for it. Told Ryan it was your questions and your deductions when we were talking and one thing led to another. He seemed to think that happened a lot when a body talked with you. Anyhow, he seemed pleased."

"Well, I'd be pleased myself, Chase, if I knew what I was supposed to be pleased about."

"Oh. Well..." he says, lowering his voice considerably and she must lean in. "The geological company that came into Laramie last summer was called Worthing and Farrell, based in Denver."

"Hmm. Denver makes sense. Did Mr Worthing and Mr Farrell come in person?"

"Yes. With two assistants. Seems Loren Bodecker hired them, brought them to town. Get this, they stayed at Donnelly's place, his ranch house."

"Donnelly's ranch? What's it like?"

"He runs about five hundred head of cattle. Nice location. Good grass and water."

"So he has a town house, where he and Bodecker stayed last summer. And he put the geological team at his ranch house. What else did Deputy Mason say in his telegram? Did this team survey any properties?"

"Mason doesn't say anything else – just that no one witnessed the geological team and Bodecker or Donnelly working together. He doesn't know anything else."

"So they probably moved around from place to place, using the ranch house as their base, while Donnelly and Bodecker stayed out of it, well out of sight at any rate. How did y'all find out who they were in the first place?"

Chase shrugs. "Don't know." And he gazes at her with his bright blue eyes.

She gets up, needing to think about the information, and paces to the hearth and back again, at the same time dreading the notion Chase is looking at her that way because he's still interested in her and thinks there might be a chance...

Loren compromised. You know what you have to do. Lamont.

Lamont and I have ways of communicating.

"Did Dillon Kerr know about this ranch house?"

"Might; don't know. Kerr would come and go to and from Laramie a bit. Although he's close to Bodecker, ain't he, not Donnelly?"

"That doesn't matter. In fact, that's good for him."

"What are you talking about, Emmaline?"

"I have an idea, Chase, a suspicion, but I need time to think about it, sleep on it."

"Sure." He gets to his feet.

"Thank you for coming by with this information," she says leading him back to the entrance.

He unpegs his hat and fixes it on his head with a wry smile. "I know Ryan's the man."

"What are you talking about?"

"Say your name and his eyes light up."

"That's ridiculous," she counters, moving towards the door. Particularly since he didn't feel the need to turn up this afternoon.

Chase follows with a comfortable little smirk on his face. "If you say so, Emmaline."

She's practically convinced of it herself. She opens the door and catches her breath as a blast of cool night air enters.

"Take care of yourself, Emmaline. You look kinda pale..."

She wishes people would stop telling her that. "Thank you again, Chase. Good night."

"Goodnight, Emmaline. And good luck."

She heads up to her room. As she reaches for a notebook and

pencil to write up the information, her eyes begin to sting. It was idiotic to think he would show up; that he would come around to thinking the book exchange was a good idea. He hated it.

Of course he did. He's a sheriff. An important man with an important job to do. Busy and important. And she's a silly little southern girl who thought she could control what was happening.

It's her own fault, and now all that's left is for her to feel utterly foolish. Something she's been all along. And there is nothing like that feeling of humiliation to really drive home the message.

Emmie...

What?

There you are. I've missed you.

What do you want?

You're not silly. Not even close. You're smart and beautiful.

I... thank you.

And you're worth every ounce of grief you give that Yankee boy and don't you forget it.

Is that meant to be a compliment, Celie?

Cliff

"She didn't tell me," he grinds out, dragging his fingers through his hair. "Why didn't she tell me?"

"Well, you were still in North Platte fetching Louis Porterfield. Something happened; or rather she did *something*..."

"What does that mean, Cam?"

"Questionable."

"She's a *reporter*."

"Perhaps unlawful..."

"Emma?" he snaps and sticks his hands on his hips in disbelief.

"Just... stay calm. For the purposes of this conversation, think Roberts."

He sighs. "Fine. Go on."

"When I asked her if she could tell me how she got this information, she said I'd have to subpoena her before a grand jury."

"A grand jury? What happened to the First Amendment?"

"For some reason she generously waived her protection under it, giving me the opportunity to subpoena her. I can't for the life of me imagine why."

"Always with the complications..."

"As I said, she recited: *When all else fails* followed by the Severinis' address in Denver. She quoted the telegram: *Loren compromised. You know what you have to do. Lamont.* And the remark by Dillon Kerr: *Lamont and I have ways of communicating.* Dillon Kerr did not know she had the information..."

"There it is. She overheard him say that last part. Where was she? – where was *he*?"

"That is the part she cannot reveal obviously."

"Kerr must have been at home," he says after wracking his brains.

"I guess that makes sense. She didn't know who Lamont was. I went to Ben and Raina for that."

"Dillon Kerr has been missing for close to two weeks. He must have returned at some point and she snooped."

"To ask her again would bring nothing new."

"Well, I'm not about to have Emma hauled before a grand jury."

"Roberts," Cam corrects him calmly.

"She snooped…"

"You mean she broke into Dillon's house."

"Yes, that's what I mean. And he being at home surprised her."

"She told us only what we needed to know."

"She kept Dillon Kerr from us, that's what she did."

"Steady…"

"I'm… fine…" There's a pause between them wherein his mind pushes ahead like a train. "Dillon Kerr came back for Eva Tarrant."

"Could be."

"Something…something…" Something occurs to him. "Nugent knows. She went to Confession. She doesn't have to reveal what she did, unless you subpoena her."

"*Confession!* Seriously? What about the First Amendment?"

"Atonement, Cam. *Penance.* An act of contrition. No hiding behind the First Amendment."

"Good grief. Well, we can kiss that goodbye then. I've got enough to think about without putting a girl and her religion on the stand."

"She must have felt terrible. I wonder why she did what she did…"

"Her father had arrived in town at the time and I detected she wasn't herself."

"A highly likely explanation, believe me."

"But this new lead she's uncovered could be a vital missing link. I guarantee you she's thinking exactly what we're thinking right this minute."

Cliff wants nothing more than to go to her and discuss it, get to the bottom of it, but...

"As for Worthing and Farrell," Cam continues, "first thing in the morning I'll wire Denver. Find out if they carried out their surveys and what they found."

"And if Bodecker and Donnelly acted on it or intended to."

"Precisely. I hope Denver cooperates."

"This ranch of Donnelly's – how come no one has ever thought of searching it?"

"This is the first we've heard of it."

"But Laramie knew."

"Perhaps Dave Ransford was in the process of investigating."

"I guess that's possible. You know, Cam, I really begin to question just who and what Donnelly is..."

"Beyond a murderer?"

His thoughts drift back to Emma. Donnelly almost killed her – twice.

"I'll be going, Cliff," Cam says. "I need to get that warrant before morning. It will be ready for you."

"And the trial?"

"I'll get by for another day. Then ask for a continuance if I need to."

"Maybe the Judge will grant you one tomorrow morning."

"It may yet be the best course. I'll sleep on it. Who knows – the Judge may want one himself. And you had better get some decent sleep yourself if you and Deloight are heading off early. If Kerr and Tarrant and this Lamont are holed up at Donnelly's ranch..."

"It could be dangerous," Cliff finishes.

"Mm..." Cam's expression mirrors his concern about the setup for potential harm. "There may even be other mavericks."

"I had thought of that, Cam. If the place looks like a fort, Chase and I'll head back to town for reinforcements."

"And don't tell Luke or Ben where you're going."

"What do I look like, a honeymoon killer?"

"Because the pair of them will..."

"I know, Cam."

"The Tribune will probably break this story tomorrow."

"Well, my leaving town won't be in it. Even Chase doesn't know yet. We'll be gone before anyone notices."

"I'll see myself out."

"Night, Cam."

A small draft of cold air disturbs the fire and then the front door snaps shut. He sinks down into the chair by the hearth and watches the flames.

No response to his book or note. No book in return anywhere, not on his doorstep, on his desk at work... nothing. He doesn't understand; he poured his heart out, went along with her crazy idea, and she's ignored it?

He needs to see her, with an unfamiliar desperation on his part, but what with one thing after another now the hour is late... and he's so damned confused.

Possibly she didn't see the book on her chair? She always goes back to her desk at some point; sits and writes up her copy... if not, then did she wait for him not knowing he wasn't going to show?

Oh God, surely not. Surely she would have come to him by now and demanded an explanation? Wouldn't she? She'd be angry, disappointed in him, hurt, wouldn't she?

She's Emma. And what goes for most women doesn't for her.

And the connection between them has shifted somehow, which can happen when pressure is applied to something precariously balanced; and now that shift is pouring on doubt and has him floundering in a flood of confusion.

She's just a young woman.

Cam. You know her. Just a young woman?

Who has you in the grip of some southern enchantment.

She is determined to have her own way.

And you are unaccustomed to not having yours.

He swore he'd fight her every step of the way but one wrong move, one little slip at the right time, could have put them at the crossroads.

Cliff

A soulless morning, caught and chilled by the long-fingered grip of a dense gray mist, signals an end to his mostly sleepless night. The mist creeps along 19th Street, obscuring Nan Morris' guesthouse but not his thoughts of Emma. Once again he's leaving town, leaving her, and every part of him screams not to. There is so much to tell her, but he needs time to convince her to listen, time he doesn't have right now.

Morning mass has concluded when he arrives at St John's church, with those few regular hardy souls disappearing like ghosts into the mist. He spends time sitting in his favorite pew, reflecting...

There is a lot that's instinctive for him about this religion, and a silent understanding between him and faith, neither of which he perceived when *Lita* tried to steer him towards it years ago; he was young and he needed to find himself amid the clamber of his upbringing and make his own way. He understands *Lita* now; he always adored her, but now he gets her and that would please her.

It all comes down to faith. This revelation has picked him up, turned him around and placed him back down in the same spot but with different eyes. Strange; it had always been missing in his life and yet he lived his whole life by it. He didn't recognize it or acknowledge it. And yet it was there, waiting to be illuminated...

Emma crashed into his existence like a dazzling star colliding with a lifeless planet. Out of the chaos, and in it, she brought order, showed his life to him the right way up; other people had their own choices to make, and that was fair, but he was choosing faith.

Why Emma did this and not someone else is a question he's

asked himself many times; the answer came in time: they are meant to be together. He believes *that* with every fiber of his being. He doesn't care if she comes from the South, from China or from Timbuktu; they have some differences to work through, sure, but it would all be worth it. Emma and Ashcliff should be together for eternity.

Now it all comes down to faith. His safety and Deloight's. Their success. Their return. Leaving Emma. Coming home to Emma.

Coming home to her...

She will be ready to listen to him then. She will be. And then everything will be all right.

Nugent appears. He potters around the altar for several moments, looks up and sees Cliff, and makes a beeline for him.

"How long have you been sitting there?" Nugent greets him.

"I was coming to see you."

"Oh?"

"I will be out of town for a while, a couple of days at most; I won't be able to attend my instruction... or church."

"I see. Well, I'm positive missing one lesson won't hurt. You can catch up on your return, just like you've done before. As for Mass, you're not the genuine article yet. I'm sure the Almighty won't hold it against you."

"So what will it feel like – when I'm the genuine article?"

"Folks describe it in all sorts of ways, so I'm looking forward to hearing your version in a few weeks. God gave you such a spirit, Cliff, a grand spirit he put in you to live the life he's given you."

Despite the affirmation, he sighs hard.

Nugent considers him. "What troubles you this morning?"

"Leaving Emma."

"But you're coming back. She'll be here."

"I can't shake this feeling about leaving her today. I think we've had a misunderstanding of sorts but I..."

"Now, now, it'll be all right. Emmaline is a grand girl. As complicated as the day is long, but grand nonetheless. Be patient a little longer, Cliff. *Omnia vincit amor...*"

He smiles. "Love conquers all."

"True as it ever was when the Roman poet Virgil put pen to

parchment and gave it to the world eighteen hundred years ago. The second half of the quote is also notable: *et nos cedamus amori*."

"And we shall yield to love."

"Love will prevail. The Lord knows what is to become of the pair of you. Believe that and your faith will carry you through. It's there to help you be strong, even stronger than you are already. The Almighty will hold you up, Cliff, hold you in the palm of his hand. Will you remember that?"

"I'll remember." He offers Nugent his hand.

Nugent shakes it, firm and yet with heartwarming regard. "God be with you, Cliff. I know you'll do a good job." Nugent flashes a grin and leaves him.

He lets the serenity of that tranquil place fill him up before he heads back out into that cold, gray mist and into town.

He shakes Chase out of bed at the Cheyenne Hotel.

The deputy splashes cold water on his face. "What time did you say it was?"

"Seven fifteen. The train leaves at eight for Laramie."

"It's Saturday, right?"

Cliff tosses him a towel. "Right. Fill you in on the train."

"Sure, Ryan."

He leaves Chase yawning into his towel.

When he finds Mac, sleepy-eyed and acting like the fog has got into his brain, he says, "Didn't sleep last night, Mac?"

"The twins ain't feelin' too good. Pat was up to them a few times. Think I'll ask Jennifer to take a look at them."

"I hope they feel better. Mac, I hate leaving you like this."

Just then, Cam wanders in, looking a lot like Mac.

"What's up with you?" Cliff asks, dreading the response.

"Meg couldn't sleep last night. She can't get comfortable. Here's your warrant."

Cam holds it out, stifling a yawn.

Cliff takes it and slides it inside the breast pocket of his coat.

"Well, I'm in two minds about going now. Look at the pair of you."

"As the Judge pointed out, it's only half a day," Cam says.

"And the continuance?"

"If you're not back by Sunday night, Callaghan will grant us a continuance."

"And the black suits?"

"Well, they won't like it, will they? Coffee, Mac?"

"Sure. Let's toast to something."

Mac pours coffee into three cups. They each take one and stand there looking blankly at one another.

"To..."

"To..."

"To a goodnight's sleep," Cam sighs.

Mac chuckles. "Let's hope this trial's over before Mrs Faraday has that baby of yours, Cam. You'll be panning for sleep like gold dust before long."

Cliff can't hold back a laugh while Cam's frown travels across his face in a comical fashion.

"To a goodnight's sleep," Mac says. And they slurp.

"The Judge doesn't believe Denver will cooperate regarding Worthing and Farrell," Cam mentions.

"We'll see," Cliff says and slurps some more.

"We witnessed the impact of the maps on the jury; imagine the impact of the report of a whole team of geologists and prospectors working off the maps."

"We'll see."

Mac grunts. "Heading off then?"

"When I've finished my coffee. Quit nagging me."

"Whatever you do, don't forget to check in with Doug Mason when you get to Laramie."

"I know, Mac."

"And don't go gettin' yourself shot."

"No, Mac."

"I'll try find Hummer for you; can't make no promises but. Come the day there's ever a dang marshal in the US marshals' office when I need one I'll faint right there on the floor..."

"Appreciate it, Mac."

Mac wanders off, mumbling. "Good luck."

"Mac…"

"Don't worry. I'll write everything down. I swear that daily report file is fatter than the Good Book. Wonder your desk don't fall down under the weight…"

Cliff and Cam exchange grins.

"See you when you get back," Cam says and heads out.

Mac wanders back again. "You still here?"

"This…" He holds out a note and Mac takes it.

"What is it?"

"A note for you know who."

Mac winks. "I'll keep an eye on her. As if she needs another. You know Ethan's got the Alliance tracking her every move night and day."

"I know."

"Well, then, stop worrying about her and get going."

He never felt less like going anywhere in his life.

SIX

That dream is o'er;
He stands upon another shore.

Henry Wadsworth Longfellow
To the Avon

Faraday

"So, Mr Sturrock..." Judge Callaghan takes the doctor's report from Sturrock's hand. He peers at the defense counsel over his spectacles. "How is Mr Donnelly faring this morning?"

Sturrock wisely sticks to clearing his throat.

The Judge opens the report. "Have you and your colleagues met with Mr Faraday yet regarding developments in the case?"

Sturrock frowns. He directs his gaze hard at Faraday. "What developments? The rubbish in this morning's Tribune, you mean?"

"I urge caution, Mr Sturrock. Sheriff Ryan has a warrant."

"Judge, how could we not have been informed?"

"I believe my instruction yesterday was that this report was to be the first thing on my desk this morning. Mr Faraday will fill you in after our meeting. Now, let me see..." He starts reading.

Faraday glimpses Dr Gus Prewitt's report being two efficient paragraphs, so it's not long before the Judge hands it over to him...

The patient has a partially-healed wound on his right hand from a gunshot wound sustained six weeks ago. The bullet grazed the back of his hand and the wound was not serious in the first instance.

Despite his stay in prison, the wound is being cared for, with the dressing being changed regularly, and is slowly healing. Mr Donnelly should refrain from tampering with it and his bandages if he wants said wound to heal faster and remain free from infection.

Sturrock hands another paper to the Judge. "This report, Judge, is from an independent doctor, one *not* associated with the court."

"I will read it, Mr Sturrock, even though I did not request a second opinion." Unimpressed, the Judge reads the second report. And grunts. "Care to read, Mr Faraday."

"Thank you, Judge."

To whom it may concern, the patient, Terrence Donnelly, has a wound on his right hand. He has had this wound for six weeks. It is not healing at a satisfactory rate, most likely aggravated as a result of incarceration. There is a risk of infection. Diligent medical care must be exercised to ensure this does not occur.

Faithfully, John Randall MD

"Mr Sturrock, advise your client that if he does not want to succumb to gangrene or blood poisoning he would do well to leave his bandages and his wound alone! This matter is concluded.

"Now, Mr Faraday, you might like to meet with Messrs Buchanan and Sturrock regarding Mr Ryan's latest exploits."

In his office ten minutes later, Faraday stands behind his desk about to square off with the black suits.

"Well, Faraday, explain this…" Buchanan, his face resembling a thundercloud, throws a copy of the Tribune on his desk.

"Last night it came to our attention, gentlemen, that Mr Donnelly has a ranch outside of Laramie."

"So, what if he does?"

"It has also come to our attention that last summer, while Mr Bodecker was visiting with Mr Donnelly at his home in Laramie, Mr Donnelly had other visitors, but they stayed at his ranch; these made up a team of geologists and prospectors from a respected firm in Denver called Worthing and Farrell."

"So? Donnelly wanted some surveying done on his property."

"Surveys for what, though, Buchanan? This Denver company specializes in determining the location of commercial commodities and precious metals."

"Our clients can do what they like on their own property."

"One of the things we intend to discover in the next little while is how much of this surveying was carried out on your client's property, how much on property he had recently acquired from small homesteaders and ranchers, and how much was intended for the heartland of the Bright River valley, for example, the Keaton ranch and the Diamond-T."

"You have nothing, Faraday."

"Buchanan, Cliff Ryan was never stood down as a deputy US marshal, he has a warrant, in cooperation with the Albany County Sheriff, to search Donnelly's Laramie ranch, and what he hopes to find is a large missing piece in the puzzle of Mr Bodecker, that is, Dillon Kerr. It wouldn't have escaped your notice that Kerr has been missing for some weeks now. It is our belief that he holed up there with a Denver man named Lamont and a woman, Eva Tarrant, who used to be Mr Bodecker's mistress. We know Kerr and Tarrant have joined up, and that Kerr is planning to extricate himself from Mr Bodecker's affairs."

"That's absurd. Why would he hang around Donnelly's ranch then?"

"It's isolated, from what we know, yet still close enough to keep an eye on what's going on here in Cheyenne. Or maybe he just likes ranches."

Buchanan and Sturrock glare hard at him.

"Gentlemen, it is not too late for your clients to change their plea to perhaps something constructive to ease their final burden."

Sturrock bristles.

Buchanan's glare, on the other hand, turns thoughtful. "Where did you get this information?"

"That is none of your concern. All I am required to do is tell you what it is. I'll let you know more as soon as I know myself."

"You are always protecting someone, Faraday."

"I wouldn't have to if your clients didn't have a history of murdering people they don't like or don't want around any longer."

"You're out of line, Faraday," Sturrock mutters.

Faraday sighs, too weary from lack of sleep to play. "I don't think so. That is all, gentlemen. Good day."

Buchanan

Laramie County Jail

"Don't think I heard you right. What did you say, Buchanan?"

"I said, Loren, that Ryan and Faraday might have discovered what's happened to Kerr."

Loren, getting slower and more dim-witted by the day, grunts. "Where then?"

"Donnelly's Laramie ranch." Buchanan observes Loren's reaction. Those cagey eyes bulge in that plump, ruddy face.

"Want to tell me what's going on, Buchanan?"

"One of Ryan and Faraday's sources uncovered the possibility Kerr has run off with your mistress…"

"Eva? Impossible!"

"I checked. Tarrant hasn't been in town for weeks. She hasn't been to see you, has she?"

"She's married to a pathetic excuse for a man. Figured she wanted to lay low, stay with him for a bit."

"She's married?"

"Sure."

"Her husband never reported her missing."

"Of course not. She's hardly ever at home usually. She's with me when I'm in Cheyenne. He knows better than to interfere anyhow."

Buchanan feels like sighing from now till kingdom come.

"She's laying low, I tell you. She wouldn't run off with Dillon. What's the attraction? He has no real money to speak of."

"Maybe the attraction has nothing to do with money?'

Loren has himself a hearty laugh. "Dillon, a ladies man!"

"Women, even mistresses, don't tend to be fools when it comes to knowing how they want to be treated, Loren."

"You think Dillon's better in bed than me?" Again, the arrogant sonofabitch cackles.

Buchanan doesn't answer, but Loren gets the message when he catches his eye.

"One more thing. Worthing and Farrell. What were they doing staying at Donnelly's ranch last summer?"

Loren actually blanches.

Buchanan gets a cold feeling down his spine. "Well?"

"They're geological surveyors."

"I know. What were they doing, Loren? What will Faraday find out when he demands that the Denver district attorney's office investigate the Company on the grounds of trespassing upon the ranches of the Bright River valley? How much did you pay them, Loren? Why – like so many other poor saps – couldn't they refuse you?"

A cruel look hardens those flaccid features. "Well, *you* couldn't refuse, could you, Buchanan – you and Sturrock."

Buchanan glares back at him, his eyes beginning to sting.

"What will he find, Loren?" he grinds out.

A fat, disgruntled sigh… "Nothing."

"Don't lie to me, Loren."

"Faraday will find a company of geological scientists who did some work for me and that's all. Does Donnelly know about this?"

"Sturrock's informing him as we speak."

"I demand to know who found this out!"

"You won't ever know, Loren."

"Not long ago if I said *jump* in this town a man like Faraday would've asked *how high*."

"Times have changed. He's offered to plea you out."

"Tell him he can go to hell."

Emmaline

Mr Quaid pounces on her as she crosses the Tribune's threshold. Was he waiting for her? His behavior is becoming quite baffling.

"Morning, Mr Quaid."

"Good, Roberts, good..."

"Excuse me, I need to get to my desk," she says, while attempting to get around him.

He steps in front of her. "What's good, I hear you ask?"

"I didn't..."

"You're early, that's what. Might as well make the most use of your half-day and get down to Ryan's office and follow up on yesterday's scoop."

"May I go to my desk first?"

"You know, about the geologists."

"I know what the scoop..."

"There's bound to be more by now."

"Yes, and I have my own theory, but..."

"'Course you do. Now..."

"I would like to check my desk. Something may've come in..."

She persists and he starts walking with her. "Get a statement from Ryan or Mac or Faraday if you have to. I want to know what's transpired since yesterday."

They reach her desk and stand before it, she sagging under the disappointment that considering she's been away from it for some time, there is nothing more than two copies of the Tribune on it.

"Don't sweat it, Roberts. Happens when you're an investigator. You don't get to write at your desk every day. You know that."

"I happen to like my desk. It feels good to sit and write at it."

"So, come back and write up what you get from the jail, write about the décor if it'll make you feel better. Consider that a fair day's work. Go home. Put your feet up."

"Not that again. Mr Quaid, I don't need to…"

"Off, off, off… get out of here and get me the latest."

She sighs, heads back across the office and out the door into the cold and the deep mist.

She's not the only one looking for a story. Inside the County Sheriff's office she can barely see over the heads of a crowd of reporters. Of course, these aren't all local journalists. Laramie, Denver, North Platte, Lincoln, Omaha and even Kansas City, Salt Lake City and eastern papers have newsmen in town to cover the trial; even smaller Wyoming towns, such as Rawlins to the west and Casper to the north. And these are just the ones she knows about.

This latest piece of news, that Bodecker and Donnelly had employed geologists over the summer, has lit a spark on what is a drab, gray morning. What they don't know is that Dillon Kerr is probably hiding out at the Donnelly ranch with his Eva.

She struggles for a vantage point, stepping this way and that.

One reporter turns after he squashes her foot and says, "Beg pardon, ma'am. Oh, it's you, Roberts."

She doesn't even know who he is.

Eventually, she must be content to listen from the back and see nothing.

But it is Mac's voice she hears.

"I'll give you this one statement and that's all. I'm busy, y'hear?"

"Sure, Mac, whatever," says someone from the front.

"Right. We're taking this latest development very serious. We've had confirmation that a geological company, Worthing and Farrell, was hired by Mr Bodecker to survey land in Albany County. Exactly which land we are in the process of investigating. Mr Faraday is seeking cooperation from Denver, where the company is based, for access to the results of the surveys and if any trespassing onto Alliance ranchland occurred."

"Where's Ryan?" someone asks.

Her heart begins to beat frantically.

"I'm getting to that. In the meantime, Sheriff Ryan has been called away to investigate the possible whereabouts of Mr Bodecker's missing attorney Dillon Kerr. He left this morning."

"He has a lead then?"

"He does and he's looking into it."

"What lead? Where'd it come from?"

"Can't tell you that for the present, Sam…"

He's left town?

He didn't even say goodbye.

Why didn't he say goodbye?

The questions continue:

"How long will he be gone?"

"It ain't for sure but one or two days at most."

"Is it true he took Deloight with him?"

"Where'd you hear that? Anyway, it's true."

"So Ryan must be headed out Laramie way?"

"Got nothing to do with that. As you can see, we're kinda short-handed around here at present. Deputy Deloight is an experienced lawman. Cliff thought he could put him to good use."

"Don't you think it's a coincidence that Ryan's investigation takes him out of town at the same time we find out the geologists spent time at Donnelly's ranch, Mac?"

"These things happen, folks. Okay, that's it. I'm busy."

She finds a nearby chair and scribbles the finishing touches to Mac's statement in her notebook while the others file past. Then Mac drops onto the chair beside her.

"Mac…"

"Emmaline." He gives her a reassuring smile. "He left early. That eight o'clock train that goes to Laramie and comes right back again…"

"I… didn't tell him about Dillon Kerr…"

He looks sympathetic. "Cam told him. The information you gave us when your pa was in town… all seemed to fit, make a bit of sense at last… well, they put two and two together. Figured you'd be doin' the same."

"Yes. Was he angry?"

"With you? Are you kiddin'?"

She shakes her head. "I know how much he wanted Kerr."

"And thanks to you he might be gettin' him. Cliff understands these things get played out and sometimes you gotta wait till your chance comes along. You're not to worry. These Laramie boys, you know same as me what they're like. They get the job done. He'll be fine. Keep Dillon Kerr under your hat for now but."

"Of course," she says and gets to her feet.

"Oh, nearly forgot," he mumbles, standing up, rummaging in his coat pocket. "He left you this."

She takes a folded note and while she's staring at it, before he leaves her, he says, "He's always thinking about you, Emmaline."

Then how did everything become so confused?

Perhaps the note will tell her. It reads...

> Emma, I need to be out of town for a day,
> two at most. May we talk on my return?
> Be safe. J.

Luke

He towels the last traces of shaving soap from his face, wondering where she's got to. Most often she's in the bedroom straightening up while he shaves... He frowns at himself in the mirror. Is it normal to want to know her whereabouts at every moment?

She appears at the bathroom door. "Ben's downstairs."

Ah, so *he's* surfaced, has he?

"I wondered where you got to," he says, dumping the towel and going to her. He puts his hands on her waist and watches that melting smile come over her face.

"I'm fixing breakfast. Where did you think I'd got to?"

He slides his arms around her and kisses her neck lingeringly. She smells like heaven; feels like an angel...

"I said Ben is downstairs," she says.

"I heard," he replies. He looks into her eyes and then kisses her mouth. Her body goes light in his arms; like champagne she's gone straight to his head. Her arms creep around his back, drawing him tight to her body and everything else is forgotten.

"What about Ben?" she murmurs.

"Who?"

Her giggle sounds like *I give up*, so he lifts her into his arms and carries her to their bed. Before he covers her with his body, he pulls a sheet over them and cocoons them like a warm secret inside it.

"Evan all right?"

"Evan? Oh..." She smiles, her eyes very bright. "Oh, I think Evan is perfectly fine."

*

He buttons his shirt as he descends the stairs. When he reaches the bottom, he sees Ben at the table, polishing off a plate of food.

"Mornin'," his cousin greets him.

"I hope you left me some bacon."

"Did I interrupt something?"

"Well, you did as a matter of fact."

Ben grins lopsidedly. "Sorry."

"Breakfast better be good."

"It is. Sorry. I saw Jennifer through the window and assumed… well, you must be feeling better."

He rolls his eyes. "I am. There wasn't much wrong with me."

Ben raises, arches and angles one of his eyebrows.

"Who do you keep that look for – your secretary? Pass the bacon over."

The bacon, the eggs and a plate of toast come his way.

"So?" Luke prompts, filling his plate.

"I went to the courthouse with Ethan. He was due to testify."

"I remember. But the Judge wanted a doctor's report on Donnelly's hand first, didn't he?"

"He got the report. Two actually, Cam told me. One from Buchanan's doctor as well, a John Randall. The Judge would only accept Doc Prewitt's. Donnelly's hand is no longer a cause for concern. The Judge adjourned court till Monday afternoon I think."

Luke eats fast. Making love to Jennifer makes him hungry.

"You obviously haven't seen the Tribune this morning."

He shakes his head, chewing some delicious bacon. "This is good. Didn't know you could cook."

Ben displays another raised eyebrow; the other one this time.

"That's a talent entirely your own," Luke quips.

"The Tribune is carrying a story about how Bodecker and Donnelly hired a geological company from Denver to survey some land up in Albany County. According to the Tribune it was last summer."

He stops chewing and swallows hard. "Last summer? During Ed Parsons' trial?"

"Looks that way. Cam has asked the Denver authorities to gain access to the Worthing and Farrell survey. He wants to know if they trespassed into the Bright River valley, onto the Diamond-T and John and Amy's place to conduct surveys for Bodecker."

"Sonofabitch."

"Are you aware of potential mineral deposits or precious metal veins under the Diamond-T?"

"First I've heard of it."

Then something occurs to him. Something he'd rather be talking to Ethan about than Ben; yet looking at his cousin across the table, there's no reason he can't talk to him as well. Apart from the fact that he trusts him, Ben's smart and he's in the mining business.

"Listen up, Ben. There's a particular clause in the deed to the Diamond-T. An agreement made between a feller called Connors and my father: Diamond Pass has to remain open. You never saw the Pass though, did you?"

"No, but Ethan mentioned it. What does the clause mean?"

"No fences, no impediments, no dams, no blowing up a hillside…"

Ben blinks. "Fascinating. Why?"

"I don't know. It's been a mystery all my life."

"You think this could have something to do with a previous geological survey?"

"Interesting you should ask that, Ben, because Connors had the land surveyed and documented by the Army so he knew what he owned down to the last square inch of dirt and blade of grass."

Ben whistles. "In order to…?"

"To keep the railroad from getting their hands on it."

"Who would stick a railroad up there?"

"No one, but railroad tycoons need more than land, they need resources, don't they?"

"What are you getting at?"

"Trying to figure it out, like I've been doing since I can remember. Bear with me?"

"Sure. Let me hear it."

"When we got to the valley, Union Pacific had begun its march across the Great Plains; that's one of the things that Pa and Ethan liked about ranching up here – easier at that time to get their cattle to market with the new railroad relatively close by."

"Makes good business sense."

"Back before the railroad, when this land was opened up, a fork of the Overland Trail cut through the grasslands about thirty miles west of Laramie, before Laramie came into existence though. It's still there. In fact you pass it on the way to the Diamond-T. And it's not all that far from our valley either. Back then everything came and went on the Overland Trail. Stagecoaches, mail, wagon trains, emigrants, livestock, pony express, all heading west."

"Must have been amazing. It joined up with the Oregon Trail, didn't it?"

"It did. Now, by Connors' time, though, the Union Pacific was on the march; the Transcontinental Railroad was coming. I'm thinking any land near a railroad corridor could be high in value, right? Any landowners thereabouts could see the railroad as a threat and they needed to be sure no tycoon could take what was theirs. So Connors made his patch as secure as he could."

"I guess it's a *theory*. For my money, cousin, the Diamond-T might've been prime ranchland but I still think it was too far from the intended railroad route to cause concern for Connors."

"Pa and Ethan paid good money for the inclusion of the survey in the property deed. Called it the Connors Bill of Sale. It has to mean something more."

"Did you ever see the original survey documents?"

"We have the deed with the clause included, all legal and binding and locked away. But as for the actual survey documents, I've never seen them."

"That's odd. Wouldn't it make sense to keep the survey with the deed?"

"Possibly. Parsons constantly challenged the Diamond Pass clause and we had to go into court a lot. He always argued that if it had to remain open then it was a kind of no man's land and he could access it, which wasn't true, and we made sure he knew it; we had no intention of yielding despite his harassment. Eventually the Judge in Laramie ordered Parsons to find something new to present or not bother."

"That's interesting," Ben murmurs. "Find something new or not bother. I wonder if Parsons ever tried to find the survey himself. I mean, the Army could still have a record of it."

"I never thought of that."

"You've never seen the survey. How do you know it exists?"

"Like a dutiful son and heir, Ben, I believed what I was told."

"Parsons could have tried to locate it but the Army probably required proof of ownership to release it. I think he wanted to know as much as he could about *why* the Diamond Pass clause existed. How did he come to know about its existence in the first place?"

"He bought half of his ranch from my father; it might have come up. Parsons was the devil as a neighbor; he fought and needled about every little thing."

"I wonder where the survey is. Still with the army? What about Ethan? – he should know."

"Ethan always said he didn't know much about the details of the Connors Bill of Sale, that Pa handled it mostly, you know, the business side of things, while Ethan handled getting the ranch up to speed. We always thought Parsons' constant challenge to the Diamond Pass clause was to harass us, but maybe what he really wanted was to get access to the surveyor's documents."

"Which begs the question, Luke: what is on the document that is so important?"

"Or, maybe what he wanted was the means to get a team like Worthing and Farrell onto our land."

"Yes, but that would mean he knew something, Luke, something about the land. Or, someone he knew did."

"Who? Bodecker? Way back then? – we're talking '67 to '68."

"Maybe Bodecker knew this Connors."

"Bodecker and Parsons certainly haven't known each other that long. Parsons must've had his uses for Bodecker, maybe this was one of them. As for the rest, I don't know."

"Yes, but what I'm saying is maybe Bodecker knew Connors and knew what potential the land had and has been slowly working his way through this 'Empire' of his and he used Parsons to try and acquire the potential he thought was there on the Diamond-T. You could be sitting on a gold mine and you don't even know it."

This comment breaks the tension and makes him laugh. "I hardly think so. Bodecker would have moved a lot quicker than this for gold."

"Okay, a slight exaggeration maybe," Ben grins. "But maybe Worthing and Farrell had some good news for him last summer. Look, from what you just said, for a long time Ed Parsons seemed to think there was *something*. You fought him all the way, and he gave you plenty to keep you busy..."

"Mart..."

"Then while you were completely preoccupied with Parsons' trial last summer, maybe Bodecker and Donnelly saw an opportunity. Enter Worthing and Farrell..." Ben finishes with his eyebrow maneuver.

Luke lets out another laugh; he reaches for the coffee pot and tips more coffee in each of their cups.

"Where's Ethan?"

"At the Keatons, talking with them about the Tribune story."

"I suppose Emmaline broke it."

"Likely. There was no byline. That reminds me. There's one more thing. Cliff left town this morning with Deloight; they think they have a lead on the whereabouts of Dillon Kerr."

"Oh? That's been bothering Cliff for some time now. Do you know where?"

"Cam wouldn't tell me or Ethan. I think they want that kept very quiet, even from us."

"And Cliff just up and left..."

"You know, cousin, it has occurred to me that while we think we might be running things, it's always been Faraday and Ryan. Arrogant sons of bitches, aren't we?"

A Taylor flaw. A Taylor strength. Depends on how you look at it. "I guess we are. And what's more, I don't care. I'll get my coat. Head over to John's?"

Ben nods. "I'll finish my coffee first."

Luke grins.

"Sorry, about before."

"Just wait till *you* have a kitchen I can come busting into first thing in the morning."

Ben chuckles. "Looking forward to it. Raina would love a home of her own."

"So where *is* Raina?"

"She went shopping."

When he returns upstairs, Jennifer is standing before the mirror wearing an elegant midnight blue dress, and pinning up her dark chestnut hair in a style all too practical to his way of thinking. He doesn't have the heart to tell her he wants to pull all the pins out; he likes her hair best when it's down, or braided over her shoulder...

"What did Ben want?" she asks.

"Mm? Oh, Ben..." He remembers his coat and lifts it from the chair by the window.

"Didn't you just speak with him? Are you going somewhere?"

"The Keatons."

"Is this about the story in the Tribune?"

He nods. "Would you mind? I won't be long. The Judge adjourned court till Monday. Breathing space at last."

She inserts the last pin in her hair and comes to him. He drops his coat at once. When she looks at him like that he loses track of his thoughts. He holds her with one arm; cradles her cheek with his other hand.

"I don't mind, and some breathing space will do you good," she says, smiling at him.

He falls headlong into her gaze, those eyes so bright and green, reminding him of rolling prairie grass in the first days of summer. He wonders if he will ever see the grass of the Diamond-T in summer again. His mind wanders for a bit; back to the life he lived and the person he was before Jennifer and the tiny prospect. The switch from that to this is complex, all his thoughts and feelings, and his very being, turned upside down and right way up... yet the Diamond-T is always present to him, in his spirit, at the heart of him.

"I will take you there," he murmurs.

"The Diamond-T..."

"You read my thoughts, don't you?"

"I see it in your eyes sometimes..."

"What's that?"

"A longing for home. I know you need to be there."

"One day... As long as I'm with you..."

She smiles and nudges her soft cheek into his hand.

"You look very pretty, even with the pins..."

"Thank you. You're not doing anything dangerous, are you?"

"I'm talking, that's all. With Ethan and John and Ben."

"And Amy and Tressa..."

"Yes, the women too," he says, grinning. "You can come, you know."

She shakes her head. "Your first instincts were right; this is something I know nothing about. But you have my support, and you know that, too."

He kisses her lips. "What will you do?"

"I have some medical reading to catch up on."

He chuckles softly. Of course, she does.

"Some patients don't give up all their secrets at once."

"Then they are lucky to have you for their doctor."

Her smile widens. "Off you go. I expect to be fully informed on your return."

"Don't worry, you will be. One thing, though, Cliff left town this morning chasing a lead on Dillon Kerr."

"Kerr! That will please him."

"You see? I'm not the one doing the dangerous stuff anymore, am I?" He kisses her cheek. "I won't be long."

Emmaline

Emmaline wanders into the bookstore on her way back to the Tribune, respite from the madness on the street and the anxious hearts of unhappy people...

"Good morning, Miss Roberts."

She clears her head, retrieves her manners and pays attention. Her greeter is the owner, Freddy Hart.

"Mr Hart, good morning."

"Misty out today. Fine type of weather for curling up with a book. Wouldn't you agree?"

"Where I come from mist is mostly warm."

"Oh," he says as if he'd like to understand the concept but can't. "May I help you with something?"

She has a powerful need to ask him if a certain sheriff bought a book yesterday, but would feel extremely foolish, particularly if he were to reply: *Sheriff Ryan buy a book yesterday? I don't think so, Miss Roberts.*

"I'll continue to browse, if you don't mind."

"Certainly. I can always tell a true book lover. A browse through the books is a recreation all its own."

He understands.

She walks along the shelves and past the tables, absorbed with thoughts about a certain sheriff. She smuggles a cough in her hand.

"Hope that fog isn't getting into your throat, Miss Roberts," Freddy Hart remarks.

Translation: don't infect my bookstore...

Just then another book lover enters.

THE HOUR of EVIDENCE

Raina!

Who spies Emmaline, smiles warmly and comes her way.

She never thought Raina would be a reader.

Which is a positively awful thing to think.

"May I help you, Miss?" Freddy Hart enquires, halting Raina's progress momentarily.

"It's Mrs actually, and no, thank you, I'm browsing."

"Seems like the day for it."

Raina's voice is pretty; light and gentle but bubbly. Like her eyes, a light and gentle blue, always dancing.

Although Emmaline and this dark-haired daughter of a Denver tycoon haven't spoken all that much since Ben brought her to town as his wife and shocked the pants of everyone in doing so, she can't help but admire the now disinherited heiress.

Today she wears a striking walking ensemble; the exquisite claret-toned cashmere skirt and matching waist are tastefully embellished with brocade and velvet of the same shade, deep trimmed at hems, cuffs and collar with color-matched fur for which some poor critters gave their lives. Her bonnet is a perfect match, fur trim included, with the addition of a beguiling jeweled spray at the front, all tied under her pretty chin with a generous velvet ribbon. Tan kid gloves and a purse made of the same velvet as in her dress, featuring a large flower of silver and black glass beads, complete the eye-catching image.

Emmaline feels every inch the local reporter, scrapping for stories in back alleys for a living, and who on earth would pay any attention to *what* kind of hat she wears with this head-turning fashion plate parading around Cheyenne.

The only thing they have in common is their height.

"Raina, how nice to see you." She thinks it inappropriate to ask where Ben might be, even though she rarely sees them apart. Nevertheless, she has to kill the urge to crane her neck and look for him.

"And you, Emmaline. I saw you come in here. I waited outside for you for a few minutes but that fog is quite unpleasant."

"Is there something I can do for you?"

"Do you have to get back to the paper right away?"

"In a little bit. Always have time for a chat."

Raina's eyes dance her appreciation and then she continues. "The train from Denver just pulled in at the depot and a crowd of people got off. I think I prefer this part of town. You live somewhere around here, don't you?"

"Not exactly. The guesthouse is a ten minute walk that way," she says, pointing at a wall of books. "I stopped in here because I…I like the books…er, are you fixin' to buy something?"

"I do love to read, very much, but not today. Actually, I was hoping to speak with you. I was on my way to the Tribune and saw you come in here. Do you mind?"

Being followed…? And stalked…? Becoming used to it.

She shakes her head. "Are you sure you want to talk in here?"

"I noticed as I came in that we are the only two."

"Oh. So we are. Even so, let's go into the corner?"

Raina agrees with a sparkly-eyed nod and Emmaline steers her as far away from Freddy Hart as possible to the furthest corner of the store. "This should do it."

Raina has dropped her voice to a murmur as she says, "You know Jacob Hunter rather well."

"Well, I… pardon me?"

"Jacob Hunter of the Bugle. He was stalking you and you fixed it so he didn't ruin Luke and Jennifer's wedding…"

"You know about that?"

"Of course." She shrugs in the same light manner that her eyes dance.

"Go on. What about that scum Jacob Hunter?"

"After his attempts to get to Luke and to you came to nothing, he's trying someone new."

"Not *you*?"

"Oh, Emmaline, this is all off the record…"

All the good stuff is. "I know, Raina, don't worry. But shouldn't you be going to Ben with this?"

"Hunter is blackmailing me."

Emmaline catches her breath. Her head-turning fashion plate is in real trouble. She gathers her wits. "He's bluffing…"

"No. He went to Denver."

"Wondered where he got to these last few days."

"Mm. He dug and dug and found out things about me, my father and other things which he will use against me if I don't give him inside information regarding the Alliance and the case."

"Oh, my. That's protozoan, even for him."

Raina winces. "I don't know what to do."

"These... er, things, does Ben know about them?"

Here, Raina's winces sound agonizing.

Freddy Hart calls out, "Everything all right back there?"

"Headache," Emmaline shoots back. "Small headache..."

"Perhaps you ladies should go home. Customers, you know."

The hoards. Clambering to get in. "We're fine, thank you for asking."

She draws Raina closer.

Raina lowers her voice even further. "My father is a dastardly man, Emmaline. Ben dealt with him in terms he understands, but even my father did not use the things Jacob Hunter uncovered to dissuade Ben from taking me away."

"Are you sure Jacob Hunter really knows as much as he's letting on?"

"He knows enough."

"Raina, you have to tell Ben."

Raina lowers her gaze and for a long moment there is silence between them. It's only when Raina wipes her cheek, opens her purse and extracts a lace handkerchief that Emmaline realizes she's crying.

"Ben loves you, Raina."

"I know," she chokes out, her quiet tears outpacing her ability to wipe them. "But we've only known each other a very short time and I haven't been able to tell him everything."

"Nor have you wanted to, I bet."

"Exactly. We're happy," she says looking up, her face awash, "*really* happy. Probably for the first time in our lives. Why would I want to contaminate this precious time together by bringing up more of my father's indiscretions and my connection to them."

"But you cannot give in to Jacob Hunter's demands..."

"Apart from anything else, I'm not much of an informer.

Hunter must be desperate. I know I'm the weakest link of you all, but..."

"Hush, now. You are nothing of the kind, Raina. You helped find and rescue Richard Taylor. Ben's father, no less. Your father-in-law! They couldn't have done it without you and that's a fact. Believe me, you are extremely important to them. And you are the shining light in Ben's world. They all adore you, Raina."

And a girl can't help her father's past indiscretions.

"Thank you, that was very kind of you, Emmaline, but right now the thought of letting Ben down..."

"I don't believe that is possible, Raina."

"Every day I think how can this man keep coming back to me, commit his whole life to me, make me a part of his future. I can't comprehend it. I wonder if I ever will."

"I suppose the concept is better understood when you have parents who model it for you. Your mother and father separated, didn't they?"

"Yes."

"And so did mine. It affects us, Raina."

"Affects us more than people realize. And now this problem."

"You can't let Jacob Hunter take over your thoughts, rob you of your natural self-confidence, twist your judgment, because..."

"At least he doesn't know how Ben and I met."

Emmaline stops and frowns. "How *did* you meet?"

Her bluntness goes unnoticed. "I'm sure he doesn't. No one does."

Ashcliff Ryan knows. Or thinks he does. But he's not telling.

"Perhaps if I knew, Raina, I could guarantee the information stayed in the right hands."

Again, Raina seems not to notice. "Hunter will ruin me if I don't agree to do what he wants."

Emmaline, God gave you a conscience and the good sense to know how to use it... She gives her head a shake to clear it of Father Nugent's image.

"What is it, Emmaline?"

"Mm? Oh, nothing... Raina, since Ben loves you, you can have no qualms now about going to him."

"Easy to say."

She knows it is. Words come cheap. And she is the last person to be dishing out this kind of advice. She digs deep...

"Raina, these are *your* secrets, and *you* are the only one who has the right to them. The one thing I truly know is you must not allow yourself to be Jacob Hunter's victim. If you are true to yourself, and trust yourself, you can be free of him."

Raina regards her intently while dabbing at her cheeks. "Is that what you did?"

"I had it on very good advice. But it helps if you know you have someone who really cares for you."

Raina's eyes blaze very bright. "I... thank you, Emmaline."

"If you want, I can turn the dogs on him."

Raina tries a smile.

"Come walk with me to the Tribune. When Jacob Hunter sees us together, he'll start quakin' in his shoes."

"He will?"

"Let me tell you something about Jacob Hunter. That's not even his real name."

Raina looks taken aback. "Then what is it?"

"Julius Holyoake."

"Oh, now you are attempting humor to make me feel better."

"I wouldn't make up a thing like that! Who could? Father Nugent also found out that our very nasty boy is Catholic. So lapsed only St Peter can save him with a Pearly Gates reprieve. Father Nugent has been on his case since the wedding and he certainly won't like what that bad boy's been up to. The good Father may not look like a vicious dog, but once that Irish voice of his gets into you and starts hunting down all the demons inside your head, snapping at their heels all day long, there is no escape."

Raina chuckles as she repairs her face.

"You see! Jacob Hunter is not so smart. He doesn't know what we know about him, *and* he's forgotten that blackmail works both ways."

They say their 'good days' to Freddy Hart...

"Miss Roberts, Mrs... er, see you again, ladies."

... and walk through the languishing fog towards the Tribune.

"Late in the morning for fog to be lingering still," Emmaline remarks. "Unsettling, to say the least."

"Unusually for these parts there is no wind today, and the sun is still pale. Takes a determined sun to burn away fog."

"A determined sun," she echoes. "I like that. May I use it?"

At the Tribune, Emmaline is so consumed with curiosity about Raina and her secrets that once inside the door she must rest against the near wall and take a good deep breath.

Off the record. Let it go...

"Roberts?"

She opens her eyes at once. "Mr Quaid. How nice to see you."

"What are you doing?"

She straightens up; gives herself a mental shake. "Nothing."

He narrows his eyes. "Well?"

"Mac gave a statement to about fifty reporters crammed into the county sheriff's office. A... Sheriff Ryan has a lead on Dillon Kerr and took Deputy Deloight to go follow it. They will be gone a day or two. Here, Mac's statement and my notes are in my book..." She hands him her notebook. "The last page..."

"And you're okay with that?"

"Okay with what?"

He goes to say something then changes his mind.

"I'll write it up, shall I? That's what you said; get the story, write it up at my desk and go home for the day..."

"Something else, Roberts..."

"Mr Quaid, I swear I don't know what's got into you..."

"In my office. Now." With a toss of his head, he urges her in the direction of his office. "Off you go..."

"I... what?"

"Just go, Roberts," he says and walks away.

Emmaline

Emmaline walks through the door of Mr Quaid's office and stops dead in her tracks. Two familiar faces greet her. Her whole being resounds with emotion, particularly at the sight of one of them.

"Mama..."

Her mama rushes across the room. "Emmie!"

Emmaline, still stiff from shock, is folded into those motherly arms. The scent of the familiar strikes her, drawing her home.

"Emmie... I know it's a shock, it's all right, dahlin."

She is set back and an inspection peculiar to mothers begins. She inspects in return. Her mama looks radiant. She hopes the Sheriff doesn't expect to take the credit for it.

"Mama, what are you doing here?"

"We're staying at the Cheyenne Hotel; do you know it?

"Well, of course, I live here, but... I don't understand."

Her father – former Sheriff of Orange County, Florida, now retired – moves forward a little. "It's a long story, Emmaline, but when I had to tell your mama..."

"When I made him tell me you were pale and not yourself..."

"Yes, well, if I was not myself it was because he showed up."

"... and not yourself," her mama persists, "I came. But not from home. Your papa and I were calling on your uncle. Papa left me there to come talk to you alone. Then he wired me before he left to meet him in St Louis, we spent a little time there together and then we came here."

She takes herself out of her mama's hands. "What were you doing at Uncle's?"

"Sharing the joy of our reconciliation. You know how your uncle and your papa always got on so well."

"So was Uncle overjoyed, Sheriff?"

Her mama closes the door to Mr Quaid's office while the Sheriff looks unimpressed.

"Well, here you both are – together again!"

"Emmie, this rudeness and sarcasm is most unbecoming and I can't abide you speaking to your papa in that manner. And it's high time you stopped calling him Sheriff."

"So, you're just passing through then?" she ventures.

Her mama regards her steadily for some moments.

"No, Emmie. We've come to take you home."

"Take me home? What are you talking about?"

"We know the signs, Emmaline," the Sheriff says, prowling about the room.

"Since when did you become the expert?"

"Emmie, stop it."

"You may have forgiven him, Mama, but I have not."

The Sheriff thinks better of speaking and instead stares at her, looking hurt.

"That look doesn't work on me."

He rolls his eyes and returns to the window.

"Emmie, your papa did the right thing. When he described your disposition, the alarm bell started ringing in my head…"

"After you spent some time in St Louis. Alarm bell? Really? The Sheriff had it on good authority, from Mr Faraday himself in fact, the trial would last three weeks. To his credit, the Sheriff was prepared to let me see this out, but you've convinced him to change his mind and to please you and keep his precious reconciliation on track he acquiesced."

"Emmaline, that is outrageous…"

"Preston, let me handle it. Emmie, this climate, this intense cold, you know what it does. You can't stay here a minute more."

"It's been a couple of months, that's all."

"But from what I hear the climate will be cold here for at least another month, probably longer. You can't stay here that long."

"Two weeks more, Mama; two weeks. I know what I'm doing."

"You led me to believe when you took this assignment it was only meant to be a short sojourn. A month at most. Why do you think I agreed to it?"

"Because I'm an adult and can make my own decisions, and because I was determined to come here whether you liked it or not and you had no say in it," she says, determined to be clear. "Why are you talking to me like I'm twelve?"

Her mama sighs. "It's so difficult to make you see reason at times, Emmie. You're a passionate young woman with more ability than any woman has a right to, but you have limitations, you know you do."

"*Me* see reason? This is not a game; this is my life. I am not an invalid you keep locked up in a sanatorium who, out of the goodness of your heart, you deigned to let out for the day and who failed to return at the negotiated time."

"Gracious, what a notion…"

"There are other women like me here. Women here have rights, they do things, they are not restricted by convention as much as we are back home."

"I understand the attraction, really I do, but you can't stay and you know it. Be honest, Emmie, you've been coughing…"

"No."

"Emmaline, you are not telling the truth," the Sheriff says.

"So arrest me!"

"Emmie, stop this and answer me properly. The cold has got into your lungs, hasn't it?"

"My lungs are just fine, thank you."

She recalls the cold in her lungs when she fell on Wednesday night – it seemed to ice a whole cake of cold nights and bitter days... A tremendous wave of heartache arcs above her and then breaks.

James…

It shudders through her.

"It's time to go," her mama says, softer. "Back to the sun."

"Stop speaking to me that way. I am not an invalid. I am not an escapee. And I am not your possession to order here or there, nor will I be the object of your fears. Am I to be locked up just to make you feel better? I don't think so! There is nothing wrong with me."

"Emmie, calm yourself. I can't believe the way you are speaking to me. I raised you and I know this is not who you are. These Wild West people have turned you into a... a... Yankee... you are even starting to speak like one."

God forbid!

"So you're my mother and you raised me, I am grateful and will always love you, but I will not be disrespected this way by you or anyone. I am a valuable employee of this newspaper. I have made friendships I will have all my life. And I'm a prosecution witness."

"I will be speaking with Faraday about that," the Sheriff says, asserting himself in the battle. "He's a reasonable man from what I recall of him."

"Oh, you never listen!"

"Mr Quaid seems to be worried about you, Emmaline," he continues. "He said as much when we arrived. In fact, I think he was relieved to see us."

"Of course you would say that, wouldn't you?"

"These people, Emmaline, will carry on without you."

She catches her breath. She wants to call the Sheriff every rude and unpleasant name under the sun, and thanks to her brothers she knows them all, but for her mama's sake she exercises restraint.

"That may be so, Sheriff, but you both need to hear what I'm saying to you. I have a place here and a job to do that is mine. And I'm good at it. You, both of you, are meddling where you are definitely not wanted. You are belittling my life and my achievements with your insulting attitude, and I will not stand for it. You cannot come here and tell me what to do. Now *go home*."

She wrenches open Mr Quaid's door, raises her chin and glares at them one last time. "And I do not speak like a Yankee!"

She rushes out into the corridor, determined to go someplace where she can pretend her parents don't exist. Mr Quaid is hovering in the lobby. He looks up with a bewildered expression.

"Your office, Mr Quaid, is free," she says and heads out into the street.

Emmaline

On busy Eddy Street she looks this way and that in utter despair. Why is it James Ashcliff Alejandro Alvarez Ryan is never here when she needs him? A more frustrating man never lived on God's earth.

She cuts into the nearest alley and has a good long cough.

She refuses to cry, however. No tears...

Out in the street again, she half-runs with little regard for her healing knee or for what people might think until she comes to the Fancy Boots Café. Here she throws herself into the furthest corner and struggles to regain her breath and steady her heart. She puts her arms on the table and buries her face in the crook of her elbow.

I'm not ready, I can't leave him. I can't, I can't, I can't.

I'm so sorry, Emmie, so sorry... but don't despair, you mustn't. There's never just one solution to a problem. You'll work it out...

Go away, Celie.

No, Emmie, don't block me out... you need me.

I only need one person and he's not here! Now leave me alone.

A voice says, "Oh, it's you, child."

Her internal rantings skid to a halt and she looks up into a wrinkled face. A gaped grin comes next.

"Mrs Landers...."

"In the flesh."

"It's been a while."

"Sure 'nough. May I sit?"

"I..."

"Much obliged. Kinda upset when ya tore in here."

"Was I? Oh, I was."

"Mm. Tell me, how goes it with yer young sheriff?"

"My...my sheriff?"

Mrs Landers chuckles. "I know which way the wind blows. Lotta folks would describe Miss Emmaline Roberts and Sheriff Cliff Ryan as a match made in heaven."

"I don't know which folks they'd be. Besides, he needs to live his own life."

"Don't include yerself in that life I take it?"

"Our paths came together for a while, that is all. But that doesn't mean it won't be hard when we take separate paths again."

"Wouldn't risk it, even for love?"

"Love?"

"Can't fool me into thinkin' ya don't love him with the kinda love that never comes to an end. I know ya do, Emmaline, and so does he."

She gulps. "Mrs Landers, I don't know where you got all this insight about us, but when James and I say goodbye and go our separate ways it will be the end. We live in different worlds that are worlds apart."

"So sure of that, are ya?"

"Yes. I admit I should've tried harder to make him see that in the beginning but..."

"Wouldn't've worked. Love is the strongest thing there is. Nothin' ya could've done about it. Funny how ya think so."

"Nothing funny about it. A person needs to realistic about..."

"Yer the only person to ever call him that."

"James? How did you know?"

"Handsome name James. In the Good Book, James is one of the Sons of Thunder. Name kinda suits a handsome man of action like yer young sheriff. He needs to be called that and called it often. By you. Dear boy."

Emmaline is speechless. Eventually, she manages to ask why.

"I told ya he needed ya, Emmaline, 'member?"

"I did what you said I should do. He no longer wears the black coat."

"Ah, that was ages ago! He's got 'lot farther ahead now. What was once barely a spark inside of him is now a flame."

"What do you mean, Mrs Landers?"

"He's a blessed man, Emmaline. He saw eternity in yer eyes the first moment he looked into them."

"Eternity. Yes… eternity." Her mind drifts back to the peaceful Sunday morning in Nan Morris' kitchen after Mass where she and Ashcliff sat and ate oatmeal and sipped coffee and talked about life and about eternity and she was falling for him…

"Mrs Landers…"

"No more questions, child. Make yer decisions, make yer peace. It's time to stop wrestlin' and wonderin' and whatiffin'. Do what ya must do."

"I feel lost, and cornered, and… and angry…"

"That's cause it's time to make a decision. But ya thought time was under *yer* control. Turned out different. That ain't easy to accept for a strong character like yers. But once ya make the decision ya'll feel better. Do, Emmaline, what ya must do."

Mrs Landers gets up and hobbles away; she opens the door of the café and closes it behind her, but fails to appear left or right through the café windows. Emmaline follows at once. She reefs open the door and sticks her head out. Mrs Landers is nowhere to be seen.

The waitress says, "Your hot chocolate is at your table, ma'am."

"But I didn't ord…" She turns abruptly.

Sure enough, at her table is a cup of hot chocolate, steam curling upwards from its chocolaty surface like a fragrant offering to the heavens.

The young waitress smiles.

Emmaline resumes her seat. And, after blowing on it several times, drinks her chocolate.

Not long after this, she knocks on Jennifer's back door.

Jennifer answers it with a book in her hand. "Emmaline!"

"Jennifer. I need to tell you something."

Her beautiful new friend smiles. "Then come in and tell me."

Luke

Amy pours them all coffee. "All I can say is who is going to escort the Severinis to church tomorrow morning if Cliff is not in town."

"Why is he always the one to do that?" Luke asks. "Anyone would think…"

Alfredo butts in. "He become Catholic… like us."

"He got religion?"

"Apparently so," Amy says, blinking at Alfredo. "I thought he was being a diligent sheriff, taking care of his witnesses."

John chuckles. "He was… is. He just found something a little extra along the way."

"I'm…"

"What?" Ben prompts.

"He never said anything."

"I guess it's something very personal, son," John concludes.

"Emmaline's Roman Catholic."

"Si," Gianni says. "Signorina Roberts."

"That's why?" Ben asks.

Signora finds her voice. "No, no. He says he want to be Catholic for him, for self…" She nods, bright eyed.

"You think you know a person," Luke mutters.

"Well, you don't," snaps Ethan, who is grumpy because for the second day in a row he didn't make it onto the witness stand.

"Cheer up, Ethan."

Ethan grunts. Loudly. And swigs his coffee.

"Why can't we take the Severinis to church tomorrow? How bad could it be? Cliff likes it."

"No, no," Signora replies with some urgency. "You no Catholic."

"No admittance," Ben says drolly.

"Well, we could stand outside and wait though. They'd be safe inside the church, wouldn't they?"

"I guess they would," John agrees.

"This we do," Signora declares. She gets up from her chair and squeezes Luke's face between her hands. "*Bravo ragazzo...*"

Everyone else laughs.

"Where your beautiful wife... *bella Ginevra...?*"

"Home," he mumbles. "Er, have you got any of those biscotti, Signora?"

"*Ah, si, bravo... bravo ragazzo...*"

Signora gives him his face back while she fetches her biscotti.

Ben is laughing at him. "You do have a way with people."

"So," he says, ignoring his cousin, "now we've talked about it, what are we deciding to do about this geological survey business?"

"Let Mr Faraday and Mr Ryan investigate it, I expect," Tressa says. Her frankness leaves him open-mouthed.

"Agreed," says John.

"Same goes for me," Ethan concurs. "Tip, as well."

"And me." Ben.

"And me." Amy.

"Well?" Ethan prompts him. "That just leaves you."

"I agree," he says. "Feels weird, is all, leaving it to someone else to do. I mean the land is ours, it's our responsibility. Shouldn't one of us go home and check it ain't being dug up as we speak?"

"No," John and Ethan chorus.

"Besides," Ethan continues, "you know the place ain't thawed out yet."

"Even if, Luke," Amy reasons, "we'd have heard something by now."

"What if the boys back home ain't in a position to get the word out?"

"Then we wait till Cliff gives us the nod. Listen, son, we're not settin' foot outside of Cheyenne till this trial is over."

Ethan has spoken. And continues to speak...

"Two good men died to keep us alive. They died in the line of duty, it's called sacrifice and I for one don't intend to ignore it. It's our lives that count. Not the grass or the dirt or the river. Even if there'd be a mother lode of gold, we ain't goin' back till this is over."

"I understand, Ethan." He more than understands. And he knows exactly why Ethan is speaking to him this way. No one missed the Diamond-T more than Ethan. And no one understood how Luke felt about being idle in the face of trouble more than Ethan. Old habits die hard.

Ethan's expression eases. "You boys should go home to your wives."

But the biscotti arrive, along with Tip, who has returned from town with some more news…

"I spoke with Clary; he's covering for Mac while Mac's in court for Cliff. Emmaline's folks – Preston and Elizabeth Roberts – are in town. They were looking for Cliff."

Ethan whistles.

"Why are they here?" Luke asks.

"That Clary didn't know," Tips reports, sitting down before putting biscotti between his teeth. "Mmm. I love these things…"

Alfredo and Gianni laugh and bring forth the inevitable pack of cards.

"Who's for a game?" Tip asks, crunching.

They all are. Except for Luke and Ben.

"Ethan," Luke says over the din, "I need to speak with you about something."

"Later. 'Bout time you both got your priorities straight," Ethan says as he picks up his hand. It appears to be a good one. "All right, you Eye-talian desperados, let's see how you handle this."

When he arrives home, Jennifer is reading on the sofa. He likes reading himself, but she reads like other people breathe. He joins her; she puts her book down and they gaze at one another.

"Tell me then."

He tells her. Like Ethan, she understands how hard it is for him to stay put and do nothing. But within her eyes he sees the unborn child secreted away and a good deal of that restlessness disappears. Just as Ethan looks out for him, it's his turn to look out for the tiny prospect. And its mother.

He kisses her tenderly.

"What was that for?"

"*Bella Ginevra.*"

She laughs daintily, her eyes shining. "Your Italian improves."

"Thank you. But I have more news. Emmaline's folks are in town."

"Oh, really?"

"Mm. You don't look so surprised."

"Don't I?"

"Why, Dr Sullivan, what do you know?"

"I'm not at liberty to say, but you will know soon enough. Although I would like to confirm something with you... if I were to ask you to name one thing you've noticed about Emmaline, what would it be? And don't say her southern accent, or that she's pretty."

"Well, she kinda is, Jennifer. And the accent's real cute."

"Come on, Texas; keep it north of the Mason Dixon line."

He laughs. "You know that was funny, right?"

"Luke."

"Can I tell Ethan?"

"Don't make me ask you again."

"Okay, okay... as long as I've known her, Emmaline is always cold. Most of what you see is padding..." He clears his throat. "...er, to keep warm.... according to Tressa."

Preston

It takes some time but eventually he finds his troubled daughter at the courthouse, seated on a bench in the corridor outside the main courtroom, her hands folded around a handkerchief in her lap, head down. There are few people around, but enough for her to blend into the background of a place people expect her to be.

"Is nowhere sacred?" she greets him.

"Emmaline, may I sit with you and offer an olive branch?"

"Oh. You may. And what olive branch?"

"I want to apologize for what happened with you and me and your mama in Quaid's office. In spite of what you think, I heard and understood every word you said. I respect you and your achievements far more than you give me credit for. I admire you, Emmaline. You fight, and you fight hard. You are an amazing young woman and I agree you don't deserve to be spoken to like an inmate or a child. And I hope you will accept my apology."

"Mama doesn't listen."

"Not nearly as well as she should. Why do you think it has taken this long for us to reconcile? You might be interested to know you share the same trait. When it suits you, you don't listen."

"And that's supposed to make me feel better?"

"I say it to help you understand yourself better and the frustration it causes for family and friends. In all your justifiable outrage at our meddling, you didn't hear our love and concern for your welfare, or our duty as parents to look out for you, or our distress if you should become so unwell it endangered your life. We meant well."

"Well, in the interests of understanding yourself better, Sheriff, and the frustration it causes, you should not have approached the situation like you were talking to a ten-year-old girl."

"Touché. And yes, we should have been more mindful, I agree. But that was your mama's panic talking. I tried to calm her fears and get you those two weeks but she became more and more agitated."

"Can you deny you were saving your reconciliation?"

"I've been trying to do what is best for everyone."

She sighs and looks utterly defeated. "Everything is a mess and it's my fault."

"It can't all be your fault; he's not here and unless you sent him away, that is definitely not your fault."

"Oh, Sheriff," she says, sniffing back tears. "I tried and I tried everything I could think of but he wouldn't give up. And now I'm in too deep and I don't want to hurt him, but that's exactly what I'm going to do. I started coughing a few days ago and I didn't know if I would make it to the end of the trial. I thought I could keep everything under control like always, but we had this strange misunderstanding before he left town and I don't know where things stand... I just don't know. He left me a note asking if we could talk when he got back, but what's the good of it? I can't stay here and he can't leave. What am I supposed to say to him that I haven't already said or tried to make him understand?"

"Hush, now, Emmaline. Hush..."

She sighs again, deeper. "You know something, Sheriff?"

"What's that?"

"The whole time you and me and Mama were arguing I know I kept saying I didn't want to leave the paper and my job, but I was thinking of him."

Secretly, he's proud of her for admitting that out loud. He says gently, "I knew."

"You did?" She puts her arm through his in a comfortable way that's also seeking comfort. She would never admit she's feeling sickly – that would be like holding up a white flag – but he knows she does and that little by little it's sapping her strength.

He pats her hand where it rests on his sleeve. "Don't forget I not only met your young man, we talked he and I, briefly but enough. He's not your average fellow."

The corners of her mouth curve up a fraction and she sniffs. "No, he's not."

He smiles at those bright eyes looking at him and wonders if she has any idea what that says about her. So he thinks it's time she heard it. "Emmaline, I used to wonder if there would be any man out there worthy of you, but I..."

She looks shocked. "Worthy of me?"

"Mm," he says with a wider grin, "he's worthy of you. Just."

"That's kind of you to say..."

"The truth is the truth. Nothing kind about it, and you should know that it's important to a father."

"Sheriff, you didn't... he didn't... did he?"

His grin becomes a chuckle. "No. But I almost expected it. I believe there was something holding him back."

Now she looks away. Hiding something from him. Keeping her secrets. Well, the fact that she's sitting here with him and talking to him at all is miracle enough.

And then, "There is something he wants me to know but I won't let him tell me."

"I see." And that's all he can say. And he feels to ask why she won't let that remarkable young man tell her would be prying so deep it would be cruel. For he has no desire to judge her or her thoughts or decisions; that's not a father's job and now that she's finally letting him be a father to her he will not cross the line. After a moment he says, "Even if *you* can live without knowing, I'm sure I don't know how Celina can."

"Celie will live," she retorts in such a way as to give him a hint things may not be so rosy there either. "Did you tell Mama about him?"

"I mentioned it. I had to, because she kept questioning my stance for allowing you to remain here until the end of the trial. She got suspicious and then asked outright. Was there a young man? And I told her there was, an extraordinary one. So then she not only pictured your health deteriorating but your whole future."

"I see."

"Her precious daughter. Lost to the Wild West. It was more than she could bear."

"You can say it, Sheriff."

He lets out a sigh. "And he's a Yankee."

"Mama... I'm never going to make her understand." A shaky sigh; tears slide down both pale cheeks. "None of this was supposed to happen. Not any of it."

"Don't fret now. Let's take one step at a time."

She blots her cheeks and dabs her eyes and looks up at him; he can just about see her heart breaking. "But I'm terribly afraid, Sheriff, that it all has to be done Mama's way."

She had that right; Elizabeth made sure all her children knew that *if Mama ain't happy, ain't nobody happy* to the core of their being before they were two years old.

"I have a feeling I might not ever see him again."

Cliff

"Doug, how are you?"

They grip hands and shake.

"Fine. What brings you here, Ryan? And you're returning my deputy. Chase…"

"Doug. What's been happening?"

"You'll be interested in this too, Ryan. I got one of my boys, Chris Dayton, posted in Bright River now. He patrols the valley ranches around the clock. Got a wire from him yesterday. Reckons one of the hands at the Diamond-T spotted some trespasses in the last few days. Dayton spent time checking it out but he hasn't seen anyone himself."

"Could be curiosity seekers – you know, famous trial…"

"Could be, but Dayton's staying on the job. Jittery cowhands ain't the most reliable lookouts. Now, Ryan, what's with you?"

Cliff tells Doug Mason about Worthing and Farrell first.

"Yeah, I sent Chase all I knew in the telegram. Faraday's investigating the company, right? We had no reports of trespasses last summer in the Bright River valley, so if there were any incidents, no one saw anything, at least no one's coming forward."

"I see. Well, the second thing, the reason I'm here – Bodecker's attorney Dillon Kerr has been missing for several weeks. We think we might know where he's hiding out."

"In this county?"

"Donnelly's ranch house to be precise."

Doug frowns. "Out there? Well, yeah, I guess it ain't a bad place to hide. Fair way out of town, and snow still about. No one would have any reason to go out there."

"Did you ever investigate it after we arrested Donnelly and Bodecker?"

"After the Maverick business you mean? No, to be honest. Thought the mavericks were all taken care of. They ain't?"

"I don't think this has got anything to do with mavericks. I think they were finished when Donnelly was arrested and if there were any left they wisely disbanded and melted into the general populace. No, this is about Dillon Kerr stealing Bodecker's mistress, a woman by the name of Eva Tarrant. Heard of her?"

"No. Why would Kerr stay so close?"

"As you say, the ranch is out of the way, but not so far out that Kerr can't keep an eye on what's going on in Cheyenne. He has some feller called Lamont from Denver working with him. I have a warrant to search the ranch. Any problem with me having Chase here come along when I head up to the ranch?"

Doug glances sideways at his deputy. "Up for it, Chase?"

"Roberts got us this lead. Think she'd like us to see it through."

"Roberts," Doug smiles, his tone mellow. "Last time I saw her she was heading back to Cheyenne; dropped by to see how we were getting on, pretty cut up about Dave. It sure was nice of her to check up on us. A girl like that don't come along every day. How is she, Chase?"

"Just the same. In the thick of it. Always asking questions."

The pair of them shares a laugh and they look like they want to continue reminiscing about her.

Irritated, Cliff clears his throat.

Doug Mason gets back to him. "Need anyone else for this, Ryan? It's a long way out of town, reinforcements will be hard to get in at a moment's notice."

"Who can you spare?"

"Well, I got this new kid. Came up from North Platte. Said he got tired of lickin' Ironpants Walker's behind."

"Who? – Nelson?"

"Sure. He said he knew you. Said you would give him a recommendation. He called you marshal so I figured if Deputy US Marshal Cliff Ryan would give this green kid a recommendation he might be all right."

Chase guffaws. Doug joins in.

"He's all right," Cliff concedes with a smile.

"Do you want him along?"

"Like you said, he's green."

"Well, he's made up some ground since you saw him last. Talks about you. Think you made an impression on the kid."

"Want to take him on, Ryan?" Chase asks with a gleam in his eye.

Things were a lot simpler when Dave Ransford was alive.

"How long does it take to get to the ranch?" he asks.

"You got winter conditions. You'll need a good hot meal before you start. Tends to get chancy up that way. The road is bad in parts. Doubles as a stock trail. And it'll get dark quick. Ride hard when you can. If the weather holds, you'll be there before supper. Train travel made you soft, Ryan?"

"No, it hasn't. Time is my only adversary, Doug. So, do you have a map?"

"Chase here knows the way."

"No offence, Chase," he says, "but I'd like to look at a map before we go."

Chase shrugs. "I'll get one then."

"Take it with you," Doug offers. "You never know when you might need it."

Emmaline

The Sheriff walks her to the Cheyenne Hotel where they are to meet her mama. Despite her own troubles, she can't help wondering…

"What do you love about Mama, Sheriff?"

He grins as he offers his arm and she takes it. "Oh, your mama got under my skin a long time ago."

"She's as bossy as the day is long."

Now he laughs. "She is that. But with the right word here and there I can completely disarm her. It's amusing, and fun to watch." His wicked words sublimated by a thoroughly charming smile uplift her spirits. He looks around as they walk through town. "But when it comes to you children…"

"You don't have to say more. I know that part."

It's when her parents meet in the dining room at the hotel, when the Sheriff kisses her mama's cheek and her mama's eyes light up at the welcome attention, that she recognizes them as a couple for the first time in her life. And she has to travel a long way back into her childhood to recall them as contented parents. Here they are as both.

Ashcliff, if he still cared, would be pleased, particularly since he should take most of the credit for her new found insight.

"Emmie dahlin…"

"Mama."

"Let's sit and drink somethin' warm…"

After yet another motherly inspection her mama's eyes lose some of their sparkle. That may be Emmaline's doing, but she refuses to feel guilty about it. Not at present anyway.

"Elizabeth, that's a fine idea," the Sheriff encourages in the calmest voice she's ever heard him use.

They sit at a table by the window where the activity in the street allows some welcome distraction from her mama's incessant watchfulness. When their warm refreshments arrive, it seems the only way to make it stop is to come right out and say…

"I have reached a decision."

"Oh, goodness gracious, Emmie, there's no decision to be made, there's only one thing to be done."

Emmaline swears in her head; these are desperate times. At least she caught it before it popped out.

Dear Mama. Kind to everyone and more tolerant than most; fighter of brave causes; loved and admired for her generosity. No woman worked harder to create a loving home, even in war and the most dreadful of times. They grew up accepting her tenacious mothering as her way of showing maternal love and raising upstanding citizens, and they mostly managed their way around it.

But in Emmaline's life there had never been a Yankee before.

"Elizabeth," says the Sheriff in that calm tone, "I'd like to hear what Emmaline has to say, wouldn't you?"

"Well, only if Emmie's about to say she's getting on the train with you and me tomorrow morning."

"Tomorrow morning?" she murmurs. "We couldn't wait…"

"Wait? For what? More cold to do more damage?"

Her mama prattles on some more but Emmaline doesn't hear all of it; her hands are shaking.

"I've always known I had to return home," she says beneath her mama's voice, "I'd like to do it on my own terms…"

Her mama stops speaking. "Emmie, you know it's rude to speak over a person. Where are your manners… and what terms?"

"The day after tomorrow."

"No."

What irony is this! One week ago she needed this vexing and bossy woman to waltz in and whisk her away and she would have welcomed it.

"Mama, there is someone I need to say goodbye to and he won't be back in town by tomorrow morning."

"He?"

"Yes, Mama, it's a he. So we will have to wait until…"

"You can leave a note."

"But…"

"I'm sure that will be fine. You write so well, Emmie."

Yes, indeed. Here is the very person who can obliterate all the guilt about leaving Ashcliff without ever having to face him again.

She exchanges glances with the Sheriff, but she can't read his expression.

"Mama, I'm not going to even try to explain this to you. I'm going to keep what is important and sacred to me intact."

"Whatever can you mean by all that, Emmie?"

"All I'm going to say is that I have to do what I must, what I have always had to do."

"And you will do it my way because I'm your mama and I know what's best. And that, Emmie dahlin, is leaving on tomorrow morning's train."

"And if I don't, Mama? What then?"

Her mama levels her eyes; Emmaline catches her breath.

"Then the excuse you've been looking for to extricate yourself gracefully from this place, Emmie, will have passed you by."

A swoonish feeling comes over her. The Sheriff slides a tumbler of water towards her and gently clasps her hand around it.

"Drink," he murmurs.

She sips, to marginal relief.

While staring at the tumbler in her trembling hand, she begins to comprehend how St Peter must've felt at the moment he realized he'd denied knowing Christ thrice before the cock crew. A cold sensation trickles down her arms, over her body and into her blood.

Betrayal.

She is not going to fight her mama on this.

Not that she could win anyway.

Or could she? She will never know because she is going to do what she must do. Save herself. And save Ashcliff.

"I have some things to finish up at the paper. And there are some people, friends I need to say goodbye to."

The Sheriff says, "I think these may be two of them now."

She looks over her shoulder. A couple of familiar faces come towards her. "Oh... yes."

Her father stands as Jennifer arrives at the table; he greets her and shakes hands with Luke.

"Keeping out of trouble, son?"

"Yes, sir."

"That's the ticket. I hear weddin' congratulations are in order."

"They are. Thank you. We heard you were in town."

"Word gets round fast."

"The Alliance has ears on every street corner."

"Well, it's good to see you both again and I wish you a lifetime of great happiness. Now, allow me to introduce my wife, Elizabeth. My dear, these fine young people are Luke and Jennifer Taylor..."

"Ma'am," Luke says.

"Mrs Roberts, it's a pleasure to meet you."

Luke's shrewd blue gaze is giving her mama the once-over, nothing less than she deserves. Meanwhile, Jennifer's fine Boston accent and New England demeanor would not have escaped her mama's notice. This would be the perfect time to add...

"Mama, Jennifer is a doctor. An awfully fine one."

Her mama's eyes go wide. "Please sit down, won't you?"

"Thank you," Jennifer replies; Luke draws chairs for them both and they make themselves comfortable. "Actually, I am Emmaline's doctor. It's a recent development."

"I see," the Sheriff murmurs.

"Then you would know why we are in town," her mama says.

"Emmaline is my patient and I am not at liberty to..."

"It's all right, Jennifer. Let's just get this over with."

"Are you sure that's what you want?"

"I'm sure. I can't stay; I have to go home..."

"You have to go home?" This from Luke, whose frown is cavernous. "I don't want to pry, Emmaline, but can I ask why?"

"You're not prying, Luke. Truth is, you were never meant to know what I'm about to tell you because I was not meant to stay in Cheyenne as long as I have. Or do the things I ended up doing. I didn't even realize just how cold Wyoming gets in winter."

Bafflement has turned into suspicion.

"I was never meant to become a friend of the Alliance, or meet Jennifer let alone become her patient. I wasn't meant to be at your weddin' and I definitely wasn't meant to..." She gulps and fights for her next breath. She will not say Ashcliff's name in her mama's presence. No matter what happens from here on in, she will keep his damyankee name sacred.

Luke comes to her rescue, murmuring, "I get it, Emmaline. I want to hear about why you're leaving."

She nods in appreciation and finds that steadying breath.

"I have this...this condition. There is something about my...my lungs and the cold. If I spend long periods in a cold climate, this climate for example, I develop symptoms that lead to pneumonia or some other dangerous complication. In temperate climates I am not affected."

On Luke's face is a look of genuine alarm.

She adds hastily, "Other than that, I am perfectly healthy."

He opens his mouth to comment, but evidently thinks better of it and clams up again.

"The cough..." Jennifer begins.

"The cough," her mama interrupts, "is usually a sign that pneumonia is next. But it was her pallor that alerted her father when he was here before. That's an early indication. Other symptoms include loss of breath, tightness in the chest...Emmie, you have experienced these?"

"Mrs Roberts..."

Her mama gives Jennifer *the look* which is both feared and revered by so many back in Orange County, Florida, including Orlando's mayor. Jennifer goes silent; Emmaline winces inwardly.

"You didn't tell anyone, Emmie?" her mama asks.

"I told Jennifer who was fast figuring out there was something the matter anyhow. Otherwise, no one else knows."

"No one?" the Sheriff asks.

She sighs at him. And shakes her head.

He rolls his eyes skyward.

"Your doctor is in Orlando," her mama continues, oblivious.

"I know, Mama. But, believe it or not, Cheyenne has doctors."

"And you have to go home?" Luke asks.

"Yes. It's warm. I won't get worse, and I'll get better faster. I cannot afford to contract pneumonia."

"May I ask how you got this condition?"

"You may," she smiles. He's being ever so polite, and he's going to need the information later. "I developed pneumonia twice during the winters I stayed in New England and my lungs have been susceptible to the cold ever since."

"If I may explain?" Jennifer asks her.

"Oh, I wish you would," she declares.

"Of course," Jennifer smiles and reaches across the table to give her hand a gentle squeeze of reassurance. "Medical research and clinical testing reveal that after a bout of pneumonia a patient's lungs become scarred and this scar tissue takes time go away. But in your case you developed another bout of pneumonia before the scar tissue had time to heal, and so now your lungs are weakened by even more scarring.

"A person's immunity to disease is severely affected by the cold, as you would know, but in my estimation, you, Emmaline, from what you have told me, are physiologically susceptible to the cold, and with your lungs weakened by the buildup of scarring you are at risk of your nemesis, pneumonia. You need a long spell in a warm climate and give those lungs a chance to heal completely, once and for all. When that is accomplished, you need to seek out ways to counter your susceptibility to the cold."

Emmaline sighs. "Thank you for explaining it. I feel much more hopeful when you explain it. I most always feel certain I will have it forever."

"We can't know the extent of the scarring, of course, but with the passage of time and taking good care of yourself, I think this problem will slowly but surely go away. Your constitution is strong; how else could you have survived bouts of pneumonia and all that you have accomplished since you've come to Cheyenne. You are certainly no weakling in my book, my friend, but unfortunately, your lungs are weakened and you may not be so lucky next time. Staying here in Cheyenne any longer than necessary is not an option for you."

Could Cheyenne be any more bittersweet?

She glances at Luke and can almost see the wheels of his mind working backwards...

In all the time of their acquaintance, through all his trials and tribulations, she has never known him to fall victim to self-pity, even in his melancholy; right now, he is a shining light in that regard, one she should keep in her sights.

"Perhaps there is a relative with a similar condition?" Jennifer is asking her parents. "These things sometimes run in families."

"Where did you receive your medical training, Mrs Taylor?"

Mama! She just won't quit.

"Boston. New York. St Louis."

The Sheriff says, "No one in the family has anything like this, even those that emigrated North and live there all year round."

"I see, thank you. Emmaline, would you like me to correspond with your doctor in Orlando? Conferring on cases like this is always useful."

While Emmaline is nodding, her mama is saying...

"Oh, I don't think that'll be necessary."

"Mama," Emmaline says, turning to her; her mama's eyes are glittering with the desperate need for control. But Emmaline exchanged a vow with Jennifer over tea and French fancies that they would always be friends, and while leaving Cheyenne may cost her many things, Jennifer's friendship will not be one of them. Better, though, to have Mama on side. "Jennifer is the smartest person you or I will ever meet. She is an exceptional doctor. Better than any doctor we know. I think it's a wise thing to have her on my case. You say yourself that two heads are always better than one, and if one of those heads is Jennifer's then I feel better already."

Her mama looks at her with some sympathy at last. Emmaline is exhausted from the tension; her mama could be so frazzling.

"Well, then, you shall have two doctors, Emmie."

"So, are you happy now, Mama, about the arrangements?"

"Ask me again tomorrow when we are on the train."

Even when you're handing them your soul on a plate there is just no pleasing some people.

Emmaline

"Guess I knew I couldn't keep you forever," Mr Quaid says after she breaks the news she is leaving town. He genuinely looks downcast at the prospect of losing her, which is heart-warming.

They reminisce for a spell.

"You were brave, Roberts," he concludes, "to take us on and then stick around when it got rough."

He ducks out after about ten minutes to attend to something and when he returns they spend considerable time looking over *Empire for Liberty*.

"Can't wait to print it!" He writes her an awfully fine reference and includes a generous bonus with her final pay.

"Do I deserve this, Mr Quaid?"

"Roberts, do you even need to ask? The Tribune won't be the same newspaper without you. I think you made it the paper it was always meant to be. I can't replace you but I'm gonna damn well try. And, you did everything I asked of you and far more – except for one thing."

She wracks her brains.

"You promised me you wouldn't become romantically attached. Even that you did with style and grace. Didn't even know it had happened until the last few days."

Her body flashes hot, then turns cold, leaving the heat in her cheeks. She slides her check and reference in her satchel hoping he thinks she didn't hear him.

"Roberts, he's a good man. Are you sure you want to run out on

300

him? And, I don't know, you kinda go well together, when I think about it. I should've seen it; he always showed an interest in you."

Does Mr Quaid honestly think she could discuss her 'romance' with Ashcliff after she spent the past two months hiding it from him? That's a newspaper editor for you.

Thankfully, their cub reporter Zachary makes an entrance, holding a largish box. "Roberts, I took the liberty of packing up your things from your desk. Everything's in here, all your papers, books and such, but you can check for yourself before you leave."

"That's decent of you, Zac. Thank you kindly."

And she relieves him of the box.

"Good luck, Roberts."

"And you."

He doffs a salute and leaves.

On the top of her bits and pieces is a parcel. "What's this?"

Mr Quaid clears his throat. "They wanted to get you something. Say goodbye. They knew you wouldn't want a fuss, so they arranged for Zac to clear out your desk and... well, you know."

"That was so kind of them." She swallows a lump. "Thank you, Mr Quaid, for everything. You'll never know how much I've learned and how much I appreciated your faith in me."

"I think I know. You'll be missed, Roberts. Make no mistake. When I think of the things you've done... January twenty-sixth was a seminal day in the life of this newspaper..."

The day she shivered in from the cold and had to restrain herself from calling him Chuck. She finds herself smiling. "Thank you. I'll miss the Tribune, every day."

He grins, his necktie still as lopsided as ever. "Sorry you had such a hard time of it. See that you get better. Send me stuff. Whatever you like. And come back in June. We'll give you a summer. And there'll be a job for you. Anytime."

Her spirits lift. "You mean that?"

"Well, I wouldn't have said it if I didn't. And there'll be no conditions either. I apologize, Roberts, I should've revoked that stupid condition when I realized what kind of reporter you were."

"No need to apologize; I wouldn't've changed a thing," she murmurs and smiles at the surprise on his face.

"I really think you mean that."

"Take care of yourself, Mr Quaid."

"Likewise."

"And take care of my story."

"I will. You'll get a copy, don't worry. I'll be in touch."

She stands at her desk and gives it one last going over. Seems to her that it looks exactly like it did the afternoon she arrived. What words have crossed its bow! What stories came into being!

She says her goodbyes to her colleagues; thanks them for the gift; tells them she won't ever forget them. Simons echoes the sentiment and suggests she open her gift.

Dispensing with the brown paper, she uncovers a notebook cover of beautifully tanned leather with her initials embossed in gold leaf on the front; inside sits one of the notebooks she likes to use, except in this one the front pages are adorned with their individual messages of farewell and good wishes.

"This... this is truly amazing," she stammers. "How did y'all manage so quickly?"

Zachary gives a sheepish grin. "My pa."

"Of course... his wonderful leather store."

Mr Quaid talked Zachary's pa into letting Zachary pursue his desired path in the newspaper business, not follow his father as a master leather craftsman. Mr Quaid is proud of the boy's progress.

"We've been scrambling around for the last hour while you finished up with the Chief," Simons explains further. "No one was going to leave for the day until we got to say goodbye, Emmaline,"

They all nod, smiling. Simons never calls her Emmaline.

"It's beautiful, thank you. I will treasure it. And my time here at the Tribune. And I'll miss every single one of you."

Will Dobson takes her hand in his printer's ink-stained ones. "You're a good girl, you are. See that you stay that way, poppet. All the luck in the world then."

Poppet? Oh well...

It's time to go.

She is no longer Roberts.

She's Emmaline.

Outside, her box cradled in one arm, she pulls the Tribune's front door closed. Her right hand lingers on the doorknob. With the noises of the street at her back, she sighs...

Goodbye, my friend.

Emmaline

On Luke's insistence, the Roberts family is to meet at the Keatons' house; Emmaline suspects a farewell. A card game is coming to an end when they arrive; Amy and Signora have tabled a large and aromatic meal guaranteed to tempt a fasting nun. While the Sheriff is greeted like an old friend, her mama is welcomed as a new one.

The circumstances of her leaving and ill-health are met with heartfelt words of dismay and disbelief.

The Severinis plead with her to stay; the torrent of Italian mentions *Signore Sceriffo Ryan*, *Padre Francesco* and *Chiesa di Santo Giovanni Battista* numerous times.

Raina rescues her and takes her aside. Looking troubled, she says, "If I had known you are unwell, Emmaline, I would never have burdened you with my problem."

"Raina, if I had felt burdened I would have told you I was busy and left the bookstore. I was pleased to help, to offer my suggestions. Jacob Hunter is a serious threat and I sincerely hope you manage to deal with it."

Raina ventures a smile. "I don't want you to worry, Emmaline. All our concerns will be behind you very soon. Jacob Hunter will cease to matter and all will be well. It's just that you mean so much to everyone here, we are going to miss you terribly."

Emmaline sniffs; at their next afternoon tea there would have been four…

When Tressa comes up to her there are tears in her eyes. "Please write to me, Emmaline, to tell me you're better."

"I'll write often. And so must you. I want to hear about Adam."

"I promise. Now you will receive more anecdotes of him than you can possible bear."

"Come visit me, Tress... you and Adam?"

"Visit? I can't think of anything I'd enjoy more, but, Emmaline, they would never allow it."

"Who?"

"Them." Tressa looks over her shoulder at all the people gathered in the room, busily talking to each other in small groups.

"Maybe they'll come too," Emmaline shrugs.

They smile at one another, then hug for a long time; it is a timely reminder that there is deeper pain in the world than hers.

During the meal her Alliance friends warm her with sentiments of love and appreciation.

Ethan stands up and makes a short speech, looking at her with soulful eyes and telling her she'll never know how much she's done for them all, how grateful they are, that she will always be part of them and she's not to be a stranger.

"We mean it, Emmaline," he concludes.

Her mama looks unsure of what to make of all this Italian flavored western hospitality and the confounded fuss about her daughter.

Meanwhile, an encouraging wink from the Sheriff helps her finds some words of reply.

"I think this has been the most interesting chapter of my life."

"And you fervently hope it never gets this interesting again, right, Emmaline?" Tip chimes in.

When the laughter dies down, she says, "I thank you for your friendship, you will be in my thoughts often, and I hope we meet again in less trying times."

Gruffly, John Keaton says, "You did good, Emmaline."

When at last it is time to leave, her goodbyes are almost as taxing on her as the cold weather.

Luke and Jennifer go with them to the Faradays, who are settling down for a quiet afternoon in their beautiful home.

She wishes Meg well for the birth of their child; Constance interrupts and sticks out her hand for Emmaline to shake. As she does so, Constance says, "You're quite a gal, Miss Roberts, but then you're southern and that speaks volumes. Get better and come back again. These folks are gonna miss ya."

Texas-raised Constance heads back to the kitchen, leaving Meg to roll her eyes and give Emmaline a hug.

"Be at peace, Emmaline. And don't let others be the judge and jury of your decisions. Only you know what's right for you."

"Thank you, Meg. You are so wise; I won't forget."

Correction. At their next afternoon tea, there would have been five…

Mr Faraday waits patiently to speak with her. He takes her hand and holds onto it. Their first meeting is clear in her mind; she hadn't expected him to be so nice. He turned out to be a friend.

"I'm sorry, Mr Faraday, to be letting you down this way…"

"Miss Roberts, it is not possible for you to let me down. No one has done more for this case than you. I wish I could have put you on the stand at least once more."

"I understand, Mr Faraday."

"We're going to miss you, more than you know. On both a personal and professional level your contribution has been extraordinary. How many leads have you found for us and how loyal you have been! Words can't begin to describe how grateful I am."

"No words are needed. It's been an honor and a privilege. Good luck with the rest of the trial. I know you will succeed."

"Emmaline," he says, his voice low and tense, his use of her Christian name clearly for effect, "I must say this…"

"I wish you wouldn't."

"Wait, another day…"

"Mr Faraday…"

"He loves you, Emmaline."

This from Mr Faraday, of all people…

Her throat dries up.

"You are freeing something in Cliff that has been struggling to see the light of day for a very long time and I have been privileged enough to witness it. He is one of the best men I have ever known and I could not let you leave without telling you that."

"I… don't know what to say."

"Then just know what to do. Wait, one more day."

"I appreciate what you are saying, Mr Faraday, really…"

He slides his hands slowly into his pockets, sensing her *but* without her having to say it, which is just as well since her throat has closed up.

"Then I will say no more about it."

He manages an unhurried smile, characteristic of him.

"Good-bye, Mr Faraday," she says, recovering. "I wish you and Meg well for the birth of your child. You will be a proud papa before you know it. And thank you for not subpoenaing me before a grand jury."

His smile broadens. "Miss Roberts, there is no one quite like you."

They leave Luke and Jennifer with the Faradays, and now there is only one stop left.

Mac is pottering about like he's been *sceriffo* for years.

"Ah, my favorite reporter. What's up?"

While her parents stand at a respectful distance and out of earshot, she explains, with a plaguing lump in her throat.

Mac listens, wide-eyed, clearly shocked.

"Emmaline, I can't believe this. Felt to me like you'd be here forever. Won't be the same without you."

"Say goodbye to Pat and the twins for me? I'll miss them. And I'll miss you, Mac. I will write to y'all. And, for goodness sake, stop working so hard."

"Now don't you go worryin' about me and work. Look at me – plain as day I'm like a pig in mud. You just get well now, y'hear?"

"That's the plan, and I will be fine. Take care of yourself, Mac. And thank you for being a friend. You saved my life. I'll never forget it or you."

"Aw, you don't have to mention that again. Glad I was on hand…" He swallows hard, his eyebrows moving from side to side. "What do I tell him?"

"The truth, Mac. My time to leave came sooner than expected. But it came. That is the truth."

Cliff

"How much further?" Nelson asks, shifting in his saddle.

"The gate marking the ranch boundary shouldn't be far now," Chase encourages him.

"How far from there?"

Chase doesn't look like he knows. Or cares to say.

Cliff recalls the map without digging it out of his saddlebag. "At this pace in these conditions from here to the ranch house maybe an hour, probably less."

Nelson doesn't sigh out loud, but the cloud of white pouring from his mouth betrays him; the kid's tired and saddle-weary. And they ate a long way back.

Cliff recalls Emma's determination and stamina during the time of the mavericks. The empty ache inside him isn't from lack of food. He's lonely for her, and it would be better not to think about her, but that's like asking the sun not to shine.

The time goes by in bitter cold, in a mixture of ice and snow. Deloight proves keen at keeping his eyes peeled; he sees critters ducking behind trees, and reports on the deepening sky, about moonrise and stars, which seems odd to Cliff. He relates well to Nelson, keeping the kid relaxed. But for the most part, they don't speak at all.

They pass beneath the ranch gate, which bears no name or marking, and proceed slowly for some time in failing light until in the distance they see corals. The whole place is quiet. On the perimeter of the ranch house yard they dismount and take stock.

"What do you see?" Chase asks.

"Nothing. You and Nelson wait here. I'll take a look around the back."

"We'll wait."

Cliff creeps along the perimeter in the gloomy dusk, scooting from tree to bush to post until he makes his way around to the back. The two-story ranch house is compact and attractively situated in a small forest. From behind a water trough he peers up at it. There, coming from one upstairs window, is the faintest of light. His heart pushes out extra beats and keeps up a fast pace. He needs to steady himself. He's waited a long time to get Dillon Kerr. A long time.

Using various objects within the yard as cover, he makes his way to the back door. And listens.

Nothing.

Time to look. The windowpane in the back door is draped but a slotted separation in the drapes reveals only gloominess within. He tries the handle next; he's half way through the turn when the high-pitched sound of a woman's voice stops him. Gingerly, he releases the handle and stays put, straining his ears.

He can't make out what she's saying; most of it is trite laughter anyway. Then the sound recedes, as if she has moved into another room. He resumes his work on the door handle. This time there are no interruptions. The door opens up for him and he slips inside.

He listens even more intensely. He can hear noises from within the house but to locate them he will have to move about in the gloom, so he allows time for his eyes to become accustomed to it before he continues. This is the kitchen; table and chairs to be cautiously negotiated.

Into a short hall.

Sounds become louder and unmistakable. He makes it to the parlor doorway from where the dying embers of a fire shed some light on the room and its occupants.

Two bodies recline on a rug in front the hearth. He recognizes Dillon Kerr, even if he is…

There's no point in disbelief. It is what it is.

And it certainly is *not* a hideout fortified by remnant mavericks. Not yet at least.

The woman springs up, laughing and twittering, luring Kerr to chase after her. He catches her and pins her onto the sofa. Things get kind of frantic and Cliff doesn't know where to look. A fleeting insight causes him to wonder if this is what Emma witnessed; she would go to Nugent with this. He doesn't blame her. Still, there is something a little more human about Kerr this way. He leaves them to it. He'll be back, with reinforcements.

Chase greets him. "Well?"

"They're in there all right."

"Wow wee," Nelson declares. "Kerr and Tarrant? What are they doing?"

"You don't want to know."

Chase lets out a laugh. "Caught in the act?"

"What act?"

"Nelson," Cliff says, thinking it's about time the kid grew up, "consider what a man and a woman half-naked by the fire in the dark would be doing?"

Nelson gulps. "What do we do now?"

"Go in and get them," Cliff says.

"Naked?"

"As long as we're not naked," he retorts and Chase collapses into laughter. Nelson gives him a shove.

"I ain't never seen a real life naked woman before."

"This'll be your first," Chase says.

"Should we wait 'til they're finished what they're doin'?"

"I..." Cliff begins and then has to stop and swallow his laughter. "Trust me, by the time we get in, they'll be finished."

Chase looks like he wants roll around on the ground; he's holding his middle, leaning back against a tree. "So, how do we go in..."

Cliff tries to grunt over his laughter; Chase falls to the ground.

"I don't think it's so funny," Nelson whines.

Cliff perseveres. "Chase, you and Nelson, go in the back way and take them by surprise. Watch Kerr for a weapon..."

"Not on him though..." Chase cackles.

"Ryan, Deloight is being stupid. Tell him he's being stupid."

"It's been a long, cold ride, Nelson," Cliff tells the kid while

Chase finishes enjoying his own joke. "Okay. The weapon, if there is one, could be anywhere. That's why one of you takes Kerr and the other keeps his eyes peeled."

"You sure there ain't no one else in the house?" Nelson asks.

Chase sobers. "The kid's got a point."

"I know. That's why I'll find another way in while you are both very cautiously and *quietly* making for the back door. I'll cover the second story once I'm inside. I'll come downstairs when it's clear."

"How do you arrest a half-naked woman?" Nelson asks.

"I don't know. How *do* you arrest a half-naked woman?" Chase returns.

Nelson blows. "I ain't telling no joke, you jackass. I'm asking. How do you arrest a half-naked woman?"

Chase is beside himself. A luxury Cliff does not have.

"You tell her to put some clothes on," he says. "Or cover herself... Now give me a few minutes before you set off."

He leaves the pair and using tree trunks and water troughs and such as cover he makes his way to the front door. How stupid can Kerr be? There are no guards. No precautions. Clearly, he perceived no threat or chance of ever being caught. Even the front door is unlocked. Cliff lets himself into a small entrance hall, and again his eyes must become accustomed to the enclosed darkness. He comes to the staircase which rises just before the parlor door. He sticks his head into the room and takes another look at the situation. They are still at it in one way or another, shadow and form cavorting and tangling in the deep ember light. Their own little love nest. Courtesy of Donnelly. How fitting.

He moves up the stairs with painstaking caution so not to disturb the treads with his weight. In the gloom of the upstairs hall he allows himself to breathe. The pale light he saw earlier comes from a room at the end of the hall, facing the backyard. He needs to be sure there is no one in there, that it's just another place for lover boy and his stolen mistress to play.

He peels back the door.

There is no sound, only what he can hear coming from downstairs in the parlor, Eva Tarrant's muffled squeals of delight and Kerr's deep-throated encouragement.

He goes from cupboard to unmade bed to washstand.

Clothes are strewn all over the place. He grabs several pieces of women's apparel and takes them with him. Then he checks the other two rooms, but they are neat and unused. The bathroom is vacant.

When he makes it to the bottom of the stairs again, he steadies his breathing and peers into the parlor. The pair is quiet now, lying by the fire.

Eva murmurs, "When is Lamont returning?"

"He's staying in Cheyenne for a few days."

Cliff strains to listen for more about Lamont.

"Pity," she says.

"You and he… Did you sleep with him, Eva?"

"Well, you were away. I was bored, sewing and cooking. He…"

"He what?"

"He… You know…"

"What did he do to you?"

"Give me your hand, Dill."

"A lady shouldn't, and a gentleman wouldn't," Kerr says, with either gallantry or annoyance that he hadn't.

"Oh, me and Lamont think all that is just plain nonsense."

There has to be a more palatable way of acquiring information. He moves back to the bottom of the staircase, shakes his head at the stupidity of the situation and sticks his fingers in his ears.

Come on, Chase. Where the hell are you?

When the muffled sounds seem to have receded, he removes one finger; satisfied that decency has returned and it's safe to continue, he resumes his position by the door to be ready for Chase's entrance.

Kerr has Eva's body pinned beneath his. "I was away for three days. He bedded you for three days?"

"Mm. Well, we didn't do it in bed at the start, Dill. That came the next morning. It kinda started in the kitchen; he came in from chopping wood that first day, I was fixing supper. He came up to me and started unbuttoning my blouse. I asked him what he was doing; he said he was gonna thank me for being such a good cook and that I should call him Kit. I said he should stop, but he was persistent and it felt kinda nice so I let him have his way. Truth be told, Dill, I thought I was gonna faint. He never kissed me on the mouth or nothin', least not at first."

"Not at first. Eva... You were whoring with him for three days?"

"Well, you know how it is, once we got started it was hard to stop. He'd get awful passionate. I liked it, Dill. I liked it a lot. You won't kill him or nothing, will you? "

"Eva, you're my woman now. You can't go being with other men if you want to be with me. You gotta stop. Say no. Mean it.

"It's hard to say no when a man comes looking for favors and they got so much to offer in return. I couldn't never say no to Lamont. You see, Dill, we kept doing it, even when you got back, before Lamont left again. I'd give him a certain look and he'd know to go meet me in the barn. And whenever you was reading downstairs he'd pull me into his room. He'd get ever so excited. I think he was in love with me or somethin'."

Cliff looks away yet again. *Hell, Kerr, are you really going to put up with this whore?*

"Eva, I'm disappointed in you."

"I'm sorry, Dill. I got fond of Lamont."

"A man doesn't want to share his woman, don't you understand that?"

"You shouldn't go into town for so long."

"I had business to attend to in Laramie."

"What business, Dill? Was there a woman there you like...?"

Oh boy.

"Women aren't business. Besides, there's no other woman, Eva. Only you."

"Dill, you're sweet. I love you, and I do prefer you to anyone, but you gotta stop going off on business and leaving me. How's I suppose to keep Lamont away from me?"

Come on, Chase.

"I understand, Eva. I do. Still, you have no idea how to be faithful to a man, do you?"

"Guess not."

"Guess I'll have to teach you." Kerr decides at that moment to give her a lesson.

Is this really necessary? Someone should tell Dill to think of other ways of showing Eva there's more to love than keeping a woman flat on her back.

Then: "Okay, you two, Stand up."

Chase!

Thank God.

Basically, hell breaks loose for several moments. Particularly after Nelson – who had been yelling *they was at it, I saw they was at it, my mama wouldn't like this* – turns up the lamp on Chase's instructions and light floods the room.

The couple is shocked. Eva Tarrant scampers about trying to cover her wanton self unsuccessfully with anything she can lay her hands on; meanwhile Dillon Kerr expresses his outrage, moving recklessly about the room as he shouts.

Cliff springs from the other direction. "Don't move, Kerr."

"Ryan!" he yelps in absolute horror. "What are you doing!?"

"Check for a weapon," Cliff says to Chase, who promptly inspects the room, tossing cushions all over the place.

"Ryan!" Kerr shouts, almost foaming at the mouth.

"Evening, Dillon. Nice fire. Put your pants on."

Cliff tosses the pieces of apparel he collected from upstairs at Eva who catches them with a stunned look on her face. "Put them on."

"Nothing," Chase reports.

"Ryan..." Kerr growls this time.

"Don't wear it out, Kerr."

"You can't do this!" he shouts, reaching for a pair of pants on a nearby armchair.

"Got a warrant, and what I find I can take back to Cheyenne. So far I found you and Mrs Tarrant here. Chase and Nelson are going to take good care of you while I have a look around."

Cliff pulls out the warrant. Flashes it in Kerr's face.

"How did you find me?" Kerr grinds out.

Nelson, meanwhile, is trying not to watch Eva Tarrant wriggle into her clothes.

"You know, Kerr, if you wanted to do this you should have run a million miles away. Chances were pretty high you would be caught. What were you thinking?"

"He wasn't thinking with his brain, Marshal," Chase says.

"Mrs Tarrant has that effect on some men, Chase."

"Marshal?" Kerr squawks.

"Term of affection," Cliff says. "Where'd you get to, Chase?"

"Sorry. Trouble in the yard. Noises. Turned out to be a critter. Timing wasn't good?"

"What timing?"

Chase shrugs an apology.

"Now, how about we tie you two up."

"I need more clothes," Eva declares, her breasts half bare as she fiddles about putting on her calico blouse and skirt.

"Need some help with those buttons, Mrs Tarrant?" Cliff asks.

She gasps. "No, I do *not!*"

"Then stop wasting time. We've all seen breasts before. Yours are nothing out of the common way, despite what Dill here thinks of them."

She hisses at him. Then turns her back on them and appears to button her blouse. They hear her murmur, "It's not polite to spy on other people."

Cliff says, "Trust me, your distaste can never be greater than mine. Now, where's Lamont?"

Kerr takes the chair Chase is indicating he should sit in. "Who's Lamont?"

Cliff shakes his head. "I don't have time for this. Tie them up. I'm searching the whole house. Keep your eyes peeled, Chase."

"Sure, Marshal."

"Sure, Marshal," Nelson echoes.

Cliff starts pulling drawers and cupboards open all over the house. A thorough search reveals nothing, except two Winchesters in a gun cabinet. He takes the ammunition and stuffs it in his pockets. Irritated, he pulls up a chair and sits down in front of the pair. Tarrant is shivering; Kerr glares back insolently.

"Nelson. Upstairs bedroom. Fetch Mrs Tarrant a coat."

"Sure thing, Ryan."

Tarrant's eyes follow Nelson out of the room.

"Chase, go through the house once more, make sure I didn't miss anything."

"I'm on it."

Cliff shifts his chair closer and gets Eva's attention.

"So, Mrs Tarrant, who is Lamont?"

"I… I don't know any Lamont."

"But he was under your skirts for three days while lover boy here was in town. You've been having the time of your life, haven't you, Eva?"

The woman looks pale and sulky in the lamplight.

"You already know who Lamont is, Ryan, so stop playing games and leave Eva out of this. She's just…"

"A whore?"

"A woman. She's just a woman."

"How gallant of you, Dillon. So then, what does Lamont do, apart from messing around with your woman?"

"He doesn't do anything. He's a friend is all."

"A friend who…" He stops and runs his eye over the voluptuous Eva.

Kerr reacts, pulling against his restraints. "Bastard…"

"Save the vitriol for Lamont, Dill. What do you say, Eva? Dill has quite a lot to be jealous about."

Nelson appears with a coat; twice he attempts to throw it on the woman's shoulders and misses.

"Nelson?"

"What, Ryan?"

"She's only a woman. Just drape it over her."

He achieves this at last, much to Eva Tarrant's relief.

"Nelson, now go stand at the front window and keep an eye on the yard."

"Sure, Ryan."

When Nelson has gone, he says, "We're not going back tonight, we start in the morning. You two can make yourselves comfortable right here. Well, I guess that's where we found you, so you should be fine."

"You're going to regret this, Ryan," Kerr grinds out.

He already does. Even as he left Cheyenne. But, regrets pushed aside, he has a job to do and he'll be doing it till it's finally over.

When Chase returns with nothing to show for his search but the Winchesters, Cliff has him watch Kerr while he unties Eva and orders her into the kitchen to put some supper together.

"Just so you know, Mrs Tarrant, lover boy here will be the first to eat it, so I wouldn't try anything clever if I were you."

"I got my pride," she says with a pout.

He expects another kind of trouble as well, so he adds, "Button that coat right up, Mrs Tarrant."

Emmaline

Later in the evening Emmaline sits beside her suitcase on the bed and draws close the box Zachary packed up for her at the Tribune. With the waste basket by her feet, she bins an assortment of notes and drafts of copy, followed by several pencil stubs, and finds some room in her luggage for a couple of books: her indispensable guide to perfect grammar and her pocket dictionary. She keeps no drafts as mementos; the only keepsake she needs is *Empire for Liberty*, and she has that securely packed already.

At the very bottom of the box is a small brown paper package; her heart leaps and begins to race, for tucked into the string is an envelope with her name written on it. *Miss Emmaline Roberts.*

Signore sceriffo Ryan's handwriting...

She stares at the package for a long, strange time, confused as to how it got in the box. To be in the box meant it had to be at her desk. How did she not ever notice a package from Ashcliff on her desk? A great many things seemed to keep her from her desk in the last couple of days. She missed something.

She never misses anything.

But she had.

She can barely steady her hands to take it. Another age seems to pass by while she stares at it, knowing on the other side of that brown paper is a small book. An inner voice, sounding very much like Celie's, is warning her not to unwrap it, but a fervent emotion is building inside her that's stronger than any warning.

She strikes at the white envelope and rips it open. She unfolds the letter and does not hesitate, forcing herself to read.

Dearest Emma,

I must beg your forgiveness because I can't meet you this afternoon. I want to, more than I can possibly express with words, it's just that the black suits are fiercely testing and examining our relationship in court and I don't want to think what Buchanan would do if someone reported seeing us together. So, in these strange and unpredictable times, this is a precaution. My one thing may not be possible for a while yet. And securing the best part of my day, the most important part of my day, Emma, will continue to stretch my imagination to even greater heights (than Nan's climbing plant).

My own Emma. I love you and I will always love you. I believe I know what's in your heart; and I know you think leaving is your only choice. Tell me you want me to follow you and I'll be there, I swear. I remain forever and always your James Ashcliff Ryan.

Those tears she had earlier refused to shed now flood her eyes.

Over and over she reads his letter, losing count of how many times, with his voice in her head reciting the words.

By and by, his voice becomes the inducement to reach for the package; she pulls the string and paper apart. A small, slender, dark red book is in her hands. The title is elegant, being embossed in gold lettering:

CLASSIC LOVE POEMS: A TREASURY

A cream velvet ribbon, scented like roses, peaks out of the bottom of the volume. She opens it at the marked page.

THE GOOD-MORROW
John Donne, 1572-1631

She caresses the page, her fingers traveling over the words he read and the paper he touched as he chose the poem for her.

The perfect poem.

The poem that has been reciting itself in her heart for days.

She reads it with eyes tear-burnt and stinging and hungry.

> I wonder, by my troth, what thou and I
> Did, till we lov'd? were we not wean'd till then?
> But suck'd on country pleasures, childishly?
> Or snorted we in the Seaven Sleepers' den?

'Twas so; but this, all pleasures fancies bee.
If ever any beauty I did see,
Which I desir'd, and got, 'twas but a dreame of thee.

These last two lines are underlined with pencil.
The poem continues:

And now good-morrow to our waking soules,
Which watch not one another out of feare;
For love, all love of other sights controules,

Again the soft pencil beneath…
And makes one little roome an everywhere.

Her chest aches as she recalls feeling precisely this way as they talked in the lamplight of her room.

Let sea-discoverers to new worlds have gone,
Let Maps to other, worlds on worlds have showne,
Let us possesse one world, each hath one, and is one.

How acutely was he listening as she spoke about their two worlds being worlds apart!

My face in thine eye, thine in mine appeares,
And true plaine hearts doe in the faces rest;
Where can we finde two better hemispheares,
Without sharpe North, without declining West?
Whatever dyes, was not mixt equally;
If our two loves be one, or, thou and I
Love so alike, that none doe slacken, none can die.

The beauty, to her eyes at least, of the early modern English complete with the Old to Middle English inflexions soothes her momentarily, and he would have known that would also please her.

Her gaze settles on the poem for an immeasurable time before she thinks to turn to the front of the book and look for an inscription. And he has written: *Darling Emma, If our two loves be one, or you and I love so alike that neither slackens, neither love can die. For eternity. James*

She feels immense sadness bearing down upon her as terrible pain, crushing her beneath its vast and cruel weight.

"My poor Ashcliff."

Time carries her forward to her next task; she slips the treasury of poems into her pocket, goes to her packed luggage and rummages until she finds a package, also wrapped in brown paper and string. After she has refreshed her face, she dons her coat and hat, muffler and gloves, and heads off one last time into the brittle cold and darkness. By the time she arrives at Luke and Jennifer's house her chest aches.

Surprise hovers behind their warm and earnest welcome.

"You absolutely should not be out in this cold, Emmaline," Jennifer says as she embraces her.

"This is important," she reassures them while absorbing the affectionate gesture like air to breathe.

Luke fixes her in front of the fire. "Enjoy!"

She manages a smile.

"How may we help?" Jennifer asks.

"I was hoping you wouldn't mind giving this to Cliff when he returns. He'll know what it is. Something we had arranged. I want him to have it." She deposits the package on the nearby lamp table.

"Of course we wouldn't mind," Jennifer murmurs.

But Luke looks frustrated. "Can't you wait till he gets back, Emmaline? You can give it to him yourself. It's only a day or two. Cliff will understand about everything and you can work it out..."

"Believe me, this is not how I intended to leave Cheyenne – before the end of the trial and on my mother's terms. But if you would just give Cliff the package..."

"Well, of course, we'll give it to him."

Luke grunts. "You leaving like this, well, it'll break his heart."

What is it with the men in this town – romance is like their hobby! She closes her eyes and takes a deep breath. When she releases it, she dispels her annoyance. "I must go."

Jennifer says, "Stay awhile..."

"Cliff is your closest friend. I understand your loyalty, but..."

Luke flinches. "And you... you who have done so much for us, gone through so much with us, aren't our close friend? Emmaline, c'mon."

She stares at him, a little stunned.

"You have our loyalty always. We want you to be happy. You have done things, discovered things, which changed our fortunes. I think we may have changed yours. I owe my life to you. So it doesn't matter where you go or what you do, Emmaline, you have to know you are always bound to us. And that includes Cliff."

She swallows hard. "I know we, all of us, share this destiny, but I was *always* destined to leave Cheyenne."

He gives her a penetrating look. "You're not in the least bit curious as to how things might turn out if you wait one more day?"

"Don't," she snaps.

"Luke..." Jennifer murmurs. A look passes between them.

"I'm sorry," he gulps, looking stricken and helpless.

She swallows again. "I understand, but there's no use wishing things were different. This is how it must be and Cliff and I both know it. We have discussed it and that's all I can say. Perhaps you don't believe me, think I'm making it up, I don't know..."

"No..." Jennifer gasps. "We would never think that."

"Then I beg you not to press me any further for the fairy tale outcome you want when I can't give it to you. I just can't. Leaving is difficult, yes, but I've worked hard and achieved what I set out to do, I deserve nothing less than a graceful and dignified departure."

They stand there quietly absorbing her outburst.

Then Luke lets out a long sigh. "You're right, Emmaline."

"There is nothing more I can say, so now I should go."

"What can you go back to," Jennifer says, "but a tidy room and your luggage."

The bleakness contained in that remark seems to ocean an endless future of more bleakness.

"What I mean is that it's your last evening with us. Please stay. I'll make fresh coffee. We could talk. About your plans if you like."

"I would stay, but I... I need to finish my packing and..."

"You need time on your own," Jennifer finishes.

She gives a nod, with a vague attempt at smiling.

"Then we'll see you home," Luke says. "I'll get our coats."

Cliff

In the early hours of the morning Cliff relieves Chase on watch; Chase drapes himself in an armchair, says he has nothing to report and promptly falls asleep. Cliff rubs his eyes and studies the upright forms of Tarrant and Kerr, their heads lolling forward as they doze. In the low lamplight, Cliff tries to spot Nelson; he sleeps curled up in the corner of the room as far as possible from Kerr and Eva Tarrant's messily clad body and tousled hair.

There is a chill in the room. Quietly, he lays another log on the fire and watches while short, teeth-like flames run along the bark and begin to consume the log.

Kerr lets out a snort, his head swinging awkwardly and then he resumes snoring again. Very romantic, lover boy.

So, if this is similar to what Emma came across, Kerr and Tarrant making love, then he begins to understand why she did not tell him about them.

She wanted them to get away and live happily ever after.

He smiles at that.

She knew he would find them and capture them.

She was protecting them from him.

His smile widens.

Emma looked beyond their licentiousness and adultery and Kerr's connection to Bodecker. She thought the intense feeling between these two lovers redeeming. He's kind of impressed, although he hopes Nugent set her straight. He probably did, which is why the guilt got to her and she had to report what she discovered but not surrender Kerr.

No one looking at Eva Tarrant would call her a dignified individual, but Emma's actions and unique insight have given this pathetic, mistreated woman far more dignity than Eva could ever have imagined for herself.

Now he's taking it all away.

For an odd moment he feels cruel, like he's crushed an harmless insect beneath the heel of his boot.

And he can't shake the feeling that Emma used this situation to manufacture a happy ending for these two as a substitute for her own.

Before dawn, Cliff gives Dillon Kerr a shake. Kerr flops about until he becomes conscious. Cliff motions him to be quiet. Then he unties him and points to the kitchen. Kerr gets to his feet, a little clumsy at first; Cliff grips his arm and steadies him, steering him past Eva in the other chair, Chase in the armchair and Nelson in the corner, and into the kitchen. The remnant of the supper fire has kept the kitchen warm. Cliff shuts the door and turns up the flame in the table lamp.

"What is this, Ryan?" Kerr whispers.

"I want to bargain with you, Kerr."

"Sure you do, Ryan."

Cliff sits in the chair next to him, close and keeping his voice to a whisper. "Do you love the woman?"

"What?"

"I asked if you love the woman."

Kerr frowns and stares hard at him. "What's it to you?"

"Answer me."

Kerr looks away and sighs. "Yes. Don't ask me why…"

"I saw why, and sometimes there are no explanations. Are you telling me the truth?"

"She doesn't know how to be faithful…"

"Yeah, I got that part."

"Not yet anyway. But she's had a hard life. Her mama died young. Her father mistreated her. When he got tired of her, he married her off to that white trash Tarrant. She discovered she couldn't have babies. If she gets pregnant she miscarries. Sad business… Tarrant abused her. She was eighteen when Loren rescued her…"

"Bodecker?"

"Hard to believe I know, but it was for his own gratification. I can see the worth in her, and always could, even if she doesn't see it herself yet, but she could one day. She needs to be taught how to make something of herself."

"I see." Maybe Emma was right.

"She's kind to folks. She works hard. And she doesn't lie to me," Kerr adds, perhaps the most important point of all.

"Mm. I got that, too. Listen, Kerr, if you give me Lamont…"

"I won't give you anything…"

"If I give you and Eva a way to escape, will you give me Lamont?"

Kerr frowns. "Are you serious, Ryan?"

"I will fix it so that you and Eva can run off together but you must answer my questions about Lamont and you must leave now, and never show your face in Wyoming, Colorado or Nebraska again."

"Something rotting your brain, Ryan?"

"Do you want Eva for the rest of your life or not?"

"Why all this sudden desire to see me and Eva live happily ever after?"

"I owe it to someone."

"You've gone soft, Ryan."

"No. Not soft. Let's say I see you and Eva through someone else's eyes."

Kerr sits speechless, staring at him, bewildered.

"I'll ask again: do you want Eva for the rest of your life or not?"

"Yes," Kerr says. "Ryan, this is plain out of character. You're downright scaring me."

"Will you do as I ask?"

"I cannot give you Lamont."

"What is he to you when I am giving you a future with Eva? I saw and heard you and Eva together, Kerr. You can't get enough of her, can you? And she's more than willing to give it to you. Will you get that from any other woman you meet?"

"I oughta be getting speeches about morality from you, Ryan. Instead I'm getting quid quo pro."

"Well, if you don't want freedom. If you want jail and a lifetime without Eva, that's your business. Like I said, I owe someone a happily ever after and you're it, if you want it."

Kerr sits back with a couple of hard swallows. Maybe it's finally starting to sink in. "I haven't murdered anyone."

"Glad to hear it. Who's Lamont and what does he do?"

"How do you know about Lamont's importance?"

"A hunch."

"He…" But Kerr shuts down again.

"All you have to do is think about Eva."

"You are the devil, Ryan."

"I'm your angel of mercy, Kerr, and it's high time you realized it. Now talk."

SEVEN

...the one face I looked for was not there...

Henry Wadsworth Longfellow
Hawthorne

Emmaline

"I'll never forget your kindness, Mrs Morris. You are an angel."

Nan Morris extricates herself from Emmaline's hold. "Hush, now, and see that you get yourself well and come visit me in the summer. I swear 19th Street is pretty as a picture in summer."

How many times did she peer up into the trees for signs of spring? Only her well-honed imagination could produce an image of summer.

She takes her parents to St John's to attend Mass and meet Father Nugent. Today the fog seems more like a clinging damp cloak, scaring her mama outright; all her movements are precise and purposeful, and she ushers Emmaline everywhere quickly, as though she is afraid her daughter will drop dead from pneumonia on the spot, which leaves her father to exercise what he can of his calming influence.

Although they attend without Ashcliff, the Severinis sit in their customary pew. Mass seems long and dreary, devoid of comfort; relief comes with its conclusion. Outside the Severinis greet her and point with enthusiasm at their bodyguards – Luke, Ben, Ethan, Tip and John, who wave or nod from across the churchyard. With the Severinis safe and secure under their protection they set off, Tip giving her a final salute.

Father Nugent draws her aside and speaks his concern for her health. "We should have been taking better care of you, Emmaline."

"Father, I have always felt very well cared for, I assure you."

"You know you will be in my prayers."

"Thank you, Father, but I will be well again very soon."

"That you will. You're a strong lass. And you have excellent parents. You know, I'm glad for them, Emmaline. The Lord wants his children to forgive one another."

"They seem very happy. And I'm happy for them, too, now."

"Good girl. And I'll be praying for you for another reason."

"Oh. That."

"Won't you reconsider your decision to leave today, and wait one more day for the lad to return? Once he knows…"

"The truth about me? Once I tell him the truth?"

Father Nugent holds up his hand in a gentle, placating fashion. "There have been more untold truths between you than God will allow. It's time for them all to be told."

But before she has a chance to ask him what he means, her parents rejoin them.

"I'm sorry you'll be missing Easter ceremonies with us, Emmaline," he says for her parents' benefit.

"I'm sure they will be splendid."

"There will be something missing for sure." He takes her hand between both of his. "You've done more good in this town, Emmaline, than you'll ever know. Take comfort from that."

"Yes, Father. And thank you for everything. We've had some good times."

He grins. "Aye, that we have. Godspeed, all of you."

They take their leave. Her enduring memory of Father Nugent will surely become his black-garbed figure standing outside his beloved church with a gaggle of children running around him.

She climbs into the buggy that will take them and their luggage to the station.

Emma, can't you imagine for even one second that our lives are not meant to be separate?

It will fade… when we part.

No, it won't. It's going to hurt, Emma, for a very long time.

Distress embraces her… the bitter kiss of her deception.

When I leave and return home, what will happen then? You wouldn't come after me?

Tell me you want me to follow you and I'll be there, I swear.

She begins to feel no longer in control of what is happening to her. There is no fight left, no ability for independent thought or action.

This is the time we have, only so many days. I will share them with you and then I have to go home.

This reality has finally come to pass; eternity seems such a long, long time and the exact opposite of heaven.

Cliff

"I've searched everywhere, Ryan, there's no sign of them," Nelson pants, "except some prints leading out the back and into the forest."

A cold wind cuts across the yard.

Chase hasn't stopped glaring at Cliff through squinted eyes since they woke up.

"How did we sleep through two people untying themselves, packing up their belongings and riding out of here?" he asks for the fourth time. "And one of the Winchesters is gone."

Again, Cliff answers him. "I told you, Chase. While you, Nelson and Eva were asleep I took the opportunity to interrogate Kerr in the kitchen about Lamont. I thought I tied him up again properly. I fell asleep. It was light when we woke. They were gone."

Chase frowns sharply. "It's out of character for you, Ryan."

"Well, what do you think happened, Chase?"

"I know how much you wanted Kerr, so I have to believe it happened like you think it did. We came here for nothing it seems."

Nelson saunters up with their horses. "Still arguin'?"

Cliff takes the reins of his and mounts up. "Not for nothing, Chase. Mount up. I have an urgent wire to send to Cheyenne."

"We could take some time to look for them," Chase persists.

"They could be hours away by now; if you want to take off into the wilderness by yourself to look for them be my guest, but I can't spare the time."

With his horse snorting white clouds, Chase mounts up. "Fine. Let's go then."

"C'mon, Nelson, mount up."

Emmaline

Emmaline stares blankly at the train while the Sheriff organizes their luggage. Her mama looks about constantly, as if warning the damp mist to stand back or face the consequences.

Imagine, Emma, there is no north or south, no conflict of duty or job, no parental blunders, nothing to divide us... I only know I'm with you. There is no other place. O Captain! my Captain! I believe in this with all my heart."

Movement on the platform distracts her, rescues her...

Bit by bit, people come forward out of the mist, until, standing in a half circle around her, is every member of the Alliance.

The Benchleys. All the Taylors. The Keatons. And the Severinis.

Overwhelmed, she stares at them, unsure what to do next.

"Oh my," her mama declares. She withdraws, and leaves Emmaline alone in the middle of them.

A suave voice from the mist says, "Ciao, bella signorina..."

They all break into smiles, followed by gentle laughter.

Amy thrusts a large heavy packet into her hands. "Very good for chest complaints, in any climate." She pats Emmaline's cheek. "God bless you, Emmaline. Write to us."

Tressa, teardrops on her cheeks, her arm linked with Jennifer's, conjures a smile. "We love you."

"And we will be thinking of you," Jennifer adds. "Always."

Emmaline can't speak, yet these people need to know what they mean to her. She tries to rally; after all, they lived to fight another day partly thanks to her; they are the symbol of her work and achievements. And pretty darn good one at that.

Ah! Luke has remembered what she said last night.

A smile forms in spite of her sadness.

She finds Luke's intense gaze and conveys her thanks, somehow, and somehow he understands. He nods, giving her a softer version of his disarming grin.

"Goodbye, Emmaline," he says. "Don't forget us, because we won't ever forget you."

No more pleadings for her to wait, no further warnings of regret, because this is the day, the one that always seemed to be somewhere in the future and is now the dreadful moment she is living.

The conductor beckons his passengers. The train's whistle screeches in her ears. She looks at each of them one last time and turns away and steps up on board, glad that her seat is on the other side of the train where they won't glimpse her distress.

She gazes out over the tracks and the yards all pale and stiff in the cold mist. *By Easter we should see a run of fine, warmer days*, Father Nugent told her last week. It seems as though tears are frozen on her cheeks for want of fine warmer days.

Her mama sits beside her. She takes Emmaline's hand in hers. "That was some send off you just had, Emmie."

"Yes, Mama."

"I'm proud of you."

"Thank you, Mama."

The train jerks and begins to move.

She gasps. Her stomach rolls. She feels weak in her legs and arms, and strange in her head.

Confused.

Something inside her is not right.

Her heart is leaping about as if trying to escape her chest; it's screaming Ashcliff's name. Calling for him.

She can't breathe.

"Emmaline..."

I know which way the wind blows. Lotta folks would describe Miss Emmaline Roberts and Sheriff Cliff Ryan as a match made in heaven.

"Emmaline..."

"Emmie, your papa is speaking to you."

I love you for eternity

"Emmaline, listen to me..."

Dance with me, Emma?

And shatter poor future wife?

A thousand dances with her won't even come close to just one with you.

"Are you listening to me?"

"I... I'm trying..."

Her father is sitting forward in his seat, his arms on his knees, peering into her face. There is a gentle smile in the crinkles at the corners of his eyes as they sparkle at her. He reaches for her hands.

"He won't forget you."

When you strip away where a person lives, what they do for a living, all the trappings of their life, what are you left with? Just them. And if you take everything about us away, we are left with just us.

It's only a notion, James. People aren't like that...

When they love, they are exactly that. We are exactly that.

The train picks up speed; an unfamiliar panic wells up inside her, which panics her even more.

No... this is all wrong... must get off...

Dance with me, Emma... Dance with me...

"Emmaline, if anyone knows how a Roberts woman bewitches a man like Ryan, it is I. It's actually the Pendleton in you."

"Sheriff?"

"In you, your sister, and your mama. All in your own way, you are extraordinary, unique, beautiful women. Believe me, Emmaline. He can't forget you, and you will see him again."

Cliff

Laramie Telegraph

MAC, FIND AND ARREST LAMONT ON CONSPIRACY. BEN KNOWS
HIM. START WITH SALOONS. BUT DO NOT HOLD IN COUNTY
LOCKUP. INFORM CAM. BACK TONIGHT. THANKS. CLIFF.

Lamont

Bored, frustrated and irritated by the slow passing of the day, Kit heads downstairs and then makes his way across the hotel foyer and through the gussied-up entrance to the hotel's saloon; it ain't open to the public on a Sunday, but for guests of the hotel, he was informed, the saloon is always open, so are the gambling tables and the girls.

Kit scans the room. He finds a suitable creature serving drinks at one of the tables. Her legs are shapely and she has dark brown hair. When she finishes serving, he goes up to her and takes her arm.

"You'll do," he says and drags her away.

"What do you want?"

"You work here, don't you?"

"Sure, mister, but..."

"How much?"

She tells him.

It angers him that he could get what he wanted back at Donnelly's ranch for free. Dillon was a lucky bastard.

He hurries the girl upstairs, shoves her inside his room and locks the door.

"Be Eva."

Ben

"This wasn't how Raina expected me to be spending Sunday afternoon, Mac," Ben laments.

"You and me both. Pat likes to go visiting Sunday afternoons. She took the twins over to see a friend. Good thing your family's all here, for Raina I mean."

"What are you getting at, Mac?"

"Raina seemed kinda jumpy when I saw her last."

"Raina?"

"Mm. She seems all right to you?"

"Sure. Maybe you remind her of someone she'd rather forget."

"She must've married you for your charm."

"Of course," he grins.

It's a cold afternoon in Cheyenne. No one's about, and yet they roam the streets, searching…

"You sure about this, Mac?"

"We've asked in every saloon in town, this is the last – the Sit a Spell Saloon. It's part of the Beresford Hotel. If that don't work out, I guess I'll have to *sit a spell* and think."

"And work on your sense of humor while you're at it."

But as they are about to step down from the sidewalk and cross the street, a disturbance breaks out. A man is being pushed out of the door of the saloon.

"Now what do we have here…" Mac mutters. He puts a hand on Ben's arm. "Watch and listen. That's the owner, Tim Beresford, ditchin' that feller. The Sit a Spell is peaceable for the most part."

"We don't want your kind in here. You touch one of my girls again or even set foot back here and I'll stick the sheriff on you…"

As the man stumbles out backwards, his luggage – a duffle bag – is tossed out after him. He staggers to the edge of the sidewalk, feeling his jaw. The man Beresford spits on the boards near the other man's feet.

Ben catches his breath.

"What?" Mac says to him. "You ain't seen a man spit before?"

"That's him. That's Lamont. I almost didn't recognize him, but that's him all right."

"Well, it's time to arrest him. You can go back to Raina now. Ah, better still, run up to the Faradays' place and tell Cam. Tell him to meet me at the 16th Street lockup, not the county jail."

Ben is flabbergasted. "How did Ryan know about the saloons and such?"

"That's what makes him Ryan and us mere mortals."

"I guess."

Mac chuckles. "He figures people out, Ben. Don't ask me how, but he does. Figured you out, figured me out, everybody he meets. Now, off you go. I got work to do."

Mac takes off.

Ben stands back and watches Lamont being arrested, manacled and led away. The man seems to be in a daze, not at all like the idiotic and bossy individual he encountered in Denver.

Seems like anyone who works with Bodecker comes unstuck eventually. He thinks back to the moment he decided he disliked Bodecker: his father was extolling the benefits of having someone like Bodecker on the board of Taylor Mining; Bodecker was smiling smarmily and Ben wanted to be sick.

On this cold and misty Sunday afternoon, with Emmaline gone the way she went, with Ryan out of town and sending him from saloon to saloon, Cheyenne feels strange and unnatural.

He hurries up town to the Faradays'.

Then he intends to find Raina and hold her close… and then find out if something's bothering her.

Faraday

"You are Lamont?"

"So what if I am?"

"My name is Faraday. I am the territorial prosecutor. You have been arrested for…"

"I know what that fool deputy arrested me for. He's wrong."

"Why did you get thrown out of the Beresford Hotel?"

"I got a little carried away with one of the old feller's saloon girls. You know they shouldn't do the stinking job if they don't like what they get."

Faraday takes a deep breath and sits back. He gave up his afternoon, his precious time with Meg, for this.

"Did you rape her, Mr Lamont?"

Lamont barks an insolent laugh. "How do you rape a whore?"

"The same way you rape any female. Without her consent, if she says no or stop, and you persist, it is rape."

"You can't rape a whore, I tell you."

So. A genius.

Mac shrugs at him from across the room.

"Did the young woman insist you to stop, Mr Lamont?"

"They don't know what they want those kind of women. I thought I was being arrested for conspiracy, so the deputy said, whatever that is, not raping a whore, which you can't do."

"Mr Lamont, when did you last see Mr Dillon Kerr?"

"Who's he?"

"What do you know about Loren Bodecker?"

"Never heard of him."

"Did you work as a desk clerk at the Denver Club?"

"Never been to Denver."

Faraday speaks to Mac outside.

"You are sure this is he?"

"Sure, Cam. Ben knows him. Said it was him for sure."

Faradays sighs. "Well, we'd better keep him here until Cliff returns. Guard him, Mac."

"Don't worry. Not like I didn't have nothin' better to do on a Sunday afternoon."

"You and me both. I'll be over at the Keaton house. I want to talk to Richard Taylor about this Lamont. See what he knows."

"Think Taylor will be up for it?"

"I'm hopeful."

"What if this character remembers he can ask for a lawyer?"

"Think of something, Mac. At the very least I don't want the black suits near him until Cliff has had a chance to interrogate him."

"Well, they won't hear about this from me and if they had any sense they'd be spending Sunday afternoon sleeping off lunch like we should be."

Keaton family parlor

Caroline Taylor sets a cup of coffee on the small table at his elbow.

"Thank you, Caroline."

"How is Meg?"

"A little tired and fed up I'm afraid."

"Oh, well, that's normal at this stage. Can I get you anything else?"

"He's come to talk to me, Caroline," her husband growls.

"Yes, Richard," she says calmly. "Call me, if you require anything."

"How are you feeling, Mr Taylor?" Faraday asks when Caroline has left them alone in the parlor.

Taylor stares into the hearth, watching the darting flames.

"Like I'll never have my life back," Taylor replies.

Faraday isn't expecting such a lucid, honest response. "Life has a way of moving itself along one way or another," he says in earnest observation.

"I guess. So, Mr Faraday, what did you want to see me about?"

"A short while ago, Mac arrested a man called Lamont. Do you know him?"

"Lamont? Kit Lamont?"

"Apparently."

"You don't seem too sure."

"Well, we have a definite identification but he's not answering my questions."

"Lamont is not what he seems," Taylor says in a low voice.

"How do you mean?"

"He was one of my keepers in Denver. He wouldn't let me leave!" Taylor brings his fist down hard on the arm of his chair.

"You were his prisoner?"

"Bodecker's prisoner. Lamont my warden. And others. Who knows where they are. You've got to put me on the stand, Mr Faraday, so I can tell the jury what happened to me, what Bodecker did to my company, how he used me…"

"Your zeal is understandable, Mr Taylor. What else do you remember about Lamont?"

"He frequents brothels. I don't know, Mr Faraday, but what is it with these men of Bodecker's. They are all about whoring; I'd hear them talking. Even Bodecker would boast to me about it. It made me sick. I'm a family man, Mr Faraday, and I know you don't think much of me but I believe that whoring is depraved and should be stopped. There should be better laws, Mr Faraday."

Faraday observes the indignation in Taylor's eyes with interest.

"Lamont was arrested outside a saloon where the owner had thrown him out for assaulting one of the saloon girls. He could be charged with rape."

"Huh! What did I tell you? That would be him then. Whoring and brothels…"

Taylor looks back into the fire.

"I understand your disgust, Mr Taylor. And it does seem to be a sickness with this group of men. Abuse of women, a vicious lack of respect. Donnelly murdered that young prostitute on the train from Omaha. She'd been with Bodecker the evening before."

"What are we doing, Mr Faraday, to our young women, when they find themselves in a predicament which would induce them to sell themselves?"

Faraday decides to be blunt. "Is that why you became infuriated with your daughter when you found out she was expecting Mart Keaton's child?"

Taylor flashes a warning with his fire-soaked eyes. "She was married."

"But you wouldn't recognize the marriage."

"No." He looks down. "A mistake. Caroline has made that only too clear to me. I didn't listen to Caroline enough in the past. In this I too disrespected a woman, the very woman I loved. My greed was my infidelity. My daughter was married to Mart Keaton. Her child is Adam Taylor Keaton. I was wrong about her and about her husband. I was wrong about my son. He came to Denver to get me back. I thought he had deserted me. He saved me."

"From Bodecker."

"Yes."

"How much do you believe Lamont knows about Bodecker's concerns?"

"A great deal, I'd say, but Lamont is not a follower..."

"How do you mean?"

"I'd hear a lot of men say 'yes and no Loren' for everything. Even I, before he blackmailed me. But not Lamont. He's different."

"He is capable of acting independently?"

"Yes. Not like the others. Loren possesses a powerful persuasion, you see. He promises you your heart's desire. Money, power, women, success, whatever it is, he can get it for you, if you do for him what he wants. Those black suits, as you like to call them, I find it hard to believe they are independent of him."

The thought had crossed Faraday's mind.

"Did you ever hear Lamont talk about Dillon Kerr? Think hard, Mr Taylor."

"That name Dillon Kerr came up often with Loren, but maybe only once I recall with Lamont."

"And do you remember that exactly – what was said perhaps?"

Taylor frowns. "That's a hard question, Mr Faraday."

"I know. I'm sorry. But anything you can recall.'

"Could've been something like, *I need to wire Dillon...*"

"And the context?"

Taylor shakes his head.

"Sheriff Ryan is on his way home and he will interrogate Lamont further; he may want to speak with you as well. Are you agreeable?"

"Don't know what help I'll be, but yes."

"Thank you, Mr Taylor."

Cliff

The train is still moving when Cliff alights with his bag. Alone, having left Chase in Laramie to return tomorrow, he hurries out of the depot. He wants nothing more than to know that Mac has arrested Lamont. Sort it out.

Then find Emma.

Mac greets him, clearly relieved. "You're back early."

"Train didn't stop all that much. Everything all right, Mac?"

"Where's Chase?"

"He'll be back tomorrow morning."

"Cam got his continuance. After lunch tomorrow."

"Well? Tell me?'

"Lamont is sitting in the interview room, like a lost soul."

Cliff nods, feeling a grin splitting his face. "Good work, Mac."

"He won't talk but," Mac adds. "Cam had a go at him. Just clammed up. What's so special about him?"

But just then Cam walks in. "Well, we have all sacrificed our Sunday afternoon. I hope it was worth it. Where is Dillon Kerr?"

"Howdy, Cam. Nice weather we're having…"

Cam grunts. "Very droll. Discovered a sense of humor in Laramie, did you?"

"I think I discovered much more."

"So, where is Dillon Kerr?"

"Will you let me interrogate Lamont before I answer that?"

Cam narrows his eyes. "What have you been up to?"

"Doing what I thought necessary."

"I'm not sure I like the sound of that. There's something you should know about Mr Lamont. He was thrown out of Beresford's before you came home for having his unwanted way with one of Beresford's saloon girls. Lamont denies it of course, but I've spoken to the girl. She claims he raped her, and from the look of her and what she described I believe her. So whatever plans you had for this Lamont, I'd factor a charge of rape into them."

"She's accused him of rape?"

"She has."

"How is she?"

"Poorly. He tied her hands to the bed. Insisted she be 'Eva'… and cruelly forced himself on her. She has an assortment of injuries, bruises, welts and marks. Said he wouldn't stop calling out 'Eva', 'like he was out of his mind', she said."

The hair on Cliff's head prickles. "Eva Tarrant…"

"What has she to do with Lamont and this girl?"

"Kerr left Lamont alone with Eva Tarrant up on the Laramie ranch for a few days. They had a torrid fling that continued in secret even after Kerr got back."

"But why should that send him over the edge like this?"

"I think it's like this, Cam. Eva was the woman who tamed Lamont down a bit. I think his normal play is rough, although as rough as this alleged rape I'm not sure. The way they behaved up on the ranch, the fact that he wants Eva and she's Dillon Kerr's woman is cause enough for Lamont to behave the way he has."

"I see. The saloon girl wouldn't see a doctor until I suggested Jennifer. She's there with her now. Jennifer said she'd stop by straight after and report on her condition."

"Do you think the girl – what's her name?"

"Ruth O'Brien."

" – Miss O'Brien would speak with me today?"

"I don't know."

Mac says, "What's Donnelly runnin' up there – a house of easy virtue?"

"Funny you should say that, Mac. Only it's not Donnelly or Kerr or Bodecker running the show. Kit Lamont owns several brothels in Denver."

Cam frowns. "But I thought he was the desk clerk at the Denver Club."

"In a manner of speaking. His seduction of Eva Tarrant was fast and it was complete. It gave Dillon Kerr more than enough reason to tell me everything he knows in exchange for his freedom."

Cam flinches. "You let Kerr go?"

"I did. In exchange for Lamont."

"Have you lost your marbles, Cliff?" Mac splutters.

"He took Eva away and intends to educate her. He actually loves the woman, although what she's capable of through sheer stupidity… Anyhow, once Lamont knows they've gone, it should prove very interesting. My bet is he wants to get back up to the ranch and Eva."

"Why is Lamont so important?" Cam asks.

"You put him on the stand, Cam, and this case gets blown wide open."

"And if I do that, what does Lamont get in return?"

"His freedom, and a chance to get Eva back."

"Kerr and Lamont will kill each other."

"No, I don't think so. They'll make Eva choose, or some other arrangement will be made…" Cliff clears his throat.

"Charmin'…" Mac chunters.

"This rape charge complicates things though."

"I haven't said Lamont gets a single thing yet," Cam informs him in a cranky tone Cliff very seldom hears from him.

"I know, Cam. It's a gamble. But once you hear Lamont's story, you may be agreeable."

Cam grunts again; repeated grunting is not something he does too often either. "Let's get this interrogation over with."

Jennifer

Beresford's saloon, 15th Street
Ruth O'Brien's room

"I'm sorry this happened to you, Ruth."

"You are so kind, Doctor Sullivan. When Mr Faraday said you were back in town, I never felt so relieved in all my life. So, how bad is it?"

"You have internal bruising and abrasions. I want you to bathe yourself religiously with this solution. You dissolve a teaspoon into water, warm water if you prefer."

"He made me bleed…"

"Yes. You've got to keep clean, Ruth. And no working. I'll be speaking with Mr Beresford." Jennifer holds up a jar. "Now, apply this salve to the welts and marks. Three times a day."

"I understand."

Ruth looks like she understands a great deal more about life than she did two hours ago, lying in her bed with her skin bruised and marked, her body abused. Her pale face is stained with tears; she cries, then stops, and then cries some more. A cycle of shock and disbelief, pain, loathing and disgust that's far from finished with her, even though Lamont is no longer a physical threat.

"Ruth, have you ever considered a different line of work?"

"Men are everywhere. Where do I go?"

"Wait on tables at a restaurant. Work as a housemaid… A respectable job, Ruth. Your chances have to be better when you don't actually put yourself deliberately into the hands of a man like Lamont, don't they?"

"Most men ain't like him."

"But some are..."

"Yes. I...I am worried about one other thing... my veil..."

"Let me assure you, Ruth, that in spite the violence upon you, your cervical cap is still in place. We won't remove it just yet. I have thoroughly cleaned you. It was uncomfortable and you've been so brave. We have done everything we can."

Ruth's eyes fill with tears. "He was so mean... he didn't care."

The firm, reassuring squeeze she gives Ruth's hand seems to help a little. "It's time to heal now, Ruth, think on that."

Jennifer finishes dressing Ruth's wounds with the salve in silence. Then she advises Ruth about the injection she is going to administer and gives it, while the young woman turns her face away.

"Now, these pills I'm holding up are for your pain, reduce the inflammation, ease your suffering. Two when you wake up. And two every four hours for a couple of days. The injection I gave you was to help you sleep, Ruth. You need rest. I'll call again tomorrow and see how you are progressing. You will take care of yourself, won't you? Is there anyone who can help you, a friend...?"

"The other girls have already been good to me. And I will do as you say. Thanks for coming out on a Sunday. Heard you were married now."

"Yes. My husband is waiting for me downstairs."

"I'm glad for you." Ruth's brown eyes flutter and close.

Jennifer watches for several minutes until Ruth is deeply asleep and all her vital signs are normal.

Luke slides his arm around her as they meet, his eyes searching hers for signs of something to worry about.

"I'm fine," she says.

He smiles and takes her satchel for her.

Mr Beresford saunters up to them. "Well, Doc?"

"Miss O'Brien can't work, Mr Beresford."

"I'm gonna have to let her go."

"Was she a good employee? Did her work? Never gave cause for complaint?"

Beresford concedes with a sigh. "Sure."

"Then you owe her a week's care in bed, Mr Beresford. And then you need to help her find some other employment."

"Aw, she'll just move on to the saloon up the street."

"Not if you help her find some decent work."

"Doc, these things happen, it's part of the job. They know it."

"No, they don't. They don't think it will happen to them. And they have to live. So do your civic duty, Mr Beresford. Help her find a respectable job."

"I'm a busy man, Doc."

"If you do this, I will not charge you for her care…"

"Now you can't go doing that, Doc, it ain't right."

"I'll leave it up to you then. Good evening, Mr Beresford."

"Doc…"

Jennifer turns and leaves the man standing with a bewildered look on his face. Luke's strides match hers after a moment and he's by her side. Out in the street evening has descended upon the town, with a thin cold mist hovering about below and the sky a deep blue awash with diamond stars above.

They stop and look up at them for a soothing spell.

She sighs. "That is certainly a sight to put everything into perspective – the universe."

"That it is." She is kissed tenderly on the lips.

"Kissed beneath the cosmos," she whispers.

"I like seeing the stars in your eyes."

"Let's go," she says, taking his hand. "I need to talk to Cam."

"Where are we headed?"

"Not far; 16th Street lockup."

They start strolling.

"Maybe Cliff will be back," he says.

"Don't remind me."

"My favorite honeymooners!" Mac's eyes light up in greeting.

Luke chuckles. "What's new, Mac?"

"Cliff got back a while ago."

"That's good."

"I thought so, too. But he and Cam are at odds, you might say."

"What did Cliff do this time?" Luke asks.

"Ah, can't tell you, but it ain't often you see Cam so grumpy."

Jennifer looks around. "So where is everyone?"

Mac thumbs over his shoulder. "Back there in Cliff's office. Went in about five minutes ago. Something big's happenin'."

"Mac, would you mind asking them to come out for a minute. I should tell them about Ruth O'Brien."

"Sure thing, Doc."

Cliff

Cam greets Luke with, "What are you doing here?"

"The town's kinda weird tonight and I'm riding shotgun for my wife," Luke retorts, not appreciating Cam's tone one bit. "Cliff, how's everything?"

Cliff is glad to see them, but before he can exchange simple pleasantries, Cam's barking, "Well, George, how is Miss O'Brien?"

"Her injuries, all of them, are indicative of sexual assault. Severe bruising, both internal and external, and some bleeding. She hadn't washed herself, probably because she was so shocked and injured, so there was good, clear evidence of the crime and of the perpetrator. I have no doubt you'll find someone who will testify Mr Lamont was the last man she was seen with. And, of course, it was reported without delay. Gentlemen, Ruth O'Brien was raped."

"And you are *absolutely* sure?" Cam asks.

"Cam, didn't you hear what I just said? She was brutalized. She told me she begged him to stop numerous times and he ignored her and kept on going. Last I heard that isn't the definition of consensual intercourse."

Cam grunts and jams his hand in his pockets. "Well, that's just great!"

Cliff sighs at the ceiling and sticks his hands on his hips.

"For Ruth O'Brien it is the worst thing that could happen. For any woman. Cam, what is the matter with you?"

"Did she put herself on the bed?"

"He asked her to and she obeyed."

"She did whatever he asked, didn't she?"

"That's what she told me, but…"

"And me. So, the jury sees she is a prostitute, that she obeyed his every whim, that it got extremely rough and she changed her mind, but he didn't want to stop. He's paying her for the privilege of using her body. Is that rape?"

"Good God, Cam, yes it's rape," she argues. "He tied her up!"

"So what? – her hands were tied."

"Oh, Cam. She couldn't fight him off. She told him to stop at least half a dozen times."

"But he is paying for a service. The use of her body."

"She's a human being not a commodity. Besides, he didn't pay her in advance. He threw twenty dollars at her afterwards, after she asked for it."

"There was a verbal contract. She told me he asked her price before they went upstairs. A good defense attorney will whittle this down to assault."

"She's lost her job!"

"And that's a bad thing, George?"

Jennifer blinks. "What are you saying? You won't prosecute this Lamont for what he did to Ruth O'Brien?"

Cliff rubs his brow. "Excuse me, but I've got an interrogation to be getting on with. See you, Luke."

"Yeah. Good to see you back. Listen, Cliff, I need to talk to you about something right away. It's important."

"Sure. But can it wait an hour? Unless it's urgent I have to do this interrogation now."

"It's not urgent. Just… important."

"I see. Meet you at my place. One hour."

Cliff resumes his seat, putting Luke's important thing out of his mind. "Right, Lamont. Let's start again. State your full name."

"Christopher Lamont. You can call me Kit."

"How old are you, Kit?"

"Thirty-two."

"And where do you live?"

353

"Denver."

"What do you do for a living?"

"I'm a concierge for the Denver Club. You know that because that's where we first met. You, the Montgomery girl and the young feller..."

"I remember, Kit. So, who got you the job?"

"Don't recall.'

"Do you know Loren Bodecker?"

"Who's that?"

"Do you know Dillon Kerr?"

"Never heard of the feller."

"Strange. He's heard of you. He says you're a friend of his. Do you know Donnelly?"

"No."

"Do you know anything about the Maverick operation?"

"Never heard of it."

"Do you own several brothels in Denver?"

"Where'd you hear that?"

"Dillon Kerr told me."

Lamont clams up.

Just then Cam strolls in. There's an expression on his face that reads *I've just been beaten up by an outraged female doctor.* And something else, something Cliff can't quite put his finger on.

He maintains his poker face. "Good timing, Cam. Kit and I were just talking about the brothels he owns in Denver. Who else knows you own the brothels, Kit?"

"I didn't say I owned brothels. You did."

"Do you know a woman called Eva Tarrant?"

"No."

Lamont is one cool customer.

"You don't know the woman you're passionately in love with?"

Lamont bares his teeth in a warning snarl. Ah...

"Eva Tarrant is the woman you can't have, isn't that right? She belongs to Dillon Kerr now, I understand."

"I don't know these people."

"You had a torrid affair with Eva Tarrant."

"What? That's ridiculous."

"No," Cliff says, sitting back in his chair. "It's true. I've been up to the Donnelly ranch and I've met Eva. I heard her talk about you."

"Bullshit," he says, but his eyes begin to betray him.

"No," Cliff says again, sitting forward. "Perhaps this sounds familiar to you. It started in the kitchen; you came in from chopping wood the first day Dillon was away in Laramie. Eva was fixing supper. You went up to her and unbuttoned her blouse. You said you were going to thank her for being a good cook and that she should call you Kit. She said stop, but you were persistent and because it felt nice to her she let you have your way. She almost fainted."

Lamont looks uneasy.

"Shall I go on? I quote: *Once we got started it was hard to stop. He'd get awful passionate.* You bathed together, got naked in the straw together, you swept her off her feet with every pleasure you could concoct and she was entirely agreeable to it. So, Lamont, do you still say you don't know Eva Tarrant?"

Lamont eyes him wildly but refuses answer.

"Fine. Let's go on, shall we? Quote: *I couldn't never say no to Lamont.* You kept up the affair with Eva Tarrant even when Dillon Kerr returned and before he sent you to Cheyenne to get an update on the trial. She'd give you a signal of some kind and you'd know to go meet her in the barn. You even had intercourse with her in your room while Dillon Kerr was downstairs reading. Quote: *I think he was in love with me or somethin'.* You excited her, Lamont, to the point where she was unfaithful to the man who rescued her from Bodecker and was prepared to take care of her for life."

Lamont glares at him.

"Are you in love with Eva Tarrant, Kit?"

"Go to hell."

"Is that why you raped the saloon girl, Kit?"

"You can't rape a whore, I tell you…"

"Frustrated all to hell. Separated. Desperate. You wanted Ruth O'Brien to be Eva because you are *so* in love with Eva."

"Go to hell, Ryan."

"But you had to tie Ruth up. You never tied Eva up. On the contrary she saw you coming and practically lifted up her skirts."

"Shut your filthy mouth."

"Now that's a comment I'd expect from a man in love."

Lamont's face is bright red, like beets.

"So what if I love Eva Tarrant," he rasps. "Dillon treats her the same way. He never leaves her alone. Always fooling around. Dill'd chase her around the house. I'd work it so that she'd run into me outside my room and I'd pull her inside where Kerr wouldn't think to look. I'd lock my door, remind her – you know – who she really wanted. She loved it and she made me crazy for her. Of course, it took the edge of Dill's advances because she'd already had some lovin'. She would put Dill off and tell him she wanted to read instead. He thought she was improving herself, so he didn't question it. Old Dill never cottoned on."

Lamont's almost wistful delivery of his licentious encounters with Eva Tarrant is beginning to make Cliff uncomfortable, but he's got to let the man feel easy about talking to him for what's to come later. And Cam needs to hear what went on up at the ranch.

"And then I'd walk in from chopping wood or taking a walk, they'd be in front of the fire or on the sofa, like there was no one else around. Evenings after supper things would quiet down till bedtime. Eva would come into my room while Dill was reading and say, *I'm sorry you was feeling left out, Kit darlin', let me make it up to you.* She would get into my bed and she'd say, *I'm yours, Kit, always and forever* and we'd arrange how we would meet the next day. Two hours later at bedtime, I'd hear her tell Dill, *not tonight, Dill, I'm so tired from all my sewing* or cooking or whatever, but I knew, and I knew she wanted me more."

Cliff glances at Cam who wipes his hand over his face to mask his dismay.

"I didn't think the ranch was a brothel," Cliff continues, thinking the way this feller runs off at the mouth he and Eva are a pigeon pair.

Lamont looks offended. "Eva ain't a prostitute. She's special is Eva. She cooks and sews and knows how to please her man. Too like a wife to be a whore."

"But too like a whore to be a wife."

"Now wait a minute, Ryan..."

"You treated her like a whore."

"No, I did not. I was fighting for her attentions, like any man would. She likes being with a man. Why should I hold that against her? It's a gift, that's what it is. I treated the girl in the saloon like a prostitute."

"Rape?"

"Well, I admit I was missing Eva."

"What did you do exactly?"

"I tied up her hands with her stockings, that's all. I went into her, she didn't like it and made a fuss."

"She said for you to stop at least half a dozen times, Kit. Why didn't you?"

"She's young. She's got to learn what the business is all about. The girls can't get squeamish and fussy when they don't like a client."

"But you bruised her severely. Made her bleed – badly."

"Can't help it if she was small, you know..."

"You wanted her to be Eva?"

"Yes."

Lamont looks forlorn.

"Eva is not small."

Cam coughs.

"Eva is perfect – everywhere."

"She would have made a fine courtesan for your Denver palaces then?"

"Eva is for me, not the clients," Lamont snaps.

"So you do intend to take her back to Denver to live with you?"

"First chance I get. She'll come. She'll come away from Dillon. When she hears what I have to offer her."

"What would that be?"

"Fine clothes, jewels, servants, wealth she's only dreamed about."

"You have a fine home in Denver then?"

"It's a palace in Capitol Hill, away from the business."

"Sounds perfect, Kit. You know, Eva will never be faithful to you."

Again he snarls. "She will. You got to know how to keep a

woman. Dill doesn't know how. I've seen how he makes love to her. She'll get bored."

"Perhaps he'll teach her there is more to life."

"He's highbrow for sure, but she ain't. She wants what I can give her. Excitement most of all."

"Thanks, Kit, I'll be back in a minute with some coffee? water?"

Kit chooses coffee.

Outside, Cam looks grim.

They stare at one another for a full minute before either of them can speak.

Finally, Cam says, "All right, Cliff, this Tarrant woman is better off with Kerr, but she could have real feelings for Lamont. And he definitely has some for her, although only God understands why."

"You heard him. She wants what he can give her. And he's probably right."

"She has a right to choose between them. But as for Ruth O'Brien... I'm not in the habit of letting rapists go free."

"Neither am I."

"And these brothels he runs. Where he lives. The man's a millionaire. A dangerous millionaire."

"Mm..."

"Can't we close them down?"

"From here?" Cliff clears his throat of his high-pitched squawk.

Cam sighs loud and long, and rubs the back of his neck. "Anything else happen at the ranch you feel I need to know? And may we keep away from his lustful exploits with that woman, my stomach is off."

Cliff

Cliff places a cup of strong black coffee in front of Lamont, even though it irks him to show courtesy to a man who just brutally assaulted a woman. Cam takes his position in a chair on the other side of the room. Cliff hugs his own coffee into his hand and takes a seat opposite Lamont.

It's evident now that the comical, prissy Lamont he first encountered in Denver with Ben and Raina was a persona, and his front desk position at the Denver Club a cover. The real Kit Lamont is to be found in the enigmatic man sitting opposite him. He's going to have to sort that out, eventually, but first things first...

"So, Kit, you'll be pleased to know a doctor has fixed up Ruth and she's feeling some relief."

Lamont shrugs. "They're all the same."

"Mr Faraday here was talking with someone a while ago who said Loren Bodecker likes to boast about his conquests. Did he frequent your brothels?"

"That's all he uses." But Lamont frowns suddenly and turns pale.

"Dr Louis Porterfield supplies you drugs for your girls and the clients if they want them?"

"Ah... he is my supplier, yes. Purely for recreation, you understand. How'd you know that, Ryan?"

"Marvin Tucker is a client of his."

"Yes, Tucker is. Tucker trashed one of my girls in Denver a few weeks ago."

"Trashed?"

"Gave her something on top of what she'd already had. The girl went crazy. The manager reported she was found unconscious in her room by one of the girls who went to check on her after Tucker left. The girl said the pair of them was loud and wild. But he just did what I've been saying all along. You pay for the use of the girl, so you use her."

"What happened to the unconscious girl?"

"She went to hospital."

"Did she survive?" Cliff asks, inwardly appalled.

"Of course... she's fine... now."

"Happy to hear it. You know, Kit, everyone in this county and in Denver and in parts of Nebraska look up to Loren Bodecker. How about you?"

Lamont's eyes bulge. "Look up to that fat old prick? Are you kidding?"

"Why not?"

"Don't need to, that's why not. My business..."

"Mm?" says Cliff sipping his coffee. "Your business?"

"I'm too successful to worry about the likes of Bodecker."

"You see that's interesting."

"I don't know why. I started my business from scratch ten years ago with money from my grandfather's inheritance. Bodecker don't impress me with his mavericks and his Donnelly and all the others who scuttle along behind him..."

Cam's head comes up.

"So you know about the mavericks."

"Everyone does, Ryan."

"But you know more."

"I ain't telling you anything."

"If Mr Faraday and I give you a way to go back to Eva and win her from Dillon, will you tell us everything we need to know?"

Lamont's eyes go big again. His mouth starts to tremble. "How... how...?"

"You tell us what we need to know and testify to it on the witness stand at Bodecker's trial."

Lamont lets out a strident laugh. "You've lost it, Ryan..."

"All you have to do is think about Eva."

The man looks set to drool.

"We could have the rape charge reduced to assault."

"But I'll still go to prison and for something I didn't do."

"Well, that's up to the Judge," Cliff says.

"Not you two?"

"No, we don't sentence people, Kit, you know that."

"So you're saying I might not go to prison for being a little rough with the saloon girl?"

Cam says, "Mr Lamont, it is possible for you to take your chances with the Judge over the assault charge, leaving the way open for you to find Eva Tarrant, does that make it clearer for you?"

"Sure. I guess. I do want Eva. More than anything. If I had her then the other thing wouldn't have happened. You know, she's got this way of tilting her hips so when you're about to…"

"Ah, I know how alluring she can be, Kit. She's a pretty girl," Cliff says quickly.

"She sure is."

"So, where were we… do we have a deal?"

"You know, if you put me on the witness stand, Mr Faraday, I can cut a lot of time off this trial."

"How so, Mr Lamont?"

"If you can get me Eva…"

"We didn't say we would get her for you."

"Well, what did you say?"

"That a lesser charge was possible so that you have the chance for *you* to get her."

Lamont frowns. "Oh."

Cliff intervenes. "You know, Kit, if you want to *win* Eva, you're going to have to do it yourself. Would she be impressed if a US Marshal came up to her and said I'm taking you away. She'd cling, scared to death, to Dillon. The Marshal couldn't make her come away. Only you can do that."

Lamont grins. "I reckon you've been paying attention to what I've been saying, Ryan."

Unfortunately.

"I know how you feel about her, Kit. Will you take the stand?"

"I ain't afraid of Bodecker's cronies if that's what you're wondering."

"Well, I was, but now you've said otherwise, I believe you. So will you take the stand?"

"All right. I'll do it. For Eva."

"Good man. So let's go back a bit, shall we? You said that you started your business ten years ago with the money you inherited from your grandfather? What made you go into prostitution?"

"I liked it. I like the women. And best of all there's a lot of money to be made. Always lots of money."

"And who was your grandfather, Kit?"

"My grandfather was an old coot. Frontier man he thought himself. Fighting Indians, taming the West. Huh! I tamed the West with a handful of girls and a decent place to screw them. Men come in from the mines or the cattle yards or off the train, all they want is whiskey, a good feed, a hot bath, a comfy bed and a woman."

"And your grandfather's name, Kit?"

"Connors. Archie Connors."

Cam nearly falls off his chair. To his credit, he asks, "The *same* Connors who sold his land in the Bright River valley to Morgan Taylor?"

"Yes, counselor. The very same Connors."

Cam ignores Lamont's sarcasm and asks *the* pertinent question: "Why do you work at the Denver Club if you make a fortune out of prostitution?"

"Well, we're getting to that, ain't we?" Lamont says. "It's all right, Mr Faraday. I know what you want from me. You're probably wondering why I would backstab a man like Bodecker. I think the sheriff here knows already, coz he's been chatting to Dill up at the ranch. Well, let me tell you something, gentlemen. Loren Bodecker don't run the Empire. I do."

Luke

He and Jennifer sit side by side on the top step of their back stoop. Sure it's cool, but they're dressed warm, and the dazzling creamy swathe of the Milky Way has become their canopy of choice for sitting under when it comes to spooning, dreaming and talking soft.

"Nearly time to go see Cliff…" he murmurs.

"Five more minutes?"

He grins; who knew there'd be a woman who loved his company so much that she counted the minutes.

In her lap she safeguards Emmaline's package till it's time. He has a bottle of good whiskey on the step beside him. They don't talk for a long while, preferring to sit with their faces touching, close and warm. Then she breaks the heady silence:

"Are you sure you want to do this on your own?"

"I'm sure. Mac and Cam agreed I should do it. It's crazy down at the courthouse and jail anyhow; better it's me on my own. And I was there when you explained everything."

"It's going to break his heart. I can't mend those."

"You mended mine."

"That was different. That was in my power to do."

"Emmaline holds all the power."

"Cliff is certainly resilient, but he really does love her and you remember how we felt when we were separated from one another."

"I remember."

She nestles her soft head into his shoulder. "I wonder what's in the package."

"Book of some description."

"Mm. I think they have a lot in common."

"Not like us?"

"Aren't we the perfect example of how opposites attract? And yet we still like similar things."

"Anything you do I like, except the… the you know."

"Blood and guts."

"That."

"And anything you do I like. Your drawing. How well you ride horses. The way you are with people. You make them like you."

"Not everyone."

"True enough," she laughs.

"Been thinking. Decided I'm gonna buy you a piano."

"A piano? Why?"

"Because I want to hear you play every day."

"A piano is very expensive and where would we keep it."

"We'll work it out."

"A piano would be lovely," she says and puts her arms around him. "Perfectly lovely."

"You can teach Evan to play it."

"If he's a son of yours, we'll be struggling to fix him to the piano stool long enough to learn. Besides, what if Evan is a girl?"

"She'll play it, if she's a daughter of yours."

"What if Evan *is* a daughter? We can't call her Evan."

"Don't see why not. Anyway, haven't thought of girls' names."

"Does that mean you're counting on a son?"

"No. Just can't think of any names for a girl. I mean, a girl's name is pretty special. You can't go calling a girl something ugly. The moment you told me your name I thought it was as pretty as you are. See, a name like that, when you haven't seen the child, ain't an easy thing to find."

She raises her head, resting her chin on his shoulder. She's wearing a sweet grin, her eyes dancing with the starlight in them. "I like Frances."

"Mm, maybe."

"Anna."

"No."

"Mary."

"No."

"Emily."

"Maybe."

"Alexandra. Alex for short."

"Maybe."

"Kate."

"My sister's name was Katrine," he says thoughtfully.

"Mm, I remember."

"I used to call her Kat. I don't think she liked it much."

"I think she loved you and she liked it very much."

"And how would you know that?"

"I just know. What was she like?"

"Funny. And kinda bossy. If I wanted to *really* tease her I'd call her Whiskers. When I think back, I think she was a loving person."

"You see, that's what I mean about you. You didn't say she had this colored hair and those kind of eyes, that she was thin or fat. You said she was loving."

"The world was deprived of a very good person."

"Do you want our daughter to be her namesake?"

"Something to think about I guess. I don't know. The way Katrine died."

"Mm. Oh, our five minutes are up by now…"

"I'll get going. We'll continue this later," he says stroking her cheek. Later, when he's holding her and all that's wrong with the world goes very far away. "The package…"

She hands it over and he stows it in one of his coat pockets, stashing the whiskey in the other.

"A kiss for luck…" she says and gives him one.

The reality comes home to him. He is about to deliver the bleakest news of Cliff's adult life, and somewhere on a train way out on a vast and lonely prairie Emmaline is sick, heartbroken and getting further and further away.

*

365

Cliff's house on 19th and Ransom

"How long have you been waiting?"

"Only a minute. Time enough to light your porch lamp."

"Is that a bottle of Old Crow sticking out of your pocket?"

He nods, feeling bleak again.

Cliff gives a small frown, like he's cottoned on that something not so good awaits him. He opens his front door. "Come on in..."

As they hang their overcoats and hats, Luke is hit with the one question he's been dreading...

"So what's the Old Crow for?"

"Thought you probably drank the last bottle."

"Almost. Thanks." He takes the bottle of straight bourbon whiskey from Luke's outstretched hand with a bewildered look on his face. "That's not an answer by the way..."

"I have some news and the only place I giving it to you is in the parlor with the fire going."

He leaves Cliff looking baffled and turning pale, and heads into the parlor. He gets some light in the room and heat in the hearth and looks up to find Cliff hanging around the doorway, sliding the hand without the whiskey bottle into the pocket of his pants.

"This is about Emma."

Luke gives a curt nod.

Cliff, meanwhile, has that calm about him that's really dread in disguise.

"Is she hurt?"

"No. She's sick."

Cliff frowns and swallows hard. "Sick... how sick? She had a cough the other morning."

"Yeah, the cough. Yesterday her parents arrived in town, after you left for Laramie and they...'

"They what?"

"Took her home. This morning."

Luke wishes he could spare a brave man this disappointment, but there ain't a damn thing he can do about it.

"She's gone?"

"On this morning's train."

"But… Explain this illness to me… I don't…"

"It wouldn't have escaped your notice that Emmaline can't stand the cold. Well, Jennifer says that made this condition she has where she gets pneumonia…"

"I'm sorry. You are going to have to start again, Luke."

Luke sits on the sofa and takes a deep breath.

"On account of not being able to withstand the deep cold of northern winters Emmaline got pneumonia, twice, in the recent past. Both times left scars on her lungs and kinda weakened them because they haven't had time to heal properly. So now when she is exposed to the cold for long periods she gets sick, like she's getting pneumonia."

"The cough," Cliff murmurs. "I asked her about it and she distracted me…"

"She doesn't have pneumonia *yet*, but that mother of hers seemed to think she was going to get it in the next five seconds the way she was carrying on."

"Will she be all right?"

"Jennifer says she will. Once she's back in a warm climate and resting and recuperating she'll be well again. Seems that in warm climates she doesn't get the symptoms and is just fine. Jennifer is gonna do some research and she has some colleagues in Boston she says will definitely help, but it is likely Emmaline will have this susceptibility to the cold all her life. She's gotta work out how to manage it, or stay out of northern winters…"

"Are you telling me she could die from this?"

"As it stands, no, but from what Jennifer tells me she's not sure if there is permanent damage to Emmaline's lungs, but even if there isn't, she can't risk getting sick. She won't survive it. Jennifer says Emmaline's view of the future would seem uncertain and limited; to her family as well. Like I said, her mother couldn't wait to get her outa here. We all asked her to wait, even Cam I think, but it seemed to me it was like she didn't have much say in the matter."

Luke can see across the room that Cliff is trembling.

It's gotta be done; he's gotta hear how the love of his life walked out on him without waiting to say goodbye…

"She always seems so strong."

"Jennifer says that Emmaline is one of the strongest people she's ever known, but she has a breaking point. Think of it this way... Imagine a perfect crystal vase but it has one tiny flaw; when you put pressure on that flaw you create a breaking point. Emmaline, as I understand it, lives her life like a person who suspects her life won't be as long as the next person's."

"Borrowed time..." Cliff murmurs, "... is what they call it."

He finally comes across and plants his behind on the edge of the cozy chair next to the hearth, shaking like a leaf.

Luke takes the Old Crow from his hand, locates two tumblers trayed on the table next to the chair and starts pouring. He sticks one of them into Cliff's hand.

"Drink it."

"For God sake, Luke, she traipsed around in snow and ice for two months."

"I know. The night I first met her you roasted her in front of the fireplace in Meg's parlor."

"She was stiff with cold; I thought she would snap. Luke, she was always, always cold. She and I trudged all over Bright River Valley looking for mavericks. She was cold the whole time. I had to make her a fire in the Stewarts' living room."

"Not to mention she rode all night with Chase from Laramie to the Diamond-T."

"Emma..." The sound seems to be wrung out of him like a cry that's been strangled.

Luke has to swallow hard to get his emotions back on track.

"She told us she hadn't ever planned to stay here as long as she did, or do the things she ended up doing, and that she didn't realize how cold Wyoming was in winter. None of it, she said, was meant to happen."

"Including me..."

Luke sighs. "She loved everything about this place except the cold."

And they down the whiskey.

When he's refilled the glasses, he says, "She'll recover, Cliff. Jennifer wanted me to make sure you knew that."

Cliff swirls his Old Crow, his expression grim.

"Preston and Emmaline's mother... Elizabeth... they were looking for you. Jennifer and I spoke with them and Emmaline for a long time. You know, I'd forgotten how some southern mamas can be. Bossy, opinionated and mule-headed as the day is long. Don't think she thought much of Jennifer neither. A Yankee female doctor not exactly to her taste. Emmaline set her straight though..."

"*Yankee?*"

"Mm. Precious, ain't it?"

Cliff blows out a long breath. "Oh, yeah."

"Preston had a word to me before they all got on the train. He asked me to tell you that you might take a shine to the south."

Cliff gives a raw laugh. "And what about Emma, what did she have to say? Anything?"

Luke breathes deep, determined to get this part right. "She was devastated. And she was brave. And she said you would understand because you had discussed it." He reaches into his coat pocket for the package. "And she wanted you to have this... she said you would know what it is, something you had arranged."

Cliff takes it. Slowly. Studies it without seeing it, saying, "She never told me she was sick."

"No one knew. Not a single soul, Cliff."

The shock of Emmaline slipping away from him is beginning to etch itself onto Cliff's face.

"I know you want to open that package. You want me to stay?"

Cliff shakes his head. "It's been a long day. And someone is staying here under house arrest. I'll have my hands full... but, thanks. Thanks for coming, for telling me, and bringing me this..."

"We gave her a fine send-off, like she deserved. She cares about us. I don't know why; we nearly got her killed. But now she's safe."

Cliff nods.

Luke gets to his feet. Cliff looks up, so forlorn while trying to keep a brave face on it that Luke sighs and throws up his hands. "It's stupid me asking if you'll be fine because you're not."

"Emma was right – we did discuss her leaving. I just never thought she'd do it this way. Without saying goodbye."

"Maybe the goodbye is in the package... and maybe there's a see you later as well. I'll see myself out."

Cliff

Cliff stares at the package knowing precisely what it is. His mind wanders to the last time they were together in Quaid's office. She was so beautiful. And she was his. He glances sidelong at the expensive glass of comfort. He pours that good sipping whiskey straight down his throat.

This cold air...

Why do you spend so much time gallivanting around in it?

To be where you are I have to be cold.

He refills the glass.

You might not know me in the tropics. I am different there...

And downs half of it.

What's that?

It's just a cough.

You didn't have it before. Not like that anyway...

No wonder she refused to hear him out. Her propensity was to turn her back on the future, always, as though she didn't deserve one, or that she would spoil his; now he finds out that under certain circumstances she couldn't guarantee she'd even have one. No wonder poor future wife was a woman she disliked. No wonder she danced with him. That was the only way she could compete; giving him an indelible memory that would shadow poor future wife for life, always resented, never defeated.

The past is a battlefield where the present can't win.

His hands are still shaking; probably because all he wants to do is hold her in them and tell her everything will be all right. He takes another sip and swallows hard. The loud gulp echoes around the room as if to announce that the wretched state of loneliness he is about to know for a very long time has arrived.

He finishes his drink and puts the glass aside. Come what may, he needs to open her package. So he pulls at the string and strips the paper away. He is hungry now for anything of her, whatever is left of her…

There are two volumes. The first… *Uncle Tom's Cabin*. And the other… *A Key to Uncle Tom's Cabin*. Both by Harriet Beecher Stowe.

He holds a volume in each hand. Looks at one and then the other. They seem old to him, not newly bought at all.

Sometime today you will buy me a book and I will buy you one. Or perhaps we each have one already that we could give one another.

He places *A Key to Uncle Tom's Cabin*, which he has never read, on his lap and prepares to inspect its predecessor.

And he flips open the cover.

Folded notepaper rests against the facing page but he lifts it to see what's beneath. As he reads what he sees his eyes begin to sting.

> Dearest Emmaline, cherish the works of Harriet Beecher Stowe. She will teach you that equality, liberty and justice have faces and names, so that when you go into the world to live out your beliefs you will never forget what they look like. With love, Papa.

He recalls that morning in Martha's, when he wanted her to see the Cheyenne he knew, the people he served each day…

Now when you're called to put your life on the line for them, it's their faces you see. Ideologies are fine, but they need a human face.

You sound like my….

Your what?

Never mind.

It was her father he sounded like.

How many ways can this girl break his heart?

In a neat yet childlike hand below Preston's message is written:

THIS BOOK BELONGS TO
EMMALINE ROBERTS AGED 10

He presses the sting out of his eyes, unfolds the notepaper and reads...

Dear Ashcliff,

As this book has had a previous owner (me!) and is bound by the original inscription, and as I have much to say until we speak again, I will write my message on this notepaper, which as you can see is proper notepaper, not a page ripped out of my notebook.

Knowing you, I think you have read this book before, but perhaps not A Key to Uncle Tom's Cabin. Perhaps you would care to read Uncle Tom again with its companion. Not that I think you don't believe Harriet Beecher Stowe but a lot of people didn't when Uncle Tom was published and she so wrote 'A Key' to provide facts, documents and corroborative statements so folks knew what she wrote in Uncle Tom had basis in fact and real life. It's enlightening and makes for truly interesting reading.

Mainly, though, I wanted for you to understand that as you turn the pages you will unlock the world into which I was born, a world that your world condemned as insupportable. Our nation went to war to settle the issue of slavery but still my world exists in moral and political conflict with the outcome. The South writhes in frightening segregation of whites and blacks. In their poverty, the Negroes and people of color are denied the democratic process the war was fought to give them. How can I look you in the eye and say when it comes to you and I my world doesn't matter. I think it does matter; I've always thought so.

All his working life my father would not bow down. He did many, many things, even before the war, and during it, before I was born and after, brave things that I have never told you about. I believe we stayed all these years because he thought he could do some good. He was rewarded with some success because while he would defend Negroes and coloreds, he was scrupulously just in his actions towards all citizens and even whites need and appreciate that. Although not all did. The Reconstruction was brutal, but he kept the peace, my father. Like many at this time, he had hope.

I am perfectly aware that prejudice exists everywhere. But it's much more than that where I come from. Your world and mine I believe will not harmonize in our lifetime; perhaps never. The politics of my world does not bend. It thrives on ignorance and prejudice, bitterness and retribution. The Redemption saw to that. And there are people prepared to terrorize innocent, liberty-hungry people. They kill, or degrade, or deny the hard-fought rights of this nation to God-fearing people.

Hope — there is never enough of it to go around. I often wonder what is to become of us? We work hard, raise our families, try to be good citizens; we build, restore and repent; we worship, we pray and we have faith. We love. We dream. Can it be enough, ever? You see, there is an evil that stalks this world, and until we drive it out it will stay comfortable. Is this a world you would want to take on for my sake? You are a very principled man, how can I let you even consider being tainted by such an association?

I know you're thinking, Emma and her family don't hold to inequality and intolerance, and that's right of course; but for better or worse the world in which it thrives has shaped my life.

Often I am torn between running away (if indeed there is anywhere to run to) or being like my father. I have not yet decided how I will choose. Too many women let go of the greater good they could accomplish to immerse themselves in domesticity. I am not unopposed to the domestic life as such, I love my family and in fact it is my duty as a Catholic woman to have one of my own, although who can say, for the future is unwritten. But what if God gifts a woman, in the time she has on this earth, with the desire to do something else? Isn't it right and just to find out?

I admire Harriet Beecher Stowe for all that she was able to accomplish. I ask myself, what can I do, no matter how small?

Ashcliff, I would not swap my time in Cheyenne for all the books in every library or book store in America.

What you have taught me is that the human face of ideology is to be found everywhere and on many different levels and in varied aspects of human existence. Wherever liberty is denied, wherever the dreams of the world are still just dreams and need someone to make them come true. Even one dream, for just one person. Just one grain of liberty for one bound heart.

I will close with some other words of Mrs Beecher Stowe, words which I often find extremely useful: 'When you get into a tight place, and it seems you can't go on, hold on, for that's just the place and time that the tide will turn.'

My greatest delight and honor will always be having known you,

Emma.

He stares for an age at her letter. It amazes and moves and dazzles him, but that's Emma herself, isn't it? He's confused about so many things. For starters, what the hell happened to their book swap? It was his fault because he couldn't meet her. Still…

Did she ever get the treasury of poems? Get to read *The Good-Morrow* and his letter? He'll never know now, will he? She's gone.

The books are clearly precious to her. Which would infer he is important to her (she wouldn't gift them to just anyone), although this is no love letter she's written; nothing like the one he wrote her.

Yet her words are tender and caring, protective, honest, and written with the utmost respect for his principles. And she wrote them before her parents came to town to take her away. So…

So she never intended this to be the last word between them, but the beginning of many words, many discussions.

This is the time we have, only so many days. I will share them with you and then I have to go home.

"Emma," he whispers. "You should've waited…"

But she didn't; she saw an opening and took it.

He flips the cover of Uncle Tom's companion volume. Again, two lines of handwriting announces the book belongs to her and she's ten years old. But below that she has written another word and Friday's date.

Eternity…

In the front of the treasury of poems he gave her he wrote the same word. She wrote the word in this book. They wrote it to each other without the other knowing. That tells him everything he needs to know. And he refuses to believe she wrote it for any other reason, such as the hereafter being the only place they'll be together.

Why wouldn't our own personal eternity begin with our earthly life?

Their discussion that Sunday morning in Nan's kitchen over oatmeal and coffee changed his life.

He closes the book; drops it on his lap. He puts his elbows on his knees and his face in his hands, digs the heels of his wrists into his eye sockets until bright lights collide across his vision.

Why couldn't she have waited for him? They would have talked, come to an understanding. But Emma never wanted to hear what he had to say, did she? His belief was that it would change everything for them, but now that her secret is uncovered, maybe it would have changed nothing.

She didn't believe the South was right for him and she knew that the North in winter was bad for her. There are other places in this world… ah, but then she would be making him choose a future that in her mind was wrong for him.

Any future with her is right.

Any goddamn place on the planet with her is perfect.

His whole body groans with frustration.

There is still so much to be done, still so many difficult things to face… he can't leave Cheyenne for some time yet; he has duties and obligations; all of it now to do without seeing her for even one blissful second. Not even the promise of seeing her.

In his letter he swore to her he would follow her, she only had to say the word. But she left no word before she left. No address to contact her at her journey's end or reach her when all the trials of the men who filled his jail were over and done with.

He knows that her health is the most important thing. But he curses himself for letting her slip through his fingers; a kind of grief washes over him, wave after wave, while he despairs of ever getting her back.

The labyrinthine tangle of complexities that is Emma had one final sting in its tail for the man who made it into the deep heart and had the audacity to think he could find the way out free and clear.

Half an hour later, Mac delivers Lamont to his door.

Mac gives Lamont a small shove; Cliff grabs his restraints which keep Lamont's hands firmly behind his back; even though he voices his complaint, he is forgotten temporarily…

"Got a minute, Mac?" Cliff asks.

Mac nods. "I got time, Cliff. I always got time."

He means for Cliff. He looks downcast, though, as if he's wishing he were somewhere else. Who could blame him?

"Emma…"

"Yep, sure… I got a message for you. She said I was to tell you her time to leave came sooner than expected."

"That's all she said?"

"Considerin' how sad she was, how frantic her mama behaved, and that she was sick, I guess Emmaline thought it was enough."

Cliff feels like punching something, or someone. Lamont would do...

"But I guess nothin' would ever be enough," Mac concludes. He shakes his head. "Talk in the mornin'?"

Cliff nods. "See you tomorrow, Mac."

He manacles Lamont to his brass bedhead, removing thereafter all his possessions from around about.

Lamont watches him curiously.

"You all right, Ryan? You look peaky. You don't have to give up your bed. I could sleep on the sofa. I won't be going no place."

"Arrest is arrest, Kit."

"Sure," Lamont smiles. "Still, you don't look the best."

"Do me a favor, Kit..."

"Sure, Ryan."

"No more talk about Eva while you stay here. The subject is off limits."

"Sure, Ryan. Anything you say. No law against dreaming about her, is there?"

"Just don't dream all over my sheets."

Lamont laughs. "Whatever you say, Ryan, but I can't be responsible for what happens while I'm sleeping. You know how it is..."

Cliff closes the door on him.

Ethan

Luke calls by so late that even Tip's fast asleep. Ethan lets him in and sits him down, asking the boy why he looks peaky.

"Had to tell Cliff about Emmaline earlier."

"Sad business," he sighs. "Emmaline's a special young woman. Blind man could see they belong together. How'd he take it?"

"Hard. Ethan, we need to talk. Something's bothering me."

"A bottle of Old Crow might help..."

"Put it in his hand myself. Listen, Ethan, I think you know why Connors made that stipulation to keep Diamond Pass open."

"Nope," he says, looking Luke in the eye. "Why would I?"

"Because you oughta."

"In that case your mother oughta too. I only know what she knows."

"And what does she know?"

"Why don't you ask her?"

"Ethan, I've outgrown the bamboozling act. What is beneath the Diamond-T? Or more especially, Diamond Pass?"

"Why Diamond Pass?"

"Because that gets all the attention in the bill of sale."

They stare at one another in silence for a moment.

"Ethan..."

"Mm," he says, taking a chair by the fire; Luke copies him.

"You know, don't you?"

"Know what?"

"What's there?"

"How would I know that? Are you crazy?"

"I'll sure as hell go crazy if I don't find some answers soon."

He grunts. "We shouldn't be talking about you going crazy."

"Ben thinks that Ed Parsons knew all along."

"Knew what?"

Luke goes quiet for a moment. He's thinking. Good time to distract him.

"So how's married life?" he asks.

Luke frowns. "You know everything's fine…" But he stops and looks like he wants to say something more only to think better of it.

"Something you want to tell me?"

Luke shakes his head.

Ethan gives a firm nod. "Good. You and Jennifer have a life that's all your own. You tell other folks only what they need to know."

"You and I sure as hell ain't married and we used to tell each other stuff all the time. Now for some reason you want to hold out on me."

"Whoa," he laughs, "that's a big call from a whippersnapper."

"Ethan, I ain't leaving till you tell me."

"I'm planning to hit the hay pretty soon."

"About Diamond Pass. I'm trying to recall what kinda rocks lie about. Ben's been telling me what kinda rocks are to be found near gold deposits. He said veins or reefs are found in quartz, opaque white rock. You usually need to dig for that. But I've seen bits of that around the place. Then there's gold that gets washed into rivers, and into sand, gravel and granite mostly, Ben reckons."

"I know," Ethan replies coolly. "It's called alluvial gold. I've seen gold panning. Even tried my hand at it."

"You never said."

"Why should I? You know, Luke, my life ain't an open book for you to pick up and read anytime you feel like it…"

"We've got this kinda stuff, lots of it."

"So have lotsa folks. It's natural. Don't mean there's gold."

"I didn't realize that I oughta've been spending my summers panning down by the river…"

"You think if there was gold we wouldn't't've found it by now?"

"You tell me, Ethan."

"Your pa and me checked out the place when we first got there. Up where the River's born. Lotsa interestin' landforms up there. True, there's bits of that quartz about, granite rocks and such. We tracked all the way down to the plains. We didn't see gold."

"No offense, Ethan, but did you know what you were looking for? Did you do the exploration? I've seen how you look for things and if it ain't on the top of the pile you say it can't be found."

"I told you I know how to pan for gold."

"What made you think to look anyway?"

"New place, who knows what's there. We *explored* – in our own way – for all sorts of things. Couldn't find anything like gold. I figured if there'd been anything valuable, Connors wouldn't have sold up and moved on. That's logical."

"Yes, but he stipulated that the Pass remain open. Why? What does that mean exactly? It's ours, Ethan? Or still Connors'? Is that what it means? We don't own it? He can come back at some point and lay claim to it? I mean, if we had the original documents, the ones the Army made, we could examine what it really means, not just what Connors put in the bill of sale for our benefit. Did Pa go to the grave with a secret?"

Stunned, Ethan lassos his response and reins it in tight. "What kind of a thing is that to say? Your pa and I didn't have secrets. And why all the interest in gold? You think it's gonna make all your dreams come true, is that it?"

The boy keeps his mouth shut; there's a strange look in his eye though.

"What are you thinking about?" Ethan asks.

"The future. My responsibilities."

"Ah. Commendable. Luke, you're no prospector…"

"But Ben is. At least, he could be."

Ethan has to swallow this; there was no stopping the boy when he got to thinking in these dimensions. There was only one problem.

"You think a whole heap of gold's gonna make you a happier person? A better person?"

"Actually, no…"

"Is that what the Diamond-T means to you now? The prospect of gold?"

Luke shifts his position, leans forward on his knees. "Ethan, I don't want to be rich. I don't want much more than I've already got. I only know one thing. When this is over and we go back, it won't be the same. You'll be there, and thank God for it. But Tip will want to spread his wings. My mother is who knows where and doing who knows what. I have Jennifer and… our future to consider. And then there's Ben and Raina. What if Tressa wants to marry again someday? Adam is the sole heir to John and Amy's place…"

Ethan stops him by raising his hand. "You're talking like a man who has an empire to run, like the future of everyone depends on you…"

The boy's face changes to a considerable shade of pale.

"I know you don't mean it that a-way, but while a little planning's a good thing, Luke, you ain't supposed to carry the burden you just mapped out. Now, I don't want you to be disappointed but I know you won't rest till you know for sure if there's gold on the Diamond-T or not. But don't think that a lump of gold's gonna take care of everyone's future, because it ain't. If you let people believe their future depends on you, then they'll expect you to provide for them. You don't want that, believe me. Wealth and riches turn families into dynasties, and dynasties turn people into slaves. Now I know your philosophy's always been that folks should be independent, a little help now and then, but free to make their own way, like you. You and Jennifer have an interesting life ahead of you. You start trying to take care of everyone, Luke, and you'll be miserable, without a shred of freedom left to speak of, for them or you. Do you get my meaning? Do you understand what I'm saying?"

"Yes. I understand, Ethan," Luke says, his voice low.

Ethan nods his satisfaction. "See what just the thought of finding gold does to a person."

The boy gives a laugh and sits back, his color returning.

"Still, I'm glad you've taken a shine to Ben. I've been hoping you would."

"Do you speak much to his father?"

"Some. Not much. Don't think Richard speaks much to anyone. When an arrogant SOB like your uncle suffers as much humiliation as he did…"

"Yeah."

But then he reminds himself that Luke suffered much more at the hands of Porterfield and Donnelly than the indignity Richard copped from Bodecker; Luke'd made such a good recovery it was easy to forget.

"Ethan…"

"Mm?"

"I don't believe you – about you not knowing if there's gold on the Diamond-T."

Ethan frowns. "Don't you trust me?"

"You can ask me that?"

"You know, Luke, here's the thing. There's gotta be other places where they should've found gold by now."

"True. Maybe that's why Bodecker and Donnelly have been so industrious about acquiring it."

"But there should have been alluvial gold. We and how many others along the River and across the valley should have found it."

Luke gets to his feet. "I agree. But something's there, Ethan. And someone knows what it is because Ed Parsons wouldn't stop and neither would Bodecker and Donnelly."

"Well, I for one don't want to muck up the place looking for something that'll only bring on a heap of trouble. I like the Diamond-T the way it is!"

The boy smiles. "Me, too, Ethan." But the smile goes as quick as it came. "It used to tell me who I was. I just haven't worked it in so long… and now I have to be who I am supposed to be without it, if that makes any sense. I feel… changed."

Ethan sighs; stands up, too, and sticks his hands on his hips. "Well, marriage is a big step."

"Marriage?"

"Sure. If marrying a woman don't change you or your life some, you might as well've stayed a bachelor. Mind you, it happens. But not with you. You love Jennifer. More than the Diamond-T, right?"

Again the quick smile. "A lot more. That ain't bad, is it?"

"Are you crazy? She's supposed to be worth more to you than a lump of dirt and grass. More than gold, too. And as for that lump of dirt and grass, well, you'll work it again. That's what we're fighting for, ain't we?"

"Sure, Ethan."

"Now go on home. As for not believing me about the gold, well, I won't hold it against you."

The boy's eyes crinkle at the corners.

"Go on home before I kick you out."

Faraday

Day Seven of Testimony
Monday morning

"So, Mr Faraday, who do we have here... let me see..." Judge Callaghan shuffles his papers, adjusts his spectacles and reads. Then looks up over his lenses. "Mr Lamont..."

"That's correct, Your Honor."

The Judge addresses Lamont, who stands straight and eager, despite his manacled wrists and rather bedraggled appearance. He's a man of medium height with a strong head of brown hair, brown eyes and a prominent hooked nose.

Cliff stands behind him, looking like a corpse. The Judge peers past Lamont to take a gander at him.

"Mr Ryan, you seem a little grim and out of sorts this morning."

"I'm fine, Your Honor," Cliff says, but his croaky voice is hardly reassuring.

The Judge looks unconvinced. "If you say so, Mr Ryan. Now. It says here in my notes, Mr Lamont, that you sexually assaulted Miss Ruth O'Brien, a saloon girl at Mr Tim Beresford's Sit a Spell Saloon down town." The Judge stops and surveys the courtroom. "Where is your counsel, Mr Lamont?"

"Don't need a lawyer, Your Honor. I admit that I got a little rough with Miss O'Brien."

"Yes, but..."

"Excuse me, Your Honor," Lamont says. "Mr Faraday here said I should get some defense lawyer or other but that will take time and I don't have time. I was rough with the girl, I gave her bruises, she saw a doctor. Oh, I paid the bill first thing this morning…"

"Mr Lamont, that will do. Mr Faraday, where is Miss O'Brien?"

"She is not well enough to get out of bed, Your Honor."

"I see. When will she be well enough?"

"I think by tomorrow morning, Your Honor."

"How old is Miss O'Brien, Mr Faraday?"

"I believe she is seventeen, Your Honor."

"A minor, Mr Faraday."

"Yes, Your Honor."

"Well, I am not satisfied, Mr Faraday. I want to speak with the girl. Have her in my chambers ten o'clock tomorrow morning."

"Yes, Your Honor."

"Mr Lamont, you admit to assaulting Miss O'Brien."

"A saloon girl, Your Honor," Lamont supplies.

"Yes, thank you, Mr Lamont; and now, sir, you may like to keep your mouth shut until you find yourself some counsel. I will see you back here tomorrow morning – with counsel. Is that understood?"

Lamont gives a sigh. "Yes, Your Honor. But this could be all over so simple…"

The Judge wags his finger at Lamont, peering over his lenses. Lamont clamps his lips together, then lifts his shoulders to draw breath, only to have the Judge smack his gavel and end proceedings. Lamont jumps and cringes and mutters, "Damn thing…"

Luckily, the Judge is too busy leaving the courtroom to hear.

Monday afternoon

"You are still under oath, Mr Benchley."

"Yes, Your Honor."

"Mr Benchley…"

"Yes, Mr Faraday?"

"Where were you on the morning Mr Donnelly arrived at the Keaton ranch house?"

"I was there visiting with the Keatons. Tressa Keaton had her brother Ben staying and I wanted to spend some time with the lad. But when Sheriff Dave Ransford arrived with news that we were soon to be under attack from these mavericks, we hunkered down for what was to come."

"And what happened?"

"Mr Donnelly happened."

Ethan relates the events of that morning. How they lay in wait. How they captured Donnelly. How a gunfight with the maverick Raz Cole ended when Dave Ransford captured him, too. How Amy, Tressa and baby Adam hid and sheltered in the basement. How, worried about his son Tip and the situation at the Diamond-T, he, Ben and Dave Ransford set off, only to be ambushed by two more mavericks. How a gunfight ensued and how Ransford was killed. How at the eleventh hour he and Ben, their ammunition all but spent, were preparing to die when Luke and Sheriff Ryan saved them, and the mavericks were dead. How Luke was ill from being poisoned by drugs and that it took weeks for him to recover.

Sturrock has a couple of questions for cross-examination.

"Mr Benchley, it sounds as though you insisted on leaving the Keaton ranch for the Diamond-T that day. Is it not true that Sheriff Ransford expressed his reluctance, given the circumstances?"

"Some."

"So, he accompanied you even though he didn't think it a good idea? In fact, your insistence in fighting these mavericks at your own peril put Sheriff Ransford's life in jeopardy, did it not?"

"Think you might be kinda mixed up, Mr Sturrock. He was reluctant to let us go alone. We had to wait till he got back from putting Raz Cole and Mr Donnelly in the lockup and leave Deputy Jim Crogan's body with the undertaker. He didn't want us to meet up with the maverick meant for Ben without him being there. And that's a fact. We didn't start this, Mr Sturrock…"

"That's all. No further questions."

"We came under attack for no good reason from Donnelly and his mavericks. If Miss Roberts hadn't got that information through to Sheriff Ransford, a lot of us would be dead, if not all of us."

"I said that will be all, Mr Benchley."

Ethan shrugs, shakes his head.

The Judge says, "Thank you, Mr Benchley. You may step down now. Court is adjourned until eleven o'clock tomorrow morning."

"All rise…"

Faraday lifts his briefcase from his desk and prepares to charge home to Meg, and he makes a good attempt at it until Sturrock and Buchanan block his path in the corridor.

"Bridger just delivered your updated witness list, Faraday," Sturrock says.

Faraday has always been grateful to be tall, never more so than when being surrounded by the black suits. "Good. See you in the morning, gentlemen." He makes an attempt at going around them.

"What about this Lamont?" Buchanan asks, through his teeth no less.

"What about him? I only have to update you, Mr Buchanan. I am not required to do your investigation for you. Good afternoon."

EIGHT

Time will teach thee soon the truth...

Henry Wadsworth Longfellow
It Is Not Always May

Faraday

Day Eight of Testimony
Tuesday morning

"Judge Callaghan, may I present Miss O'Brien."

"Thank you, Mr Faraday. Miss O'Brien, please sit down."

In Judge Callaghan's chambers, Faraday seats the girl in the more comfortable of the chairs before the Judge's desk. She can barely move without grimacing. The Judge notices everything.

"Just answer my questions truthfully, Miss O'Brien."

"Yes, Judge," she stammers, unsure where to look.

"You can look me in the eye, young lady. I don't bite. I have daughters of my own. I know how it is with young ladies."

"I'm no young lady, Judge."

The Judge scrutinizes her for a moment before diving into his notes. "It says in my papers that you work for Tim Beresford in his Sit a Spell Saloon on 15th Street as a saloon girl, correct?"

"Yes, although the doctor told me I can't work there anymore."

"Because of your injuries?"

"Yes, sir."

"And you entertain upstairs as well as downstairs?"

At the bluntness of this question Miss O'Brien swallows hard. "Yes. I need the money. I haven't saved enough to get by yet."

"For how long, and how many clients have you had?"

"Two months. And a few. Mr Beresford wanted me to get some experience before Spring roundup."

"When trail cowboys come into town."

"Yes, that's right."

"Do you have a home, Miss O'Brien?"

"I stay at the saloon. I have a room."

"Your family – where are they?"

Miss O'Brien shrugs, but the gesture causes her to grimace.

"What happened to you yesterday afternoon, Miss O'Brien?"

She shakes her head.

"Miss O'Brien, if you want the man who assaulted you to be punished you must tell me what happened…"

"I… he…" Ruth O'Brien draws a huge breath. "He approached me, wanted… you know, I told him how much, he accepted, we went to my room, he told me to undress and get on the bed, I did as he said, then he tied my hands to the bed with my stockings, he… he pressed my feet to the bed with his knees, my feet are bruised…"

She is only one tear away from sobbing; she takes another deep breath.

"He sat on top of me. He told me to be Eva. He put it inside me, pushing and pushing… it hurt so much and I told him to stop… I wasn't ready… I told him to stop over and over… but he wouldn't. He kept on and on. His hands hurt my body… he didn't kiss nice… it hurt, like biting. After him telling me to be Eva over and over and pushing till I thought I would die, then he got what he wanted. He still didn't stop, he kept on, hurting me… at last he stopped and got off me. He untied me, pushed me off the bed and told me to get out. I demanded my money. He shoved me into the hall and threw the money at me. I had no clothes on, he wouldn't let me get dressed. I'd never been treated this way before. I didn't know what to do, what was happening to me… I should never have done what he wanted, but I didn't think he would be so rough and mean. He wouldn't stop. I was so stupid…"

Ruth O'Brien puts her head into her hands and sobs hard.

Faraday offers her a clean handkerchief.

"Did he beat you, Miss O'Brien?"

"No."

"Did he speak violently to you?"

"No. He wanted me to be this Eva. He was speaking to her, he wanted to make love to her, instead he… he did this to me."

"Did you at any stage refuse to do what he wanted?"

"A couple of times, in the beginning, before he got on me and held me down. I tried to fight him off, Judge, but he had me tied up. I couldn't get away. And when I struggled it seemed to make him more... you know... determined."

"And when you tried to refuse him in the beginning, what made you go along with what he wanted from you?"

"He said it would go easier on me if I just did what he wanted."

"Miss O'Brien, have you ever experienced rough treatment from a client before?"

"Sometimes a man will get rough under the influence, but you learn how to handle that. Not this man though. He wasn't drunk. He was mean. There was no feeling in him, except for this Eva."

"Do you believe you were raped, Miss O'Brien?"

"I said stop so many times and he didn't, but that's what I'm there for, ain't it? I was so stupid."

The Judge doesn't answer; he stares long and hard at the girl.

Finally, he says, "Miss O'Brien, you are a minor, do you know what that means?"

"I'm too young."

"It means that now I can do with you as I see fit..."

Ruth O'Brien sits forward, plaintively, despite her pain. "No, please, Judge, don't send me anywhere. I'm looking for a respectable job. Honest. There are people helping me. Even Mr Beresford said he'd help. I'll find a good job and never set foot inside a saloon again."

"That's very commendable, Miss O'Brien, and I'm glad to hear it. But once you lose your self-respect it's a long road back to respectability. Do you understand?"

"I understand..." she murmurs.

"I don't know what set you on this path to begin with, Miss O'Brien, but it was a dark day."

"It was, Judge."

"Then I suggest you find employment with a respectable business that will protect you and educate you to such a degree that you will not be tempted to stray. You are to attend night school, Miss O'Brien."

"School, Judge?"

"You heard me, young lady. When you have a respectable job, you enroll in night school. Learn what's worth knowing about the world you live in. And I want a report on my desk every two weeks about your progress, is that clear?"

"But, Judge…"

"Mr Faraday, are we clear on this point?"

"Ah…"

"Speak to the clergy in town. Find out who would be willing to keep an eye on Miss O'Brien for a few months until she gets herself on track. A little religion wouldn't go astray either."

"Yes, Judge."

"Miss O'Brien, who is your doctor?"

"Dr Sullivan."

"Excellent. Mr Faraday, would you please inform Dr Sullivan of these requirements for her patient. I think I can also count on Dr Sullivan to see the thing done. Now, Miss O'Brien, the man who assaulted you will come before me in approximately fifteen minutes. You are required to be court. Are you willing to give testimony?"

"Say all this again to more people? How can I ever be respectable again, Judge?"

"You chose the path, Miss O'Brien. The court can only do so much. It's up to you where you go next."

The clerk, who has instructions to accompany Miss O'Brien to the witness room, escorts her out of the Judge's chambers.

The Judge sits back in his chair, peering at Faraday over his lenses. Then he removes them and peers some more.

"So, Mr Faraday, what is your charge against Mr Lamont – rape or assault?"

"Rape, Judge."

"Good for you, Mr Faraday," the Judge says with a hint of a smile. "That will be all." He knows as well as Faraday that rape will be difficult to prove. Lamont has procured a sympathetic defense attorney. "You never disappoint me, Mr Faraday," Judge Callaghan murmurs as Faraday leaves his chambers.

Faraday pretends he doesn't hear.

In court

"Mr Lamont, you are charged with rape of a minor, how do you plead?"

Defense counsel Andy Marks, replies, "My client pleads not guilty to rape, Your Honor. And he had no idea how old the girl was. He admits to being rough with her because he wasn't of sound mind at the time."

The Judge frowns. "Not of sound mind, Mr Marks?"

"That's correct, Your Honor. Mr Lamont was grief-stricken at losing the woman he loves."

"Did she die, Mr Lamont?"

Lamont looks up. "Oh no, Your Honor. We are forced apart."

"Mr Marks, this is no legal defense. Mr Lamont either raped or assaulted Miss O'Brien, and disappointment at not being with his inamorata is not a mitigating circumstance."

"Very well, Your Honor. My client still pleads not guilty."

"I have the relevant statements in front me, Mr Lamont, and they match. Yours and Miss O'Brien's match. Only she accuses you of rape and you admit to assault. Mr Marks?"

"Your Honor, I petition the court to have the charge of rape reduced to the lesser charge of assault in the fifth degree which in Wyoming Territory carries a penalty of one week in the lockup. Mr Lamont paid Miss O'Brien for her services. She willingly went with him, carried out his wishes and then changed her mind at the last moment. Miss O'Brien tried to renege on her part of the agreement. Mr Lamont held her to it. That does not constitute rape, Your Honor."

The young and perky Andy Marks has an interesting quality to his voice. He makes a person listen to him.

"A business deal gone sour, Mr Marks?" the Judge suggests.

"Precisely, Your Honor. When Miss O'Brien lay down on the bed and offered Mr Lamont her body for his pleasure, she had no right to pull out of the deal and he had every right to fulfill the obligations on his part. He did so, despite Miss O'Brien's unwillingness. In her profession, Your Honor, there can be no doubt that pulling out just as a client is fully aroused and ready to fulfill his part of the agreement would incur the client's displeasure and depending how far along the protest occurs, it would make it almost impossible for the client to not fulfill his part of the agreement."

The Judge blinks.

"Mr Lamont was vicious, Mr Marks."

"He was a fully aroused adult male who was at the last moment being denied what he was paying for."

The Judge frowns. "Mr Lamont is a human being, Mr Marks, not a wild bull elephant."

"Studies have been done, Your Honor, where..."

"Ah, spare me the studies of the scientific world, Mr Marks. Mr Faraday, I will hear from you now..."

Faraday feels tugging on his coat; he looks down to find Ruth O'Brien, her face awash with tears, shaking her head at him.

"Ah, one moment, Your Honor..." He sits and faces the distressed young woman squarely. "Are you sure about this, Miss O'Brien? – because everything his attorney is saying is fully refutable."

"No," she mutters. "Enough. This attorney will destroy me..."

"You can't let him scare you. Please, Miss O'Brien, you have to trust me on this. I've been at this game a very long time."

"No, Mr Faraday. Let him have his assault in the fifth degree."

Faraday makes yet another plea. And another.

She shakes her head firmly. "I will do as the Judge says. And I will make something of myself. I can't do it though if every detail of what happened is spread across town and through the papers. I...I can't do this anymore."

"Mr Faraday..."

He gets to his feet. "Yes, Your Honor. The prosecution has decided it will be satisfied with the lesser charge. However, it would make recommendations to the court that the punishment for this lesser charge be more substantial than one week in the lockup. Miss O'Brien is black and blue and suffered greatly at the hands of Mr Lamont. This was no bar room brawl. This assault was premeditated and brutal."

Ruth O'Brien quietly sobs. Faraday takes a deep breath.

"And, Your Honor…"

"Continue, Mr Faraday."

"The prosecution would also recommend the defendant pay punitive damages. Miss O'Brien has suffered and will continue to suffer severe personal loss as a result of his assault. She has no income; she has medical bills to pay; she suffers from loss of self-esteem, and needs money to restart her life. She can no longer work at her former job, she is a minor and is under a court order to find respectable employment as well as attend night school. With the reduction of the charge, the defendant will be able to resume his life as normal after a few weeks none the worse off. The example this sets to the rest of the community regarding the treatment of women is poor at best."

"Objection. Miss O'Brien is a saloon girl, Your Honor."

"Your Honor, Mr Marks has already forgotten, it seems, that Miss O'Brien is a naïve seventeen year old girl who was brutally sexually assaulted."

"Overruled, Mr Marks. Mr Faraday, thank you for your recommendations. These will be taken under advisement."

"Thank you, Your Honor."

"Regarding Mr Lamont, are there any circumstances the court should be aware of, Mr Faraday?"

"Yes, Your Honor. Mr Lamont is a key witness in the Bodecker-Donnelly trial and is required to give testimony over the next few days."

"Very well. Mr Lamont, this court finds you guilty of assault in the fifth degree. As the county jail is full at present, and taking into account Mr Faraday's recommendations, I sentence you to one month in the Territorial Penitentiary in Laramie. This will ensure that you are close at hand if you are needed for the trial. Mr Marks, where did your client spend the last two nights under arrest?"

"Your Honor, my client has been under house arrest with Sheriff Ryan."

"In his *home*?"

"Yes, Your Honor."

"Your Honor, if I may elaborate?" Faraday says.

"Please do, Mr Faraday."

"Your Honor, it is in the interest of the trial and Mr Lamont's welfare that he be given appropriate protection. Mr Ryan and his deputies are providing that."

The Judge sighs deeply. Faraday knows how he feels.

"Is Mr Ryan agreeable to continue this arrangement for the time being, while Mr Lamont is required to give testimony?"

"He is, Your Honor."

"Then once again we are very fortunate that Mr Ryan is our sheriff. As for the case for punitive damages, I find in favor of Miss O'Brien. The defendant will be required to pay damages in the amount of $550..."

Ruth O'Brien lets out a sob.

Lamont gasps. "But, Judge..."

"...in the amount of $550. Miss O'Brien, I suggest you go down to the bank this afternoon and open an account if you don't already have one. Mr Lamont will be writing a check for the full amount within the week. Isn't that right, Mr Lamont?"

Lamont's face has slipped into his neck. "Er... Yes, Judge."

"Excellent. Anything else, gentlemen?"

"Your Honor, the usual penalty for this charge is one week," Andy Marks replies. "I appeal against the severity of the sentence."

"Of course, you do, Mr Marks, but I will not be moved. We are finished here, gentlemen." He smacks his gavel loudly and sweeps from the courtroom.

Faraday sinks back into his seat. Across the way, Marks is patting Lamont solicitously on the shoulder, but Cliff – grim-faced and pale – appears from nowhere and drags Lamont away.

Ruth O'Brien watches with morbid fascination.

She says, "I've learnt my lesson, Mr Faraday. And thank you for what you did, standing up for me like that. I can make a fresh start now. I promise I will use the money wisely. And make you and the Judge proud."

What can he say to that?

"I believe you will. Good luck, Miss O'Brien."

Faraday

Faraday is pouring coffee when Cliff wanders into his office and sits down. He looks – in a word – awful. Faraday walks over to him and offers him the coffee.

"Thanks," he says and sips it.

Faraday pours himself another. "What happened to our friend?"

"My roomie?"

Faraday chuckles. "Haven't heard that expression since college. Living with a man like that, it probably feels like college."

"Mac's looking after him for a couple of hours."

"Well... You got your wish."

"I know you tried your hardest, Cam, but the outcome was expected."

"It's not something to be proud of or pleased about. Even though she has received a fresh start, Miss O'Brien deserved a better justice."

Cliff blows a sigh; gets an impatient air about him. "Sure, Cam."

"I think we should change the subject because you and I will never agree on this."

Cliff twists in his chair. He doesn't respond. He's lost interest...

"There's an expression..." Faraday says. "You look like hell."

"I'll be fine in a day or two, so let's forget about me and concentrate on Lamont."

Faraday sits at his desk. "Lamont will keep. You on the other hand... I know how you feel..."

A shadow of disbelief falls across those tortured blue-green eyes. Another slurp of his coffee. "You do?"

"In a way, yes. I've told you before I had to ask Meg to marry me three times; she accepted on the third. Twice she coldly refused me. At the first she told me she didn't love me and she would never have me."

"And yet you tried again..."

"I didn't believe her of course... I loved her passionately; it wasn't possible, surely, that she didn't return my feelings. So, I made some improvements which I thought would impress her. I asked her again. She laughed; she gave me a two-page list of all the things that had to be done – that I had still to do – before she would ever consider a proposal from me. Well, any attention is better than none, particularly as she had gone to so much trouble. So, I went through the list and, short of compromising myself, found that there were indeed things I could improve on. I wondered, in fact marveled at her. How could a twenty-year old woman be so astute?

"In the meantime, having completely dismissed me from her life, having sent me on my way with the impossible list, Meg continued her social life as if I'd never happened. I was utterly miserable. Probably the gloomiest stretch of my life. Then, when she discovered that I'd given up my ambition for politics to focus on being a prosecution attorney, her attentions began to swing my way. That warm-hearted, delightful Meg who I knew existed below the surface of the cold, ambivalent Meg became interested. I knew I'd been handled but it didn't matter. I asked her once more."

Cliff flashes a wry grin. "I know how much you love Meg, but I just can't picture you getting down on one knee and proposing."

"Third time I didn't go down on one knee." Faraday grins at the memory. "I wrote Will You Marry Me on a calling card and left it at the front door of her home. Her mother was livid; her father laughed for two days straight and Meg marched into my office downtown and demanded I ask her properly or suffer the consequences. Refusal, of course. Eternal refusal. I told her that I would only do so if her answer would favor me. What would be the point of you knowing that, she said furiously. I replied, calmly, that if she could no longer find fault with me, then what reason could she have for refusing me. None, she said. You know, she didn't believe I could change, that was her trouble. I had to make her believe in me.

"And there are my own thoughts on Meg herself. Indeed she was stalling, but for her own sake as well. She wouldn't be rushed; she took time to consider everything. Meg prepared herself. Some people say that I should never have given away my own ambitions for her, but Meg caused me to resort to introspection, not something I was glad to do at first, and I realized what a man wants to do with his life and his true calling are not necessarily the same thing. I never considered myself callow until she made me look at myself."

"I can't even imagine you callow at the age of five."

"I have never once regretted my decision."

"She *will* let you sit on the Bench one day, won't she, Cam?"

"I believe to that path she is most open and agreeable," he says, grinning.

But Cliff is not in the mood to find amusement in the persuasive powers of the woman in a man's life. A frown deepens the shadow of unhappiness over his face. "She left, Cam, she could have waited a few hours, a day more..."

"Her mother would have none of it."

"That's what I keep hearing, but..."

"You didn't tell her, did you?"

"No. She wouldn't let me. And it had to be done right. I planned my next attempt for when I got back from Laramie. I was determined. Wasn't the only one with something to tell, was I?"

"Will you go after her?"

"Does she want me to? Do I even want to?"

"Do I even need to tell you? If not for this trial, you would be long gone, but you're stuck. Upset, and frustrated. See what the next few days bring. Give yourself and Emmaline a chance to come to terms with what has happened. There is no doubt in my mind she was deeply distraught about leaving you."

"I thought you said you didn't have any advice for me when it came to Emma."

"I thought of some."

Cliff's laugh is somewhat bitter. "I'm not the one who's sick, am I, so why am I complaining? I knew Emma had to go home, but I figured on an understanding before she left. That was my goal. But this…" He gives his head a shake.

"You two have had quite the tussle, haven't you?"

"And the only thing I regret is leaving for Laramie on Saturday morning. Nothing else. Because that tussle, Cam, is the best time I've ever had."

They pass a long moment in silence.

"So, Cam… what's next? – in the case, I mean."

"You're going back on the stand."

"Denver?"

"Precisely."

"Finally. Alfredo Severini?"

Faraday nods. "That way we can introduce Lamont slowly to the jury."

Faraday

"Sheriff Ryan, why did Marshal Dan Hummer swear you in as a deputy US marshal?"

"Marshal Hummer had been on a mission to locate Loren Bodecker, Ben Taylor's father Richard, and the scientist who drugged Luke Taylor, Louis Porterfield. Up to that point in time, Marshal Hummer had had no luck in locating any of these people. He asked me for assistance and swore me in as a deputy US marshal. Neither of us believed that Loren Bodecker had gone south to a warmer climate for health reasons, which was the statement put out by his attorneys."

"You had a specific reason to go to Denver?"

"I had a hunch that Denver was where Loren Bodecker could be found."

"So you and Marshal Hummer proceeded to Denver. There was a third party who accompanied you."

"Yes. Ben Taylor. Since we were searching for his father Richard, Hummer thought it a good idea to have him along."

"Now on the way to Denver, is it not true that your train was hailed down en route with the express purpose of giving your party an important telegram from the sheriff's office here in Cheyenne?"

"Yes, we received a telegram."

"And what did this telegram say?"

"It said: *Kerr ordered by interested party to send Tucker mile high pronto. Took the 9.30 am stage today. Investigate at once.*"

"How was the information in the telegram gathered?"

"At a conference with newspapermen earlier that day, Dillon

Kerr, Bodecker's senior attorney in Cheyenne, dropped a telegram in the street which read: *Kerr. Send Tucker mile high pronto. Loren.* Luke Taylor found it and handed it in. The telegram came from Denver. It confirmed we were on the right track so it couldn't have come at a better time."

"Refresh our memories regarding this Mr Tucker, if you would."

"Marvin Tucker is one of Loren Bodecker's lesser Cheyenne attorneys. By lesser, I mean not well known."

"What did you and the others do as a result of receiving the telegram en route to Denver?"

"We interpreted the telegram to mean that Loren Bodecker had ordered Dillon Kerr to send Marvin Tucker to Denver because Bodecker needed Tucker to do a job for him. Although Tucker left in the morning the same as we did, he was traveling by stagecoach which meant we could make Denver before him, then stake out the stage depot and wait for him. Then we would follow him until he led us to Bodecker. This is precisely what happened."

"Your Honor, People's exhibit 11a: the telegram picked up in the street by Mr Taylor; and People's exhibit 11b: the telegram sent to Mr Ryan on the train to Denver alerting the marshals where Mr Tucker was headed. The People offer into evidence both these telegrams."

"Thank you, Mr Faraday. Proceed."

"Sheriff Ryan, once in Denver did Marvin Tucker go directly to Mr Bodecker?"

"No. He spent two hours in a brothel on Market Street before he led us directly to Loren Bodecker."

"And what was this place he led you to?"

"The place where Marvin Tucker led us was the Denver Club. This is a large private club for wealthy men and boosters and such to meet, find accommodation, entertain guests and conduct business."

"What did you do then, Mr Ryan?"

"Marshal Hummer gave me the warrant for Loren Bodecker's arrest. I took the warrant because I was to be the one who would find Mr Bodecker and make the arrest. Marshal Hummer would see to Bodecker's minders and other security matters. I gained entry into the club and arrested Mr Bodecker in Room 2D; he was not alone though; Marvin Tucker was with him. I noticed that Tucker had a huge wad of money in his possession and I took Tucker and the money in as evidence of further criminal activity. I suggested to Tucker that he had just been paid off for something. He denied it but later at the Union Station lockup, where we incarcerated Bodecker and Tucker, I searched through the wad of money and found a piece of paper with a name and address on it."

"How much money, Mr Ryan?"

"Five hundred dollars."

"And how did you proceed when you discovered the name and address?"

"Marshal Hummer and I decided that I would investigate the address and he would deal with the state's attorney when he showed up."

"And your suspicion about the address?"

"After all we had been through with the mavericks, Marshal Hummer and I suspected this was the address of a hired gun."

"Objection, Your Honor..."

"Overruled."

"A hired gun for what purpose, Mr Ryan?"

"Objection. Calls for the witness to speculate..."

"Overruled. The witness had acquired a deep understanding of circumstances by this stage and his opinion is relevant. The witness will answer."

"The purpose of the hired gun was to kill Mr Donnelly."

"Order... order!"

"So, Mr Bodecker orders Mr Tucker to Denver and pays him five hundred dollars so that Mr Tucker can do what exactly?"

"Locate the hired gun residing at the address found in the money and give him his instructions to kill Mr Donnelly."

"Order... order!"

"Mr Ryan, what name was on the piece of paper you found in the wad of notes?"

"Alfredo Severini."

"And the address?"

"Beecher Street in Highland, north west of Denver."

"Your Honor, People's exhibit 12a: the five hundred dollars found on Mr Tucker…"

"Order… order!"

"…and People's exhibit 12b: the piece of paper with the name and address of Mr Alfredo Severini which Mr Ryan found within the wad of money located on Marvin Tucker's person in Mr Bodecker's Denver Club apartment. The People offer these into evidence."

"Thank, Mr Faraday."

Proceeding as normal, Faraday allows the jury to eyeball the items before he places both pieces on the evidence table.

"What did you do with the address, Mr Ryan?"

"I went to investigate it, aided by Deputy Allan March from the Union Station police precinct."

"Who or what did you find at the address?"

"The Severini family. Mother – Signora Rosa Severini – and her two sons, Alfredo and Gianni. I took Alfredo away for questioning regarding what Loren Bodecker would want with him."

"Did Alfredo Severini admit to you what Mr Bodecker wanted with him?"

"Eventually. With his mother's help. They are a good family. Alfredo had got mixed up in something and his mother wanted to make things right."

"Into what exactly had Alfredo got himself mixed up?"

"Mr Donnelly had hired him for his team of sharpshooters. He wasn't a maverick as such, but a hired gun nonetheless. He hadn't killed anyone or done anything wrong in his life; his family needed money and he thought this misguided way of getting it would help. He was still waiting for his first job. And he was nervous. Donnelly had already given him some token amount of money up front to entice him and have him ready and willing to do as he was told."

"What evidence do you have that Donnelly had recruited Alfredo Severini?"

"The Severinis were able to produce the circular that Donnelly had been distributing around the market gardens looking for recruits among the low paid workers."

"Your Honor, People's exhibit 13: the notice for recruitment of sharpshooters circulated by Mr Donnelly…"

"Thank you, Mr Faraday."

"Continue, Mr Ryan."

"Two days previous to my calling on the Severini family, Bodecker had sent Alfredo Severini a note. The note said: *You will be contacted soon with a job. Be ready. Maverick.* However, Donnelly had already been arrested and could not have sent it. Looking at the handwriting, I found it was a match for the writing on the note found in the money with Alfredo Severini's address on it. This new note was also written by Loren Bodecker."

"Objection. Your Honor, these notes could have been written by anyone."

"Your Honor, in order to make this perfectly clear to the court, the handwriting was examined independently by several people." Josh hands him a sheet of paper and he reads from it: "Mr Tom Follows, the school teacher, and a handwriting expert. Two of Mr Bodecker's own staff, who would only do so if they were promised anonymity. And Mr Donald Digby, one of Cheyenne's most experienced telegraphers, who is quite familiar with Mr Bodecker's handwriting. Mr Follows and Mr Digby are willing to testify if the court wishes them to do so."

"The court does not. Objection overruled, Mr Buchanan."

"Your Honor, People's exhibit 14: the note written by Mr Bodecker, using Maverick's name, and alerting Alfredo Severini."

"Thank you, Mr Faraday."

"So, returning to the note, Mr Ryan, you have stated that you believe Mr Bodecker had every intention of assassinating his own partner, Mr Donnelly. Why?"

"To stop him from talking about all their alleged murders, their alleged schemes and their alleged conspiracies."

"Objection…"

"Your Honor, I believe Mr Ryan used the word *alleged*…"

"Overruled, Mr Buchanan. Proceed, Mr Faraday."

"Mr Ryan, while you were searching for and arresting Mr Bodecker and then investigating the Severini family, what was Ben Taylor doing?"

"He was searching for his father, Richard Taylor."

"What was your suspicion regarding Richard Taylor?"

"The general thought was that he'd got caught up with Loren Bodecker to the detriment of his family, but this was not my considered opinion…"

"Objection. We have heard nothing but Mr Ryan's considered opinions since he took the stand."

"Your Honor, if the witness may be allowed to finish his statement…"

"He may. Objection overruled. The witness will continue."

"I began to believe that Richard Taylor was being blackmailed by Loren Bodecker and even held against his will."

"So how was Richard Taylor located?"

"Ben Taylor and his wife, Raina Montgomery, located him."

"And were your suspicions correct?"

"Yes, Richard Taylor was being held against his will in a quiet section of the Denver Club at the direction of Loren Bodecker. A number of Bodecker's men were Richard Taylor's keepers. They fed him, gave him Mr Bodecker's instructions, took him out of his room when Bodecker required it, and deprived him of liberty."

"Why did Richard Taylor succumb to such treatment?"

"He was warned that his wife Caroline and son Ben would be killed if he didn't do as he was told. Originally, Mr Bodecker had suckered Richard Taylor in with promises of money to help expand his mining business. This was a ruse to get Richard Taylor's family under his control, extending the range of his control of Luke Taylor and the Alliance."

"Richard Taylor didn't know what had happened to his wife and son?"

"According to Luke Taylor's testimony of the discussion between Bodecker and Donnelly in Omaha, Ben Taylor was to have been murdered by a maverick, which as we have also already heard, never happened because of Dave Ransford's heroic efforts; and Caroline Taylor was supposed to have been so terrified that she would never leave her home, but she was rescued by Luke Taylor and together they managed to see her to Cheyenne, where she was given protection."

"So if Richard Taylor was being held against his will and deprived of liberty in the Denver Club, how did you extricate him?"

"Objection, Your Honor. How is this relevant?"

"Your Honor, the relevance will become clear."

"Short, concise, relevant, Mr Ryan."

"Yes, Your Honor."

"Overruled. The witness will answer."

"Ben, his wife Raina and I infiltrated the Denver Club by diverting the desk clerk whose name was Lamont. Ben and I roamed the corridors until we found the room where Richard Taylor was being held. He was unwell, extremely disoriented and didn't know what was happening to him. We explained who we were, what we doing there and smuggled him out."

"And your suspicions regarding Richard Taylor were confirmed at this time?"

"Yes. Richard Taylor revealed to us that Loren Bodecker was holding him against his will. He expressed concern for his wife and was fearful of leaving because of her. We were able to reassure him. With this done, two of our mission objectives had been achieved. Locating and arresting Loren Bodecker. Locating and extricating Richard Taylor. The state's attorney and other city officials gave their OK on the warrant and we were ready to return to Cheyenne."

"Your third mission objective – to locate and arrest Dr Louis Porterfield – was that any closer to being achieved?"

"No, that needed a different tack altogether."

"Your Honor, I request that Mr Ryan continues with this testimony regarding the arrest of Dr Porterfield and its significance to this case after the luncheon adjournment."

The Judge takes out his watch and peers at it. "Good heavens," he murmurs and haphazardly stows his watch back in his pocket. "Request granted." He taps his gavel. "Court is adjourned for forty five minutes."

"All rise."

All do. The Judge sweeps from the court as though he's late for a crucial appointment.

Forty-Five Minutes

Cliff checks that Donnelly and Bodecker are secure in the holding room while they await their lunch.

As he enters the room he catches Bodecker sneering...

"Lamont the desk clerk? I got nothing, Buchanan."

Buchanan glances over his shoulder and in a *let's change the subject* tone of voice says, "Same fare every day, Ryan. My client could use a change of diet."

The bailiff enters, as if cued by a stage director, carrying a tray of sandwiches and several apples.

Cliff nods politely to the bailiff and says, "They might as well get used to monotony."

Buchanan gives a bitter smile and Cliff walks out with the bailiff, who locks the door behind them and then stands adjacent to one of Mac's burly prison guards.

*

As Bodecker lifts one of the sandwiches and inspects it like it's last week's fish, Buchanan launches another attempt...

"So, Loren. This Lamont..."

"Told you already. He's a desk clerk at the Denver Club. And that's all I got to tell you."

"I need to know what you know, Loren. I need to know what Faraday and Ryan are about to unleash."

Donnelly looks like he wants to say something; Bodecker gives him a filthy look. Donnelly sinks his teeth into a sandwich instead.

"Who says they're going to unleash anything? Anyone'd think you are scared of them. You'd be better off finding out what's up with Ryan. He looks as sour as a maiden aunt."

"I have a maiden aunt, Loren," Buchanan says, both offended and annoyed. "She's anything but sour. In fact, she's probably the nicest relative I have. As for Ryan, his personal problems don't interest me. Now let's try this again. *Lamont...*"

*

Cliff strides across town and into his office. Mac is there, with Lamont manacled to one of the legs of the interrogation room table.

"Howdy, Ryan," Lamont says as Cliff enters and Mac slips out.

"Have you eaten?"

"Mac says lunch'll be here any minute."

"A little bird told me Bodecker's staying quiet about you, Kit," Cliff remarks , leaning back against the doorframe. "Why is that?"

"Beats me. Could be he's scared."

"Could be."

Lamont chuckles. "The difference between me and Bodecker right this minute... I got one month in a lockup and then I go get Eva. He's got a whole lifetime in jail and no Eva ever; even if the unthinkable happens and he goes free, still no Eva."

The hairs on the back of Cliff's neck prickle. "That better not happen, Kit."

Again Lamont twitters, slyly. "It won't, Ryan."

Mac rejoins them. "Cliff, this letter just came for you – express from Denver."

"Worthing and Farrell?" he asks hopefully, taking it.

Mac's eyes glitter. "No. I think it's personal."

"Thanks, Mac." He retreats into his office, closing the door, examining his name and the county jail address on the front of the envelope, knowing the handwriting as well as his own.

He rips it open. Unfolds the sheets. Emma's handwriting flows across the white expanse, filling the painful void between them.

Dear Ashcliff, I'm sorry. I am so sorry. Do not think I am smug about this; I am in agony. When the train moved out of the station, gathering speed, I began to feel the cord that has bound us together these past weeks pulling and pulling. It hurt terribly. I know I should have waited for you to return to say goodbye properly. Forgive me, please. I would come back to you in an instant if I thought it was the right thing to do. My mother rushed me out of fear and concern, and I didn't take a stand. We are so different on this point - family. Your upbringing and mine could not be more different. I was raised in a large family; my extended family and relations go on for days. And you, an only child, as extraordinary as you are, might struggle to grasp the bond between twins. For me to disregard my family's concerns and the insistent demands my mother makes upon my life, which she preaches are for my own good, would require something beyond powerful.

One thing I know, we are two people in transition. I did my job at the Tribune to the best of my ability, but I don't belong in Cheyenne so I am going home. You have told me you are in the process of making decisions which will affect your whole life. You need the space and freedom to make them.

I know you believe I should have told you about my condition. Truthfully, it was my insurance that I would not succumb to the temptation to stay, and for that reason no one could know about it. But I did succumb and pushed out my departure till the end of the trial. I didn't foresee the intervention.

Our book swap went seriously awry. I never did find my beautiful treasury of poems. I thank you for it and for what you wrote. But I didn't know of its existence until the evening before I left when I sorted through the things from my desk which Zachary boxed for me. That morning in Mr Quaid's office you didn't seem keen on the swap, and you were so busy with work, when you didn't show, I thought you had changed your mind. It was terribly confusing; I didn't know what to do. I didn't understand what had happened until I found the treasury in the box.

Do not come South. Do not be tempted. Do nothing for my sake. I don't want you to. Do not open up the scars that will have begun to heal. I do not want to feel this empty and bereft in my life as I do now. What is the point of possessing something grand only to have it taken away because no matter how we look at it or how hard we try, it would never be right? Once we learn to be without each other, all will be well. We are not destined for one another, James. Believe that. Trust me on this.

I do not hold you to act upon those feelings you expressed towards me, although they do me the greatest honor. You have a life so full of promise; you must realize it with the woman who will fully commit herself to you in that task. She will 'hear you out' gladly I'm sure because she will be the right woman for you. And you will both live a long and happy life together.

I apologize for the mistakes I made; for the things I kept from you; for any foolishness you had to suffer. I don't suppose it matters now what you think of me. This will be my last communication with you. And our lives will take separate paths, as they should. All that is left is to wish you everything good and blessed for the rest of your life. Sincerely, Emma.

He can't stay the trembling in his hands. His eyes sting and fill with tears; he doesn't bother to catch them as they fall on the page.

*

Josh flies into Faraday's office, half-eaten sandwich in one hand and an envelope in the other.

"This telegram just came for you, Cam."

He's gone before Faraday can thank him.

Faraday opens the telegram.

```
CAM FARADAY, DISTRICT ATTORNEY, CHEYENNE, WYOMING, HAVE
SUBPOENAED GEO REPORT ON YOUR BEHALF, WORTHING AND FARRELL
GAVE IT UP IN LIEU OF FACING COURT AND EXTRADITION, EXPECT
REPORT BY URGENT DELIVERY WED MORNING, GOOD LUCK, DOUGLAS
CLARKE, OFFICE OF STATE'S ATTORNEY, DENVER,
```

When he rises to his feet and lets out a great *whoop!* Josh flies back in again, his eyes large behind his spectacles.

"Cam?"

Trying to restrain the triumph leaping out of every cell in his body, he rasps, "We got the geo report!"

"Ah," Josh says, his eyes settling back behind his lenses. "Good. Excellent."

"It will be here tomorrow morning by urgent delivery."

"I'll keep my eyes peeled for it, Cam, don't you worry about that…" Josh leaves again, pushing up his spectacles and grinning.

"Oh, yes, this is a great day…" Faraday sits down and stretches back in his chair, ready to eat a bite of lunch now.

He's chomping into it when Constance, cheeks flushed and hair slumped into some kind of atrocious mess, falls through his door with Josh hot on her heels.

His mouthful goes down his throat is one giant gulp.

"I'm sorry, Cam, she…"

"Constance?"

"Mrs… Mrs Faraday," she puffs. "The doc is with her."

Faraday feels the blood drain from his head. "The baby…"

"The baby is coming…" Constance pants.

"I… I've got to go…" But he seems to be stuck to his chair.

"She's askin' for ya."

"Meg…" he sighs in a kind of wonderment.

"Doc Chestnut… Sullivan, I mean… is there."

"It's early." He gets to his feet at last. "The baby's early…"

"The young doc said it ain't *too* early. She said…"

Josh appears before him. "Instructions, Cam?"

"… the baby is a good size…"

"I'll handle the afternoon session, shall I…"

"…for Mrs Faraday to deliver."

"Cliff can second, when he stands down…"

Somebody please throw cold water on him. "Stop!"

"Certainly, Cam. My apologies."

"Er, Mr Faraday?"

"Yes, Constance?"

"No need for panic. First babies ain't never that keen to make an entrance. I just look this way on account of I had to run so many errands. Take a deep breath. Honest. A good deep one… There ya go… Me and Mrs Faraday do this a lot…"

She breathes. He breathes.

Josh says, "You're not to worry, Cam. Cliff and I will handle this. I'll inform the Judge and take care of things. And I know where you are if I need you. Off you go with Constance. Go on…" Josh hustles him out, draping his coat and muffler over his arm. "And here's your hat. You can check on us later, if you have a chance. Or send someone. Now, good luck and don't worry."

Faraday is still deep breathing as he leaves the building.

Thirty-Five Minutes

As Sara steps down onto the platform at Cheyenne Depot, her whole other life comes rushing back to greet her. Home seems so close now. The ranch and the house; the herds and the horses; all her things, her memories, even Morgan. But home is not where her son is, apparently. According to the New York financial pages he's here. Somewhere. Which is also deeply cold, like New York, but the air is different. Purer. Crisper. Quieter. Even as the conductor starts yelling…

"All aboard for Laramie! Train departs in ten minutes. All aboard for Laramie!"

A young porter approaches her. She hands him her ticket and when he returns with her bags, she asks, "I wonder if you would happen to know where I might find my son – he is quite well known here in Cheyenne these days. His name is Luke Taylor."

The porter grins. "I know where all those Alliance folks live."

"All?"

"Sure, ma'am. The Keatons and the Omaha Taylors live on 18th and Evans. The Benchleys live on 17th and Evans. The Cheyenne Taylors live down town on 16th."

"The Cheyenne Taylors?"

"Sure," he grins again. "Luke and Jennifer Taylor. That's who you're after, ain't it?"

"Luke, yes…" *Jennifer?*

"Where would you like these bags, ma'am?"

"Would you keep them in the luggage room till I call back?"

"Sure, ma'am. Hold onto your ticket."

With her luggage taken care of, Sara wanders into town in a daze. How is she not to make a complete and utter fool of herself?

*

Andy rounds the corner and ducks down the lane, happy as he could be with Lamont's treatment; the man was being fed and treated well, despite the trying nature of his personality. His stature as key witness in Faraday's case against Bodecker had ironically humbled him slightly, that and the promised jail time in Laramie. And Andy is very pleased to have such a client. On the one hand it hasn't been simple to set up his law practice amid the turmoil that is Cheyenne at present. But, on the other, suddenly a lot of folks are thinking about legal representation in lawsuits against Bodecker. He's got to keep a strong, ethical and dynamic profile for when those thoughts turn into action.

He takes the next corner at his usual enthusiastic pace only to slam into a tall man in a black suit. He begins to apologize, but very quickly he's told *to shut up and listen.*

He rights himself, straightens his hat and takes a step back. This is Buchanan. One of the black suits, as the Tribune has dubbed Buchanan, Sturrock and company.

"Excuse me?" Andy says, taking note of the cold stare in Buchanan's dark eyes.

"You represent Lamont."

"And that's your business because..."

"Lamont is about to take the stand against my client. I want you to tell me everything you know about him, Marks."

"Really, Buchanan?" Andy throws in a look of disbelief for good measure.

"That's *Mr* Buchanan to you."

"Age before beauty."

"What are you, the court jester?"

"Court jester? Nice pun, *Mr* Buchanan."

"Cut it out, Marks, and tell me everything you know about Lamont."

Andy does cut it out. He pins Buchanan with a death stare, and says, "You'll have to ask your client. Why don't you?"

The cold eyes narrow on him, whereupon it occurs to Andy that Bodecker, the arrogant sonofabitch, might be giving Buchanan a very hard time.

"Faraday wouldn't put Lamont in Bodecker and Donnelly's firing line unless he thought it would draw Bodecker out."

"I can't help you, Buchanan. I can't discuss the case…"

"The rape…"

"Assault… Look, Buchanan, I don't know what your game is, but if you intend to kill or maim me for information, you're wasting your time."

The dark eyes open up. "Kill you?"

"What I *do* know is why Faraday keeps all his key witnesses, shall we say, below the horizon."

"I ought to smack you in the mouth," Buchanan grinds out.

"Why do you let Bodecker kick your ass around? Oh, right, the rumor must be true – when you work for Bodecker he's got something on you. Is that true, Buchanan?"

Buchanan's expression darkens even further; his complexion turns red as he restrains his anger.

Andy holds up a conciliatory hand. "No hard feelings, Buchanan. I can see you're just trying to look after your client. We defense attorneys have to stick together. So I wish you luck." He straightens his hat. "Good day, Buchanan."

Andy sidesteps Buchanan and goes on his way, his heart beating so fast it bangs against his ribs. If he's learning anything from Faraday, and Ryan for that matter, it's when to hold back and when not to. He'd won his case for Lamont, but he had the sneaking suspicion the whole incident was never beyond Faraday's control. Maybe Buchanan is beginning to feel that way, too.

*

"Sara?"

"Yes. Your mama... remember me? The woman who raised you."

His face blanches and he gives a halting laugh as his natural self-assurance wanes; it will return soon enough; it usually does.

"Has it been that long?" she snaps.

He stands back and bids her enter the house.

She steps through.

They stand there looking at one another.

She sees a boy who is her son and yet he is some other man.

"What has happened to you?" she murmurs, her heart beating strangely now.

Gently, he put his hands on her shoulders and smiles his disarming smile.

Not knowing what will come, she reminds herself to be strong.

"Many, many things," he tells her quietly.

She takes another deep breath for courage. "Are you married?"

The answer is in his eyes.

"I don't understand," she stammers. "I don't see how... I... I think I need to sit down."

He sees her into a chair at the kitchen table.

She turns her gaze around the room. It seems cozy, as though this house is truly a home. "Whose house is this?"

When he doesn't answer, she turns her gaze back to his face; he is studying her.

"I can't believe you're here," he murmurs.

"Edith would have come, but she can't travel in the cold months. Luke, you have to tell me about..."

"Jennifer..." he murmurs, so sweetly gruff and with a shine in his eyes that her heart produces an uncomfortable beat.

"But you were supposed to marry Kelley..."

"Well, that was hardly possible, now, was it?"

"I... you are twisting my words."

"No, I'm not. I was supposed to marry Jennifer," he says slowly, as though English isn't her native tongue, "and K, had she lived, was supposed to return to New York and live with Edith and write, as she planned to do."

"I don't know Jennifer."

"You will. I promise. She'll be home soon. I was at the courthouse earlier; she went to visit with Meg Faraday."

She feels something akin to panic swirling in her chest. "But I don't understand."

"I know I promised you a letter explaining everything, but..."

There's loud rapping on the door, interrupting him.

"Stay right there," he says, "don't move..."

Move? Where would she go?

When Luke opens the door, a long-limbed woman with hair resembling a lopsided bird's nest walks right in.

"Constance," Luke says, frowning at the sight of her.

"Sorry for bargin' in on ya like this – how do, ma'am – but the young doc said I should tell ya Mrs Faraday's gone into labor and she's stayin' there till the baby's born."

This Constance woman puffs and pants and tries in vain to push her unruly hair into place. Luke mutters an exclamation that would appear to express the magnitude of the event.

"That was unexpected," he remarks as he turns to a water pitcher on the table.

"Ain't that the truth," says this Constance, as he pours water into a tumbler. "So, what should I be tellin' that wife of yours?"

"Tell her I'll be along, if you wouldn't mind, Constance," he says calmly, handing the woman the water.

She takes the glass and downs the water. "You're a treasure. Might as well've been ridin' drag I felt so dern thirsty."

"Know what you mean."

"'Course ya do. Well, I better be off. Seems to be a day for runnin' errands." She snaps her hands together, making Sara jump. "We're gonna have a baby!"

When this Constance is gone, and Luke has closed the door, Sara is still staring open-mouthed at the place where the woman had been standing.

"Sara?"

"Mm..."

More sharp rapping on the door! They both flinch; Luke hurries to open it, explaining, "It's not usually like this."

There's a telegram boy on the other side. "Telegram for Mrs Jennifer Taylor." The boy thrusts an envelope forward.

Luke takes it and tips the lad a coin from his pocket. He closes the door, studying the envelope. Then, as if he remembers she is there, he pockets it and looks up.

"I think it's time you met Jennifer."

"I want you to tell me how *you* met her. Right now!"

"There'll be time for that later. Let's go..."

"Where?"

"The Faradays."

"But the Constance woman said they're having a baby. Hardly the time to go barging in unannounced."

"Yeah, you're right. I'll take you to Ethan instead. Relieved to see you, I reckon. I'll call back when I've checked on Jennifer."

"Ethan? That... that scoundrel! I think I'd rather see Amy and John if you don't mind."

"Sara, trust me on this. Start with Ethan. Work your way up to the Keatons. And since when has Ethan been a scoundrel?"

"Since the day he was born! And he will probably draw his last breath as one!"

*

Josh Bridger appears at Mac's desk trying to catch his breath.

Now what?

"Josh..."

"Mac... where's... Cliff...?"

"Well, he's takin' a break somewhere I guess. He was here ten minutes ago. Can't have gone far though..."

"Where?"

Mac frowns. "Is this urgent? – cause he ain't feelin' all..."

"Meg Faraday is having her baby. Cam has gone home. I'm in court this afternoon and when Cliff's finished with his testimony, I need him to second for me while the Severini boy is on the stand."

Mac swallows a lick of panic and says, "Oh, is that all..."

Twenty-Five Minutes

"So, Mrs Raina Montgomery-Taylor... what have you decided?

"That you are a blood-sucking leech and you deserve to have your backside kicked from here to Canada."

"Ouch."

"I know things about you, Jacob Hunter."

"So what? I know stuff about you..."

"Yes, I know what you know about me. But you really should be more interested in what I know about you. You see, I did some research. Tit for tat, you might say. I know people, I have connections."

"What just a minute, you..."

"You got a sixteen-year-old girl in the family way before you left Pittsburgh for college. You left her high and dry. Threatened her you would ruin her even further if she told who the father was."

"How did you...? No one knows that..."

"Well, it's all about *who* you know, isn't it? In college you mounted up some hefty gambling debts. Got yourself into some serious trouble. You have a scar on your right side where someone who came to collect got violent. Your reputation for cards and the ladies meant you had to leave college and find a job. You've been a newspaper hound ever since. The editors give you all the jobs no one else can stomach. Should I go on...? You look a little pale..."

"No. You can stop. What are you going to do?"

"I thought we would strike a deal. You forget what you know about my father and I'll forget what I know about you."

"You think this is so clever..."

"I think you have met your match, Mr Hunter. You see, my life is in a far better place than yours right now. I am surrounded by people who love me. Strong people. They are not afraid of you. And if my father got wind of what you propose to do, believe me when I tell you he would have no qualms about striking you down. I can furnish you with a list of the names of the people who have felt his wrath in the past. You, on the other hand, have no friends to speak of, you are alone here, and The Bugle would happily ditch you the moment you proved a liability to its reputation. So, do we understand one another, Mr Hunter?"

"I don't believe this…"

"*Do* we understand one another?"

"Oh, I understand bitches like you. Does your husband know what kind of woman you really are?"

"I never realized just how alike my Ben and I are until this moment. Good day, Mr Hunter. I trust we won't ever have to speak again."

*

Ruth enters the church and catches her breath. After a small hesitation she immerses the tips of her trembling fingers into the holy water font and makes a shaky Sign of the Cross; it's been a while. She fixes her gaze on the large crucifix suspended high at the opposite end of the church, and makes her way toward it.

In the stillness and serenity, all those once-loved sights and smells welcome her. It wasn't till the Judge insisted Mr Faraday find someone to put her back on the straight and narrow that she realized just how far she'd strayed. To her credit, she eventually remembered where she could turn for help. She didn't need Dr Sullivan or Mr Faraday or even the Judge.

Gingerly, she kneels at the altar rail, the altar itself gleaming before her, and joining her hands tight, she bows her head.

O God, forgive me. O God, help me.

The words dart and run round and then lodge in her mind.

And this is just to find the courage to speak to the priest.

She hears a noise – a cough – coming from the body of the church and glances behind her. Of all people she sees Sheriff Ryan, sitting in a pew several rows from the back. She looks away. Too late! He knows she knows he's there. Embarrassed, she squeezes her eyes tight, and hopes he drifts away. But she can hear footsteps.

And then he's behind her.

"Miss O'Brien?"

She turns slowly and raises her eyes.

He looks pale and ragged and unhappy. Pitiful, like her. But even so, she detects the profound kindness in his sad eyes.

He makes a pathetic attempt at a smile. "I know Father Nugent. Allow me to introduce you?"

She uses the altar rail to get her steady on her feet. "What are you doing here, Mr Ryan?"

"Rough day."

"I… I wouldn't want to hold you up."

"You won't."

"I didn't know you were Catholic," she remarks as they turn their back on the altar.

"Not yet. At Easter."

Very slowly they walk the aisle.

"How lovely."

"I didn't know you were a Catholic either," he says.

"I… Something made me forget for a while."

He gives her another sad smile. "But something also made you remember."

Her hearts skips. "Yes."

"I… Forgive my forwardness, Miss O'Brien, but it so happens I need a sponsor. At Easter. Would you do it?"

She frowns, not sure what he's asking of her. "I'm sorry, I don't understand."

"At the ceremony, I need a sponsor. A couple of people have volunteered, but I keep telling Nugent – Father Nugent, that is – I'll know who the right person is when I see them."

"You… you can't… you couldn't possibly think…"

"Mm. It's you."

*

"Ethan, now Luke is gone, we can talk and I want you to tell me what he's been up to, because if I know anything in this world, it's that if he's been up to something, you've been right there beside him, egging him on…"

"Sara, what are you saying? Well, actually, you got no idea what you're saying…"

"Well, I might if someone would tell me the truth!"

"We haven't lied about anything, Sara. We told you there was gonna be a weddin' and we asked you to come."

"You're going to tell me everything, from the beginning."

"I…" he stops and grows calm again. "I won't tell you about Jennifer. That's not my place, but everything else is open for discussion. You know, Sara, I think I might've missed ya."

She moves her head from side to side, as stubborn as always. "Don't even think of buttering me up, Ethan. And I want to know what's going on at John and Amy's house."

"Okay, you got every right to be riled up, but a lot's happened, Sara, and to take it all in you gotta be calm."

Sara parks herself in the comfortable chair by the fire, joins her hands in her lap and stares up at him. "Very well, Ethan. I'm calm."

He drinks in the sight of her after what seems like an age, amused by this New York air she's acquired, clears his throat and sets about stoking the fire. "You look kinda fancy, Sara."

"What is it about trying my patience you find so amusing?"

He stokes some more. "So how did the boy look to you?"

"Older," she snaps. "Not a boy at all."

"But not sick?"

"No. Far from it. He looked like a man who has recently been married should look. Happy and content. Ethan, I should warn you. This marriage…"

"Uh, we ain't discussing the marriage, remember…"

"Ethan, you approved of it. How could you? What must Amy and John feel?"

"He loves her, Sara," he says gently. "She's the one for him."

Sara grips the arms of the chair. "How is that possible? He loved Kelley."

"That was a good idea, Sara, in theory. Reality was a whole lot different."

Her eyes go to the fire and follow the flames. "I miss her, Ethan."

"We all do."

Her eyes flash at him. "Not Luke."

"Are you crazy? He grieves deep and private for her. I think he grieves because the world missed out on a special person."

"When he sent me the telegram to announce his marriage, I didn't treat it seriously because it was inconceivable to me that he would even find someone to replace her. I really don't understand it, and frankly nothing short of a miracle could make me..."

Because when Morgan died she let a lot of herself die with him. Couldn't see herself as anyone other than Mrs Morgan Taylor. Still a young woman, she knotted herself to his memory, clung to it, and never let go. But how does he tell her that? And he's kinda worried Tressa will end up doing the same thing over Mart.

Scared to look back.

Scared that all the sacrifice and loss would be for nothing.

Scared of betraying it.

Not realizing it's their job to make it count for something.

Hasn't been a day when he himself didn't miss Morgan. Some days he'd even forget that Luke wasn't Morgan. But Morgan left him with a big responsibility – the future of his son – and Ethan had to make every day with the boy count. And raising the one that wasn't his gave him insight for raising his own, made him a better father. Even Red Sky had said so.

"You don't replace people, Sara," he says. "You make their life and their death count for something and move forward, leaving the past where it belongs."

*

Josh finds Cliff walking down the church path. He looks downright peaky, yet there's a humble air of satisfaction in his demeanor that gives Josh cause to hope that the man is not as ill as Mac made him out to be.

"Cliff, I'm glad I found you."

"Sure, Josh. Something happen?"

*

Luke lets himself in because no one will answer the front door. He sticks his head into one deserted room after another until he finds Constance in the cool confines of the pantry slouched on a chair with her feet up on another. She looks exhausted.

"Oh, ya made it," she says, not moving.

"Constance, are you all right?"

"I'm done runnin', I can tell ya that."

"Where is everyone?"

"Upstairs. The doctor's been and gone. Left the young doc to keep an eye on Mrs Faraday for a bit. Good idea in my opinion. She calms people down, your wife does."

"Listen, hate to disturb you, but could you go up and tell my wife I'm here?"

She manages a smile. "I reckon for you I can. There's coffee on the stove and cake on the buffet."

He helps himself to neither; instead he waits at the bottom of the stairs for Jennifer. When she emerges, her cheeks are flushed to ripe rosy pink and her eyes are dazzling and vivid with excitement.

She stops on the bottom step. "The baby is coming!"

He gathers her into his arms. "I heard something like that..."

Her hands come around his face and neck and she kisses him.

"Why is it so quiet?" he asks.

"Meg is doing well. But are you aware that Cam's upstairs and that Josh is taking over in court this afternoon?"

He frowns and shakes his head. "Cliff is on the stand, so I can't see a problem."

"Cam told me he is expecting Alfredo to be up next."

"Mm, well once Buchanan sees that Cam's absent it could get interesting."

"You'll be there, won't you?" she asks as if he'd be doing them all a favor. "You have finished testifying…"

"You don't want me here with you?"

"I… yes, I do want you to be here. Later, for Cam's sake."

"Cam?"

"It's not easy being the expectant father, you know."

"I should watch and learn, is that it?"

"Barring complications, which I don't expect, Meg still has a while to go…"

"I'm not needed in court, Jennifer," he tells her. He frowns as he recalls Sara's unexpected arrival.

"What?" she whispers.

"A couple of things. My…"

"Your?"

"My mother just got into town."

Some of the dazzle disappears from her eyes. "Oh… Is she well?"

"I think so."

She makes no further inquiry, so he continues, "And a telegram came for you…" He releases one of his hands to retrieve the telegram from his pocket. "I think it's from Frank."

"Frank?" She takes it quickly and stows it in the pocket of her skirt. "I'll read it later."

But he stays her hand and says, "We said we wouldn't do that, remember?"

She looks into his eyes and holds his gaze for several moments.

"Do what?" she murmurs at last.

"You're trying to hide something from me."

"Hide something? Luke, I put it in my pocket for later."

"You don't want me to know what it says."

"That's ridiculous…"

"No, it's true."

"You don't believe me?"

"Well, Jennifer, if…"

"Are we going to fight about this?" A flare of annoyance puts the dazzle back.

"Fight? You and me? Well..."

"Let me begin by saying it is for me to choose when I open telegrams with my name on them. You have no right to demand when I open anything addressed to me. So, what do you think about that? And please remove your hand."

"I wouldn't dream of putting my nose where it doesn't belong," he says, relinquishing his hand from where it restrains hers in her pocket.

"It's just a telegram," she insists.

"From Frank."

She stiffens and looks entirely miffed. "Accusations?"

"Wouldn't want to get in the way of personal family business." He pulls away from her and steps back. "I'll be back later to learn how expectant fathers do their part."

Her eyes flash at him. He glares at her. She glares back with her chin raised. Discussion closed.

He walks away; once he's lifted his hat from the hall table he glances at her over his shoulder, feeling weird.

*

When the door closes behind him, Jennifer winces. She reefs the telegram from her pocket and glares at it.

"Fine! *Fine!*" she declares, barely muffling her outrage. "You think I'm trying to hide something. Well, let's do this your way and see what happens!" She rips it open.

DEAR JENNIFER. HAD A WIRE FROM PROVINCETOWN. DERMOT IS EXTREMELY ILL. JOSEPH INSISTS YOU COME...

She doesn't read any further. She doesn't need to. All her suspicions are correct, and the distress pulsing through her true. Spurred into action by it and a familiar deep-seated defiance, she tears from the house, down the front path and onto the street where Luke is sauntering away, smacking at bare branches as he goes.

"Luke..."

He stops and half turns.

She rushes up to him, her eyes filling with annoying tears.

When she reaches him, she smacks the telegram into his chest where his hands have to gather it up before it falls. He regards her with surprise and confusion, and simmering annoyance that's hard to bear.

She backs away and then turns away.

"Jennifer... Jennifer, come back."

"No," she says over her shoulder. "You were so desperate to know what Frank wanted. See for yourself."

"You can't..."

She stops and turns, clenching her fists. "Left up to me I would never have opened it. Thrown it away. Lost it. Accidentally dropped it in the hearth after supper..."

He begins to walk towards her.

Welling up is misery as familiar as defiance. She walks away again, quickly.

"Jennifer, stop..."

"You wanted it this way."

"Not this way."

"It's too late and I have nothing more to say to you." She makes it into the house and closes the door, locking it behind her.

*

He takes several futile steps this way and that and then gives up; he stands there feeling utterly lost. So he reads the damn telegram.

DEAR JENNIFER. HAD A WIRE FROM PROVINCETOWN. DERMOT IS EXTREMELY ILL. JOSEPH INSISTS YOU COME. I KNOW YOU AND LUKE WILL WORK IT OUT. SENDING ALL OUR LOVE TO YOU BOTH. FRANK.

"Shit."

He crushes the paper into his coat pocket and squeezes his eyes shut only to see Jennifer's miserable face. He swore he would never get angry or impatient with her over this.

Swore to her.

When he tries to re-enter the house, the door is locked and he has to knock several times before foot-weary Constance opens it.

"You again?"

"Constance, would you mind..."

Constance rolls her eyes. "Newlyweds..."

This time he follows her up the stairs, ready for when Jennifer, looking mutinous and unhappy, appears in the upstairs hall.

"What do you want?"

"May we do this over again?"

"Why?"

"Because I was an idiot."

"Was?"

"Was, am... I'm sorry."

"I see."

"I'm starting again."

"Don't expect..."

"My mother arrived today; she's well but she's in a state of disbelief about our weddin'..."

She opens her mouth to interrupt, but he draws her against him and silences her.

"...and, I left her with Ethan to come here and deliver this telegram, which I think is from your brother, so I thought you'd want to open it right away. You can send me away if you want, but I should warn you that my mother is impatient to meet this Jennifer I went and married. I don't want to go back and have to tell her that my wife is no longer speaking to me, I think that would give her some kinda perverse satisfaction."

"I am trying to get a baby born..."

"I don't know what to do about Dermot either; I mean, can we really toss this into the fire and pretend it'll go away?"

"And what if I leave you here with your precious trial and go to Provincetown?"

Leave him here?

"What are you talking about? You're not serious."

"No?"

Crestfallen, he murmurs, "We said we would never do that."

"Fifteen minutes ago I would have sworn an oath that you and

I were the most perfect couple of the face of the earth. But that was fifteen minutes ago, you've already broken one promise to me in that time, and now I can't even imagine how I could have held such a fanciful notion as…"

"Because you love me and you know I love you and there's nothing fanciful about it."

"Your mother won't *ever* accept me. And there is a man on the other side of the country demanding of me what I am not in the least prepared to give. But, for now, I have better things to do, so I'd appreciate it if you would leave."

He cannot hide his dismay. "Okay, I'll leave." He releases her and steps back. "And wait for you at home… your house, I guess… maybe I should wait at Ethan's…. I'll be at Ethan's… or maybe the Keatons'… I'll be at the courthouse, yeah, the courthouse and then…" He shrugs. "Wherever…"

He turns and hurries down the stairs.

"Luke…?" she calls after him with a tremble in her voice.

"I'm leaving," he hollers from the bottom of the stairs. "I'm doing what you want."

This time he slams the door behind him and throws himself on the porch seat.

Now what?

Fifteen Minutes

"How is she?"

"Apprehensive."

They look at one another squarely.

"How are you holding up?"

"Better."

Cliff is happy for him. "Cam, you'll be a great father."

"How can you tell?"

"Looking out for people comes natural to you. And you don't mind giving advice."

Cam's expression, having been stunned into gravity by what is about to happen, suddenly lightens. "Thank you."

Cliff grins. "You're welcome."

"About this afternoon... If I leave Meg now she'll panic."

"Mama and baby come first. Of course."

"I know you can handle it..."

"You just want to *hear* me say Josh and I can handle it."

Cam nods.

Cliff rubs his brow. "I think Judge Callaghan is feeling sorry for me at the moment, so..." He shrugs. "We'll handle it."

"Buchanan knows you're not yourself."

"Let's face it, Cam, everyone knows. It's like old news."

"Hardly," Cam says with a wry smile.

"Well, I had a letter from Roberts. She sent it from Denver."

"Ah. There! She's missing you already."

Sadness fills his recesses, like the sea trickling into a tender tidal pool then leaving an enormous gouged out cavern in its wake.

"No, I think we're done."

"I don't believe that for a second."

"She convinced me. That's all that matters."

"Well, you're not convincing *me*. And it matters to us all."

"I appreciate that, but we are done. Anyhow, on a positive note, I found a sponsor. I believe she'll be perfect."

"She?"

"Did you know Miss O'Brien is Catholic?"

"*Our* Miss O'Brien?"

"The same."

Cam is busy frowning. "How on earth did you manage that?"

"I'll fill you in later. By the way, Luke was sitting on your front porch looking like I felt this morning. He told me he and Jennifer are no longer on speaking terms. What happened?"

"I've been so preoccupied with Meg... I don't know. Granted, George seems on edge."

"I thought I could persuade him to come into court, get his mind off it, but he said he had to see Ethan. Then he took off apace. Honestly, Cam, who has the time or the inclination for a trial today..."

"Did Josh tell you Denver is handing over the geological report?"

He gives a sharp nod. "About time we got some real support from Denver. Ah, must go, Cam. Good luck. And give my regards to Meg."

*

"All right, Meg, you can relax now."

"Well?"

"You are doing just fine," Jennifer tells her, smiling and drawing the sheet down. "Try to rest between the contractions."

"Why does it feel as though I'm going to die?"

"You won't die. I won't let you die."

Jennifer's glance collides with Meg's cherry brown eyes.

"I'm sorry, Jen," Meg says softly, reaching for her hand. "That was very stupid. I won't ever say it again. I promise."

"Hush, Meg. I know it's hard. And you're becoming weary."

"The baby?"

"A strong heart beat."

"How much longer, do you think?"

But Meg's body is responding to her own question with the onset of another contraction. Jennifer places her hand on Meg's belly. Meg goes white.

"This... this is the..." Meg can no longer speak.

"The strongest yet."

For the first time since the onset of her labor, Meg's groans completely fill the room.

"Now we're getting down to business."

*

In the gentlemen's restroom in the courthouse, Cliff splashes water on his face, letting the fresh feeling seep in; he finds his comb and slides it through his hair until it stays where he wants it. Trouble is, even his own hair reminds him of Emma. The way her fingers played with the tips... he got it cut short on account of her...

There's a thump on the door. He drops the comb.

"Two minutes, Sheriff."

*

"It's about time you showed up."

"I'm here, Ethan. Where's Sara?"

"Laying down for a spell. You don't look so good."

"Jennifer and I had a disagreement." He slumps into Ethan's good chair by the hearth.

"And what have you done to fix it?"

"Don't start on me, Ethan. I tried to fix it. She ain't listening. Ethan, I…"

"You, what?"

"Something's different."

Ethan takes the chair opposite. "How so?"

"I left myself open. I mean, I let myself get too vulnerable. I don't like it. She can hurt me and I don't like it."

Ethan sighs. Cracks a smile. "Not many men can actually articulate that thought, son. I'm proud of you."

"Well, I ain't proud of me. I don't know where to go. Can I stay here?"

"Nope. You belong with your wife. Thought the reverend made that pretty clear."

"It's her house. *Her* house. She doesn't want me; she made *that* pretty clear. I ain't doing that again, Ethan, letting myself be susceptible to what she says or does or wants. Got more important things to do than being tossed around like a ship at sea till the storm passes over. I got other things needing my attention."

"Sure you have," Ethan says. "When it comes right down to it, a wife ain't that important."

"I didn't mean it that way."

"Sure you did. You can't waste your feelings on your wife because when it comes right down to it there are more important things needing your time and energy."

"Will you stop doing that?"

"I'm just staying what you said."

"No, you're twisting my words so I'll see the other side of it."

"Used to work when you were knee-high. Listen, you big lump, you told me you loved that woman more than the Diamond-T, has that changed in the last thirty minutes?"

"Something has."

"I'm only gonna say this once today. Nothing in marriage stays exactly the same from day to day. Life butts up against you. Every day needs doing for, whatever it brings. Understand?"

"Little things, yeah…"

"Sure, the little things bring more undoing than most folks will admit to, but when you got a big thing on for the day, you think of all the little things that you did for and what really matters. If you love her, if you can't see the rest of your life without her, then all that energy you were fixing on other important stuff, you'd better put back where it really belongs."

They stare at one another solidly for several moments.

"What if I can't get past the feeling that I don't want to be vulnerable to her?"

"You go down that road and this marriage will be over in less than a year."

"I can still love her."

"Won't be true love. Won't be honest. You'd be holding back and that's not what you vowed to do, is it?"

His thoughts drift back to their weddin' day, two weeks ago this Thursday, and the vows he made and the way he felt when he made them. The look on her face telling him she believed with all her heart that he meant them with all of his heart.

Ethan's voice cuts through...

"And she'll know. Believe me, they don't miss much in that department. See, it's about who you are, Luke. The way you love gives the vows their meaning. I don't think you could go through with it, holding back till it didn't hurt no more. You wouldn't even be alive. You wanna turn out like Jennifer's father?"

Luke goes cold. "She told you?"

"She told me. As much as I need to know, I reckon. She said you would need me to know. She's a wise one that girl of yours. She said one day what her father did to her could come between you or make trouble for you. Is that what's happened?"

He nods, stunned.

"Well, then, I repeat the question. You wanna turn out like Dermot Sullivan?"

"I'm nothing like him," he murmurs, coldly.

"You think a man who loved his wife the way Dermot did was a hard, cruel despot from the beginning? I'm here to tell you no. When his wife died he went down the road you just described and refused to be hurt ever again, that's my thinking, and someday I hope Jennifer understands that. But you – you should understand it now, so you don't do to Jennifer what Dermot did. I know she's a complicated woman, and it won't be easy some days. But do you love her or not?"

Luke, amazed at Ethan's bottomless well of wisdom, stammers, "She... she scares me."

Ethan chuckles. "Hell, there ain't a man alive who ain't scared. But after a while you get used to it. I kinda figured they were made that way for a purpose."

Luke frowns, amused and bewildered. "What purpose?"

"Keep us in shape. Keep us human."

"Ethan..."

"You want to be happy, don't you? And Jennifer to be happy?"

"From the beginning all I wanted was to see her happy."

"So think about Dermot every time you got doubts."

"I didn't have doubts – till now."

"You really despise Dermot Sullivan, don't you?"

"I..." But the hate firms like a ball in his gut. "Yes."

"Well, Jennifer knows it and *it* scares *her*. Reckon you gotta do something about it, son."

Just then the door to one of the bedrooms opens and Sara emerges.

"Thought I heard your voice," she says pertly. "Now we three can talk at last."

"Feeling refreshed after your nap?" Ethan asks her.

"Mightily," she fires back.

Luke exchanges a glance with Ethan, who says, "I'll make fresh coffee."

Cliff

Judge Callaghan stops him in the corridor.

"It never rains, it pours! Mr Ryan, I have told Mr Bridger, as Mrs Faraday is having her baby, I will grant a recess until tomorrow morning, but he seems to think that it's not necessary."

Cliff adjusts his necktie for the tenth time.

"A little to the left," the Judge suggests.

"Thanks." Cliff tugs to the left. "How's that?"

"Acceptable. Did you hear me, Mr Ryan?"

He straightens up respectfully. "Certainly, Judge. But Mr Faraday gave Mr Bridger specific instructions to carry on, so that's what we're doing."

"Very well," the Judge says.

He nods and waits for the Judge to depart, after which it feels as though his inside will collapse in on themselves and bring him to his knees. He tells himself to think about Easter. That's it. Whenever Roberts gets the better of him, he's to think about Easter and the salvation of two souls. His and Miss O'Brien's.

Suddenly, the Judge is before him again.

"Judge?"

"Mr Ryan, if I find out that you have let that young reporter get the better of you..."

He swallows, hard. "That's not going to happen, Judge."

The Judge nods brusquely. "Excellent. Carry on."

In the courtroom, back on the witness stand, he regains some equilibrium; perhaps he can even convince himself that the young reporter hasn't got the better of him. Meanwhile, it's Josh he feels sorry for, filling Cam's shoes and facing the black suits. Yet he and Josh have worked together before with a successful outcome, they can do it again.

"Mr Ryan, you arrested Dr Porterfield as soon as you arrived in North Platte?" Josh asks him.

"Pretty much. I asked a neighbor if he was home and then went in and got him. I escorted him downtown."

"Did you seek Sheriff Walker's co-operation in apprehending Dr Porterfield?"

"Yes. Acting as deputy US marshal I sought his assistance."

"As soon as possible?"

"Yes. As soon as I apprehended Dr Porterfield for attempted murder."

"In what way did Sheriff Walker co-operate?"

"He agreed to lend me his lockup for Dr Porterfield while I continued my investigations. For this, he gave me a junior deputy as my assistant."

"What was the nature of your investigations, Mr Ryan?"

"I hired the photographer in town to take pictures of Dr Porterfield's laboratory and the basement where he poisoned Luke Taylor almost to death. And I gathered evidence from the house."

"This is the same Dr Porterfield to whom the accused Mr Donnelly took Luke Taylor after the incident on the train wherein Mr Donnelly murdered Miss McClements?"

"Objection…"

"Sustained."

"I will rephrase, Your Honor: The same Dr Porterfield to whom Mr Donnelly took Luke Taylor after the incident on the train when Luke Taylor saw Miss McClements murdered and was wrongly accused?"

"Yes, the same Dr Porterfield."

"So, on Mr Donnelly's specific instructions, Dr Porterfield was to drug, terrorize and incapacitate Mr Taylor to such a point that Mr Taylor would be unable to escape while the Maverick attack on the Alliance was both imminent and taking place?"

"Yes."

"The same Dr Porterfield you had to leave behind so that you could hurriedly extricate Mr Taylor from North Platte to safety, and install him as a key witness in this case?"

"Yes."

"And after you and Marshal Hummer arrested the accused Loren Bodecker in Denver, why did you think Dr Porterfield would still be there at his house of drug-induced torture in North Platte?"

"His laboratory was full of expensive equipment and drugs at the time we left. I believed that once the heat died down on Donnelly, and not knowing that Bodecker had been arrested, Dr Porterfield would return for it."

"And is that what he was doing when you apprehended him?"

"Yes. The court has already viewed the photographs I had taken on my return. Dr Porterfield's laboratory was full of small boxes, some half-packed up ready for his departure."

"Your Honor, if I may refresh the jury's mind…"

"Go ahead, Mr Bridger."

Josh goes to the evidence table and picks up the pictures relevant to the questioning. He holds four, two splayed in each hand, and stands before the jury, whose eyes are riveted to them.

"Objection, Your Honor. I fail to see what relevance Mr Ryan's apprehension of Dr Porterfield has to do with anything."

Josh leaves the pictures of the handrail of the jury box. "It's simple, Your Honor. Mr Ryan returned not only to apprehend Dr Porterfield, but also to retrieve evidence of what Mr Donnelly and the doctor had inflicted upon Luke Taylor. These photographs are proof indeed that Mr Taylor did not make up his story, that Dr Porterfield is not some alchemist from a children's fairy tale, or that Mr Donnelly's orders to destroy Mr Taylor a myth. The relevance is supremely clear."

"Your Honor…"

"Overruled, Mr Sturrock."

"Your Honor, the prosecution would like to offer into evidence People's exhibit 15a to 15j, these…" Josh returns to his desk and points out two boxes sitting on top of it. "… which are two of ten boxes which Mr Ryan had carefully removed and brought back from Dr Porterfield's laboratory."

"Thank you, Mr Bridger. Continue with the witness."

"Mr Ryan, would you please tell the court what is contained in these boxes?"

"Some contain drugs and others equipment for making the drugs. There are also notebooks and schedules."

Josh begins to unpack the boxes. He lines up vials of morphine. Tips out dried up mushrooms from paper packets. Groups small bottles of this and that. Scientific equipment. Notebooks…

"These are the tools of Dr Porterfield's trade?"

"Yes."

"And Dr Porterfield the cruel scientist and these deadly objects are, in turn, the tools of Mr Donnelly's trade?"

"Yes."

"Mr Donnelly deals in murder and torture and kidnapping…"

"Yes, he does."

"You've seen it with your own eyes."

"Yes, I have."

"And there is no doubt in your mind that Mr Donnelly had no intention of releasing Luke Taylor from Dr Porterfield at any time?"

"There is no doubt in my mind."

"That this code *round up and drive,* et cetera, was just a game?"

"Mr Donnelly reveled in a sense of power in the game he'd created. He intended Mr Taylor should die a slow and distressing death while he unleashed death and destruction upon the Alliance."

"Thank you, Mr Ryan. No further questions."

"Your witness, Mr Sturrock."

Sturrock springs to his feet. "Thank you, Your Honor. Mr Ryan, you honestly believe that your exploits are legendary, don't you?"

"Objection. Your Honor, Mr Ryan is not required to believe his exploits are legendary. He only has to do his job. How others interpret his performance is their business and not relevant here."

"Your Honor, if I may be allowed to finish…"

"Mr Bridger's objection is sustained, Mr Sturrock, since I do not believe that the direction in which you are headed is in the best interests of this court."

"Yes, Your Honor, but…"

"Mr Ryan's credibility has been discussed many times…"

"I beg to discuss it further, Your Honor."

"Be that as it may, Mr Sturrock, the evidence is clearly before us. In his capacity as Deputy US Marshal, Mr Ryan sought Sheriff Walker's co-operation and got it, apprehended Dr Porterfield with all this paraphernalia in his possession, the same paraphernalia present when Mr Taylor was his guest. Move along or allow Mr Bridger to call his next witness." And the Judge gives a firm nod of his head.

"No further questions, Your Honor." Sturrock sits down, looking miffed. Buchanan leans across and whispers something to him. Sturrock nods.

Cliff catches Donnelly's eye; surprised, Cliff stares back at him only to discover that Donnelly isn't seeing anyone at all.

"The witness may step down. Call your next, Mr Bridger."

"The People call Alfredo Severini."

"Objection, Your Honor. This person Alfredo Severini's name is not on the witness list."

"Approach, gentlemen."

Josh, Buchanan and Sturrock congregate at the Judge's bench.

The Judge lowers his voice but loud enough for Cliff to hear as he slowly steps down from the witness stand: "Mr Buchanan, we've been over this before. Several witnesses for the prosecution are under witness protection. Clearly, Mr Severini is such a one. Now, let's have no more of this…" Voice raised again, he declares, "Step back, gentlemen. Objection overruled. Proceed, Mr Bridger."

As Cliff takes his seat, the one next to Josh's, he hears a woman's deep, trembling sigh. He turns to see Signora Severini in the front row directly behind him, her dark brown eyes dilated by fear. She seems to sense him looking at her. The last thing he thought he'd find himself doing is winking at her, but that's exactly what he does. Her jaw drops slightly. Then all at once her expression warms and her eyes crinkle at the corners. So, when Alfredo walks past her a moment later, looking to her for reassurance, she smiles her encouragement, bossily nodding him forward to get the job done and redeem the Severini name. Alfredo's glance lingers on his mother's face even after he's sworn in and Josh approaches him.

Luke

Luke hears the back door close and takes himself off the sofa and through to the kitchen. He half doesn't expect it to be Jennifer.

"What happened?" he says at once.

Guardedly, she says, "Meg had a girl..." She straightens and declares, "They have a daughter."

"A daughter..." he grins. "That's great. How's Meg?"

"Everything went well. Mother and child are perfectly healthy."

"And Cam?"

"Relieved. And very happy."

She doesn't look happy though.

"I believe Meg could use my help tonight. Leave Constance to look after the house and Cam. I thought I'd pack some things and stay over."

He swallows hard. "I see."

"I didn't expect you to be here."

"It's where we live."

"You didn't seem to know earlier..."

"Well, this is your house and you can throw me out anytime you want."

"Fine," she snaps, her eyes flashing. "Leave whenever you feel like it. I won't stop you."

She charges from the door to the stairs without a second look.

He waits with a stomach full of wriggling worms for her to come down again.

"You're still here."

"It's just a fight, Jennifer."

"You and I don't fight."

"I think over Dermot we do."

"I really do not have time for this," she says, shifting her small bag from one hand to other.

"Let Cam and Meg be alone with their baby girl for a while."

"What does that mean?"

"We have some things to talk about. Jennifer, I'm not about to let anything break up our family. I'm sorry about before. I... You scare me sometimes."

"It's this house... I knew it was a bad idea."

"It ain't the house, Jennifer. You're not listening to me." He takes a step towards her. She doesn't cringe exactly, but she doesn't look too comfortable either. His fear preys upon him, twisting what had been clear thinking into more confusion. He can't look at her. "I thought we were secure. I thought we... *I* got it wrong..." Again, he feels fear's sting. "I will always take care of you and our child... at least, you probably won't need me, but the child will. Er, look, I'm not saying the things I meant to say, what I wanted to say... maybe you'd better go to Meg. I have to work out what to do next."

When he looks up from his confusion, her face – awash with tears – shocks him.

"Lily..." she murmurs.

"Sorry?"

"They named the baby Lily."

"How can you not love me anymore?" he rasps. "How can you be so in love with me one minute and want me out of the house the next?"

"I didn't mean for it to go this far..."

"For what to go this far?"

"You... you keep saying things... they aren't true. But I don't know how to stop you saying them. And the more you say the more I'm confused."

"You're confused!" he shouts and she jumps.

He rubs the back of his neck, utterly bewildered. "I'm sorry. I didn't mean to shout. What... so what have I said that confused you?"

In a shaky voice, she says, "You're leaving me?"

"*You* are leaving *me*," he points out.

"Are you leaving me?" she repeats, slowly this time.

"Do you want me to?"

"What kind of an answer is that?"

"I don't know what I'm supposed to say, all right?"

"And I am?"

"Yes, you're the girl. And I lost confidence in my ability to do this hours ago."

He pulls out a chair and sits down, exhausted.

"Do what?"

"Jennifer, I've apologized over and over and you won't forgive me. I don't know what else to do except say it again. I'm sorry things got out of hand. And why would I want to leave you? I thought this was our home."

"It *is* our home," she grinds out. "Our home... yours and mine."

Progress at last! And something very simple occurs to him.

"Then I will be here when you get back."

He goes to her, tries not to let the tragic beauty of her tear-stained face get the better of him, and plants a heartfelt goodnight kiss on her damp cheek.

I will be here, my stubborn, insecure wife.

But to be this close and not be drawn in is difficult to say the least. He hesitates. Studies the lips he's kissed a thousand times. Looks into those prairie grass green eyes. And thinks to himself: would *that* fix everything? It would for him, but for her?

She moves her lips as if to speak, but he covers them tenderly with his own.

Sara

The Keatons' House
Amy's kitchen

Even now, now that she knows exactly what has transpired all these
months, Sara still doesn't feel any better. What has happened to her
son! His guilt over Kelley, his vow to avenge her murder, his love
for this Jennifer, his involvement with her, his trip to Omaha and
finding Caroline, helping her, becoming a key witness against Loren
Bodecker, getting himself almost fatally entangled with the vicious
Donnelly, being rescued by his friend Cliff Ryan, arriving home in
time to save Ethan and his cousin Ben, whom he once vowed he
would never accept, then bringing Ben into the Alliance, trying so
hard to get well again after the drugs, setting up in Cheyenne for
the trials, getting married, being married, giving testimony...

"Don't be disappointed, Sara." Amy gently places a cup of tea
in front of her. "Drink this. You'll feel better."

"I doubt that. I haven't even met her yet."

"She is delightful, full of character, so talented, and a very good
person."

Sara shakes her head. "How can you accept this? He loved
Kelley. I don't understand."

Amy sits back and despite that ever-stoic expression, regret
does lurk in her bright gray eyes. "We wanted them to do
something they couldn't do. And they tried... Well, I think Luke
tried. I think my daughter never truly recovered from her long-held
resentment of him. Not until it was too late anyhow."

"How can you speak of her that way?"

Amy smiles sadly. "Sara, I don't think it does anyone any good making Kelley out to be a paragon. John and I have heard Luke explain what happened to them and if you could have seen his face. I know in my heart he wanted it to work but he couldn't make it happen."

"But she loved him, Amy."

"Reluctantly, I think."

Sara folds her arms. "Well, I don't believe it for a second. I think he let this Jennifer distract him."

"Well, she certainly is a beautiful young woman, but no more so than Kelley. A different personality. One that suits Luke. He's not a shallow young man, Sara. You know that. He fought his attraction to Jennifer for a long time to try and make it work with Kelley. I believe him when he says that. His sense of duty has always been strong."

"Not strong enough."

Amy sighs. "I'm not sure I can change your mind on this. You seem set about it. Would have helped if you'd come to the wedding when Luke asked you."

Sara watches as Amy gets up and moves about her kitchen.

"You and I, Sara, have been friends a long time. I know how much you loved Kelley, but she's gone. She's with her brother. We who are left have been busy doing other things while we mourn them. Staying alive in the main. John and I have a prime job looking out for Tressa and Adam. We owe Mart that. And we intend to see it done. We gave Luke our blessing to marry Jennifer when he manfully came to us and told us how it all came about. He didn't have to do that, but you raised him well, Sara. He's been brave and true through all his struggles. The world is a harsh and fearful place at present. Jennifer is strong. And he deserves some happiness."

Sara sips her tea. "It would help if I could actually meet her…"

"Meg Faraday is having her baby. Jennifer is her best friend and a doctor. I think the delay is to be expected."

"I think you like this young woman, Amy."

"She has been a good friend to the Alliance for quite some time now."

"How can you possibly say that when the intended alliance…"

"Sara, she's been there for Luke when he's needed her."

"What are you saying?"

"You should be very, *very* grateful. You know, I can't believe Ethan hasn't managed to convince you."

"Ethan? Ethan has been in on this since the beginning. I wonder about his loyalty."

"Sara, forgive me, but I think you've been in New York too long. And I don't appreciate you coming back and telling us we've been doing everything wrong. You should've been here! You should've seen for yourself! And you should know if you give Jennifer any grief, John and I will take her side. I... I'm just warning you."

"Amy, I didn't mean to..."

But Amy wears a fierce frown as she walks out, muttering, "Think I'll check on Adam."

Jennifer

Engulfing her like a tidal wave, it twists her in its euphoric surge and then releases her on a more familiar shore. All the while she clings on. And is clung to. Her heart and her breathing seem to be fighting with each other, but it is another's heart beating against hers and that other's breathing in syncopated rhythm, centering her body and brain and desire in the one place.

He has broken through. Did he know all along?

"This won't solve our problem," she murmurs, catching her breath.

But her partner in tidal waves is not the slightest bit interested in speaking. His desire-intense eyes flash at her and then he covers her with kisses. She forgets that kisses are not words. He wants her convinced that words are not the only form of communication.

And he's very good at it.

She takes his face between her hands as he sucks air into his lungs. His eyes are closed. She adores this face. Vulnerable to her, transparent… his loving soul, his brazen spirit, and resolute heart. She releases him; holds his body instead. His head finds the hollow of her neck and nestles there, his warm shallow breaths caressing her throat.

"Sweetheart," he whispers.

Her heart skips more beats… he's never called her that before.

Always Jennifer.

She grins into the lamp lit darkness. "Yes?"

"When the time comes remember this."

"What time?"

"The next time you doubt that I love you more than anything else in this world."

Now, the words…

"Promise me."

"Yes."

"Say it."

"I promise."

He feather kisses her neck, sending tingles around her body.

"You called me sweetheart."

"Did it work?"

"Yes," she grins.

"Jennifer, when we… when I had my hands on you before I think I noticed something."

"Oh?"

"You feel… I don't know… bigger around the middle."

She laughs. "Lucky for you that's the baby making himself at home and I don't have to feel offended you think I'm getting fat!"

He gives a low, delighted chuckle. "He's going to be some kid."

An hour ago she could have sworn that marriage was not on her list of proficiencies; but now… while there is definitely room for improvement, perhaps she is better at this than she thought. All she has to do is listen with her heart, and not to her fears, which cast her back to the frightened child she was before he came.

Cliff

When Cam enters the living room with a look of contented exhaustion on his face, Cliff finds himself relaxing; his muscles disengage and all his insides let go of themselves. He hadn't realized how tense he'd become till now.

"Well?" he says. "Constance wouldn't tell me anything…"

"Meg's fine," Cam announces. "We have a daughter."

Cliff reaches for his hand and shakes it with heartfelt gladness. "Congratulations."

"I can hardly believe it," Cam mutters. "She's beautiful. And tiny. The doctor said the last thing Meg needed was a large baby in any case. But she's perfect."

"That's the miracle of them, I guess," Cliff reflects.

Cam slides onto the sofa and draws his hand across his face. "We did it."

Cliff gives a laugh and puts himself in the armchair nearby. "What have you named her?"

"Meg's always wanted Lily for a girl. I never really did, until I saw her. Lily will do. I think we should tack on Margaret, after all her mother went through for her."

"Lily Margaret. That's very fine. So, you're keen to get back?"

"What?" Cam says, utterly distracted.

"Back to Meg and the baby…"

"Yes… By the way, what happened in court?"

Cliff grins. "Josh seemed to think it wouldn't be proper for him just yet to come over and tell you. He sends his very best regards and congratulations. Says he'll see you tomorrow." Then, in short punchy sentences to hold Cam's patchy attention, Cliff relates the afternoon session.

"So Alfredo held it together right through Buchanan's cross?"

"Absolutely. He was nervous. Then after a time he got fed up with his own nervousness and showed his mettle."

Cam sits forward. "Thank you."

"For what?"

"I know you did something."

"I told you – Josh stood up to Buchanan and Sturrock. He was very good. With Alfredo as well."

"Mm." Cam's careful brown gaze seems to digest him.

"Well, it's been a long day."

"We have a lot of those." Cam sits back again, expelling a meaningful sigh. "Where's Lamont?"

"At home. Pete's watching him."

"Is he behaving himself?"

"Pretty much. About tomorrow…"

"I'll be there. You heard that the Worthing and Farrell report should be arriving tomorrow?"

"Mm. Luke and Ethan need to see it."

"What time's court?"

"Ten. The day *after* tomorrow."

"What?"

"Josh talked to the Judge in recess. He said we needed a day to analyze new evidence and that you would need another day to be with Meg. The Judge agreed."

"Bless him."

"Josh or the Judge?"

"Either… both. You're right. Josh did just fine."

Another day to have Lamont as his houseguest. Another day for the black suits to investigate Lamont. Another day to delay the show-stopping secret that is Lamont's testimony – the one he sacrificed Emma to get. Another day to find things to stop thoughts about her devouring him…

"You haven't seen George, have you?" Cam asks.

"No. Thought she was with Meg."

"Oh, she assisted at the birth and stayed for a good while…"

"She has a home to go to now, Cam."

"I know. But I think Meg would feel better if she were close by."

"Maybe she went home to get herself back on speaking terms with Luke."

"I forgot about that. I wonder what happened."

"I don't know. I'm sure they'll work it out and Jennifer will be back. Well, Cam, I'll be going home to my houseguest."

They both rise and head towards the door.

"Sorry about the delay," Cam says, "you know..."

"At least I can't complain about going home to any empty house."

Cam opens the door, nodding philosophically. "In your new career I insist that you complain and complain often. Goodnight, Cliff. And thanks for coming."

"Give my best to Meg."

A brief shake of hands and Cliff's walking down the Faradays' front path and into the street. The chill never used to bother him. Now it reminds him of Emma. And if someone were to ask him how Cheyenne feels without her...

Like salt that's lost its saltiness. Like a broken compass. Like a carriage with broken springs.

Thin. Adrift. Wrecked.

NINE

Oh pardon me, my friend,
If I so long have kept this secret from thee;
But silence is the charm that guards such treasures,
And if a word be spoken ere the time
...they were not meant for us.

Henry Wadsworth Longfellow
The Spanish Student

Josh

Wednesday

Josh gathers up the backlog of cases and takes them into court. Brash and confident Andy Marks, the new defense attorney in town, is his opponent, excellent experience even though the cases are small matters. As for yesterday afternoon, he thought he handled himself admirably; the experience in a major murder trial was invaluable, even if brief, because he had to deal with the black suits.

Today, however, he has to take Cam's place in court and simultaneously keep an eye out for the Worthing & Farrell report; and although he has briefed the clerk to alert him as soon as it arrives at the courthouse, no matter what, he finds himself frequently glancing at the courtroom door.

He and Marks are into their second case for the morning when the clerk brings the Worthing & Farrell report to him. He places it with his case files and as soon as possible calls for a recess.

The Judge asks him to approach the bench.

"Mr Bridger, we have three more cases. We are making excellent progress. We'll have them all done by lunch…"

"Yes, Your Honor, but I have just received the new evidence I told you about for the Bodecker trial."

"You have a recess of fifteen minutes to get the information to Mr Faraday. After that, we have three cases to hear before lunch. Understood? That is all, Mr Bridger." The Judge taps his gavel. "This court will recess for fifteen minutes."

"All rise."

His Honor sweeps from the courtroom as is his wont.

Josh receives a cool look from Andy Marks as they pack up their files. He comes across to Josh's table, his hands in his pockets.

"Counselor," Josh greets him.

"Bridger. Thought you and Faraday might like to know that Buchanan is becoming fidgety about Lamont."

"How so?"

"Lamont is my client, Bridger. His welfare is my paramount concern. If anything should happen to him…"

"He's under the Sheriff's protection."

"I understand that and I think I have a fairly good idea of what kind of sheriff Ryan is, but you didn't see the look in Buchanan's eye when he held me up in the alley yesterday."

Buchanan threatened him?

Josh scrutinizes Marks' expression and comes to the belief he is genuine.

"He wanted information about my client," Marks continues. "I told him to put his nose back where it belongs, but the longer Faraday keeps Lamont from the witness stand… well, I'll let you work out the rest."

"I see," Josh says. "I'll pass on your concern."

"You do that, Bridger. Good day."

Josh arrives at the Faradays' front door, feeling breathless and somewhat nervous. He knocks; Cam himself opens the door.

"Josh. At last. How goes it? Come in, come in. You look a little pale…" Cam waves him inside and Josh hurries in.

"Congratulations on your daughter, Cam." He shifts the report from his right hand to his left in order to offer Cam a congratulatory shake.

Cam grips like a vice and shakes enthusiastically. "Thanks, Josh. Would you like to see her?"

"Well," Josh hesitates, pushing his spectacles up his nose, "I would like to, Cam, certainly, but I only have fifteen minutes, half of which is used up. Here is the geo report from Denver…"

Cam takes it from him. "Excellent," he exclaims and then starts peering into Josh's face. "Something the matter, Josh?"

"Andy Marks has informed me that Buchanan was demanding information from him about Lamont. Marks is concerned about Lamont's welfare. I tried to reassure him, but Marks is…"

Cam holds up his hand; Josh stops speaking. He is being studied. The famous Faraday fathom. There's no escaping it once it's upon you. Josh adjusts his spectacles and waits.

A calmer, graver Cam then speaks. "If you wouldn't mind telling Cliff, and then have him come see me as soon as possible."

Josh nods. "Certainly."

Cam's mouth twitches. "The sky won't fall in if the backlog isn't completed by lunch recess."

Josh blinks. "How did you…?"

"Judge Callaghan makes me feel from time to time the way you look right now. The sky has yet to fall in when I didn't comply. Besides he gets hungry."

Josh relaxes. "Yes…"

"You will do two cases at the most. You had better get moving anyhow. How is Cliff this morning?"

"I saw him briefly around the courthouse. He looks the same as yesterday."

"Grim."

"Gloomy."

"Miserable."

"Precisely."

"Well, let's pray this report gives him something to cheer about. After lunch I want you to call back again."

Josh nods as he heads for the door. "What about Buchanan?"

"Leave that to Cliff."

Up close, Cliff looks even gloomier, but he's not impatient or grumpy. He listens with close attention to Josh the way he always does. If Josh isn't mistaken, there is something almost serene about the sheriff and the way he's handling the disappointment of Roberts' departure. Hard *not* to look unhappy when you're that miserable, so much of what a person feels eventually shows on their face, but it is even more difficult not to *behave* like a miserable s.o.b. That's an active decision – not to take it out on everyone else.

Cliff

On his way to Cam's, Quaid stops him in the street, looking like he has plenty on his mind and intends to say it. At the last minute Quaid ushers him to one side to avoid a four-woman delegation of the Women's Temperance Society Cliff didn't see coming.

They both tip their hats at the ladies, who beam at Cliff...

"Sheriff," one of them, Clara Whittaker, says.

...and pierce Quaid's thick skin with their renowned *we got our eye on you* glower.

"What'd I ever do..." Quaid mumbles, gazing after them.

"I'd give them a free advertisement if I were you."

"Now there's an idea. That's what I like about you, Ryan, you think like a newspaperman."

"What do you want, Quaid?"

Quaid faces him. "Thought you'd come see me by now."

"I'm busy."

"You're always busy."

"What does that mean?"

"Nothin'. I just thought you'd have come see me."

Cliff sighs. "What about?"

"Roberts. What else?"

"I'm trying not to think about Roberts. Why would I subject myself to talking to you about her?"

"Because she's a keeper, and you're letting her get away."

"Fine. I'll say this. If I find out that you ever invoke that stupid rule that your female employees are not permitted to become romantically attached while they work for you, I'll shut you down."

Quaid's jaw drops.

"Wouldn't want to shut down the only paper in town that manages to print the truth once in a while, would we, Charlie?"

"As if you... Hey, once in a while? What the hell..."

"Good day."

Cliff takes off, only to have Quaid step in front of him.

"Ryan, I'm sorry. And I can hear your frustration talking. But Roberts was young and sassy and good-looking. And Southern. I could see every feller in town falling for her and me losing my reporter. You never even entered my head in that regard."

"Just dandy."

"You wanted to run her out of town in the beginning, how was I to know? You should have said something..."

Cliff rubs his brow. "Yeah, I should have. But she wouldn't let me. So just let it go."

"She'll regret it for the rest of her life. You didn't tell her about...?"

"No, I didn't tell her. Now drop it, Quaid..."

"Don't let it go, Ryan, or you'll regret it for the rest of your life too. She was really cut up about leaving. A girl like that doesn't come along every day. You know, she never once tried to straighten my necktie; there ain't a woman in this town who hasn't tried to straighten my necktie or looked at me like I should."

"Look, I appreciate your concern. And I know how highly you regarded Roberts and in your own way you probably miss her..."

"I offered her a summer job, heck, we owe it to her," he blurts out. "And to publish anything she wants to send my way. People will read anything she writes, especially after they get an eyeful of *Empire for Liberty* in a few weeks. She didn't say no to either."

Cliff regards him for a long moment. "I intended to wait until after the trial, but you and I need to talk. I've made some decisions. Waiting for the right time, I guess."

"Sounds serious. When did you have in mind?"

"I'll swing by the Tribune for lunch."

"I'll send out for sandwiches. A whole bunch of them. And pie. You look like you could do with a feed."

"Fine. Thanks. But don't bother with the pie."

Jennifer

Mr Beresford spots her the moment she enters his saloon and for some reason approaches her with eager strides.

"Dr Sullivan."

"Mr Beresford."

"You're looking for the O'Brien girl."

"I need to check on Ruth, yes. After the court order from Judge Callaghan to see to Ruth's welfare…"

"You'll be happy to know the priest came and saw me. Father Nugent. Said he'd found some appropriate accommodation for the girl."

"Very glad to hear it. Where?"

Mr Beresford gives her the address.

"I'm sorry the hearing didn't go her way," he adds. "But the good news is the priest is also helping the girl find a job."

"You know, Mr Beresford, we all share this world. It's not your world or mine, it's everyone's, and we all deserve a chance at making the most of it. Ruth sacrificed the justice she should have had so that the world would give her a chance. I think we are duty bound to see that she gets it, don't you?"

Mr Beresford smiles. "Now, Doc, not everyone holds that view. Some of us think you make your own luck. Wouldn't expect you to think like that, being a doctor an' all."

"Ruth wasn't born a saloon girl, Mr Beresford. She didn't come out of her mother's womb wearing sequins and feathers and black lace garters…"

"Steady there, Doc…"

"Ruth was a precious child with a future, the same as every child conceived."

"I hear what you're saying."

"Then you understand that kindness, justice and liberty are rights due to every child throughout their whole life, even in the dark times."

The man's mouth slackens in patronizing fashion. "She was only roughed up a bit, Doc. She'll get over it."

Jennifer raises an eyebrow at him. "She was raped, Mr Beresford."

"Well, the Judge didn't think so."

"Is that what you think? How convenient for you. All I can add is that I'm glad Ruth O'Brien no longer works here."

Mr Beresford sighs. "There'll be another come along to replace her."

"There will be your chance to do something honorable – don't employ the next one, or the next or the next. And there are laws regarding prostitution and underage women. I'm surprised the Law hasn't come after you, Mr Beresford."

Nettled, he says, "She lied about her age."

"Of course, she did. Now, excuse me, I need to find my patient. Thank you for your time."

Mr Beresford gives a begrudging nod and Jennifer makes her exit.

Ruth seems settled in her new room at the boarding house. It's a warm, bright, sizeable room which she could happily call home, if presently a little sparse with but a small bed, a table and two chairs.

"Father Nugent said the landlady – one of his parishioners – is very strict about who comes and goes and who lives here. Think it'll take some getting used to after living in the saloon and other places all this time."

"I can well imagine." Jennifer examines the bruises and marks on Ruth's body, letting her talk. Ruth never lets on that she hurts except for a passing grunt every so often.

After a little more young girl's chatter about her strict new landlady, Ruth says, "Something happened yesterday."

"Oh?"

"Yes, I went to the church – that's how I met Father Nugent. You'll never guess who introduced me to him."

"Who?"

"Sheriff Ryan."

Jennifer looks up. Ruth gives a childlike nod.

"True, Doc. He was there in the church. He asked me something odd."

"Good heavens… what?"

"To be his sponsor. He's becoming a Catholic."

"Oh… yes… I heard about that. And you are Catholic?"

Ruth looks at her hands. "A while ago now. Didn't seem to matter to Mr Ryan though. Father Nugent was a little shocked at first. Mr Ryan said he was… adamant?"

"Yes, adamant."

"That it should be me."

"And do you want to be Mr Ryan's sponsor?"

"Not at first. I mean, look at me. I thought maybe he was mad or something. But he meant it. Said he'd been looking for ages. I'm kind of confused about why he picked me."

"Well, although he might not always appear to be, Mr Ryan is a crusader from way back."

"Crusader?"

"These days it tends to mean a person who champions people's rights and liberties, that kind of thing."

"But Mr Ryan's a sheriff. He arrests people and puts them in jail."

Jennifer smiles. "I've known Mr Ryan for some time now. Trust me, he's a crusader."

"Guess he is then, if he wants me as his sponsor."

Jennifer sits beside her patient on the bed. "I think it will be very beneficial for you. He's a good person. And you need something to occupy you while you get your life back on track."

"Are you a church-going person, Doc?"

"Not usually. Things happen in life that seem to turn people away from practicing religion."

"Mm. Father Nugent says that too. But he says once the seed is planted in you, it never really leaves you. It's like a calling card tucked into the pocket of your soul always offering you an introduction or an invitation. I like that. It makes God sound like a friend rather than a mean old judge. I said that to Father Nugent and he says God is a faithful friend, but you still got to pay attention. I thought since my life had reached rock bottom it couldn't hurt to pay attention."

"That's lovely, Ruth. I'm proud of you."

Ruth smiles, a little life-weary grin. "Mm. Mr Ryan told me his grandmother was Catholic but he never really paid attention either, until recently."

"I see. Are friends allowed to attend the ceremony?"

"I'm not sure. I've noticed Father Nugent thinks very highly of Mr Ryan. So if Mr Ryan wants friends to be present I think Father Nugent probably won't mind."

Jennifer grins. "Delightful."

"I never thought Mr Ryan was humble, him being such an important man an' all, but I think he might be. Anyway, somehow I'm supposed to help him. Look at me! Look at who I am! I still can't believe it. But I got to because Mr Ryan says it's right."

Mr Ryan would.

Luke

The Taylors' house on 16th

Ethan rubs his hands together vigorously. "It's all set, I've arranged for Jennifer to meet Sara in one hour at the Keatons. Where is she?"

"Out attending to a patient. She'll be back soon."

"Hope you don't mind me organizing things. Sara's not herself. Thought we'd better get this over with, before she blows up or somethin'."

"I don't mind," Luke says, but his stomach is churning. He pretends to tidy the pile of newspapers on the kitchen table.

"You get that thing…you know… sorted out?"

"We're back on track," he replies. "We spent some time with the Faraday's last night. They're happy. The baby's nice, kinda small."

"Babies born before time usually are. You probably don't remember Tip was one of those pre-mature babies. Look at him now."

They grin at one another.

"I remember the day Tip was born," Luke says. "I remember I wasn't quite sure what a baby should look like. Red Sky asked me if I wasn't too disappointed Tip wasn't a foal. I just remember liking him straight away."

Ethan's chuckling. "He was a good baby. Even for one with only two legs."

"Did you never think of having another?" Luke asks.

Ethan starts. "You never asked me that before."

Luke shifts his feet. "Well, I'm asking you now."

"Why?"

"Because we're talking about babies."

"Mm. Because you're married and it's natural, that's why."

Luke stares at him. "It was just a question, Ethan. If you don't want to…"

"Red Sky wanted lots of babies, but Tip was the only one that came along. She had you and Katrine to mother and she loved you like you were her own children. Made her happy thinking about you and Tip being brothers. That's how she saw the pair of you the moment Tip was born."

He grins, loving the talk about Red Sky and Ethan telling it.

"Funny, I've known you all my life and I never thought about it before…"

"Ain't nothing strange about it. Like I said, you're married and things are different."

If there was anyone in the world to whom Luke wanted to spill the beans about the tiny prospect, it was Ethan. Some secrets have a way of wanting to be shared…

"Somethin' you want to tell me, Luke?"

Uncanny old cowpuncher. Luke learned to wise up to him long ago. But as he studies those experienced eyes, and realizes that for the first time in his life he shares the same adult responsibilities as Ethan in caring for a family, his resolve wavers a little. He opens his mouth, remembers that he couldn't disclose the secret without consulting Jennifer, and shuts it again.

"Well?"

"I'm sorry about Red Sky."

Ethan folds his arms, shifts his feet. "It was all a long time ago. So. How are you gonna handle this meetin' between Jennifer and your mother?"

He shudders inwardly. "Haven't thought about it."

"You haven't thought… Listen, Mr Married Man, you better think about it…"

"Ethan, that ain't helping."

Ethan grunts. "Well, I'll head on over there. Make sure everything's ready."

"That ain't helping either."

Sara

The Keatons' house on 18th & Evans

Sara agreed to be introduced to Jennifer at the Keatons'.

One thing Sara had observed since her return – the Alliance has become a good deal closer than it used to be. Such as living in each other's pockets. A larger, more formidable and in some ways odder Alliance than she could have imagined.

And they *all* wait in the sizable kitchen for Luke and his bride to walk through the back door.

Tip and the Italian boys speak constantly and rapidly, jangling her nerves. She overheard Tip talking to Ethan about giving them jobs on the Diamond-T. The boys' mother, Tip argued, would make the best cook they'd ever had on the ranch. Ethan didn't seem opposed to the idea at all.

What about *her*? As part owner, didn't she have some say in who worked on the ranch?

The biggest surprise of all is the Taylors.

First, there's Richard Taylor, Morgan's brother, a man to whom she took an instant dislike thirty years ago, an opinion upon renewing the acquaintance she has little reason to change. He has said barely two words. Such a pathetic figure of a man. What would Morgan say, she wonders; nobody has a care about Morgan.

And then there's Caroline, who seems genuinely relieved to meet up again, but tends to overcompensate for her husband, which is irritating.

Ben, however, is a thoughtful young man, who has the dark blue eyes of the Taylors. His choice of wife speaks volumes for him.

Tressa seems happier when Ben is in the room; and Adam adores him, stretching out his little arms to be taken up and affectionately attended to by his uncle. How had Richard produced such a young man? Oh, the boy isn't perfect by any means; he looks a little sour from time to time, no doubt a remnant of Richard's parenting. According to Ethan, however, Ben is doing just fine.

But what are they all doing here?

"We are all in this together," Caroline had told her.

How comforting.

When Ethan warned her that the Omaha Taylors, as they are apparently called, were back in their lives, she spent the night coming to grips with it so that when they met she would be composed and rational – not the harpy she tended to be in her imagination. And it worked. She was civil.

Now, curious is she to see Luke with these estranged relatives.

However, waiting in that crowded kitchen, it is Ben's young wife who says, "I think all of us sitting around like this would terrify anyone, even someone as calm and clever as Jennifer."

"I agree, Raina," Tressa says. "So, let's all go, and leave Aunt Sara and John and Amy here to meet them."

There are rumblings and mumblings of agreement and then they all get up and leave.

The silence is deafening.

"John…"

"Now don't start, Sara. I know this ain't easy. But no one's had an easy time of late. So just don't start…"

Sara blinks. "Why are *you* so nervous?"

"We want you to like her for Luke's sake," Amy blurts out.

"She is *my* daughter-in-law, Amy."

Amy flashes her gray eyes. "Fine. We'll leave. Come on, John, we have things to do."

John frowns. "What? We do? But…"

"Come on."

Amy coerces him from the room. It wasn't the plan. Amy reminded her of Kelley when she did something as spirited as this.

Now she is alone and the kitchen suddenly seems huge and like it's had its bones stripped and then re-fleshed with everything

Amy. She even has herbs growing in abundance by the window. She's made herself – and therefore them all – at home here.

A few moments pass; the backdoor opens and her son walks through it. He smiles and sits down opposite her at the table.

"Sara..."

"What happened to Jennifer?"

"Sara, if you had even the slightest notion how hard this is..."

"Did something happen?"

He shakes his head. "Trying to do this the easy way."

"Honestly, Luke, do I look like the evil mother-in-law to you?"

"Honestly? – just a bit."

Sara sighs long and hard. "Do you remember when you first decided to call me Sara?"

"Yes," he says cautiously.

"For me it was an unhappy day. Luke, whenever a son says the word 'mother' it reminds him this woman gave birth to him, raised him, sacrificed herself for him and always wants what is best for him. Am I or am I not your mother?"

His eyes grow bright. "You're laying guilt on me?"

"Answer the question."

"Yes, you are my mother."

"You undertook this marriage without..."

"You took yourself off to New York and didn't come back."

"Don't take that tone with me. You undertook this marriage without me, knowing I was still grieving over Kelley."

"We all still grieve, Sara."

"Not you apparently."

"That is untrue. I loved her as much as you did."

"And this is how you show it?"

"I wasn't *in* love with her. Marriage to K would have been unfair. She wanted to go back to New York with Edith. She told me so. We gave each other our blessing to go on with our separate lives."

"She loved you... was *in* love with you."

"For a while. But she knew, she told me, that we never loved each other enough to make it work. Why won't you believe me?"

"Because your head was turned by this other woman."

"Listen to what I'm telling you, Sara."

"You broke her heart and then you betrayed her with another woman."

"Is that what you think of me?"

"I'm disappointed in you."

"Is *that* what you think of me?"

"It is."

He gets to his feet. "Then we have nothing more to say to one another."

"Sit down."

"Go back to New York, Sara, and wallow in your grief and self-pity, and leave K's justice and the survival of the Alliance to those who actually care about it."

He storms out of the kitchen, the back door rattling shut behind him.

Sara's nerves jump, and then she starts to tremble.

What's the matter with everyone?

Ethan appears before her.

They stare at one another for a long time. Seems to Sara that she has known Ethan longer than anyone else in her whole life. Perhaps no one knows her better than he, which is strangely comforting. She watches as his eyes grow moist.

"I know I ain't the boy's real father," he says and clears his throat, "but I raised him like he was my own."

"I raised him, Ethan."

"Yeah. You did. To be the man we knew Morgan would want him to be. He's that man, Sara, and then some, and you can't see it?"

"After what he did..."

"What he did..." Ethan sighs hard and looks at the ceiling. "Give me strength."

"Are you praying, Ethan?"

"Yeah, I've taken to prayin'. I prayed every minute that the boy was still alive till I had him, sick but safe, in my arms, and every minute after that till he got better, and every minute after that that Jennifer would come back into his life and make him happy. Yeah, I've been prayin'."

Sara stares, astonished.

"The boy almost died, Sara. We almost lost him, the way we lost Katrine. Lost him, Sara. Do y'hear?"

"Yes, I... I hear you."

"Do you? Are you truly hearin' me, Sara?"

"Yes, Ethan, yes... But no one bothered to tell *me* my only son was gravely ill, did they?"

Ethan rubs the back of his neck. "No. Maybe we should've done that."

"Oh, you think so, do you? How could you, Ethan? How..."

"Sara, I'm... sorry. I'm sorry."

Another long silence falls between them. She has to forgive him, because he's Ethan and because she can see he means it right down to the marrow of his bones, although resentment and reluctance are almost choking her. She pulls herself together.

"I think I understand, Ethan, although I can't excuse it, but I will never condone the way he betrayed Kelley with this Jennifer."

Ethan throws up his hands. "He didn't. Can't you get that through your head?"

"Don't speak to me that way, Ethan."

"Well, listen to what I'm telling you. He didn't betray anyone. He tried his best with Kelley but it didn't work out. It wasn't to be."

"His behavior is disappointing."

"What behavior? Falling in love?"

"All I know is if he had tried harder Kelley probably wouldn't be dead."

"God Almighty, is that what you think? Now we're gettin' to the gist of it. You think it's his fault. How wrong can you be!"

"Really?"

Ethan actually laughs at her. "I know you're disappointed in me, Sara, but now you've turned the tables. You are way off the mark. There ain't a person alive, including John and Amy, who thinks that. What put that into your head? It weren't there before, when he took off to San Francisco and you to New York."

"I've had time to think. And then his telegram came. And I've listened to all your explanations."

The back door opens and there appears a graceful and refined young woman with a face as charming as a porcelain doll, hair richly colored like chestnuts and large green eyes.

Now what? Who is this? Yet another interruption?

Sara sighs and looks away…

"Ethan," the young woman says, "for some reason I can't get Luke to budge from the back porch. Nothing will persuade him…"

Sara's ears prick up. That is a New England accent.

"Sara," Ethan says.

She looks up.

"Sara, *this* is Jennifer. Jennifer, this is Sara."

This is *she*? This is who he married? And she's a *doctor*?

While Sara's insides storm, the young woman's green eyes show no emotion whatsoever.

She holds out her hand and says pleasantly, "How do you do, Mrs Taylor? I'm very pleased to meet you. I hope you had a pleasant journey from New York."

Sara doesn't take her hand to shake nor even clasp it the way she is expected to do. She doesn't say or do anything. All these years she often wondered about the woman he would marry. When it occurred to her that woman would be Kelley, everything seemed to fit into place, like all the pieces of a puzzle. This woman, however… This Jennifer is nothing like Sara could've ever imagined.

The young woman lowers her hand and glances sidelong at Ethan who winks. "I apologize for keeping you waiting. I had a patient to see," she explains. "And yesterday, my friend Meg Faraday had her baby…"

Sara stares, her head suddenly swimming with questions.

"As I said, Ethan, I'm not sure how to get Luke back in here."

"I'll fetch him," Ethan says.

When Ethan is gone, the young woman asks, "Is that fresh tea in the pot?"

"No."

"I'll make some, shall I?"

Ethan

"You left them alone together?"

Ethan grasps the boy's shoulder; he can feel him trembling.

"Just for a bit. I think there's no other way. You don't have to worry about Jennifer; she can take care of herself. You know, this is interesting. I kinda get the feeling that the shoe would be on the other foot if you were meeting Dermot."

The boy nods unhappily.

Ethan gives him a shake. "Good. And if it's any consolation to you, I saw the look in Sara's eyes when I introduced her to Jennifer." He grins. "She got one almighty shock."

Luke manages a smile. It's gone again as quick as it came. "You didn't hear what she said to me."

"Your ma? Aw, there ain't much about your ma I don't know. Including what she thinks of you. She's just upset is all."

"No. She *blames* me."

"What put an idea like that in your head?"

"She just said it to me. I broke K's heart and then betrayed her with another woman. My own mother said that to me..."

Ouch. That had to hurt pretty bad.

"You got a notion to rush in there and rescue your bride from the wicked witch?"

"I knew this was going to be tough, why am I so surprised?"

"Your ma's just a little confused right now. You know, she's been a long time without your pa. Good chance she once thought Morgan would be around when you came home with the woman you wanted to marry."

"She doesn't trust me, Ethan, or you for that matter."

"She knows I'll take your side. Lotta things get churned up at a time like this. The past. Regrets. Recriminations. All her dreams for you. What you ended up doing. She wants you to be like Morgan."

"Pa…" he mutters and walks off to another part of the porch. "He would've liked Jennifer, wouldn't he?"

"In all honesty the only person that matters to is Sara."

"But if that's how Sara thinks…"

"All she can see is that Morgan would've wanted someone like Kelley for you. Rancher's daughter. Someone to consolidate what Morgan began. She's been wanting that for years. Like it's the job Morgan left her to do."

"Fucked that up then…"

"Might surprise you to know Morgan wouldn't have thought that at all. Sara's got that wrong. Like I said, all mixed up. I know we taught you to honor your heritage and that don't change, but your likeness to your father only goes so far. You're your own man, Luke. You know that. And it's your life to live the way you see fit. Morgan would've said the same – in fact, I'm saying it for him.

"If there's anything this business with Parsons, Donnelly and Bodecker has taught me it's that sure it's important to fight for what's yours, but you can't hold on so tightly to it you forget what really matters. Tip matters to me. And you matter to me. And Sara. You're my family. The Diamond-T is just the dirt and grass Morgan and me bought to make a good living from and raise our families. Morgan would've wanted you to be the rancher he was if that's what *you* wanted. Seems to me Sara's got the heritage that lives inside of a man mixed up with the dirt and the grass. It's what's inside the man that counts."

The boy comes back to him, slowly, with thinking steps and expression to match. "Thanks, Ethan."

"Don't mention it. Now, whatever your ma accused you of before, you can't let it get to you. It ain't your problem, it's hers."

"Yeah, I see that now."

"Good. Now go inside and be with your wife. She's been missing you. And Sara needs to see the two of you together to really understand."

Luke

He returns to the kitchen. Sara's restless gaze converges on him as he enters, but he looks for Jennifer. She's pouring boiling water from the kettle into Amy's teapot. Her eyes flick sideways in his direction; she smiles and softly exclaims, "You came back."

His heart gives a leap. She's pleased with him. He goes to her, takes the kettle from her and lumps it back on the stove.

"I came back," he concurs, finding delight in her lively – and relieved – expression. He turns to Sara. "So, *Mother*, what have you and Jennifer been talking about?"

Glowering at him, Sara says, "How you two met."

Jennifer tables the teapot. "We were up to when I operated on your leg."

"And you captured Wilson Cutter in the medicine pantry."

"And Cliff gave you such a scolding."

"And you stood there and let him."

"I thought you deserved it."

"Did you? You never said before."

"You got cross when I snipped your brand new union suit."

"A Texan wears long handles, if you don't mind," he laughs.

"Oh, pardon me. Of course. I'm being a blue belly again."

"Then you and Duffy had me wear that short nightgown."

Sara jumps in with, "What were the rest of us doing while this was happening?"

"Seems a long time ago," Luke murmurs.

Jennifer starts pouring tea into Sara's cup and two others.

"Is Ethan joining us?"

"He had something to do."

They take a seat, fresh tea fragrance wafting about them.

"So, what are your plans for the future?" Sara asks.

"Until the trial ends we are taking one day at a time," Jennifer replies.

"No plans at all?"

"I wouldn't say that exactly. We were married because being apart wasn't good for either of us. We needed to be together."

Sara looks strained as she asks, "How do you plan to practice your career and take care of home and family?"

"That is a way off yet," Jennifer says.

"You have nothing to say on the subject?" Sara accuses him.

"Nothing you want to hear."

"Clearly the pair of you can't live on the Diamond-T and ranch when you have other ambitions."

"Sara," he says, as patient as he can be, "we just got married. When the trial is over and the future belongs to all of us once more, then we'll make some serious plans."

"So concerned with the Alliance, aren't you, Luke, yet you…"

"Don't say it, Sara," he murmurs, his heart aching. "You can say what you want to hurt me, but I won't let you say it in front Jennifer."

He can feel Jennifer's gaze on him. Sensing she might fly out the door at any moment, he reaches beside him for her left hand and holds it between both his on the table where Sara can see. Their hands joined; her wedding ring.

Her cool slender fingers remind him of those earlier days. He looks at her, remembering…

"That night I cut my hand and you stitched it up. See – here's the scar."

She takes his hand and draws it towards her to inspect. "Mm. You can tell my hands were trembling."

"I like having a memento."

"I'd prefer it was a neater effort on my part."

"So, Jennifer," says Sara, "your family…"

She had to bring that up. Especially as what to do about Dermot had yet to be decided. And especially as Luke had already told her plenty about the Sullivan family, including how Jennifer's mother died.

"My brother and his family are very pleased," Jennifer says.

"And your father?"

Oh boy. If there's one thing that really gets Jennifer's ginger up it's to refer to Dermot as her father.

"Unwell at present. He lives in Provincetown."

"I'm not familiar with that town."

"Cape Cod..."

"Does he know?"

"To be honest, I'm not sure."

"You're not in contact with him."

"Mrs Taylor, the man you refer to as my father disinherited me and disowned me when I was eighteen. I was well on my way to becoming a doctor and I defied him in every way possible. And while I feel that your judgment is sure to lean in favor of him, regardless of what I might say in my defense, I make no apology for my actions. And now, according to my brother, he is quite ill and asking to see me. I have yet to make the decision to go to him."

"What is holding you back?" Sara asks, sincerely.

"I have no love for him."

"That must be difficult."

"Not really. There is no feeling between us at all."

"Between a parent and child there is always feeling, whether you know it or not. How can any parent be indifferent to his or her offspring?"

"I don't understand it myself. It seems incomprehensible. But it happens. Happened to me in fact."

"I'm sorry to hear that. My own father passed away many, many years ago now, but I still miss him. He was older when I was born, so by the time I married Luke's father and Papa moved back East, I never saw him again."

Luke can't believe his ears.

"He was Danish by birth, my mother American."

"Luke mentioned that."

"Sullivan – isn't that Irish?"

"My father's ancestors were Irish and English. My mother was

Irish born, but there was French in her background somewhere, so I'm told."

"What was her name? Do you look like her?"

"She was Aisling, and her portrait reveals a striking likeness."

"What a comfort that must be to your family."

"To my brother I believe."

"America's a strange place. If we were in Europe, you would be either French or Irish. I would be Danish. And yet here we are – all muddled up and mixed in. A bit of everything. Luke has French blood, too. His grandmother on his father's side. Lara Proulx was her name. Her family were Quebecois…"

"Luke has told me about her. And what about Ethan?"

"Oh, Ethan has been Texan since God created the earth," she declares, then sees Luke's frown of disapproval, clears her throat and continues with, "but he married Red Sky, a true friend and I miss her still. She was the daughter of Black Wolf, a Comanche chief no less, an extraordinary and beautiful woman. And so we have Tip. A fine boy."

"Tip is wonderful. And Ethan is a very good man."

"Ethan is Ethan…"

And she takes him for granted.

"I know I take his goodness and his loyalty for granted…"

Luke bites his tongue. Hard.

"He has been a good friend to me," Jennifer says.

"Oh, he'd walk through fire for you two. I suppose I shouldn't have expected anything less from him." She sips her tea, and then asks, "Why did I never know of your relationship?"

"For a long time we never told one another how we felt."

"We pretended it hadn't happened."

"And we were friends."

Luke considers going into detail but the strain of bringing K and all the complications into this conversation is beyond him. The tale of his whole life since Mart died on that terrible day in March last year is too much to tell, too much for Sara to understand, if in fact she ever could.

He says, "The time came to face up to our feelings and we did."

"Ethan knew, didn't he?"

"Yes, Ethan knew. Cam and Meg Faraday. And Cliff."

"How much encouragement did Ethan give you, I wonder."

"Wasn't needed. He knew without me having to say a word how I felt. Could tell by just looking at both of us. But he let things run their course. The way you wanted. And they did. Only some things you can't control. Sara, you don't know how many bad days are behind me thanks to Jennifer. She has kept me safe all this time..." He can't be sure his mother even understands what that means. Her eyes are grave and sad; she's struggling, but he can't help that. The truth will set her free... eventually. "There is nothing else ahead of her, Sara."

"You love the Diamond-T," she argues softly.

He swallows and firms his hands around Jennifer's. "Not ahead of Jennifer."

"You don't know what you're saying..."

"Do I look like a child to you? No, Sara, this is the way it is."

"You think she loves you more than her profession?"

"I'm right here, Mrs Taylor..."

"We'll see, won't we?"

"Sara, there's such a thing as a fine line..."

"These things need to be discussed in a marriage..."

"And why would you think we haven't done that? I want Jennifer to be a doctor for as long as she wants and she knows it. It's part of her and the world needs her. It will probably mean we go to St Louis or back East or someplace else. Wherever we need to."

Sara stiffens. "And what of the Diamond-T – your heritage?"

"Apart from ranching there are other things I want to do with my life. Now I know you've always had trouble understanding that, but marrying Jennifer should make you realize now how serious I am about it."

"But what on earth would you do in St Louis or Boston?"

"I have some ideas."

"For God's sake, Luke, you are a rancher, like your father. I've never told you this before, but you are better at it than he was!"

"Thanks. I appreciate the compliment. But it doesn't change the fact that the ranch will always be my heritage but only part of my life."

"A significant part," Jennifer says.

"You know nothing of ranching," Sara says to her.

"I'm sure Luke can teach me what I need to know."

"Yes, but if he had…"

"Ah, we won't go into that," Luke says, cutting her off. The last thing Jennifer needs to hear is that, in Sara's opinion at least, K was a far more suitable wife for a rancher. "And what about you, Sara? Are you still calling the Diamond-T home these days?"

She seems stunned. "Of course."

"I wasn't sure. I think you liked New York, being with Edith."

"Edith reminds me of Kelley. When I'm with Edith I feel Kelley's presence all around us. And I worry that when I am back on the Diamond-T all I will feel are the ghosts of happier times leading me to despair."

"But she's in heaven, Sara. She's free, like she always wanted."

"Heaven? So that's how you came to terms with it."

"How else? Not you?"

"No, not me," she mutters, glancing this way and that, fiddling with her shawl. "She was taken for no good reason and I'm still angry about it. And since when did you believe in heaven?"

"Some of what Mart taught me finally sunk in while I was in San Francisco searching for answers."

"You've changed, Luke. I think I hardly know you anymore."

And who is this woman who used to be his mother?

"What are you fighting for," she persists, "doing all *this* for?"

"The men on trial had K murdered. When they're convicted and punished, I'll have ensured K has the justice she deserves. What did you think I was fighting for?"

Her mouth goes slack with shock. "This is not about the Diamond-T and the Alliance?"

"You know I'd never turn away from a fight to protect them."

After a pause, she mutters, "You surprise me."

"Why? Because you thought I'd forgotten K?"

"Yes," she says, almost resentfully.

"I did not betray her with Jennifer. We tried, Sara, but K didn't want me. Can't you accept that? I had to. You must believe it. K knew what she wanted before she died and it wasn't me. I'm sorry there weren't any witnesses at the time we discussed it, so you have to believe me. Can you do that?"

She wriggles unhappily.

"Accept it, Sara," he says gently. "For your own sake."

"No."

"I know how much she brought to our lives. But you can't live in the past."

"Easy for you to say. You found something to replace her."

Luke hears Jennifer's shocked intake of breath above his own.

Hurt speaks a harsh language.

Holding tight to her hand, he digs deep now, very deep. He's got to, for all their sakes.

"Jennifer has a far different place in my life than K ever had. Nothing could replace Mart either but I've found other friends who have shown they care about me as much as he did. No one gets replaced, Sara. Our lives change and people move in and out, some stay forever, some are here for a while. Some we see every day and some we have to look into our hearts to see. I swore to K she would always be in my heart and she is. I have never broken that promise to her and I never will. But Jennifer is the love of my life. I can't imagine loving anyone or anything more than her."

"Oh stop!" She clutches at her shawl, trembling and teary-eyed.

"Sara, this will destroy you if you don't let it go. It nearly happened to me. But I had Jennifer to save me. And you have us."

"I...I had such dreams," she says, crying.

"I know. I'm sorry they didn't come true. But you can dream other dreams. I promise you this will not be a dull life. There'll be grandchildren one day and a whole world will open up full of life and joy and adventures that will amaze you..."

"I've never heard you talk like that before."

"I have hope, Sara."

His eyes fill with stinging moisture as they meet Jennifer's green ones. Their gaze lengthens pleasantly. There are hurdles, no doubt about that, but he can't imagine a minute of life without her.

He hears Sara say, "Grandchildren?"

Jennifer's eyes dance.

"Someday," he grins.

Jennifer

"You look peaky," Luke says as he draws her up the stairs by the hand. "Very peaky. Sara makes *me* peaky some days, well, often."

"But I'm fine... and what about Meg?"

"You're all done for the day, at least till supper time. Meg has plenty of help. You, *bella Ginevra*, need some sleep."

"Supper is hours away. I could put my feet up on the sofa..."

"Nope. Bed. We'll be removing your clothes..."

"I beg your pardon?"

"And putting on a nightgown. The shorter the better."

"Oh, I see what this is."

"Tucked up in bed for some lunch, then off into dreamland."

"Revenge."

"You got that right, Doctor Sullivan." They reach the top of the stairs. "Is that a giggle I hear?"

It is now.

"I see your strategy. You plan to distract me with your giggles and your wiles and all that beauty, but I'm onto you. I refuse to be distracted."

And for the most part he remains focused on his goal. She provokes him along the way, with a look, a caress or word; his blue eyes sparkle with amusement, but he proves unyielding.

"Happy?" she asks when she's sitting up against her pillow with the bedclothes up to the ruffled neckline of her nightgown where he arranged them.

"Only one thing would make me happier."

483

"Lunch?"

He feigns hurt at the notion.

"Fishing?"

He pretends to be wounded.

"Wrangling wild horses in the high country perhaps…"

"Horses? Now you're playing dirty, Mrs Taylor. C'mon, let's see what else you got."

She leans forward and kisses him, once, twice, lingering over a third…

"Happy now?" she murmurs.

From the look on his face he appears quite contented.

And yet, of all things, he says, "I'm proud of you, Jennifer."

"Thank you," she smiles, "but for what?"

"The way you talked with Sara about your past and Dermot."

"Oh, I see." She locks onto his train of thought. "It's beginning to feel less burdensome than before."

"It doesn't scare you like it did."

"Well, I'd rather everyone didn't know about it."

No one who hasn't experienced the humiliation and shame of such a childhood could truly understand how it feels. Most of her life has been spent hiding it; she hungered sometimes to know how it felt to have a childhood where recalling it was a joyous exercise…

"Sweetheart…"

"Mm?"

"I said: but you discussed it with my mother."

"I know," she whispers, anchoring herself in those blue eyes and firmly back in the present where she has all the joyousness she could wish for. "You were very good with her. Why do you call her Sara? She is your mother after all…"

He gives a sheepish laugh. "She would be happy to know you think so. The reason is simple. Whenever I do things to displease her she brings my father into it – what he would expect of me, just as she did today. When I was twenty, after I returned from San Francisco, she was pleased to see me but kept hounding me about staying where I belong. She insisted we were all partners in this legacy of my father's and should work and act like it. I said, fine, partners! Sara my partner, I declared, and I've called her Sara ever since. I think she wishes she'd never said anything."

"That must make her feel a little insecure, especially since she's on her own."

"She has Ethan – no one is more loyal than Ethan."

"I'm sure she appreciates him, deep down."

"I hope so. Sara's known a long time I might not turn out like she wanted and kept hoping something would happen to tip things in her favor. She pegged all her hopes on K to influence me. Even on the memory of her."

"Poor Sara. Imagine how it will feel when our child's dreams and yours are conflicted."

He chuckles delightedly. "I can hardly wait." His eyes sparkle. "You know we're gonna have to have a girl, someone to carry on your beautiful face."

"This is my mother's face."

"It was very good of her to give it to you."

In spite of his heartfelt compliment, she feels herself frowning. Her mind has begun to swirl with filaments of thought she can't formulate or grasp long enough to comprehend. Usually such abstractions involve her mother, as though her mind yearns to make sense of something that should exist but doesn't... all she knows of her mother is this.

Loud knocking on their back door shatters her reverie.

"Sit back and rest," Luke says. "I'll be back with lunch."

He kisses her cheek before he leaves.

She smoothes her hands over her belly. Her body is changing, sapping her energy in order to create the growing new life within, whose very presence is yet undetectable to others. She tires in the afternoons and morning sickness is taking the edge off her sense of well-being. To give life, she must concede hers. And while Luke is bound to her, she is utterly bound to her baby; nothing must come between her and the tiny prospect. This is their shared destiny.

Luke

Balancing a sandwich, two raisin cookies and a glass of milk on the black tray with the rose picture on it, Luke sets off up the stairs. As he walks through their bedroom door, he spies her sitting up and smoothing her hand over the covers, where the baby would be.

"Everything all right?" he asks, sitting beside her.

She looks up as if she just noticed him.

"Hungry?" He places the tray on her lap.

"Oh, my. That's some sandwich."

"Ham, cheese, tomato, cucumber and Amy's corn relish, but no raw onion because it no longer agrees with you or you with it."

"Mmmm. Delicious. Thank you."

"You were rubbing your belly."

"Just thinking. Who was downstairs?"

"Ethan. Cam's called a meeting with Ethan, me and Cliff over at his place soon as we all get there. We can eat lunch first."

"Where's *your* lunch?"

"Ate it while I made yours. Had to keep up my strength."

She giggles in that elegant way she has and then looks into his eyes. "Take the tray a minute, Luke. I want to talk to you."

"Had a feeling you were working up to something." With the tray transferred to the nightstand, he budges up closer to her. "Feeling all right?"

"This is our baby."

"I should hope so." He studies her vivid green eyes with a growing sense of needing to stay alert. "Say what's on your mind."

"My mother…"

"Mm…"

"Frank tells me our mother loved him, and Joseph and Miles, very much. Even now he can remember things about her. She was a loving mother, a loving person. Frank says she loved Dermot."

He smiles sympathetically but, liking Frank's reasoning and recalling his talk with Ethan, he says, "You think Dermot would have gone to pieces like he did when she passed away if they weren't in love?"

She catches her breath. "It is beyond me to see Dermot as a person who loves."

"I know."

"But my mother… she loved me in her womb, the way I love our baby. She loved me."

"I think that's a fair assessment. She loved you and she was looking forward to meeting you, same as we look forward to the tiny prospect's arrival."

"We?"

"Fair to say it's something husband and wife both look forward to, a baby on the way."

"Then what you are saying is that Dermot… that Dermot…"

He holds her troubled gaze. "Dermot wanted you, just like your mother."

"But it's not possible. He hated me the moment my mother…"

"He blamed you, stupidly."

"If he loved me as he waited for me to be born then he should never have rejected me. What he did was irrational and bitter."

"I think if it were me," he says carefully, "I would've blamed myself. Maybe Dermot did that too. But it seems logical, since he loved your mother, he must have loved you as he waited for you to be born. I think all that love made it all the harder to bear."

She stares at him, fathoming the logic – for if it is logical then she can't, and won't, refute it.

"He loved me?"

"For nine months."

"Eight," he is corrected. "I was early. Hence the trouble…"

"You weren't trouble. You were a sweet, innocent baby your whole family longed for."

"I was loved."

"You were loved."

"Not supposition?"

"I can only tell you what a husband feels when the woman he's completely crazy about is expecting their baby. Proud. Happy. And anxious…" A wondrous thought fills his mind and transforms into emotion as he gathers her in his arms. "You know what I think?"

Her expression leaps, as if mimicking her heart. "Tell me."

"I think there was so much love for you when they waited for you to be born it was more than enough to make you the lovable, compassionate, desirable woman you grew up to be."

A kiss of dreamy tenderness is placed upon his lips.

And she whispers, "That's the most beautiful thing I've ever heard anyone say."

"This heart of mine could never tell you anything other than the truth."

She smiles; a tear spills from her eye and trickles over one dainty freckle. "It always does, my darling."

Cliff

True to his word, Charlie had the sandwiches piled high, devouring most of them while Cliff did the talking. The final agreement was reached. They shook on it; the official paperwork would soon be completed. And all that was left on the plate were crumbs.

Now he hurries from his lunch feeling as though a piece of him has been transported out of Cheyenne. His leaving begins, although essentially it began the day he met Emma... Mrs Landers steps in front of him and brings him to a jarring halt on the sidewalk.

"Mrs Landers!"

"Sheriff... ya look kinda in a hurry there."

"Is there something I can help you with?"

"Now ya come to mention it, I sure could use one cuppa hot chocolate."

"Hot chocolate? *Now*?

She turns her irresistible grin on him. "And a small chat."

"About?"

"Now I know yer busier than most, but this won't take long. There's always a table at the Fancy Boots."

He succumbs. "Okay, you got me. Lead on."

Her grin broadens. And although he suspects this is about Emma and wishes it wasn't, Mrs Landers may know something about her that he doesn't and should.

At Fancy Boots Café she finds them a table.

He holds her chair for her while she sits and then takes the seat opposite. He orders her a hot chocolate and coffee for himself, since his went cold when talking with Quaid.

"How's yer friend doin'? – the one who gave me this here fine scarf…"

"Now, Mrs Landers, I know you know all about Luke and Jennifer so you don't have to pretend with me."

"Oh. Guess Emmaline told ya 'bout that, huh?"

He nods, amused. "Luke and Jennifer are fine. Married. You probably read about it. And now that we've broken the ice…"

"'Bout Emmaline. Yer not supposed to give up on her."

What is it about Mrs Landers… "It's what she wants."

"Wasn't what she wanted when her folks came into town. Ran away from them, she did. I brought her here. She was one mighty confused young woman. The thought of leavin' ya was breakin' her heart."

"Mrs Landers…"

"Hush now, James, listen to me…"

"*James?*"

"She was sick. So she had to go. But she wasn't goin' to. She wanted to defy her parents and her illness and stay. But that weren't right. I told her to do what she had to do. And she knew, she did. Knew she had to go home and get better. So she left. She didn't tell ya goodbye, so what's that sayin'?"

"Mrs Landers…"

"She won't love no one else the same way or as much 'cause she ain't s'posed to. She won't be happy unless she's with the man I'm lookin' at. James and Emma share their destiny is what's written in heaven. You gonna rewrite that?"

Emma love someone else? He swallows his panic.

"Emma wrote me a long letter from Denver. She told me in no uncertain terms it was over between us. I'm supposed to understand we are *not* destined to be together."

"Not her job to know destiny."

"And it's yours?"

She blinks. "All I'm sayin' is Emmaline ain't qualified."

The hot chocolate and coffee arrive. Cliff drinks his with as much gusto as Mrs Landers drinks hers.

"Want her well, don't ya?"

"Of course," he says, frustrated. The thought of Emma being ill is more than he can bear, but bear it he must, alone and unable to help.

"Then let her get well. Let her see her family and make her decisions. She has a twin. They got a close bond… rare and peculiar. And for some folk, home's the place to be when makin' decisions, the big unexpected ones in partic'lar. But don't give up on her."

They're going round in circles. "You can lead a horse to water."

"So I heard." She grunts. "But did ya tell her what she needs to know?"

"How do you…"

"Well, can't be helped. What's done is done, and the future is everythin'…" She becomes still as though she's listening to a distant sound. "Her heart is cryin'… Yer not to forget her, James."

"Why do you call me that?"

"To remind you in your heart of who you are and who you are meant to be," she says in a voice that doesn't sound completely her own.

Where'd that come from? Weary from bewilderment, and just plain weary, he says nothing.

They finish their drinks in silence.

Mrs Landers licks her lips. "That was mighty fine, Sheriff. Much obliged."

He smiles. "You're welcome."

She gets to her feet and he follows.

"Don't forget what I said. It's important."

"If you think I'm going to spend one more iota of time or energy thinking about Emma, you'd better think again."

She considers him with an open expression. "That's just the hurt talkin'. Ya ain't *stopped* thinkin' about her, not since the moment ya laid eyes on her. Fight for her, James. Don't give up."

"She doesn't want me."

"Dear boy, is that what ya truly think? Search ya heart. She's right there. Always. Hold onto her tight. Yer not to forget her."

When she's gone, Cliff sinks back into his chair; he studies the dark ring of coffee staining the bottom of his cup. He can't let himself want Emma for even a second. He'd made progress; he isn't about to unmake it and have to start all over again.

Luke

"All right, you two," Cam says while rubbing his hands together, "I have here on my desk the Worthing and Farrell report which spells out in no uncertain terms what lies beneath the Diamond-T."

Ethan frowns. "Come again?"

"The report of the secret geological exploration undertaken by Worthing and Farrell that Bodecker and Donnelly undertook illegally of your property last summer."

"*Under our very noses?*"

"You want to tell us, Cam," Luke says, "or do we read it for ourselves?"

"How come we never noticed?"

"Because they covered their tracks, Ethan," Cam explains. "Extremely well. They had to, or risk being caught."

"Well, ain't that just dandy..."

"What does the report say?"

"It says that on the advice of Ed Parsons it had been observed quartz rocks were to be seen all over the plateau, down into the valley between the plateau and Diamond-Pass. It says that digging equipment was used to discover if this quartz in its subterranean state could be gold-bearing. And so, last summer, in the valley between the plateau and Diamond-Pass, Worthing and Farrell punctured a gold-bearing reef of quartz ore."

"What the *hell* are you talkin' about?"

Ethan's strident disbelief confuses Cam for a moment.

"I'm speaking of gold, Ethan, on your ranch."

Ethan swears long and hard, causing Cam's eyes to bulge.

"See, Ethan, I told you Ben knew what he was talking about!" Luke declares, striking his knee.

"The report says that eventually erosion would have exposed the reef. And it would be extremely profitable to mine."

As Ethan is still too stunned to speak, Luke asks, "How far down is it?"

"Ten feet just in the area they explored. Apparently, it would eventually become exposed on the surface, and some of it would eventually get swept into rivers and streams. Apparently, *eventually* is a non-specific but rather lengthy period of time – very lengthy. Therefore, you haven't discovered any outcrops or alluvial gold because the primary reef has yet to be eroded and weathered. But speculators and prospectors, and those men who think they're prospectors, follow clues."

"We are sitting on a gold mine?" Ethan croaks.

"Well, allow me to explain about that. I know you've both been wondering about that clause in the deed of the Diamond-T: you can't fence the Diamond Pass area, et cetera. Worthing and Farrell traced the agreement Connors made, and went to the Army for the original survey – because they are geological surveyors they were allowed access to it – and found you never owned that tract of land between Ed Parsons' side of the Pass all the way through the valley to the plateau. In short, it can't be fenced because it was never yours."

Luke feels stupid, glances at Ethan and is relieved to see he looks as stupid as Luke feels. He clears his throat. "Then who?"

"Christopher Lamont."

"What in the Sam Hill is a Christopher Lamont?" Ethan drawls.

"He is, in fact, Archie Connors's grandson."

Luke shakes his head. "All right. I'm confused. Is anyone else confused?"

"Count me in," Ethan quips.

"*We* own the *whole* of the Diamond-T, Cam. That's what the deed states. I went to court half a dozen times with Ed Parsons and proved we did."

"I think you'll find it couldn't be proved that you didn't."

"What's the difference?"

"Good question."

"And how did Archie Connors know there was gold there?"

"Another good question."

"And why didn't he mine it back then?"

"All pertinent questions…"

"How about answering a few…"

"Archie Connors had every intention of returning from California and mining for gold, but he never made it back. Then he died, leaving a will in favor of his grandson, Christopher Lamont.

"The point is that because Bodecker found out you didn't rightfully own it, he stepped up his campaign to remove you from the Diamond-T altogether. I believe he had Miss Keaton murdered purely as revenge for your victory over Ed Parsons. And, germane to her murder was the need to have you all scattered, demoralized and defenseless so he could bring about the culmination of his plan. Unhappily for him, the Alliance is never without courage or determination…"

"Cam," Luke implores him, "make *sense*."

"As much as I would like to say more, I can't for now. You need to be in court and hear the testimony of Christopher Lamont."

"But, Cam…"

"And I need you to be patient. I have told you this much because you have a right to know that what will be revealed in court tomorrow is paramount. And, I've told only you two because you are the owners of the Diamond-T."

"I only own one quarter," Luke corrects him. "My mother the other quarter. Ethan the other half."

Cam's eyes him speculatively. "You fight tooth and nail for just one quarter of the ranch?"

"I don't care if it's a skinny sow's wallow, it's home, Cam, and it's mine. Besides, in my mother's will…"

"The remaining quarter is to go to you upon her passing."

"Yes."

"Tip inherits from me," Ethan mumbles, still in a state of shock.

"I know there is a lot at stake here."

"It's not just about the…the gold," Luke says, not liking how awkward that sounded coming from his lips. "I don't understand how the deed works. The place is ours but not ours? The tract mentioned in the report includes extremely valuable grazing lands. Now this Lamont can just go in and dig it all up whenever he feels like it?"

Ethan gives a firm nod. "That was my next question."

"Gentlemen, Lamont has become key to this case. I know what's at stake, believe me, but to win this outright, beyond all reasonable doubt, to prevent the case dragging on, particularly when the black suits present their defense case, we will need to expose the deed, this Connors Bill of Sale, to scrutiny, and your ownership of the Diamond-T."

Ethan barks a laugh. "Now won't Sara be thrilled about that."

Luke coughs. "Did we not mention she's arrived in town?"

"Oh? She should've been here then."

"Don't worry, Cam," Ethan says. "She ain't in any mood to be hearing somethin' she's not nearly ready to hear."

Luke meets Ethan's flashing eyes. "Looks like we don't have to worry about the gold, Ethan."

"And your heritage just shrunk."

"How can that be right," he murmurs.

"Huh! It ain't right. We've been working that land till the sweat stopped comin' and now we don't own it? Nothin' right about it."

"How come you didn't know?"

"Back in those days your pa handled that side of things. I had more know-how with the cattle and the breedin' stock."

"But you were there when the deed was signed."

"Sure I was. My signature went on it, same as your pa. Morgan signed first, said it was all in order, and then I signed, having faith it was as Morgan said. But I wasn't there when it was all worked out."

"But why would Pa agree to something strange like that: keep the pass open. Did he even question it with Connors at the time? Did you, Ethan?"

"I mentioned it."

"And?"

"All your pa said was it didn't matter, we got the best grazing land. And we were secure, set up for life. I had no reason to figure he meant anything else but ranchin'. We set our sights on producing the best beef. And the clause didn't matter. And then Morgan came up with the idea of selling off some northern acres to raise money for improvements to the ranch and our stock, and Nathaniel Collins, Amy's cousin, thought he'd do the same. Ed bought 'em up quick smart; he was a greedy bastard from the get-go... Now what's that look on your face for?"

"Just thought of something...

His mind has come alive with the kind of instant illumination that happens when an idea pops in and makes itself at home.

"There could've been another agreement, Ethan."

"*Another* agreement?"

"A secret one maybe..."

"Between Connors and your pa you mean?"

"That's what I'm thinking."

Ethan shakes his head. "Don't think so."

"Face it, Ethan, I don't think Pa told you everything."

"Why would he do such a thing?"

"If Pa said to you the clause didn't matter, that we were set up for life, then maybe he knew what the clause meant. Pa handled the business arrangements because he was good at it, so it makes sense he wouldn't sign up to something he didn't feel right about or that was a mystery."

Ethan grunts. Frowns his begrudging agreement of this point.

"So maybe Connors told Pa about the quartz ore. He'd found someone to look after the land and the quartz who was honorable and who had the perfect motives for keeping the agreement: ranching and the prospect of gold."

Ethan whistles. "You got some imagination. Morgan agreeing to that? That would make him and Connors partners." He shakes his head. "And why would he leave me out of somethin' like that?"

Deception bordering on betrayal? Or deception to err on the side of caution? Either way Ethan had been shut out; he has to be feeling let down by a man whom he trusted completely and considered his best friend.

Luke wishes he'd never had the illuminating thought; wishes he'd kept it to himself, at least for Ethan's sake.

"I reckon Pa took a secret to his grave," he murmurs.

"I see what you're thinking. But I'm old and ugly enough to take what Morgan can dish out any day, past or present."

What does that mean? He decides he'd rather not know and mutters, "Sure, Ethan."

"Well, go on. What else have you got in that head of yours?"

"Er, just this. Connors must've been a mighty unusual man not to want to dig the place up back then. Could be it was gonna be expensive and he needed to make some quick money for equipment and labor, since you said yourself, Cam, the gold has to be mined from deep beneath the ground. Meanwhile, Connors' potential gold mine sits all safe and secure till he comes back for it."

Ethan whistles again. "Begs the question, don't it, what kept Connors from comin' back?"

"Yep, I reckon. So now I'm thinking let's move forward some years. Imagine this: Ed discovers this Lamont is snooping around in the period after Lamont inherits; this alerts Ed to something out of the ordinary; it takes him a while but he works it out.

"Sure, he's always harassed us about water and boundary riders and so on, but he really stepped it up, didn't he? – what he did to Mart? Remember he was madder than a rattlesnake and twice as mean when we refused to renew our water contract with him, probably because he couldn't poke around on our land without trespassing. So Ed decides to take the land off us by any means possible. How Bodecker and Donnelly figure in all of this, I guess we'll have to wait and see."

"I guess," Ethan murmurs, not noticing, as Luke has, the unsettled expression on Cam's face.

"In the meantime," Luke says, getting to his feet, "I'm gonna ask Sara why Pa agreed to that clause, and if there was a second, secret agreement between him and Connors."

"Will she know?" Cam asks in a quiet, thick voice.

"My mother was very determined I should marry the girl of *her* dreams and keep me on the Diamond-T till the day I die. For me that has to mean more now in the light of this news."

Ethan stands up. "Maybe I'll come along."

"I'm countin' on it."

"This can't get out," Cam reminds them.

"It won't," Ethan says, plonking his hat on his head.

"One more thing. I need the deed itself," Cam says.

"But it's at home."

"Cliff will need to accompany one of you to bring it back."

Ethan rushes to declare, "I'll go!" And does a double take in Luke's direction.

Luke hasn't moved a muscle; didn't intend to.

Ethan folds his arms and unleashes that canny grin of his.

"Well, well, well," he mutters.

Cliff, who a person could be forgiven for forgetting he's still in the same room as them, says, "We'll leave in an hour, Ethan. There's a train at two."

Ethan nods. "Meet you at the depot. Luke and I need a minute to decide how we're gonna play this with Sara, then I'll fetch her from John and Amy's and take her back to Luke and Jennifer's for our talk. I'll let her know where I'm going and why on the way."

"Sounds like a plan," Cliff says with an attempt at a smile.

Of course, Luke would've gone if Ethan didn't feel inclined to volunteer. But as desperate as he feels right now about the deed, his heart is elsewhere. He'd been wondering how the test would come and what it would feel like…

On top of her vulnerable state of mind and the stresses of her condition, Jennifer had made it clear on the day he proposed she didn't fancy a husband who thoughtlessly took off at the first sign of adventure. She needed him, by her side, till she was ready to make her decision regarding Dermot.

And that's where he intends to stay.

Luke

He finds Jennifer fast asleep where he left her, all the food but for half a cookie eaten. Loveliness radiates from her as she slumbers. Peacefulness, too. He was never more aware of her condition than he is at this moment. Used to be only the Diamond-T made sense of his life. But that has all changed. More precious to him than anything, including gold, this beautiful woman and the child she carries. Now it is they who define who he is and his place in the world, shaping his destiny in ways he never would've imagined.

He pulls the door to a gentle close and heads downstairs to wait for Ethan and Sara.

When they arrive not long after, he leads them into the parlor, shutting the kitchen door behind them.

"Where is Jennifer?" Sara asks, looking about.

"We won't be interrupted," he replies and she glances sharply at him.

"What is this all about, Luke? Ethan is behaving strangely."

She's trying his patience; still he takes her coat for her, finds a place to drape it and exchanges glances with Ethan, who gives his head a small shake meaning he hasn't said a word to her about the gold.

"Take a seat, Sara."

She takes the sofa. "Ethan says he has to go home with Cliff Ryan and fetch the deed to the ranch because Mr Faraday needs it for the trial."

He draws up a chair close to her.

"What are you doing? What's this about?"

"There's no use pretending any longer, Sara."

"Pretending?"

"That you don't know what the *don't fence the Pass* clause in the bill of sale is all about. I know you know."

"Well, I don't know how you can know I know something when I don't know what you are talking about."

Ethan, sitting beside her on the sofa, gives a low chuckle. "That don't work on the boy no more, Sara, and you should know *that*."

Restraining a grin, Luke continues, "Likely there's gold in quartz ore under the Diamond-T and you know, don't you?"

Her face goes blank, either from shock or something else he can't be sure.

"G...gold?"

"Sara," he begins carefully, "there's no point in hiding any longer because Ethan and I figured it out with the help of a geological report Cam Faraday got sent to him from Denver. The people who made the report are geologists who carried out an illegal exploration on the Diamond-T last summer and covered it up. The men in this company had access to the original survey Connors had done for him by the Army."

She frowns, as if confused.

"Story goes like this, Sara... Ethan and I believe Connors knew about the quartz ore and so did Pa, and the two of them made an agreement to keep quiet about the potential gold until Connors could return with mining equipment. Connors didn't care about the land in a pastoral sense; Pa could have that, ranch all the cattle and horses he wanted. Connors couldn't feel secure no one would find out about his discovery; he needed a trustworthy partner to keep it safe till he got back and then help him mine. That was Pa. Connors would make the investment, Pa would offer protection and a decent beef steak. The rewards would be great. Now tell me it's not true."

"Land sakes, what a tale!"

"Sure, it has all the makings. Well? Tell us it's not true."

"How would I know?"

"Because although I might keep some things about my life from Ethan, I would share all my secrets with Jennifer. It's what husbands and wives do."

"Good man," Ethan says. "So, Sara, Morgan didn't tell me about the quartz or this agreement with Connors, maybe he died before he intended to tell me, I don't know. And I don't know why he didn't neither. But we think you've known all along."

"I… I don't appreciate this…this inquisition."

"It's all out in the open now, Sara, or it will be at the trial tomorrow when Cam puts a feller named Christopher Lamont on the stand. Lamont is Connors' grandson. He's been wanting his quartz, but Ed Parsons got in the way."

She studies her fingers for a very long time, and they wait with sorely tested patience. Then…

"The acres included in the clause span an area for the mining. Archie Connors didn't want it fenced or treated any different because he didn't want to draw attention to it. He was supposed to return within two years and begin mining. Morgan and I expected him sooner. The clause would've become redundant then, long before anyone could give it a second thought. And we were all to reap the rewards. But Morgan was killed and Connors never returned. The clause became this…this oddity instead and…"

Her words die away, leaving shock and bewilderment in their wake. It's a long while before either he or Ethan can speak.

Ethan finally clears his throat. "Why didn't you tell me?"

She looks at him imploringly. Ethan goes to water and sighs.

"All this time… you didn't want the gold?" Luke asks.

"I didn't like Morgan's plan. I…I know what gold fever does to men. I could never be sure if the gold was there, even though your father was certain Connors was telling the truth. I couldn't risk you and Ethan and Red Sky and Tip, my precious family, being destroyed by the prospect of it. We did it tough sometimes, yes, but it was never beyond what we couldn't handle…"

Ethan grunts. "You didn't want Richard getting his hands on it," he remarks, so shrewdly Luke is shocked into wondering why he hadn't thought of it himself.

"That's…true," she confesses. "And neither did Morgan."

Luke groans. "It was tough, Sara, damn hard, and seems to me you're as guilty of keeping our families apart as Uncle Richard is."

"Easy, son," Ethan croons. "She did right there."

Luke clasps and unclasps his hands; sits back and sits forward. "I'm sorry. You're right, Ethan."

"It wasn't just about Richard," Sara exclaims.

"Oh?"

"Ethan, you remember my brother..."

"Fred?"

"Frederick, yes. He got caught up in the gold rush in California. It ruined him, drove him mad looking for gold, and the little he found he was murdered for."

"You never told me any of this," Luke bursts out.

"I told you about your Uncle Frederick, that he died young."

"Yes, but I'm thinking of pneumonia or scarlet fever – not because he was bumped off for his gold."

"Very little gold," she stresses. "Frederick was an intelligent young man with such promise. But he went crazy looking for gold, ruined himself with women and drinking in the mining camps and gold towns. My father was heartbroken, and he made me swear an oath never to put riches before honor, fairness and kindness, or wealth above education, self-discipline, good sense and hard work.

"I couldn't break an oath I swore to my father! I tried but couldn't make Morgan understand. So I was determined to teach you those things that are the true riches in life – honor, fairness, kindness, education, self-discipline, good sense and hard work. Your life's happiness would spring from these. So the gold is there on the Diamond-T, and if we had mined it what would I've taught you? How to be entitled and pampered? It could've ruined you.

"Oh, you wouldn't have your Jennifer now if I'd let that happen. That young woman is your match in every way, but not if gold had run your life. What she loves most about you, my son, is that you are honorable and kind and sincere. I could see that in her eyes. And she has me to thank for it. Gold, Luke, drives men to the brink, your father included. And you don't want to go there."

Luke's throat is so dry by now he can barely swallow. "But all this time, all through the trouble with Ed, you never said anything... Ed knew, Sara..."

"I believed Ed would kill us for it, if he ever found out that it was leased land. But he did find out, suspected at the very least..."

"Didn't it ever occur to you the quartz was what the trouble was about all along?"

"It crossed my mind once or twice, but I didn't know he suspected. I thought the same as you; he was a cattle baron, greedy for our land. And, I never gave the quartz much thought. When Morgan died and Connors never returned I let the prospect of gold slip away and I pushed it from my conscious thought long ago. I had dealt with it, what was the point of thinking about it."

Ethan gets to his feet.

She looks up at him, forlorn. "You're angry with me, Ethan?"

"Kinda." He gives her a smile anyway. "I understand why you did it. I have to go now, Sara."

She nods. "I'll be here when you get back, Ethan. We can talk then."

"Sure, Sara," he says. "I won't be long."

Luke walks Ethan to the door.

"Go easy on your mother."

Luke nods, not trusting himself to be able to speak.

Ethan clamps a hand on his shoulder. "I know it's a shock. But, well... Luke, she's had so much loss in her life. First, Fred to the gold, then Katrine, and your pa. All for chasing dreams. The cost was too high for her. She didn't intend to sacrifice more."

"What about the Keatons' sacrifice? And what am I supposed to think about Pa now?"

"Will it be enough for now if I say we'll talk when I get back? I need to think."

It's frustrating, but he agrees.

"Take care of things while I'm gone. Take care of Sara."

"I will. You'll tell Cliff?"

"If he asks."

"He'll ask. I'll talk to Cam."

Suddenly, earnestly, Ethan looks him in the eye. "We've got to look after her, son."

Luke nods, his stomach churning. "We will. Don't worry."

When he's seen Ethan off, he returns to the parlor.

Sara is crying into her handkerchief.

"Don't cry, Sara..."

"You're ashamed of me, angry, disappointed, and shocked."

"Shocked, yes..."

"Oh, Luke, you have to know I didn't mean any harm."

"I know."

In the silence of their distress, swirling patterns of his harshest memories grasp his mind and pull him back in time... to his childhood, the last time he saw Katrine and his Pa... to Mart and all he suffered... to K, her senseless death... to his own near-death at the hands of Porterfield. He shudders violently; shakes himself free.

"What are you thinking?" Sara whispers; she's studying him.

"I... Sara, I don't know who Pa is anymore. And all the stories I was taught... are they true?"

"They remain whatever you were taught; they never change."

"I wonder."

"No, no..." she sobs, shaking her head.

"You can't tell anyone of this, Sara, not even John and Amy. We promised Cam. Promise, Sara."

"I promise."

"And, Sara?"

"Yes?"

"I'm only going to say this once, but I have to say it. You should've told me and Ethan about this when Ed began taking us into court."

Tears pour from her eyes.

"And, Sara?"

"What?" she chokes.

"You were so desperate to keep me on the ranch, so desperate for me to marry K. Is this why?"

With little heaves she weeps, not answering him.

"You have to tell me and then we'll put it aside forever."

"I...I truly loved that child. And I... truly believed you were perfect for one another..."

He waits while she attempts to compose herself.

"I... never wanted you to leave the ranch because since your father passed on I've been as scared a mouse as you could find. Never wanting to venture anywhere for fear of what might befall us. Sometimes I would be torn... leave the ranch and the dilemma

504

of the quartz ore behind, or stay because I couldn't bear to leave. This was Morgan's dream. My Katrine died in the making of that dream. My sweet baby taken from me. I couldn't turn back. How could I turn back and have her die for nothing… or turn away and dishonor her memory? I stayed for her, Luke, don't you understand? We stayed for your sister, for all that she was and for what she could've been and never had the chance."

His heart cracks hard down the center; his eyes flood with tears. How could he have been so blind to his mama's grief and her pain? When he sobs, Sara reaches for his hand and squeezes it.

"This morning, Luke, you said to me that now I could dream other dreams. That life could be full of amazing adventures. It was exhilarating to hear you talk that way. I felt a sense of hope.

"I realize you think I wanted to keep you on the ranch because of the quartz ore, but in fact I was scared of change, of losing you. If you had married Kelley, you would never have strayed. Life would have gone on, grown from the seed planted all those years ago into a proper destiny in return for all that was sacrificed. Not this… Luke, not this."

Full of regret and terrible heartache, he can't speak. They sit for an age in drowning silence.

Sometime later he realizes Jennifer is standing in the doorway; she looks as though she's been watching him. Softly beautiful from her sleep, she stands like a beacon in his shadowy world. That hasn't changed in all the time he has known her. And she smiles at him, setting his heart to beating again long after he thought it had surely stopped in the agony of his heartache.

"Is everything all right?" she asks.

Sara looks up then. "Jennifer, my dear…"

"Luke, I need to go to the Faradays and check on Meg and the baby."

He nods. Finds his voice. "We were just heading over there ourselves. C'mon, Ma, let's go."

...Dermot

Provincetown, Cape Cod

Dermot wakes with his nightclothes clinging to his skin. Damn these night sweats! Cold and uncomfortable, he lies there momentarily before he coerces his broken down body out of bed. His hands are shaking as he extracts a nightdress from the bureau and as he peels the wet one off. The night air nips at his clammy skin; shivering, he hurries to get the fresh one over his head.

The bedclothes need pulling back to let the air dry off any moisture; with this done, he dons his robe. He pours himself a glass of water, spillage inevitable. The window in the sitting room draws him forth to overlook the bay.

Tonight a full moon casts its silver-white light over the dark body of water and catches the gentle shore break in its luminous glow, mesmerizing him for a timeless interlude.

Six weeks, seven weeks, eight… nothing. Where was that damn girl? He couldn't prevail forever. He should prepare himself for the eventuation that her heart is so hardened towards him she will never come.

THE END OF VOLUME FOUR

THE GRAND SAGA OF THE WEST & GILDED AGE

THE LIBERTY & PROPERTY LEGENDS™ by Terri Sedmak

America 1880's. Lives taken, justice sought. Love won and love lost.
Friendships forged and families fractured. As terror grows, heroes rise.

ଔVolume One
HEARTLAND
On the Side of Angels

Adventure and romance will not be denied
anyone who has the courage to be free.

ଔVolume Two
EMPIRE FOR LIBERTY
Dangerous Lullaby

Deep in the heart of the Legends...
Their darkest hour is coming.

ଔVolume Three
FIRST COUNTRY
Tinged with Rose

Unlock your heart... The grand saga of
The West & Gilded Age continues.

ଔVolume Four
THE HOUR OF EVIDENCE
Deceived

The scales of justice are poised... All eyes are
on Cheyenne, Magic City of the Plains.

Two volumes of outstanding adventure and romance remain until the stunning conclusion!

Visit www.terrisedmak.com
Explore www.pinterest.com/terrisedmak
Follow www.facebook.com/terrisedmaktthelibertyandpropertylegends

'Fast paced and riveting' - *Midwest Book Review*

'Recreations of 19th century America are evocative' - *Daily Telegraph*

'A creative, insightful and poetic writer' - *Keystone Creations*

'Compulsive reading' - *That's Life! Fast Fiction*

'Spritely and engrossing saga... ample conflict, a captivating historical
context and enduring romance. Sweeping historical fiction.' - *PS News*

'One of the best fiction stories I have read.' – *Kate Matthew, NSW Writers*

'Be prepared for an insatiable need to keep on reading!' - *VANCOUVERgirl*

www.ingramcontent.com/pod-product-compliance
Lightning Source LLC
Chambersburg PA
CBHW030745030726
47497CB00001B/136